SAILS OF SUNSET

SAILS OF SUNSET

BY

CECIL ROBERTS

AUTHOR OF 'SCISSORS'

WILLIAM HEINEMANN LTD
MELBOURNE :: LONDON :: TORONTO

First published September 1924
Reprinted 1924, 1926 (*twice*), 1931, 1933, 1934
1935, 1936, 1937, 1939, 1949

823

PRINTED IN GREAT BRITAIN
AT THE WINDMILL PRESS
KINGSWOOD, SURREY

TO
HOLBROOK JACKSON

SAILS OF SUNSET

CHAPTER I

I

THERE was a flutter of applause along the Venetian salon, applause that stirred the heavy air of the June night until the steady candle flames, in the gold candelabra on the frescoed walls, wavered to and fro, spilling their wax in extravagant consumption. The famous tenor had just finished singing; the sostenuto passage pulsated in its diminishing pianissimo until the lungs of the bull-necked maestro were exhausted.

A general movement followed after the applause. The hundred guests of Count Cesario Casmiri chatted, the gentlemen bending politely over the seated ladies, who fanned themselves, scarcely rewarding their efforts. At the far end, talking to the wife of the American Consul, stood Count Cesario, a figure of agitation. A bachelor, and deprived of the assistance of an hostess thereby, he felt that he should be running round exchanging brief pleasantries with his guests. He was rightly proud of his gifts as an host. This old palace on the Grand Canal, for instance. Had Venice, the city of palaces, anything finer to show, any greater example of the glory of Sansovino ?—omitting always the great façade of the old

Library, running up, like a screen of lacework from the Zecca to the restless coloured Piazza di San Marco.

So much merit could he claim for the material part. No salon had richer ceilings or rarer tapestries. Poor he was, but the foundations of his family's greatness still endured. In himself the stamp of his lineage was apparent. There was small need to declare that, of that oligarchy, makers and rulers of a mighty Venetian State, a Casmiri had always been a member. Generations of conscious prestige were preserved in the calm of his dark eyes, in the chiselled strength of his face and firm sensuous mouth, in the very wrinkles of his skin, like parchment in its yellowy pallor of age.

To-night, for to-night was a rare occasion, he had opened the old palazzo and felt a tremor of the vanished greatness of his line. He would later, following the summer migration of the Venetian nobility, go to his villa near Verona. Now he was living on the top floor of the palace, attended by his housekeeper, and gondolier-valet. It was perhaps too characteristic of the disastrous spirit of the age that even his gondolier was no longer a gondolier, nor, in his part as valet, a true valet. He steered the motor-launch, fussed over its petrol engine, and in the rôle of valet his services extended to the kitchen.

To young Peter Neville, lounging on the balcony overhanging the moonlit canal, there was something immeasurably pathetic in this determination to awaken the glory of the past. Beautiful, yes, of a kind that man would never create again, lacking the leisure, the economic ease, the tyrannical power to impose individual desires upon enslaved masses of men. This determined revival of Count Cesario's in celebration of his sixtieth birthday, was a gesture of despair, a childish protest against an unromantic age. To-night the old ghosts would walk, for were not the frescoes, the tapestries, the ceilings and mosaic floors, the gilded corridors and pillars part of the old stage ?

Even the Grand Canal and the moon clung to their romance. Why should not he, Count Cesario, walk a few moments in the gay fashion of his ancestors ? Let the lute be plucked, let the tenor sing, and fair ladies suspend the flutter of fans while that wonderful pure note seemed to pierce their bosoms with the cry of suppressed desires.

Alas !—the moon was faithful, no doubt ; not so the romantic Grand Canal. As Peter Neville leaned over the balcony, held in the enchantment of the Italian night, the spirit of the age again interposed. From under the high arched Rialto bridge—an architectural wishbone, his brother, Sir Roderick, had facetiously called it—came the steamer, with a shriek of its vulgar little syren, its freight of tourists borne towards the Ducale and the Molo, where they would disembark and parade restlessly down the rectangular Piazza, or sit consuming ices at one of the tables of Florian's.

Peter Neville watched the fussy little steamer pass under the balcony, out from the shadow of the palazzi, with the moon-silvered track still troubled by the passing of other vessels.

Then he turned, conscious of someone quietly coming to his side. The light from the salon blinded him as he looked from the sable Italian night ; and for a moment the silhouette in the arcaded window was unfamiliar. He drew back a little into the shadow of the wall, surprised by a low laugh.

" Peter—you are most unsociable to-night ! " said a voice, attractive though slightly hard in tone.

" Maud ! I couldn't see who it was."

He pushed the wicker chair forward and she sank into it, with deliberate dignity, delayed and ostentatious.

Lady Neville always moved like an actress. ' Born to open bazaars for charity ' had been his brother's description of her. It was just, to her sense of deportment as well as of duty. All her life she had desired dignity. She was a violent reaction from her native environment. The desolation of a vicarage in Lancashire had fanned the passion for a flat in Paris. Rescue arrived in the shape of Sir Roderick Neville. She had never quite recovered her breath from the miracle of that escape. Her real life dated from a dinner party in her aunt's house in London. It had been all the more wonderful because Cupid came as swordbearer to Sir Perseus. Andromeda had almost fainted, not in relief at the loss of her chains, but in the disturbing dominance of her deliverer. Had he come but to transport her to a new desert she would have gone gladly. An incredible force had shattered her self-sufficiency. She was in love and for the first time tasted the bitter relish of obedience. But she soon reasserted herself with the rest of the world, restoring the balance skilfully.

To Sir Roderick she was just a woman ; to the world, and that was everybody else, she was a managing woman. For this reason no one ever suspected the romance that coloured the relationship of Sir Roderick with his wife. His love for her was a steady possession ; it made him unconscious of any other world than that of which she was the light. Peter thought it could not last, but pessimistic speculation was frustrated by a new interest so tremendous that the two characters in this little drama became supers. The stage centre was taken by the son and heir.

With the coming of Ronnie the universe was completed. Peter felt this, and was also thankful. He was relieved of the family traditions, a legacy that menaced his bohemian desires. Ronnie made many things possible. The choice to marry or remain single, to administrate or lounge, to rusticate or wander. Blessed be Ronnie, son and heir to the Neville traditions ! By a single act of birth Peter was relieved of all his ancestors. He knew Maud would never believe in the sincerity of his joy. To her this ancestral nihilism was unnatural. Roots ! Foundations ! These were the sacred, fundamental things. No ! there was something inscrutable about Peter. He baffled her. If only he would seek relief in consultation or confession.

Lady Neville placed her fan on the balustrade, picked up her lorgnette, and, half turning, surveyed the long salon within, where the shaded candles clustered like little moons under the expanse of the ceiling.

" How beautiful these Italian girls are ! " she said. " Do they ever go out in the sun, I wonder ? Peter, if I were a man I should fall violently in love here. Look at that girl, what wonderful shoulders ! "

" Is it worth the sacrifice ? " he bantered.

" Peter, how can you ask ! Love is worth any sacrifice."

" I don't mean love—I mean those shoulders. Are they worth the sacrifice of so much sunshine ? "

Lady Neville looked at him with deliberate scrutiny.

" Peter ! " she exclaimed, sharply.

He looked down into her eyes, his own slightly mocking.

" Peter, I sometimes wonder if you're capable of being in love."

" Is not love a state of incapability ? "

He fenced with her, cheating her instinct for analysis.

" That's witty, but it is not an answer."

He smiled, and made no comment, peering over the balcony. Another steamer sailed under the dark arch of the Rialto bridge, the rays from its lamps flung in coloured patens on the molested water. The eddies travelled outwards towards the banks, and the chafing of the gondolas, moored at the worn steps beneath them, floated up.

" How wonderful the steel prows of those gondolas are," he said, " they look like polished halberds. It was an inspired law that made them paint the gondolas black."

The opening chords of the piano cut across his words. Lady Neville rose.

" That's Signor Zambra again," she said, then, looking directly at her brother-in-law, " Peter, you're keeping something back. You are tantalisingly secretive. All the way home from Chioggia, this afternoon, you've been in a dream. It's no business of mine, but I'd like to think there *was* something."

He laughed, and she was quick to notice it was an uneasy laugh. She watched him, deriving pleasure from her examination of his handsome face. He was so magnificently virile ; animal, she might have said. His mouth was firm yet mobile, and his eyes, very dark, always seemed full of laughter. And then, he had the Neville nose ! Sometimes, when stirred, the nostrils twitched, something after the manner of a faun's. He was slim for his twenty-five years, but in dancing with him she had divined the steely strength of his shoulders. There was passion latent in that body. He moved with a springiness of the loins characteristic of young mountaineers. She saw all this in him, and wondered how the spirit kept it so chastened. Surely sometime—

He moved uneasily, conscious she was searching the sex in him. To-night, of all nights, he felt unsafe beneath her scrutiny.

" I want to hear Zambra too," he said, ignoring the drift of her words, " Shall we go in ? "

Defeated again, she let him lead her into the bright salon. They found Sir Roderick, very concerned about their return to the Hotel Danieli : they must not be late, their packing was still incomplete, and a few purchases had to be made in the morning before they departed for Milan.

" There's a host of gondolas at the steps. We had better go now, I think," urged Sir Roderick.

" But we can't, dear, we must say *Buona notte* to the Count—and I want to hear Zambra," she whispered, for the maestro had taken his preparatory breath and a hush fell upon the assembly.

There was something medieval in their subsequent departure. The high pillared portico was illuminated by a solitary lamp encased in a magnificent wrought-iron cradle. The pale beams fell upon the scarf-wrapped heads and fur-clad shoulders of delicate ladies. One by one the black gondolas came out of the darkness into the arc of light where the green water lapped the marble steps. Silently propelled, they glided in, with shining steel-toothed prows, black-cabined. Behind, on his *poppa*, stood the gondolier, skilful and deft in the manipulation of his swanlike craft. At each prow there rocked a lantern sending lurid reflections rippling across the Canal in macabre designs.

When the Nevilles' gondola came, Sir Roderick handed in his wife. Peter refused to enter the cabin, preferring the diminutive chair outside, whence he could see the curved sweep of the palaces on either bank. While Sir Roderick and his wife chatted within, Peter was trying to come to a decision. All the evening he had been perturbed unreasonably, foolishly perturbed, he told himself. He had always followed his inclinations, and here was the strongest he had ever known, yet he hesitated. What excuse could he make ? He did not want to go on to Milan with them to-morrow. He wished to remain in Venice. Not Venice actually—but to go back across the great lagoon to the place of this day's excursion.

Early that morning the Count had taken them in his launch out along the Lido strand, across the lagoon, beyond Malamocco and the long sea wall dividing its calm waters from the Adriatic, until they had come to Chioggia. Peter had known the fame of the old-time fishing town, from the artists to whom it was a magnet. He too, an amateur of the palette, had wandered far in search of colour yet found here something surpassingly beautiful in the kaleidoscopic glamour of the fishing boats, in the indescribable confusion of rigging and folded sails. The bewildering riot of colour drenching these boats, staining the water, overflowing to the quays, walls and roofs ; the babel of voices, the dirt, the smells, the hammering—not elsewhere had he seen it, so vivacious, so pregnant with voluptuous life. It feasted the eye, throwing fitful illumination on lurid phases of history, on the splendour of the Venetian State, the pageantry of her maritime power, the proud exultation in physical prowess.

All this flowed in upon him, stirred him, inspired the artist in him. Yet in this his experience was not uncommon, his companions were entranced by it, though not equally, for he brought to it the more delicate, trained consciousness of the artist, receptive yet critical, enthusiastic but selective. It had been a day of enchantment, remarkable even in a region where the sea had conspired with man to create something flower-fragile and of perishable beauty, but strong as a dream, actual though tangible.

Nevertheless, the explanation sought by his sister-in-law, sought too, at this moment, by himself, was not geographical nor artistic. Something had happened, swiftly, without perceptible action or surprise, yet something so momentous that his twenty-five years were suddenly dwarfed into one moment of unfathomable experience.

It was not a lightning flash, lighting a new world briefly, then plunging him again into familiar darkness. His revelation remained, it stirred him now, he was a bewildered captive in an enduring vision. He who had prided himself on his freedom was now captive. It hurt him, he resented the breaking down of his reserve. In a moment he, a master of life, a disdainer of it at times, had been made a suppliant. Should he surrender or fight for his liberty, grimly ?

And then, in deeper confusion, he discovered he no longer coveted liberty. He was willingly captive.

" Peter ! "

He started. A moment gone he was sitting at a table in Chioggia ; now the vast dome of Santa Maria della Salute at the mouth of the Grand Canal towered over him. Maud's voice brought him back to reality—or was the other reality ?

" Peter—I've spoken to you twice and you've not taken the slightest notice ! Roderick suggests that we break our journey to Milan at Verona and spend a few hours there."

He was being driven to his decision. He looked across to the Palazzo Ducale, its marble façade glimmering in the moonlight ; he followed the thread of lights, beyond their hotel, along the Riva degli Schiavoni. Now, in the darkness of the canal, he would decide. After all, was he not free ? He could change his decision to-morrow if he wished.

He heard himself speaking, was vividly aware of the forward stoop of the gondolier on his *poppa*, of the living darkness of the cabin, and the vigilance he would have to meet within it.

"Verona—yes. I've been thinking, however—if you don't mind—that I'll not go on with you to-morrow."

He caught his breath. How absurd was this diffidence at speaking his mind !

"My dear fellow," said Roderick, "you're perfectly free, of course. It's delightful having you with us, but if you—if you— " He hesitated, searching for the relieving phrase. Peter took the opportunity eagerly.

"I do want to paint. There's wonderful material out at Chioggia. I've had it in my mind all day."

"So that's your secret, Peter," called Lady Neville from the darkness. "It's Art ! "

But there was a question in her intonation. She was wholly satisfied now. She knew it was not Art. She had got to the bottom of him at last. He was not Peter the imperturbable, he was Peter the vulnerable. It filled her with a curious gratification ; her instinct had been sure throughout. This man's denial of his sex, his deliberate reproof of all her attempts to bring his temperament into accord with his enveloping physical attraction, had baffled and disconcerted her. She had never yet failed in her analysis of men, and it was annoying that her own brother-in-law should threaten her first defeat.

She lay back on her cushions looking at him. What kind of a lover would Peter make ? And as she asked she was vividly alert to the answer, so that something within her, whether a momentary impulse of vanity, or of conquest, she scarcely knew, gave an agonising stab of jealousy. It gave her next remark its tang.

"Peter knows we don't wish to drag him with us, I'm sure."

Their gondola had now floated into the small canal, under the narrow bridge, skilfully timed to drift on the hotel steps. Peter sprang out, and offered his hand. As

Lady Neville passed into the lighted doorway he fancied she was smiling ; he was certain she had pressed his hand, an intimation of her pleasure in his self-betrayal.

II

After Lady Neville had left them in the lounge, tne two brothers talked, making final arrangements. This spring they had met after a separation of three years. Their former meeting had been at Roderick's wedding, when Peter acted as his best man. In appearance, as in temperament, it was difficult to believe these two men were brothers, save for one distinguished and common feature, the Neville nose, which for generations had been long, slightly arched from the bridge, with satyrically curved nostrils. But in all other details they differed. Peter was five feet eleven inches in his socks, Sir Roderick was two inches shorter, and his height seemed even less in comparison owing to his rotundity, a cause of some anxiety but not a sufficient cause to interrupt his enjoyment of food. Also, whereas Peter had black smooth hair, so smooth that his neat long head always shone immaculately, Sir Roderick's crisp brown hair wished to be curly, and stern disciplinary measures had affected it much as a drill sergeant affects a recruit ; his hair kept its form rigidly, so that it gave the appearance almost of a wig, having nothing individual in its shape. Ten years divided the brothers, in experience as well as opinions. It was clear that Sir Roderick was a Neville, like all the Nevilles, and it was becoming clearer that Peter was not a Neville, and was growing less and less representative.

Peter was a Rochefort in every way. His mother was heard in his voice, seen in his calm smile, above all present in his preposterous outlook. For so Sir Roderick deemed it, reserving the opinion that Fate had been wise in making him, and not Peter, the ninth baronet. The Nevilles had always been aristocrats of a particular nature. They were ever men of affairs, however much their breeding and social status had made them men of Society. They had, from the beginning, traceable in the portraits at Neville Court, been handsome men with a splendid sense of their worth. A Lord Chancellor, two Bishops, three Generals, an Admiral, and one Colonial Governor had made the name distinguished. They had, with the right instinct, married beautiful women of sound family and good substance.

Sir John, the fifth baronet, had married his daughter to a duke, and Sir Philip, the sixth, probably affected by this costly alliance, had gone into business. No ordinary business, of course, such as would sully the creed of supreme independence. With true foresight he had founded a bank, chiefly, at first, for the quiet accommodation of careless friends, hard pressed until the fulfilment of their expectations with the decease of their relations. Thus quietly the business had grown. To-day, throughout Meltonhamshire, Harbyshire and Minstershire, there was a branch of Neville's Bank.

People liked banking there, it was, in the best sense, a family bank. It took a personal interest in your welfare, in other words, in your securities. Its managers knew you, your local prestige, your important family connections ; and they never kept you waiting, every clerk immediately showing you direct to the manager's room, where a coal fire burned brightly in an open iron grate, and the leather on the arm-chairs was worn by generations of Neville's clients.

There was something so well-ordered about the Neville family. Eton and Trinity College, the world tour, marriage at twenty-five, Justice of the Peace for the County at forty, not less than two sons, and not more than two daughters, this was the routine and reward of those who served the great god Security.

But we may not forget Nature. Unhappily it did not forget Sir James, the eighth baronet, and the father of Roderick and Peter. It was distressing to Roderick to realise that his father had been somewhat of an unusual man, certainly a most unusual Neville. He had been a good banker, a good father, but a cautious mind and a steady life had not averted a violent end. He was drowned in the sinking of an Atlantic liner while on his way to transact some banking business in New York. The old line had not ended there, however; Roderick had assured the continuity, and to make doubly sure Peter had followed later, but not alone. Susan came with him, his twin sister. They had delayed coming, and then were precipitate. He, Roderick, had appeared precisely one year after marriage, as a proper son and heir should do ; a ten years' wait for a brother or sister, and then, suddenly, both !

Looking at Peter now, as he sat in the lounge chair, legs crossed, his head tilted back, not in contemplation of the rococo ceiling, but of his cigarette smoke, Sir Roderick realised more than ever before that his brother was not really a Neville. He was dark, he was sleek with rest-less eyes and teeth too noticeably ivory. Sir Roderick looked down at his own limbs, stouter, more English, more—he was almost going to say, well-bred, when natural pride in the fact that his mother was descended from a Rochefort checked him. There was French ducal blood in them both. Sir Roderick would not deny that, his gratitude was restrained only by Peter and Susan.

For three years this brother of his had been leading a

nomadic life in Italy. He had ambitions as an artist. Surely such hopes were for poor men with nothing but genius ? Peter was not necessary to the banking business, it was more convenient that he was absent, for it gave Sir Roderick undisputed sway, but Peter should have done something for the family, either in the Army or the Civil Service. He was a poor younger son and must make his own estate. As it was, he was doing something merely for himself, if sketching and painting in obscure corners of the earth could be regarded as doing anything.

An irritating fellow ! He could appreciate Maud's half-hidden annoyance. So good-looking—handsome even, he might marry well, as Maud again thought. Yet here he was, with three years of fruitless wandering in Italy. He was now putting off his return indefinitely. Well, Peter led his own life, thought Roderick, gratefully, and pleased with his own in comparison.

" When may we expect you home ? " asked Sir Roderick, knocking the ash off his cigar.

" Oh, I don't know quite. I'll wander about here for a while. Venice has been painted to death, but I think there's plenty left for individual taste. I thought of getting together a Spring Show in town. But I'll be home soon. I've not seen Ronnie yet—and there's Susan."

" Ah—Ronnie," sighed Sir Roderick, with deep satisfaction. " Ronnie's going to be a fine boy—a fine boy."

" How old is he now, two years and what— ? "

" Two months—chubby little beggar ! Peter, why don't you marry ? You're not a man until you're a father."

Peter laughed. " There's plenty of time to qualify," he retorted. " When did you last see Susan ? "

" Susan ?—oh—er—we rarely see Susan—she's in town mostly—doesn't seem to care for the country life."

Peter smiled. He could see Susan revolting against the order of Neville Court. It was Susan's home, so Maud reiterated. Susan had her own rooms, her own horse-box ; and Susan had her own views, which upset all the other admirable arrangements.

" I'm uneasy about Susan," began Sir Roderick.

" Susan ? Oh, she's all right, I'm sure," cut in Peter, cheerfully. "You can't say Susan's a worry."

" But she is ! " said Sir Roderick, gravely. " Why ever she behaves as she does, I cannot understand ! A woman doctor—who on earth wants a woman doctor ? It's unnatural ! "

" I don't see that," argued Peter, lowering his gaze, and watching his brother's worried expression with amusement. " A woman wants a profession these days, and there's nothing unnatural in women wanting doctors of their own sex. If I were a woman— "

"You'd have a man!" interrupted Roderick, impatiently.

" Why ? "

" Why ?—why, because—well, for the reason that— " he floundered, searching for a presentable reason. Peter waited while the search was prosecuted, then—

" You see, Roderick, there's no reason except custom, or unpleasant reasons."

" Ability—brains !—that's the reason," Roderick rapped out. " What do women know about— "

" Has Susan passed her Final ? "

" Yes."

" They're the same examinations as the men pass ? "

" I suppose so."

Peter smiled affably. " Then the brain power's equal, I suppose ? "

Sir Roderick twitched up his body. He was not good at argument.

"Oh, if you like to debate about it, you'll make a case. But let me tell you that you're flying in the face of Nature. A woman's function—"

"Is the home," added Peter, dryly.

"Exactly," said Sir Roderick, firmly.

"And marriage?"

"Of course!"

"And children?" continued Peter, calmly.

"Why, certainly!"

"Yet a girl may have no opportunity of marriage or no desire."

"It's unnatural of a woman not to desire," defined Sir Roderick.

"There have been, and are, thousands of nurses and nuns—would you call them unnatural?"

"Certainly not—that's a vocation—a call, if you like."

"And they have a right of choice?"

"I don't deny that—" said Sir Roderick, slowly.

"Then so has Susan, if she wants to follow a profession."

"But a *woman* doctor," protested Sir Roderick.

"I might say a *man* doctor. Surely a doctor's just a doctor? The day's gone when a woman was content with being amused or amusing. The fact that she can become a mother should not preclude her from becoming anything else."

Sir Roderick stirred uneasily. He never shone in discussion.

"We shall never see eye to eye on this," he said, in a tone that inferred his brother's limitations. "What's the result in Susan? She wears clothes like a man, she resents my help or suggestions, she knows every Tom, Dick and Harry by his Christian name. Do you think a man wants to marry that type of woman?"

"Marriage again!" laughed Peter. "And do you think Susan wants to marry that type of man? Susie'll go halves in life all the time. The modern woman——"

"I don't approve of the modern woman," said Sir Roderick grimly.

"She wouldn't approve of you, Roderick."

"That's personal!"

"So is your opinion, Roddy,—anyhow, old Susie's happy, I'll wager. Well, I suppose we'd better go to bed."

The two brothers crossed the lounge in silence. On the wide landing of their rooms they said Good-night, Roderick a little stiff, feeling he had been at a disadvantage.

Confound Peter!—he always made his wrong-headed reasons appear so right. He detested artistic people, they could argue the devil out of his own. What a world, what a muddle it would be if the conventions of sensible society did not keep them in their places! He'd tell Maud all about it. She was so level-headed, she always saw exactly as he did. It was a comfort to have a wife like his. No fantastic notions, no silly doctrines of woman's independence! Maud had been perfectly right about Susan from the beginning. And about Peter. He was always safe in taking Maud's opinion. She was so sound about everything.

III

Peter Neville found his bedroom intolerably stuffy. As he turned the switch the large room was flooded with light from a central chandelier of Venetian glass. The door was panelled with printed notices and instructions to guests in Italian, French, German and English. Over his bed, from a small hoop attached to the top of the back-frame, fell the *zanzariere*, the muslin-net without which, in the mosquito season, experience had taught him never to accept a bedroom. Crossing the tessellated floor to the double shutters of his window, he flung them out and open.

The enchantment of the vista thus revealed made him incautious of mosquitoes attracted out of the night by the brilliance within. Throwing off his coat, and waistcoat, the heat still worried him, and he turned from the window and stripped himself, the floor striking delightfully cool to his bare feet. Going to the window again he leaned out : he was not overlooked, and the night air was refreshing to his skin. Venice was still awake, reluctant to close her eyes on the splendour of the night.

Men and women walked beneath his window, along the broad marble pavement of the Riva degli Schiavoni, that quay of the old Dalmatian traders, bordering the lagoon which opened out from the mouth of the Grand Canal. He saw them come, tired, down the steps of the Ponte della Paglia, bridging the small canal running in at the side of the Molo, between the dark high walls of the Doge's Palace and the Prison, connected by that Bridge of Sighs so beloved of tourists. They walked along, their voices rising in the still night. White-clad sailors, making their way in twos and threes along the Riva towards the battleship stationed off the Public Gardens, sang snatches of Italian airs, and to supplement them, somewhere out on the lagoon, a serenading party was singing to the accompaniment of mandolines.

Away to Peter's right, in the bright moonlight he could see the broad platform of the Molo, with long rows of gondolas huddled together, a few lanterns still lit at their steel-toothed prows. Beyond the Molo, on the Piazzetta leading to St. Mark's, he could see the two famous granite columns, bearing the Winged Lion, and St. Theodore on his crocodile, brought centuries ago from Syria ; those two tragic columns between which, in the lurid days of Venetian glory, unhappy victims had been hanged in the name of the Great Republic. Their place was peaceful enough to-night, with the marble wing of the old Library jutting out behind, its beautiful double colonnades glimmering in the moonlight.

Peter listened to the singing of the sailors, happy bronzed peasant lads, as they climbed the steps of the next canal bridge, and descended again to the broadening pavement with the inevitable equestrian statue of Vittorio Emanuele, and its fringe of steamers, fishing trawlers, and miscellaneous craft that plied on the lagoons. Away across the Grand Canal rose the noble pile of the church of Santa Maria della Salute, with its massive dome and broad descending steps, a true platform for the pageants beloved of the Venetians.

But it was the vision opposite which held Peter Neville entranced at his open window. It was too beautiful, too ethereal for reality. Across the lagoon, smitten here and there with the silver track of a passing gondola, on the shadowy horizon, clearly silhouetted in the bright Italian heaven, star-spangled in its depths, floated the island church of San Giorgio Maggiore. He could discern its great Palladian façade, its copper-hued dome, and the red-brick campanile, crowned with a stone colonnade and a tapering spire surmounted by a golden angel. It had lost its gorgeous colour in the moonlight, but the night had touched it with a new splendour, as it rose delicately into heaven, a thing of romantic grace. And to its natural beauty it added another enchantment, speculative this time, but more potent because its origin was emotional and not architectural. Beyond that statuesque campanile, mile on shadowy mile, stretched the great lagoon to Chioggia.

Chioggia! Strange that a few hours ago it had been only a name and place unknown, and now it was etched on his burning memory, its name a spell upon his blood, its streets and quays unforgettably known. Scarcely three hours had been spent there, three hours of aimless wandering in its churches, along its canals jammed with the fishing fleet, and down its wide Corso. They had laughed and gossiped, the Count making an infallible cicerone. Here had Goldoni dwelt and found the vivacious people of his comedies. Here had they publicly read Tasso on *festa* days. Here the fisher-girls went in procession to the church of S. Andrea.

And then they had seated themselves at the small tables outside the hotel on the quay. From its corner you could look down the wide Corso Vittorio Emanuele, and, to the left, across the little harbour, and the Porto leading out between the Pelestrina sea-wall and Sottomarina, to the Adriatic. Northwards, beyond the leagues of calm-sun-burnished water, down the lagoon lay Venice on the hazy skyline, the place where he now stood, remembering, pierced with longing to hurry back.

They had given their orders and were talking gaily. Immediately in front of them lay a fishing boat, its bright-hued sails drawn up to dry in the sun. On its gaudily painted prow a picture of a red St. George, slaying a purple dragon, gave the vessel its name. The deck was littered with old nets, blackened floats, coils of rope and all the untidy impedimenta of the fisherman's calling. Three men, one half-naked, burned a deep red by the Adriatic sun, lay asleep, the only moving thing aboard being a cat. Suddenly a voice caused Peter Neville to turn and take notice of the boat.

It was a voice of singular attraction, speaking the beautiful Chioggian dialect, which he could scarcely follow.

But in vain did he look for the speaker. It was a woman's voice undoubtedly, a young woman's voice of rare quality. Then a gruff voice replied, and this time he could see one of the men half turn his head towards the hatch-door. So the first speaker was below.

With pretence, Peter kept in the flow of conversation at the table, but his mind was alertly elsewhere. He wanted to hear that voice again, wanted to see to what kind of a woman it belonged. A whole minute elapsed, and then the conversation between the man on deck and the hidden speaker was renewed. He listened intently, impatient with the chatter of his companions. There was a sudden burst of laughter, deep and hearty from the man, ringing and melodious from the woman, and suddenly, as Peter frankly turned, she came up out of the hatch into full view of the deck.

She made an arresting movement of wild beauty as she stood there, her back to the flaming sunset-sail, her bare throat and face almost the colour of the boarded deck. Her hair was uncovered, and bound with a single scarlet braid, crossing the brow and temples and catching the black lustrous hair in a loop over the pink ears, and behind the head. Her brow, from which the jet hair lifted in a level line, was smooth and finely shaped, and long black eyebrows, delicate but firm, emphasised the flawless contour of sunburnt cheeks, and marked the eyes, heavily lashed, in which a vital fire glowed and flickered from the source of her mirth.

She stood there, with head thrown back, the red full lips parted, her small teeth gleaming. Her gesture was challenging yet artless, it represented a natural abandon to her mood, now of bantering mirth. You felt it might as swiftly turn to an equally powerful gesture of defiance, or supplication even. Her young breasts, firm and rounded, rose under the tight scarlet bodice, open low at the neck, showing the shaded channel where the brown flesh took a softer hue. Her hands rested leisurely on her hips, full but symmetrical, in keeping with the litheness of her carriage, and the strong suppleness of her shapely arms and small straight ankles.

Peter saw all this, wholly and almost as unemotionally as an artist learns to see, an appraiser of points and defects ; but when, in turning curiously to his seated group, she looked at him, the artist was suddenly erased and the whole man leapt into passionate being. It was a calm look, not challenging nor timid, that held his eyes, speaking consciously to him, so that his heart seemed to shake him as she held his gaze. Then, as suddenly, she looked away, turned, and was gone from view below.

But she had not left the same world as on her coming ; he could see her going down there, see her moving, though out of sight, see every line and movement of her, knowing that she knew he was still looking towards her. And somehow he was assured she still saw him, as clear there in the darkness of that cabin as in the sunlight of the day.

They had paid the waiter, and with a clatter rose from the table. Mechanically, obsessed, he rose too, talked with them, walked with them, though what he said or whither they went he neither cared nor knew. The afternoon wore on, they re-embarked on the launch and turned towards Venice. As they rounded the stone molo he caught a last glimpse of the fishing boat, inanimate, afire in the sun, with its suspended sail and untidy tackle. He watched it cut off from his vision, tried to imagine it through the stone seawall, and held it in his sight out across the lagoon.

Her name, her life, what were those things to him ?

Why had she suddenly struck him, as a strange hand might strike a harp and set it quivering with formless music ? All the long afternoon, all the long evening, and now, here, in the silent moonlight, he was asking himself this, finding no answer, yet conscious that instantly his life had blossomed into an incredible romance. Maud's penetrating chatter all the evening had not shaken this obsession. He was still obsessed, as he leaned now at his window, looking across San Giorgio and the lagoon to Chioggia. To-morrow he should have gone to Milan, homewards to England ; and he was not going. Why was he not going ? Why ?

He shivered, slightly chilled in the night air. A clock struck one, and the single note roamed over the still water. He closed the shutters and turned towards his bed. But when he had switched out his light he knew he would not rest, for still in the darkness of his room he could see the radiant sky, the moored boats, the beautiful figure and face of that Italian fisher-girl. And in his ears still, that free laughter was ringing, those challenging eyes holding his through the darkness that brought no sleep. The morrow slowly came through leagues of night, and with the morrow— ?

Finally, towards dawn, he turned and slept.

CHAPTER II

I

AT breakfast the next morning Sir Roderick made no allusion to Peter's sudden change of plans. Lady Neville, joining the brothers somewhat late, asked Peter whether he intended staying at the Hotel Danieli or moving elsewhere.

" It must be delightful not to know your own mind. All my life I've wanted to feel perfectly free," she said gaily.

' My dear," responded Sir Roderick, looking up from his plate, and peering over the rim of his gold eyeglasses, " if there's anything you would detest it would be not having a definite plan of action for the day. Why, you always mortgage your life for at least a fortnight ahead ! "

" That's a safeguard against the tedium of existence. But look at Peter. Last night on the Count's balcony— at least I think it was there—he suddenly decided to discard all plans for England and turn beachcomber."

Peter, carelessly covering his bread with marmalade, deliberately refrained from betraying himself. Clever woman ! she was at it again—on the Count's balcony, at least she thought it was there ! She thought nothing of the kind, she knew his changed plans had an earlier origin. That was a sly shot about beachcombing. He determined to face her.

" I'm going this afternoon to Chioggia. It captured my fancy with its fishing boats and narrow street."

She looked at her brother-in-law archly, as he spoke.

" Well ? " he asked, seeing her suppressed smile.

" Peter, you dear, you make romance out of nothing."

" Nothing ? " he queried.

In a second he realised he had made a slip. She had caught him. Lady Neville was too astute to vaunt her success.

" I always feel you're a little mysterious," she explained. Sir Roderick picked off his pince-nez.

" She means erratic, Peter," he said, with a paternal air.

Sir Roderick was hopelessly in the dark as usual. Peter knew exactly what she meant. Put into words, with utter frankness, she would have said—' Peter Neville, brother-in-law, you are twenty-five years of age, a fine set-up fellow. For three years you've been out of view, and knowing you and seeing you, I am certain that in those three years you have gained some experience, bitter or otherwise, of my sex. I can hear it in your voice, see it in your eyes. There's the hot blood of youth pulsing through you for all your outward Neville self-possession. There's the tremendous lover locked up in you, urged by all the Latin blood of your mother's race. You'll do things that dear old Roderick cannot conceive, be struck by passions he has never known. Despite yourself, you place a compelling force on women who interest you. I don't interest you, your code holds you from that, but if I did I should not be able to help myself, and I should not want to. Some men are civilised and companionable, that's Roderick. Some are barbaric and possessive, that's you, Peter Neville, despite your ancestors and your traditions. Away from your native haunts you are the male, unrestrained, a nice male, I know, but combative, although you've no club in your hand and no cave to throw your woman in. And while all my being wants to outwit and thwart you, because I can't indulge in primitive passion, yet I'm envious. I'd like to put on a bearskin and live in the sun, to rear fierce children and exult in your physical prowess, to cower before your anger and share the transport of your passion.

' That's you, Peter Neville, for all your ancestors and your sham self-possession. There's something tells me you are going to that life. You're breathing deep before a desperate plunge. And I hate you for it, because I can't follow, for I believe in duty and caution and Society and all the other imprisoning things that take the zest from life.'

That is what she would have said to him, and suddenly he felt self-conscious, sitting there at breakfast in that heavily decorated Venetian room, with all the signs of an elaborate, refined society about him. He moved his legs uneasily and put a thin finger down between his soft collar and his neck. Sir Roderick had risen.

" I'll go and settle the bill," he said, and they watched him go, in silence. Suddenly Peter faced her. He would make her agree now.

" Well—wouldn't you ? " he asked her, directly.

She blanched a little at his clear assumption of her knowledge. It was useless to fence.

" Can a woman say, Peter ? You're young, you're single— "

He laughed. " You talk as if you were twenty years older instead of my age."

" It's often dangerous to one's liberty to have no responsibilities," she said, enigmatically. For the first time she felt uncomfortable. He was reading her now, the tables turned.

" It may be now or never—do you counsel never ? " he pressed.

" Peter," she said quietly, gathering up her purse and some letters. " I'm not sure that we either of us know what we're talking about. We always think it's now or never, that's the tragedy of love, when it should be now *and* ever."

" And why not, Maud ? "

She hesitated, but his eyes held her, and she confessed half-breathlessly—

" You're so animal, Peter."

He flushed then. Did he deserve that, although there was no reproach in the tone ? An awkward pause followed, and she rose, abruptly.

" I really must go and see my maid," she said, and went.

II

At four o'clock that same afternoon he was free to shape his adventure. They had gone, with much fuss about the luggage, with trunks and bags and packages, with Felix the valet and Janet the maid, with a lifting of hats from the hall porter and his staff. They had departed from Venice, leaving Peter behind, standing, as it were, in the wash of their passing. One hour later he, too, was departing, but his going was obscure. No one who had met the Peter of the breakfast table would have known this Peter who walked forward on the upper deck of the lagoon steamer bound for Chioggia. In the morning a Savile Row tailor and a Piccadilly shirt and shoemaker had contributed their anglicising effect. But now, in garments reduced to simple necessity, in a pair of flannel trousers and a jacket, with but a plain white shirt, open-necked, a black felt hat and white shoes, he was an Italian from any small place.

His soft slouch hat suggested the peasant. In his hand he carried a canvas hold-all, strapped to his paint box and folded easel. Experience had taught him that good clothes encountered suspicion among simple natives. As an artist he courted obscurity amid the obscure. The apparel of the fashionable Englishman lay in a trunk stored at the hotel. Apparently it was a young Italian of the bourgeois class who booked his fare to Chioggia.

The heat of the April afternoon lay upon the shimmering water as the steamer quietly glided from the Riva. The pink and grey façade of the pillared Palazzo diminished as they turned down the Lido channel. But they were not bound for that popular strip of sand, beloved of bathers. Suddenly the steamer swerved to the right seeking the straight broad channel to Malamocco, marked by *pali* clamped in threes and weather-worn. On his left the long low strip of the Lido was now clearer. It cut the skyline, dividing the Adriatic from the calm lagoon, standing as a barrier to Venice against the open sea. On it the large hotels reared up, white, luxurious palaces for the traveller, veritable castles on the enchanted marge for young honeymoon couples.

They were now passing the little island of La Grazia, which seemed to float on, rather than have a basis in, the burnished water. Once it had sheltered religious hermits in its peaceful cloisters, but now it was a retreat for consumptives. The lagoon was dotted with small islands on the right. The level sweep of water faded in distance where sky and lagoon had an imperceptible union in the heat-haze. On the left, the long line of the sandy Lido kept clearly in view. They had passed the island of San Clemente, and drew nearer San Spirito, between them and the treeless Lido. The old home of the Augustinian monks, for whom Palma Vecchio and Titian had painted, lay sadly deserted under the radiant sky, its ugly powder magazine seeming an added insult of Time.

Next, Poveglia the deserted, rode into view, once the home of the intrepid fishermen who had so gaily cut the throats of the Franks when King Pepin made his ill-fated attack on the Republic. That same Republic ruthlessly destroyed it later, rather than that it should fall as spoil to the hated Genoese who had seized Chioggia, and affronted Venice with such insolence.

They were running into Malamocco now, the old village on the sandbank which had once boasted its own Doge. As they neared the wooden pier the steamer aroused the usual temporary commotion, where its call was the only distraction in the hot sleepy day. From the wooden pier a dozen bronzed urchins dived and threshed the blue water to silver foam. They swarmed up the warping ropes and begged money from the passengers, handsome little beggars with the heads of cherubs and the swift movement of water rats. A party of eight nuns, clad in brown with black mantillas, walked down the gangway. A dozen empty hen crates were flung ashore. The spasmodic shriek of the syren and they were moving up the lagoon again, with Venice, silver on the skyline, its campanile quivering in the haze.

They were not alone on the water. Long low boats, propelled by gondoliers, glided by, their decks almost awash, bright with double cargoes, mirrored in the iridescent water. Odd fishing boats rode by, their sails like butterflies' wings, blazing as with heraldic colours. Now the Lido broadened as Forte Alberoni jutted out into the lagoon, standing guard over the break in the long sea bank, where the Porto opened into the Adriatic. A battleship rode at anchor, its awnings drawn against the afternoon sun. About its stern a swarm of happy sailors splashed in the tepid blue water.

Then once more the long, narrow bank between the sea and the lagoon, the Littorale di Pelestrina by name, where man had assisted Nature with a vast sea-wall, the murazzi, built in 1618. It was the last great work of the Republic to ensure that the Bride of the Adriatic should not be overwhelmed by her husband in his tempestuous moods.

There was a similar herd of brown urchins around the pier at Pelestrina. The village gossips, presided over by the village oracle, all with their hands in their pockets and their sleeves rolled back, watched the forced labour of the cargo porters. They would be standing there in the same listless fashion next year or any year. One did not work in the heat even if one had not an eye for all this lazy beauty. The little steamer thrashed its way out again towards the next open Porto, of Chioggia, the deepening blue and green of the water revealing the sea channel.

And once again Peter Neville could see Chioggia. It lay there, on the near horizon, stretched out, crescent-fashion, across the lagoon. To the left, beyond the open sea channel, the sea wall ran on again, this time past Sottomarina, with a small lagoon dividing it from Chioggia. There, protected from the sea by the hook of that sea-wall, an actual island in the lagoon, but connected by a bridge to the mainland running beyond, Chioggia lay in the heat haze, its harbour wall immediately guarding it. The canal, the Vena, used by the fishing fleet, traversed the island. Some high chimneys cut the skyline on the right.

Those chimneys were the only modern jarring note in a picture of flawless beauty. On the one hand the wine-dark Adriatic rose to the horizon, on the other the great lagoon ran almost to infinity across its leagues of sapphire water. Here and there the winged sails of a boat hovered in the still air.

The approach to Chioggia had been quickened for Peter by a lively old woman, beautiful with her sun-shrivelled face. He had helped her along the deck with a box and she began talking to him in artless fashion, with the candour and inquisitive wonder of the Italian peasant.

" The signore is an Americano ? " she asked, when he responded to her voluble thanks.

" No—I am English."

" Ah, signore, ah ! Then you will not know New York ? " she said, wistfully, he thought. She clutched her black umbrella and put a brown gnarled hand under her yellow apron.

" Yes—I have been to New York. Do you know it ? " he replied.

The old woman shook her head.

" No, signore, but I hear much about it. It is a mar-vellous city. My son is there. He has been gone twelve years and he has never forgotten me, the Holy Mother preserve him ! In five years he will return. He has saved, and he has kept me. I am eighty-eight, signore, but I cannot die until that blessed day."

Peter looked at the calm, dignified old face.

" Perhaps he will take you back with him," he said.

The wrinkled mouth puckered into a smile.

" No, signore, I shall die in Chioggia, and he will not return to America. All his letters are of home. He saves hard. He longs for the sun."

" But there is plenty of sun in America."

" Ah, maybe—but not our sun, signore," and she lifted a withered brown hand towards the sky, " He wants that ! "

So even these old peasants knew the spell of the land. He turned away, and suddenly saw Chioggia looming up

over the rail. Instantly he stepped forward. Was *it*
there as yesterday ?

No, the harbour was empty. The vessel had gone ;
and in that moment he realised the utter folly of this
return. How should he find her, and when he found her,
if so fortunate, what then ?

He stood thinking, wondering, as the steamer was
warped in, and deep within him he felt the answer, felt
it in his blood. They would meet. The force that had
drawn him here would compel it. There were some
things beyond human direction.

CHAPTER III

ABOUT a dozen persons left the boat when it moored at its final stage for the night. It would leave early, at dawn, on the morrow with fish, poultry and vegetables. Two sailors were hastily throwing ashore the returned empty hampers and crates, whose smell attracted a couple of thin cats out of the shadow. On the quay itself there was no one to be seen. Along one side of it stood a newly-built hotel, of white stone. The side of the building was in the main street. It faced an open square leading across the picturesque Vigo Bridge, rising from steps at either hand to its central arch.

From that balustrade, north, one looked out across the harbour to the great lagoon and the sea-channel—the Porto di Chioggia ; to the east lay the long Canal of San Domenico, giving access to the small shallow lagoon, separating Chioggia from the sea-wall where Sottomarina bordered the sea. Over the Vigo Bridge was the tiny church of San Domenico which they had visited the previous day, attracted by Baedeker's recommendation of its painting by Carpaccio of St. Paul. At the corner of the hotel a number of chairs and tables stood unoccupied. In the cool of the evening, when the social life of the town began, they would be filled.

Peter decided to take rooms at the hotel. It had a modern air, and although that was no recommendation to an artist, it was probably clean. Through the plate glass window he could see a young Italian in the waiter's perpetual evening dress. It had that much pretension to form.

Peter went in, and the proprietor, aware that the boat had arrived, waited in the hall. In a moment he realised the stranger's need. Yes, he had beautiful rooms for the signore. He led the way up the stairs, turned into a long corridor, opened a door and bade his patron enter. It was a large room, in semi-darkness, for the windows were shuttered. The smiling padrone skipped across the concrete floor, and flung out the shutters with a flourish.

" Bella vista ! " he exclaimed, indicating the view.

It was, admittedly, a beautiful view, worthy of those overworked words in the Italian vocabulary. The windows looked out over the harbour and the wall of the molo, to the vast lagoon reflecting the reddening evening. Far away on that heat-obscured horizon lay Venice, but now the lagoon and the sea were merged into one hemisphere of colour. The sails of a number of fishing vessels, half-furled, floated like a crimson screen, renewed in shaken mimicry below.

The padrone stood waiting for the signore's expression of satisfaction. Yes, it was quiet. It faced due north and was therefore the coolest room in Chioggia. No, there were no *zanzarieri* to the bed, they were not necessary, for there was a wind from the Porto, and mosquitoes abhorred the sea wind. They had many artists and the signore would therefore be in capable hands.

Peter took the room. In reply to a query, he could not give the length of his stay, perhaps a week, perhaps a month. The padrone bowed, smiled, and raised his hands ecstatically.

" Ah, signore, that is always the reply, and it is always
a long time. I have known the signori to stay six months.
Chioggia la bella ! It is hard to go ! "

He bowed himself out. Peter put his valise down on
the table near the window. Voices below caused him to
look out. Abruptly he turned away. Of course it was
not ! He might never see her again. It was possible the
vessel did not belong to Chioggia.

There was a tap on the door and a girl entered with
towels. She curtsied as she came in, a well-built, dark-
eyed girl of about nineteen, with wooden pattens on her
stockingless feet.

" Is the fleet out now ? " he asked, indicating the
harbour.

She halted at her work and smiled.

" Si, signore, but it will return at sunset, they are only
beyond the Porto to-day. It is a poor season."

She spoke slowly, with a Chioggian accent, softer than
the Venetian, and he was pleased to find that he could
understand.

" Do the local vessels have any particular sign ?—I
noticed one the other day—yesterday, with St. George
and the Dragon on its prow. It had russet sails, with a
yellow— "

" Si, signore, it was here," she said, eagerly pointing
below, " the *San Giorgio*. It belongs to Signor Delfino.
He owns many bragozzi."

She felt happy in being able to give him information.
Had the signore been along the Canale Vena ? The boats
moored there for refitting and unloading, bella vista !
She went out, with another curtsey. He wanted to ask
' Do you know who was the black-haired young woman
on board the *San Giorgio* yesterday afternoon ? Do you
think she would let me paint her ? Had she— ' No, he

could not ask those questions. He must be patient and observe.

The day was deepening now. Away over Venice the blue grew less intense and was shot with purple. Following the stream of colour to its western source he found a sky of bronze falling to a fierce crimson horizon. Already the intrepid moon hung over the Adriatic in a colder sky.

He unpacked his valise, washed, and went down to dinner.

In the dining-room he was shown to a small table in the corner. There were not more than a dozen guests present. A stout old gentleman, accompanied by his stouter wife and a pale, pimply youth with glasses and stiff flaxen hair, occupied the centre of the room. They spoke German with a Zurich accent, were quiet and homely. Not so the bald Englishman at the side table, with his faded little wife. He exuded self-importance. He informed the room, via his wife, that the Italians could not cook. They drenched everything in oil. He was tired of veal and spaghetti. Half-way through dinner Peter was very tired of him. At home he probably ate tinned foods and drank coffee essence. National dignity urged him to demonstrate before the Italians. His tired wife tried to soothe him and smiled at the harassed waiter compensatorily.

The noisiest and gayest party was that of four Harvard undergraduates. They were clean-looking young fellows, with cheery faces, and a well-groomed air. They were deriving fun from the Italian of one of themselves, named ' Stuffy,' who pluckily conversed with the waiter, all smiles and bad French. Also, very quiet and happy in the opposite corner, were a young bridal pair. English, he could recognise from their new-tailored clothes. They were engrossed in each other, and Peter saw the sparkle of the girl's love-lit eyes above the rose-shaded table lamp.

They were all tourists, he noticed, so he would not be troubled by his fellow-guests. Their haunts would not be those of one such as himself, free of the language restriction.

He was the first to leave the table, and hatless, he strolled out into the semi-darkness. The moon had not yet risen from the bank of cloud, whence it silvered the ripple at the Porto's mouth, where the sea current broke the calm of the lagoon. There was not a sound, not even of the *cicala*, that fretful monotonous insect of the Italian landscape, for there was no vegetation near. Down the Corso a few lights glimmered, but the flags were empty, except for urchins. It was early yet.

He crossed the small square and turned down the quay of the Vena Canal. In the gathering darkness the fishing vessels were magnified in size and confusion. The masts towered up like a wintry forest. Below, the furled sails were lost in the night. From a few hatchways a feeble yellow light rayed out. He walked on down the length of the island, picking his way with caution amid the hawsers, floats and tackle. A long row of arcaded houses ran by the side of the canal, and these were frequently intersected by narrow streets running through to the parallel Corso. They were dark, with a few odd lights, and doorways in which the lounging figure of a man or woman was silhouetted. He was in the fisherman's district now. Soon the canal turned at a right angle, bringing him to the bridge, connecting the island with the mainland. It was a continuation of the straight Corso, leading to the railway line to Rovigo beyond.

There were signs of life now in the Corso, but he struck away across the wide street and plunged down an alley. It was still hot with the day's sun, and a general store, open to the street, tainted the air with mingled odours of

fruit, fish and garlic. He had heard the twanging of a
pair of mandolines and knew he should find a group
around the performers. He had spent long nights in
Tuscany sitting under plane trees while the mandolinists
played and gossiped.

The sounds were more distinct now. He could hear a
babel of voices, and a light streamed out across the cobbles.
A dozen half-naked boys, with bright eyes and black
tousled heads, clustered about a doorway. It led down a
passage at the side of an inn, styled the *Trattoria del Sole*,
wherein, through a dimly-lit room, he could see men
drinking, their throats bare, their faces hidden beneath
soft-brimmed black hats. Familiar with the nature of
the music, singularly alluring despite its metallic pitch,
he walked down the passage.

It opened on to the inn yard. Under the timbers that
leaned to the back wall of the house a great vine had netted
itself, so closely that it shut out the night above. From
this green roof hung a few electric lights. Above their
circular shades clustered the shadowy leaves of the vine.
Three large open windows overlooked this yard, each
filled with a small group of men, leaning out on their
elbows, their wine glasses on a table within.

It was a strange, but to Peter, a familiar scene that
spread before him. On the mud-beaten floor nearly
twenty men and some four girls were dancing. The dim
light fell upon them from the vine-rooftree, as they moved
in a slow, jumpy step, to the indefinite time of the two
mandolines. The men, for the most part, were dancing
together, as often he had seen them in the village inns,
for the girls were a little shy of dancing except with their
acknowledged lovers.

Many of them to-night were youths, slim but mus-
cularly built, with strong thighs and lithe, graceful

movements of their bodies. They were clad in thin brown cotton trousers and spotless white shirts, rolled back at the elbows, with open necks showing strong tanned throats. Hatless, with tumbling black hair, their eyes had a strange light, half-smouldering, half-languorous, as they danced.

They might have been figures moving in an hypnotic dream, so intense their clasp of each other's swaying body, so rapt the expression of their faces. The four girls, dancing with their young lovers, moved like thistledown carried on a strong wind, the youths holding them embraced, every line of their soft bodies dissolved in the harder figures. The compelling male strength, made pliant and rhythmic by the music, had an irresistible impulse to which the women surrendered, their heads falling back a little, their tight bodices pressed up to the adamant chests of the men, their contiguous limbs yielding in movement to the superior force.

Near the entrance several youths were lounging. Three old women, in shawls, sat gossiping on a bench, against the wall. A couple of children, tiny creatures that should have been asleep, clambered about the knees of a gnarled old fellow, his face burned with seventy years of sunshine.

" Buona sera " said Peter, to the lad on his right.

" Buona sera, signore," he responded, shyly. His companions looked half sullenly, half suspiciously. The padrone made his way from a corner, beaming. Peter ordered a flask of chianti and three glasses and asked the young men to drink with him. They appeared reluctant, standing as cattle stand, their minds ponderously wondering. He knew this look of old, had met it in the inns and byways of many Italian villages, but it would go speedily as he gained their confidence and they lost

curiosity. One youth, franker than the rest, seated himself at the table. Peter filled his glass.

" It is early yet ? " he asked, alluding to the half empty
floor.

" Yes, signore. They have just started. You're an
artist, signore ? We get many here in the spring and
autumn," he went on, not waiting to be answered.

They talked easily. The others watched them a while,
then slowly the remaining chairs at the table were occupied.
Peter filled their glasses, and ordered another flask, after
which he pulled out his cigarette case and handed it round.
Their eyes glistened at the sight of the English cigarettes.
Ten minutes later, Peter was laughing freely among them.
He had the gift of securing confidence.

The floor was filling now, more men were dancing, the
women still scarce. The mandolines began a lilting tune.
Peter turned to the youth at his side.

" Will you dance ? " he asked, rising.

The youth stood up shyly, and without answering
slipped into Peter's arms ; they glided off. His partner
was a slim boy, the down scarcely showing on his brown
face. Like most of his companions he was dark, his hair
curling crisply over his small round head. He hardly
spoke as they danced, his eyes like an animal's, affectionate and sad. So light was he on his feet, and so
completely self-surrendered, Peter might have been
dancing with a nervous school-girl.

His name was Marco Migone, he worked with his
father on a boat, netting on the lagoons. Yes, he knew
most of the vessels in the fleet and the men on them.
The *San Giorgio* belonged to Jacopo Delfino. He was a
rich man and owned twenty-three boats as well as a steam-
trawler. Perhaps the signore had seen his house on the
Corso ? It had once been a palazzo occupied by a Genoese

general during the famous siege. It had some marvellous frescoes, so he was told, for he had not been in the rich bragozzi owner's house.

Peter directed the conversation back to the *San Giorgio*. No, they did not carry women on board, or rarely, so he could not say who the young woman was—perhaps one of the men's daughters. Oh yes, all the girls were glad to pose for the artists, save those with lovers, who did not always like it.

While they talked, the dance grew faster and faster. The dancers were losing themselves in the strange rhythm, which became an obsession. In the dim light the whole room appeared to palpitate. An acrid odour rose from the ground-swell, caused by the movement of the dancers. The music seemed removed, and took on an Eastern atmosphere. It was no longer Italian, it was barbaric. A girl swept by, held close in the arms of a powerful man, her dark loose hair clouding his face, the veins of his temples suffused.

Faster and faster they whirled. It grew dark, the maze increased. It was almost a riot now, the strings of the mandolines were being torn and uttered a plangent cry. Peter looked at his partner. His eyes were somnolent, in an hypnotic fashion, his body inert but still moving, as if obedient to a demoniac spirit that seemed to have entered the assembly. They were abandoned to the lure of the dance, with the earnestness of children. A woman's displayed hand rested protectively on her bosom, her lover's mouth brushing her hair.

Suddenly the music stopped. The dancers halted, stood transported awhile, then disengaged, half-sighing, and walked from the floor. The laughter and the chatter broke forth again. Peter and his partner rejoined their table.

"Did you tread on the signore's feet, Marco ? " cried one.

"Pulling Marco's hard work, signore," laughed another.

Marco flushed sensitively beneath his tan, and with a little animal jerk pushed a tormentor off his chair.

"He dances as well as a girl," said Peter. "But all you lads are born dancers. Where are your glasses ! "

By eleven the inn-yard was full. Fathers and mothers, accompanied by their daughters and babies, filled every form and table. The mandolines were now augmented by a castanet player. The music was wilder, the fervour less restrained.

It was towards the end of one of these macabre dances, when the dust from the floor had risen in a fog that dimmed the figures and hung clouded under the electric lights, that Peter suddenly started and abruptly broke the conversation. Fearing to betray himself, he joined in again after a moment of fruitless, desperate search. They had been lost immediately in the shadowy maze. He waited for the dancers to come round. The minutes went by but he saw them not. In his tense apprehension he feared the dance would stop too soon. Furtively, he searched each approaching couple.

There !—gone again ! It was the woman of the *San Giorgio* !

"Marco ! " He placed a hot eager hand on the lad's arm. "Tell me—that couple—who are they ? "

Marco's eyes wandered indefinitely.

"No !—there,—in the black-velvet bodice, red hair-band, with the boy."

Marco found them.

"That's Rocco, the nephew of Signor Delfino, who I told you about, in whose house— " he explained, tortuously.

" Yes, yes—but the girl, who is she ? " asked Peter, impatiently.

Marco's eyes rested leisurely upon her.

" Oh that's Lucia," he explained, " she's dancing with her cousin. He's on the *San Giorgio*."

Peter turned to the table again. He did not wish to make them curious. The ingenuous Marco had noticed nothing. He was too flattered by the attention of the signore to think of anything else. Secretly he nourished ambition as a guide. He liked the English signore who was so friendly and had such kind eyes.

When twelve struck from a distant tower, Peter rose from his table, bidding his companions good night. They gave him a cheerful, friendly response. He wanted to be alone in the cool night with this vision of her radiant beauty. What hair, what dark eyes ! He could see her mouth now, the small teeth parted in the smile of her scarlet lips. She could not be more than twenty-two, for all her mature beauty.

Marco watched the Englishman go to the door and disappear down the passage. Swiftly he followed, pressing his way through the loungers. Peter had just gained the street.

" Signore ! " he called.

Peter turned. It was Marco, his eyes shining, holding his hands interlaced, nervously.

" Pardon, signore—if I might suggest for an artist some places ? I know the beautiful places."

He stood there, in the moonlight, apprehensive of his temerity.

Peter hesitated. He did not wish to be troubled with a guide on his expeditions. But there was something pathetically anxious about this Italian lad.

" Thank you, Marco," he said, " but I hadn't thought of work just yet. I've only come to-day."

Marco bowed, showing two even rows of teeth.

"As the signore wishes," he said, quietly, his face shadowing.

"But I'd like to be shown round," said Peter, relenting. "When are you free ?"

"I am at your service any time, signore. I work with my father," he said, as if explaining his freedom. "To-morrow—I can take the signore across the Porto, to the murazzi and the Littorale di Pelestrina. I have a boat."

"Good," assented Peter. "We'll bathe and fish. To-morrow—at ten ?"

"Sì, signore, thank you," Marco smiled, and bowed deeply.

"Buona notte, Marco," cried Peter, going.

"Buona notte, signore," responded Marco, and then, singing his thanks as he bowed anew, "Grazie, signore, grazie."

Peter walked on, down the broad Corso, past the lighted cafés and the groups seated at the small tables extending to the middle of the flagged road. The strong moonlight cast firm shadows from the buildings. Nearing the harbour, he could see the lights on the mastheads of some of the boats on the lagoon, and on the sea-bank, where the Littorale ended, a green light flashed intermittently for ships making the Porto.

Peter halted in the small piazza at the end of the Corso. Beside him stood the sign of the mighty Republic, the Lion of St. Mark, on a column. He had seen it in a dozen proud cities, in Verona, in Padua. What a wonderful race these Venetians were ! He was looking now across the Porto leading to the open sea. The grey mass of Forte Caroman, on the spit of the Littorale, lay shadowy at the water's edge, and, not far distant, the light on the promontory marked the sea channel. Its raised beam was thrown across the water and scattered emerald reflections where the sea broke the calm surface of the lagoon. Through that very porto Venice had been delivered from terrible defeat when gallant Vittor Pisani sealed up the Genoese Navy, which had entered the lagoon and seized Chioggia, thus turning the tables on Admiral Doria who awaited the surrender of blockaded Venice.

On his walk from the inn down the Corso, Peter had passed the huge granary built to withstand the strain of such sieges. It was now a fishmarket. Yet the real features of Chioggia remained as they were in that time of stress in the fourteenth century. The hardy, handsome fishermen and the boats they sailed had not changed in type. For a thousand years Chioggia had boasted of its beautiful women, its virile men.

When Venice rose from the sea, while the emperors ruled at Rome, and the eagle went with the legions marching over the known world, ships such as these, manned by men such as these, were upon the sea and the lagoons. These men and women of Chioggia still kept the Greek grace of their early Illyrian stock. They were aloof to the Romans as to the Celts; the Huns pouring down the Trentino, sweeping the Roman Empire to red ruin, could not touch them in the fastnesses of the shallow lagoons. In vain Attila and Alaric threatened their destruction.

Peter could see in these men and women the pride of a long, unbroken line. There was a natural dignity in their carriage, a courtliness in their speech and gesture, a reserve in their attitude that proclaimed a race of proud birth. He read all this in the face of Lucia. Outwardly, in the costume of the Chioggiotte, she was a woman of this old race, but with something additional. What it was lacked a name, a definition. Imperial—perhaps that was the term. Her look revealed a race of seigniors.

The grace with which she had danced! Throughout
Marco's chatter he had watched her. The tilt of her head,
the swing of her young body, the lambent beauty of her
eyes and face! He could see her now, with the widening
swirl of her skirt, the soft shapely arm wound round the
neck of her partner. And despite his ardent desire, he
feared to speak to her, to approach her. When that time
came he would lose whatever command he now held over
himself. A force greater than his own will, something
before which resolution, thought of consequences—all
would sink impotent beneath the flood that took their
lives in its remorseless sweep. Nothing could avail him
then, the ties of society, the call of duty, or the weight of
tradition. They would all be useless, ignored, beaten
down in the track of Destiny.

Destiny! Standing there, at the harbour's edge, his
sight soared to the star-strewn dome of the night. Lower,
the waters mirrored the moonlight through league on
league of space, beauty and quiet. An atom, a moment
of consciousness, limited but perhaps the intenser for its
limitation, he stood there, minute beneath the unfathomable night, an observer of beauty drawn from the centuries,
passing to the centuries. Why not live this moment, live
it in the full sweep of his emotions, his ardent desire?

In the still night he trembled. Caution, Reason, the
things of the world said " Go! " Therein lay safety.
But in his heart, voicing the beauty around him, the deep
desire within, came a whispered " Stay! " and he knew
it was the voice of Life, fulfilling, perpetuating itself.

A door opened in a house under the arcades by the
Corso. A shaft of yellow light was thrown across the
piazza. Voices broke his reverie, and turning away from
the harbour he saw two men come out of the doorway.
It was evidently an inn. Within, the dim light falling

from the low ceiling of the room, Peter could see a number of black-hatted men seated along a wooden table laden with chianti flasks. With the beam through the open door came the music of an accordion. The two men halted in the piazza. Suddenly, as if urged by the quiet beauty of the night, they raised their voices in song.

The words were indistinct, the melody perhaps from a folk-song. The piazza had been transformed into a stage. They raised their hands to heaven, embraced each other, and sang lustily in good voice. Then silence again, and the two mysterious performers moved on, irregularly, down the Corso. Peter tried to imagine two British workmen, emerging from an alehouse, singing in the moonlight. It would have given him no feeling of romance, of the dramatic, as these men had done, only a feeling of disgust at the hideous noise and depravity.

He walked on to his hotel, fearing the porter would not be up. A sleek-headed waiter let him in.

" Has the signore heard the singing ? " he asked.

" Those two sailors—oh yes—from a folk-song wasn't it ? "

" No, signore—not those men, they were from the trattoria. We have had real singing—*bel canto*—on the Molo to-night. The girls and their lovers have been serenading. The fleet sails to-morrow morning, that is why," he explained, as he locked the hall door.

" At what time to-morrow ?—I'd like to see it."

" At eleven, I think, signore. They are going down the Adriatic, as far as Zara, I hear. When the shoals are scarce they have to go south for several days."

This Italian was communicative. At moments he lapsed into French, so bad that he was almost unintelligible.

" The signore speaks French ? " he asked with an

apologetic smile, " I learn with much labour. It is the accent. But I am ambitious. I want to go to Paris. And then to London, when I can speak English. But pardon, signore, you are tired."

" I am interested—why do you want to go to Paris, and to London ? You would miss the sunshine."

The waiter shrugged his shoulders. " It is money," he said simply.

Peter laughed. So they were not happy here.

" We are poor in Chioggia, signore. There is nothing but fishing. It is hard work and dangerous. I know, I am the son of a fisherman and worked five years on the lagoons. Often we starved. So I came here. There is always food where the *signori* come."

He smiled pathetically. His dark young face slightly tragic during this confession.

" Tell me," said Peter, speaking in French to give him the desired practice, " do the fishermen own their boats ? "

" Sometimes, signore, pernaps a family, a father and his sons, or brothers, own a boat between them. If they are lucky they may have two boats or three. Signor Delfino has twenty-three ! He is a rich man, his fathers owned bragozzi before him. He lives in the palazzo off the Corso. Has the signore seen the frescoes there ? Signor Delfino is very hospitable to visitors. On Tuesdays and—"

Peter interrupted his informant.

" He has a daughter, has he not ? "

The waiter's face wreathed itself in smiles. He clasped his hands together ecstatically, his whole body swaying in his enthusiasm.

" Ah, signore—la bella Lucia ! Have you seen her, signore ? " he asked eagerly. " We are all her worshippers. She is beautiful, she is rich, she is kind."

He leaned forward, as if imparting great information.

"She was here yesterday, signore," he said, dramatically, pointing to the door. "She was on her cousin's boat. I heard her singing to him and teasing him as he dozed. She is full of mirth, la bella Lucia. The artists, they all—"

The artists! Then he was not the first! Peter abruptly broke in on the fluent adorer.

"She will be married soon, with such wonderful assets," he said, lightly, turning towards the stairs. "The catch of Chioggia!"

The waiter turned serious at once.

"Ah no, signore. There is none in Chioggia. Who should there be? Her father guards her. She has every accomplishment. The great maestro, Signor Zambra, teaches her to sing. Once a week she goes to Venice for her lesson. I have not heard her, but my friend, Luigi, says—"

Here words failed him. He rolled his eyes upwards in ecstasy and sighed. Then, recovering, he added pathetically, "There are many poor *nobili* in Venice. Her father is of proud blood. He is ambitious for her. Who knows?"

Peter agreed. Who knows? Bidding the voluble little fellow good-night, he went up to bed.

CHAPTER IV

AND Lucia, the object of so much heart-burning and speculation, was she all unaware ? She was now in her twenty-first year, and in no way differed from her sex. She had loved often, loved joyously, ever since that day down by the quay young Luigi Spinelli, coming off his boat, and still clad in his cotton trousers and crimson jersey, had suddenly taken her into his arms and kissed her fiercely. He was fifteen and she was sixteen then, and amazement at the sensation had prevented her boxing his ears. It would have been easy to do, for he, too, stood astonished at his audacity, and shaken by his emotion. But she had teased him too often.

She had enjoyed talking and laughing with Luigi. He was a strapping, handsome lad, with strong shoulders and a fine skin, under whose bronze the blood readily flushed. On this occasion Lucia would have escaped, as often before, if it had not been for her hair. She had put it up, and the sight of her sweet young neck, in its beautiful curve from the slim shoulder, had been too much for Luigi. He kissed her, stood a moment amazed at his fortune, and then fled.

That was four years ago, and she would not claim she had never been kissed since. Lucia enjoyed life to the full. She tripped up and down the quays, gossiped on board the ships refitting after their unloading, played

pranks on her father's old sailors, who adored her, and
was never so happy as when courted by half-a-dozen good-
looking lads, who followed her in silent worship and, at
the most, as it grew dusk, pressed her tiny hand in their
own. Even those opportunities were rare, for Bianca was
never long away. Bianca led a worried life trying to
make her old bones as active as Lucia's. She was a kind
of chaperon and attendant to Lucia, authorised by her
master to keep a cautious eye on his wayward, motherless
daughter. She assisted also in the household, which
contained one other woman who acted as housekeeper and
whose husband made himself useful in the kitchen and
small garden.

The surveillance grew less as Lucia grew more in need
of it. At eighteen she wholly outwitted Bianca, and at
twenty had established her independence. Her father
watched her growing liberty, but being a man of sense
he saw that his daughter would not lightly lose her
head. She was often in love, nevertheless. Generally
they were handsome young fellows with little to say for
themselves, but in their eyes admiration found expression. Yet there was a note of fatality in their wooing.
It could have no satisfactory end, for the Signorina Delfino was the daughter of a rich man, so far as riches were
accounted in poor Chioggia, and a proud man, for was
not the Signore descended from those Delfinos who had
given a Podestà, or Governor, to Chioggia in the early
days of splendour?

Lucia, at the dance whither she had gone with her
cousin, had seen Peter Neville seated at the table, talking
with Marco and the other youths. Had he but known,
the tumult her appearance had caused in him was no less
than that aroused in her by this meeting. She had not
expected to see him again. When she first saw him

seated among his friends outside the café on the quay she
knew he was a tourist, one of those who came by the
morning boat from Venice, walked along the canals, and
looked at the picture by Carpaccio in the Church of
San Domenico. Perhaps they traversed the Corso as far
as the towered gate, La Torre, leading to the mainland,
taking on their return the Duomo of Santa Maria, with its
fourteenth century reliquaries.

If the weather was not too hot, they climbed the high
campanile whence they could look over the lagoons to
Venice, south towards Rovigo and Ravenna, west towards
Padua and the blue Euganean hills, and east across the sea
to the Dalmatian coast. If the party comprised an artist
then they would be sure to visit the south side of the
Duomo, where an untidy public garden filled with acacia
trees was bordered by a stone balustrade, overlooking a
narrow canal. It had a famous shrine, where of old the
fishermen had prayed to the Madonna.

This handsome young Englishman, for such she guessed
he was, had attracted her gaze from the moment when she
emerged from the hatchway, where she had been gossiping
to the men, overhauling in readiness for the sailing of the
fleet in a couple of days. She liked the stranger's clean-
cut profile, and the fine texture and fairness of his skin.
In a glance she had appraised the athletic lines of his body
as he sat there, carelessly, one leg crossed over the other,
a thin brown hand fingering his pipe.

He had removed his hat and she loved, at once, the
way in which his dark shining hair went up from the forehead, defining clearly the attractive head and the back of
his neck, close-cropped and tanned with the sun.

All this was but a moment's vision, for he turned to look
at her, his eyes on hers. He had seemed to look through
her, so that she turned swiftly to avoid embarrassment.

While she spoke she was aware his eyes were still upon her, and perhaps this gave a certain wildness to her laughter, an aggressive touch to the posture of her body. She wanted to look again, but dared not, and fled below. When she came up, her heart palpitating at the possibility of another encounter, he had gone. Her pleasant apprehension had been unnecessary. She would never see him again.

And now she had met him at the *Trattoria del Sole*. She realised what this meant. He was staying in Chioggia, was an artist probably. In which case she knew she would meet him, for Chioggia was not so large, and she knew the haunts of the artists. At this thought she had blushed, and looked at her cousin as he danced with her, but he was smiling at a friend who had just passed them. When the Englishman left the room, she was about to make her way towards Marco, who had talked to him. He would know something ; but before she had been able to leave her cousin Marco had gone out.

She turned to the table where the stranger had sat. Luigi Spinelli was there among his friends. His eyes were upon her, eager for recognition. Lucia's look invited him to her side, and to his joy she consented to dance.

" Who was that Inglese ? " she asked, breaking across Luigi's dream, as he held her tenderly, his eyes trustful and tender as a dog's.

" You are sharp, Lucia—how did you know he was English ? "

" I didn't, I guessed," she corrected him. " He was too lightly built for a German and is not pale enough for an American."

" I don't know anything about him," confessed Luigi, unhappy in his inability to answer. " I think he's an artist, for he asked a lot of questions about the boats and where we go."

" He speaks Italian ? "

" Easily, we could understand him."

Then there would be no language difficulty when they met. She remembered the young American last year and that absurd flirtation, when they could not exchange a word ; but he had nothing to learn and much to teach about kissing, and since it had been their only method of conversation she had indulged him more than she had ever intended.

Luigi was dismissed at the end of the dance. He was happy and envied.

The entrancing stranger was still in Lucia's thoughts when the cousin left her at the door of her home, a large house off the Corso, dignified by the name of the Palazzo Delfino. In part of it, still remaining with its well-preserved frescoes, had lived that Delfino who had so stoutly championed Venetian rights during the occupation of the hated Genoese. It was he, Paolo Delfino, who had sat on the Doge's left hand on the great triumphal platform erected in the Piazza San Marco.

Lucia found her father seated in his favourite chair, playing his favourite game. Night after night he could be found there, the chessboard before his knees, and his old opponent watching him from the other side. He had fought Dr. Antonio Galuppi for thirty-five years. There was not a move he could not anticipate, not a move the dottore was not prepared to counter. It might be thought that between two such familiar antagonists the fortune of the game brought no changes. But the supremacy of either was never sure.

To-night, as on thousands of nights, they sat there in the dark room, its gloom exaggerated by the pale flames of the two candles burning in the sconces on either side of the board. They always played in candle-light, although the room had a Murano glass chandelier hanging over the dining-table.

Seated thus, they made an arresting picture, one which the observer would have dated with some difficulty. They might have been a couple of Venetian *condottieri* poring over the disposition of the armies in the long battle with Carrara's forces ; their heads might have been found a dozen times among those of Tiepolo's senators in scenes of Venice's splendour on the walls of the great Council Chamber in the Doge's Palace.

Delfino was a man of some sixty-five years. As he bent slightly forward, the fortune of the moment reflected in his smiling face, he made a handsome figure. His head was covered with a wealth of hair, almost silvered, which swept from the forehead backward in a mane, augmented by the bushy growth over the temples. To-night, with the soft light of the candles glimmering over it, there was a silver aureole which softened into the darkness around. The face was bearded, silver also, well trimmed to a point, revealing a somewhat fastidious taste. The nose was aquiline, and of a prominence which on occasions, when his antecedents were unknown to the observer, had caused him to be mistaken for a Jew. It was a nose of decided character, of a man whose will was adamant. Something of the passion, generally quite somnolent, of this striking man could be seen in the piercing level glance of the eyes, which were as those of a hawk, clear green and ringed. Aroused, he was a menacing figure, before whose fury men gave way, conscious of the tiger-heart, but those moments were rare. Kindly, with an active sense of humour, his life was controlled by a continuous love of justice and moral wholesomeness.

" There, dottore," he said, moving his knight, and leaning back in the carved ebony chair. He rested his strong hand upon the lion's head that scowled on the end of the chair arm. His eyes glinted in the candle-light, as he looked up at the dottore, deep in perplexity.

" That's something new for you ! " he cried.

It was seldom they spoke, being serious players. Dr. Galuppi leaned over the board. He was a dark man, with clean-shaven face and deep-set blue eyes. His years were about seventy, all of them spent in Chioggia, and he had superintended the birth of most of the men and women of the town. He was poor still, for he had a habit of forgetting to book his fees or the number of his visits, which, known, made him much called upon.

Yet he had all he wanted from life—good food, a comfortable home, kept by a housekeeper as old as himself, the love of a glass of wine and a game of chess. And he had a great dream, carefully preserved in his romantic old heart. Fifty years back he had loved passionately and in vain. He never married, cherishing the tragedy of this episode, until it coloured his whole life and softened his nature, making him the champion of all young people, especially if they were lovers. The absence of Dr. Galuppi at a local wedding was unknown, it would have been regarded as the dire threat of a malign Fate.

At this moment of challenge his tanned old face was grim, the thin lips compressed, one finger rubbing his brow while he experimented thoughtfully.

" H'm," was all he replied to his friend's comments. " H'm, let me see, friend Delfino,—let me see."

He had just spoken when a footfall caused the players to turn towards the door at the far end of the room. It was lit by the moonlight pouring in from the long open casement through which, against the bright sky, rose a delicate black tracery of masts and rigging, belonging to the boats lined up in the canal.

The door swung open abruptly and into the patch of moonlight stepped Lucia. Arrested by the darkness, she peered down the room towards the table and the candle-illumined players.

" Father—and you, dottore ! How late you are ! " she cried, advancing.

Jacopo Delfino rose from the board as his daughter entered.

" That's only a little trick of yours, Lucia, to have the first word, so that I can't say how late you are ! "

He put his hand under her chin, lifting her young face upwards, and looked down at her affectionately.

" I suppose you've danced all night and worn out your cousin ? " Then, placing his arm around her waist— " Look at the poor dottore there ! He'll not go to bed to-night unless we order him away."

Dr. Galuppi rubbed a veined hand down his lean thigh, and blinked over the board. Then he peered at Lucia, smiling at him, her young face aglow and, he observed, more freshly beautiful this night than ever.

" Your good father, Lucia," he said, slowly, in his deep voice, " always imagines I am at the end of my resources. He is an experimentalist, I am a strategist. Sometimes Fortune favours the intrepid, but I have proved that it never deserts the skilled. But for to-night I have had enough. By to-morrow, my friend, you will find yourself checkmated."

He rose cautiously, in order not to shake the board.

" And what's the latest gossip among the young folk ? " he asked, as Lucia fetched his stick and hat from a chair.

" Nothing, dottore, except there's another painter here."

" Another ! " grunted Galuppi. " There've been artists coming to Chioggia regularly since I was a boy. They all

paint the same places, in the same way,—the Vena, the
Ponte Vigo, the Canale Lombardo—pah! Whatever
becomes of all the pictures they paint? Every gallery in
Europe must groan with Chioggia. Well, it's a good
thing for all the handsome lads and lasses. They get
more out of the artists than they do out of the sea, I'm
sure!"

He bowed low to Lucia, with an old-world grace and,
escorted by Delfino, walked briskly towards the door.

"To-morrow night, my dear friend," he said, halting
in the doorway, "To-morrow night you will find I am a
man of resource, of infinite resource. At nine, as usual?"
he asked, shaking Delfino by the hand.

"At nine, dottore—your doom awaits you," laughed
Delfino, throwing back his fine old head, exultant.

"Merciless wretch!" cried the dottore, "a rivederci!"

"Buon riposo," responded Delfino, as his guest crossed
the threshold of the small courtyard, opening on to the
wide Corso Vittorio Emanuele. Delfino waited until his
guest had gone some distance. The Corso was not yet
deserted, for the lights of the cafés down towards the molo
were still burning. He bolted the courtyard door, walked
up the stone steps leading to the loggia, and locked another
door. A moment later, Lucia joined him, holding both
candles. He took one and, together, they ascended the
broad stone staircase, long grotesque shadows playing over
the groined ceiling and the walls decorated with armorial
bearings, records of the days when the old palazzo had
been the Governor's residence.

On the landing the fleet-owner kissed his daughter
good-night.

"The fleet goes out to-morrow at full tide," he said,
looking at her closely. "It will be Paolo's first time as
master. Will you come down to the molo?"

He did not fail to see the dull obedience of her reply. There was no delight, no real assent in it.

" Yes, father. At eleven ? "

He nodded, and went towards his room. Lucia watched him sadly. Paolo, always Paolo ! Would he not see it was useless, impossible ! Detested Paolo, tall, massive, swarthy Paolo. She stood a few moments, statue-like in the long corridor, stiller than the flame of her candle. She could see the black hair on the back of those strong hands, the growth in his nostrils, the blue-grey of his shaven cheeks, and the consuming fire of his hungry eyes. Handsome Paolo, some women called him. But to her, repulsive. Never ! never ! she vowed to herself.

In her room, Lucia paused in the semi-darkness, calling back the scene of an hour agone. The rhythm of the dance, the plaintive cry of the mandolines and the violin, the intense expressions of the dancers, the fog of dust whirled up from the floor, they were all part of her vision of him, seated there among the boat boys. Clearly she saw the sweep of his hair, the fine brow and dark eyes.

Moving to her window, she looked down on the canal, beyond the small garden with its sentinel cypress trees to the black moonlight-diapered mass of rigging and masts. The beauty of this scene had been hers from girlhood, she was a child of the sea and the lagoons. Her life was the life of these fishermen, she was the daughter of a fleet-master. What then, could she have to do with a strange young man, of foreign race, of unknown name ? What could he have to do with her ? It was folly to build dreams on such drifting, hopeless material.

There, down the canal, at her left, rose the Campanile. It stood erect and immense, black against the bright sky, keeping watch on the lagoons and the sea. When the boats were far out it was the first sign of home, in storms the lightning played about it, an accusing finger thrust into the black heavens. On hot sunny days the air sang through the arches of its bell tower, and on festival days it was clangorous with its five bells, whose voices in sweet interchange called across the waters, a sound familiar and dear to the fishermen, for were not these the voices of the saints, protecting them? Loudly called *San Felice*, softly joined in *Santa Maria Assunta*, boldly spake *San Francesco* and sweetly *Santa Maria del Carmine*, while over all soared the voice of their patron, *San Rocco*. In unison they flung far their voices, a warning and signal in storm, a joyful peal on festival days. Those bells had called generations of fishermen to prayer. They broke into a tumult of joy when Chioggia celebrated some great day in its history. Lucia knew that noble tower well. From it she had watched the sailing of the fleet in the silver dawn, and seen the sails return down the path of the sunset, into the home canals.

But now it was not of its beauty, or its bells she thought. Its strong silent shape was the symbol of remembered tragedy to-night, and an old story had for her a new meaning. As a small child she could remember the sensation created when Ursula Bossi in a paroxysm of despairing passion, had thrown herself from its balustrade, and lay broken and terribly disfigured on the cobbles of the Campo Duomo, two hundred feet below. For a week the story of her hapless love was related at every doorway and along the canals.

When Emilio Bossi walked down the Corso he saw the eyes that watched him, felt the silence that closed about his presence. He had betrothed his daughter to a young Tuscan farmer. In vain she pleaded, prayed, threatened. Was he, Emilio Bossi, the apothecary, to allow his daughter to marry young Zannone, handsome maybe, but one of a poverty-cursed family of lagoon netters? She had a dowry of four thousand lire! Why, the whole Zannone family could not raise five hundred! He loved his daughter, but he loved prestige. This Zannone affair was making him ridiculous before his neighbours.

So he drove his relentless bargain. On the eve of her marriage, a distracted girl borrowed the keys of the Campanile, and flung herself within fifty yards of the altar that would have bound her to a life worse than death.

Poor Ursula Bossi! Her name was now a legend almost. The once prosperous shop of her father was empty and boarded up. Bossi, shunned and childless, had gone forth from Chioggia a broken man, and Zannone himself was drowned at sea, a year later, in a storm that took seven of the boats.

Lucia looked at the Campanile, and a prayer hovered on her lips for the soul of unhappy Ursula. It stood there, as it had stood for hundreds of years, indifferent to the restless tides of life surging beneath it. In her love-dream Lucia had little difficulty in assuming the rôle of Ursula. She saw and pitied herself, driven desperately to a supreme sacrifice for love, and, touched by the romance of martyrdom, she enjoyed the sensation her death would create.

Then, awake to the absurdity of her thoughts, she turned from the window, and slipped out of her clothes. Letting fall the heavy cloud of her dark hair, she brushed, plaited and braided it, then stood a moment, naked and sylph-like in the faint candle-light. Her young hands gathered up the knotted tresses, and in a moment of contemplation, she pressed them to her bosom, standing motionless. In such an attitude of virgin beauty had Botticelli beheld his Venus wave-borne to earthly shores.

Upon Lucia's face there glowed the light of wonder, and all her pure young body shone, curve on curve of soft beauty falling to hidden shadows.

Thus for a moment she paused, body and mind caught in the transitory radiance of her thoughts. Then, swiftly, her hands let fall the gathered tresses, her white bed gown shrouded the lily figure, and the candle flame vanished under her warm breath. Soon, dreaming, she smiled as she was carried down the tide of night to the new dawn.

CHAPTER V

PAOLO FINGHETTI had been up and at work since five o'clock in the morning. Three times had he walked along the Vena Canal where the boats were lined up, all fitted in readiness for sailing. It was for him a day of achievement. Old Jacopo Delfino had relinquished his mastership of the fleet. For thirty-five years he had gone out with it and there had never been, in the memory of the Chioggiotti, a more skilled sailor, either in the handling of boats or the following of shoals. But he was growing old, and the rigours of winter fishing were telling upon him. If only Lucia had been a boy ! That was his thought, again and again. The disappointment at her birth had been intense, but Jacopo was a man of balance, and through all the years that Lucia grew to womanhood no hint of his disappointment was ever revealed. Nay, to cover his grief he increased his watchfulness over her, and slowly, under the influence of her joyous nature, his days were brightened. A new ambition now took the place of the old hopeless dead one. The house of Delfino should still rule Chioggia and control the fleet through a sound marriage.

In Paolo Finghetti he saw the means of consolidating Lucia's position. He, Jacopo, would soon pass from the scene of his labours, but not, he hoped, before he had seen the coming of a grandson, a child destined to increase the fortune of his house. With Lucia's marriage to Paolo the control of the fleet would be united. He was the owner of twenty-three bragozzi. Paolo's father, Giovanni, the Sicilian, held nine. This marriage would place under a single mastership thirty-two of the best fishing boats known in Adriatic waters. It was an amalgamation growing more essential each year. New conditions were menacing the old supremacy. Down at Ancona a company had taken control of a large fleet. They had had fierce disputes over their fishing grounds. The men of Chioggia and the men of Ancona had come to blows three times in the last twelve months.

Only last month the *Santa Lucia* of Chioggia had rammed the *Conte Contarini*. Had it been an accident ? After the altercations, the letter-writing between lawyers, Delfino, shrewd in all things, had seen that the *Santa Lucia*, sailed by a fierce-tempered Chioggiote, had been the aggressor. It had been a matter of tangled floats that had almost ended in bloodshed. The Ancona company was wealthy, they threatened litigation. Having a deep distrust of legal justice, Delfino paid their claim. The need of a young powerful controlling hand was imperative. Fortunately in Paolo Finghetti he found a suitable successor.

The new fleet-master, as he walked down the fondamenta, or canal side, on this sunny June morning, was a figure of romance. Painters had sketched him, for he epitomised the fierce masculine strength of the fisherman. He was taller than any of his companions, a heavily-built fellow standing six-foot-two on his bare feet. His scanty clothing scarcely veiled the splendid symmetry of his limbs, which still revealed the lines of youth despite their growing strength. A red-and-white ringed cotton shirt clung thinly to the heroic back, the spine channelled in ridges of muscle, mounting to the herculean shoulders.

The shirt was sleeveless, so that every line and sinew of his powerful arms stood forth, bronzed and hard as ropes. Such a figure had probably once posed in the studios of Michael Angelo.

The head captivated all artists. It was sullen, aggressive but handsome in its massive Sicilian way. A broad low brow was lost in a thick mass of black curly hair, close-cropped and almost shaven at the nape of the thick neck. The eyes were dark and heavily lashed, the strong jaw set squarely. His fleshy nose was broad, and the lips finely turned, but with a thickness slightly negroid. He was undoubtedly handsome but marred by a certain coarseness, a predominance of the physical.

Among the rough women of the port Finghetti was admired, among the men, feared. He spoke very little and was well-tempered until—but they had only seen him lose his temper twice, and the story had spread throughout the town, emphasising the legend of his strength. A drunken deck-hand had once defied his order, and found himself thrown across the donkey engine, over the gunwale, and beyond the fondamenta, up against the wall of a house, as if he had been a melon. The dazed man realised he was fortunate in escaping with only a broken arm. Had his head gone first, he would have crumpled up with a smashed skull, so powerful was the impact at the end of his twenty-foot flight.

The other memorable occasion had been in Finghetti's seventeenth year, when he had quarrelled with and thrashed an Ancona fisherman for speaking disparagingly of the Chioggian fleet. Only the intervention of the terrified crews, drinking in the trattoria yard, had prevented the young bull from breaking every bone in his adversary's body. Ancona knew him and feared him. It held him in honour also, for in addition to strength, which always commands admiration, he had swum for half an hour in a wintry sea, holding up an insensible Ancona seaman, washed overboard from a bragozzo.

This radiant morning, as he walked along the canal, his alert eye surveying each boat at its moorings, he was a proud man. At twenty-six he was the most important fellow in Chioggia, for old Delfino might be now considered out of the race. But one thing remained. This fleet must be inalienably his. Lucia must be his wife. To make this end easier of attainment he had been ridding himself of obstacles. He had sent back to her native Calabria the woman he kept for four years. He was tired of her, and of late she had been emphasising her claims upon him. A thousand lire, and the relinquishing of all right to the boy, had enabled him to send her off satisfied with the bargain.

Maria, his first woman, the plaything of his passionate teens, had been married to one of his crew, grateful for the small dowry and the permanent job assured by his obliging disposition. The new husband had not foreseen the responsibility of keeping a son whose physique now at six years was remarkable for a seven-months' child. To a man of Paolo's powerful way, little difficulties such as these were easily brushed aside; and no man cared to open a subject upon which Finghetti was obviously unwilling to talk.

Jacopo Delfino had not been blind to his fleetmaster's irregularities. While he looked with great disfavour upon these past episodes, he realised that youth was inconsiderate in its hours of passion, and gave little thought to the future. The lives of these fishermen were a long battle with Fate. They laughed at Death and Poverty, and the vigorous spirit within them suffered little repression during its respite from battle. It was natural that so magnificent an animal as Paolo should attract what he had no inclination to reject. His passion was purely physical, short-lived, and uncontemplative. His was no mental ailment, only a superabundant vitality running wild over conventions never rigorously upheld.

In his favour, Delfino remembered the reforms Paolo had effected in his life, on the realisation of future responsibility. He had revealed no weakness of sentiment or will, and Delfino could not withhold admiration from one so ready to assert self-discipline. In Paolo he saw a man of unbending purpose, of a will to hold supremacy. The fortune of Lucia was safe in his hands.

One hour later, after Paolo's early morning survey of the fleet, in a state of clamour, partly arising from necessity and partly from exhilaration, he went on board the chief boat, the *San Giovanni*. Its beautifully curved prow was elaborately painted and decorated with a shield bearing a rough and vivid picture of the young saint. Along the gunwale ran a floral border of crimson, blue and green. The great russet-coloured sail, half-hoisted at the stern, merged into yellow, with concentric rings of mauve, purple and orange. In a circular patch of the last colour was painted a vermilion cross on a ball. Paolo looked at his vessel with pleasure, and, so intense was his admiration of her lines, he was startled when he heard Jacopo Delfino's voice behind him.

" All ready, Paolo ? " asked the old fleetmaster. " You see I haven't been able to keep away. I've been thinking of you since sunrise."

Paolo smiled at him, his red lips parting in a manner that relieved his heavy expression.

" Yes—we could sail now if it wasn't for the tide. I'm just going to eat. Will you have some ? "

Delfino nodded and followed him down the hatchway,

but before leaving the deck he gazed at the beautiful boats all about him, in their infinite complication of rigging and vivid sails. He sighed deeply, and then went below.

Several hours elapsed before Lucia sought her father on the canal. She had deliberately left herself only a few moments before the sailing. She knew she would find him on the *San Giovanni*, and Paolo would be there, alternately self-important and ingratiating. In her presence he did nothing but smile and swagger about, displaying his strength ; he increased her annoyance by his refusal to answer back to her banter, which she knew deeply wounded his pride.

Luigi was on the boat next to the *San Giovanni*, so she purposely stayed talking with him, as he hung over the side, his bare arms folded, the breeze lifting the black ringlets over his brow. Paolo and her father came down the canal as they stood laughing together. She left Luigi and joined them.

" Lucia mia ! where have you been ? " began her father, " Paolo is just going. I'm sure you want to wish him success."

Paolo smiled, waiting for her to speak. Lucia turned to her father.

" Paolo knows you've great confidence in him," she said. " Men don't value women's ideas about their work. But, for all our sakes, I hope Paolo will be in luck." She looked at Paolo as she said the last words. He had suddenly become serious, and actually seemed nervous.

" Lucia—I want success for one reason," he said, quietly.

Her father had been accosted by a friend. Paolo stood a little nearer and looked down into her face. She knew his meaning. He was so clumsy with his hints, but she would not help him. She returned the look, gaily.

" Which is ? " she asked.

" Lucia mia—don't you know ? " he pleaded. " You must know ! "

" I know you're very ambitious."

" That means nothing to me now. Lucia, won't you send me away happy ? "

The great fellow was almost tearful. What an actor he was, she thought. Then her fierce resentment of his clumsy selfishness, of his tactlessness aroused her. Her eyes glinted.

" Hadn't you better learn to handle the fleet first ? "

The dark blood rose under the lash of her insult, but he forced a smile to his face.

" What do you mean, Lucia ? " he pressed.

" What you should have the sense to realise," she said, shortly. He laughed then, with a flame in his eyes. At this moment of tension her father joined them. Already a number of boats had entered the harbour.

Jacopo Delfino held out his hand, and then, half to cover his emotion at this passing of his command, and half to convey the warmth of his feeling, he embraced Paolo on each cheek.

" A good catch, a safe return, my dear Paolo, a rivederci," he said huskily.

" A rivederci ! " responded Paolo, a little self-conscious in the moment of realisation. He looked beseechingly at Lucia.

" A rivederla, Lucia ! " he said, still hoping she would show him some encouraging sign. She veiled her hostility as well as she could, but defiance still lingered in her eyes as she said " Addio, Paolo."

It was dismissal. Well, he was a slow man, but his purpose would be gained one day. He sprang aboard. The boat was already drifting from the quay. As it rounded and the sail luffed in the breeze he stood a few minutes by the bow, shouting to the men, a stalwart figure in a maze of colour and graceful canvas.

Lucia and her father walked along the mole of the harbour with its view of the Porto and the sea beyond. The leading boats had come out of the west lagoon, had tacked and were now heading for the dark, green mouth of the Porto. On they came, boat upon boat, irregularly spaced. Now in the stronger breeze they raised their sails, with a rattle of pulley blocks, flaming in the sunlight.

Outside the Porto, a small boat rowed by a youth turned north to run up the line of the Pelestrina sea-wall. The rower stopped as the fleet, crowding sail on sail, came out. Now they were running in the narrow channel south of the promontory, where the light which Peter had watched the previous night towered from its base, a quaint cylindrical reservoir, with horizontal stripes of red and white. Across the Porto, still higher, on the white octagonal tower of the Forte San Felice, was the companion light. They marked with their intermittent green or red flashes the Porto, in high and low tide barred with a dangerous shoal.

Beyond, two light-buoys, green to the north and red to the south, floated, one mile distant from the shore lights, thus marking in a square the treacherous entrance.

Peter and Marco, beyond the shoal in their small boat, looked inland towards the floating pageant. A few vessels had passed the narrow channel and were spreading fanwise as they gained the open sea. Behind, with sails of russet, orange and vermilion, the fleet crowded, narrowed in the sea-way. Beyond them, on the mauve horizon, hazy in the unclouded splendour of the noon, floated the Euganean Hills, blue beyond the plain of Padua. Nearer, bright on the skyline, was the picturesque Campanile, surmounted with its grey cupola, to the south, and beyond, the smaller campanile of the Church of the *Madonna di Marina*, rising above the diminutive houses of Sottomarina. White-walled and red-roofed, with its crouching batteries, and the low forts guarding the entrance, these lagoon-dwellings lay like a child's cardboard model, silhouetted against the turquoise sky and the burnished waters.

" That's the *San Giovanni* leading," cried Marco, resting on his oars. Peter watched it speeding forward, the brightening foam rising and falling back from its subtly curved prow. Half-a-dozen men in gaudy vests stood on its littered deck. Behind it came the host of vessels lifting their russet-hued sails like proud banners in the blaze of the noon. The surrounding water was stained with their sunset hues, broken in restless reflections. How they glowed upon that sapphire flood, the vast blue vault above them, the faint pink line of Sottomarina running low beyond, with the sea widening as they sailed forth. They were tacking now, interweaving in a dance of changing colours, butterfly-winged.

Peter found himself stirred by the romantic beauty of this argosy. It was part of this miraculous Venetian picture, of the cloudless radiant sky, of the vast lagoon lying like a crystal mirror, dotted with the channel pali, and boats gliding to Venice with their cargoes of vegetables. Northwards stretched the long low sea-wall of the Pelestrina ; to the south ran the houses and Venetian chimney-stacks of Chioggia. Westwards rose the symphony of colour on the indefinite line where sky and lagoon merged. A thousand years of custom had wrought the harmonising shape and colours of these boats ; they were an equal part of the beauty through which they sailed.

Marco dreamed over his oars. He too watched the fading vision, held in the spell of its mystery and beauty.

"They'll turn south now, signorino," he said, as the sails slowly veered, revealing their full spread to the watchers.

"Perhaps they'll go as far as Zara, or north to the Piave if the shoal's there."

Peter turned from the fading pageant.

"When will they be back?" he asked.

Marco paused in his rowing, and shrugged his shoulders.

"Six days—perhaps five—as luck runs, signorino. Paolo Finghetti will go south—he has no faith except south."

"Paolo Finghetti—who's that?"

"The new fleetmaster, signorino, old Jacopo Delfino's man. Paolo has taken the Signore's place. He grows rich and tired."

"What do you call rich, Marco?" asked Peter, with a suppressed smile. He remembered Tuscan tales of peasant wealth.

"Signor Delfino has twenty-three bragozzi. Paolo's father has nine. Paolo's fortunate. They're rich at Ancona, but not as Paolo when his thoughts are things."

"What do you mean, Marco?" Peter turned to the frank brown face of this simple lad. Marco rested again on his oars, and rubbed his bare chest before replying.

"Paolo will own the fleet, signorino. He is a ravenous one. With his father's and Signor Delfino's boats, who can refuse him anything? Other boats have ill-luck. He has money to lend, the lendings cannot be paid, the lendings grow. Ecco! the boat is his! He sees far. He lives with his back to the sun." Marco grimaced as he pronounced the final words.

" But if his father owns only nine boats out of—"

Marco smiled in assured wisdom.

" Scusi, signorino," he said, leaning forward, " you don't understand. Signor Jacopo Delfino has twenty-three boats. Jacopo was fleetmaster, Paolo is fleetmaster, as Jacopo wished it. Paolo already takes care of the dowry ! "

He grimaced, and began stabbing the water in angry strokes.

" You mean Lucia will— " began Peter.

Marco turned his eyes heavenwards and sighed.

" Paolo lives with his back to the sun and his face is dark to us," he added, giving an angry tug at the oars to emphasise his feeling. " Where will you bathe, signorino —we are a mile out from the shore now."

" Here then, Marco. I'll swim to the Littorale. A mile's about my limit."

Marco headed the boat towards the land. Peter kicked off his shoes and in a few seconds stood naked in the soft warm air of the blazing noon. He paused at the prow awhile, watching the lucent sea below, its blue-green surface undulating and unbroken. The air played lightly about him, warm and caressing. Behind, Marco sat motionless, admiring the lithe symmetry of this Englishman, poised like a statue of bronze against the radiant sky. Suddenly the statue moved into glowing life. The muscles rippled, the shoulders broadened, the arms spread wing-wise. There was a swift arch of the supple back, a shimmer of light, and the diver leapt, arrow-like, then turned and fell through the sunlight to the broken surface. Slowly Marco followed the foam-track made by his padrone's glistening arms.

As Peter neared the strip of sand where ran the great length of limestone sea-wall, he turned on his back and floated until Marco had rowed within speaking distance.

" It looks deserted, Marco," he called. " Where's the nearest village ? "

" Pelestrina, signorino."

" Then can I have a sun-bath in safety ? "

" Sì, signorino, we often bathe here, there is nothing until we come to the Forte Caroman."

Peter stood up in the shallow water and waded through to the hot sand. Marco dragged his boat out of the surf, and laughed when his master rolled himself in the sand like a dog.

" I suppose you think I'm quite mad ? " called Peter, standing up and shaking the sand from his limbs, " but it's sheer joy to get rid of civilisation for a few moments. Why don't you bathe ? "

This was the hint for which the envious Marco had waited. Off went his singlet, his quick fingers loosened the belt at his waist. He kicked the fallen trousers from his feet, and ran joyously into the water, where he flung himself full length with a great noise. Peter watched him lazily. Like all these Venetian lads he swam swiftly, without effort.

In a few minutes he had returned, and stood squeezing the sea water out of his hair, a brown wet figure cutting vividly into the blue sky. From such a vision of sunburnt grace had Titian taken his colours and the lustrous limbed men and women of his canvases. Peter rolled over on to his stomach, revelling in the animal pleasure of the sun's heat. Marco had followed his example and lay inert, like a young merman, surprised in his noonday siesta on the sea marge.

Presently, so still were they, the lizards joined them in their basking. They could hear nothing but the faint murmuring of the sea, the shrill cry of those tireless insects, the cicale, in the bushes, and the fainter sound of the wind stirring the pink sea-holly. For a long time they watched the brown reeds and green thistles checking the flight of the foam-drift borne towards them.

Peter was happy again. Sir Roderick and Maud were gone, they had taken with them all the absurdities of their complex civilisation, their niceties of rank, their unbendable conventions, their insensate ambitions for being something and doing something. Here were quiet and beauty, here were sunshine and rest, with the radiant heaven above and the warm laughing sea below. He tried to imagine Roderick lying naked with himself and Marco. The thought was too incongruous. Roderick naked was quite unimaginable. He would have a horror of himself as God had made him, and, actually, Roderick, white as an earthroot, would have been a blot in the landscape, an agonised blot, for Roderick, burnt and blistered in ten minutes by this sun, would have writhed in pain.

Peter looked at his firm bronzed figure. Months of sun-exposure had given him this freedom of light and air. Like Marco he was a sun-child, a lover of these wild spaces, of the amethyst lagoons and the golden strands, of the fierce sunlight, and the blue-green sea. Here men wrestled with Nature, walked proud limbed, eagle-eyed, creatures of passion and exhilaration : the women no less proud and beautiful, bearers of sturdy children.

And they would expect him to go back, to grey skies and cold days, to modes of thought and dress, to all the minor hypocrisies, to dinner-parties and stiff collars, to—

Peter rolled over on to his side and slept.

CHAPTER VI

WITHIN three weeks of his coming to Chioggia the young
English artist was a familiar figure to all the fishermen
along the canals, and also to the women, sitting on cane
chairs at their open doorways. For he had an extraordinary way with babies and small children. There
was a scamper whenever he was seen coming down the
shady arcaded streets that traversed the island town from
canal to canal. Nor was his popularity among the
fishermen due to his foreign cigarettes, nor, among the
children, to his habit of finding all kinds of sweets in his
pockets, that also included a penny and a piece of string
with which he did amazing tricks. These little assets
helped but they would have been useless without a manner
that gained their confidence.

The Signorino was daily looked for. On La Vena and
down the calli he came regularly, making sketches; he
could be found in the squero, or ship-building yard.
There was a smile for him at every door, and on old
Madre Pappini he had conferred earthly immortality.
He had drawn her sitting by her melon baskets, and for
days the women had flocked to see the wonderful likeness
by the young Inglese.

Moreover, he frequented the Trattoria, and his appearance drew a special bow from the padrone. Had he not
presented a twenty-five lire note one evening to the
Punch-and-Judy man giving a performance to the children

in the yard of the Trattoria del Sole, so that he should play an extra hour ? Dio mio ! after that every father on board his boat had a bow and a courteous invitation for the Signorino.

Lastly, he made a friend of the dottore. This was an accident. He had carried a young cherub, who had cracked his head with a fall from the upper window of a warren holding twelve families, to the doctor's surgery. In the course of a quarter of a mile's walk, an escort of three—the lad's mother, sister and a famished dog, swelled to a multitude which halted, chattering like monkeys, before the gaily frescoed front of the Signor Dottore Galuppi's house.

Ten minutes later the mother and the boy emerged, the latter unrecognisable under a turban of bandages. The escort, still more swollen and voluble by this time, followed the proud urchin home. Peter remained within, detained by the genial old doctor, ever eager for a gossip, who had heard much of his visitor in the last few days.

He led the stranger through a dark room, that from its appearance had once been a music room, out on to a little loggia, covered with a pergola, which overlooked the maize fields on the mainland towards Brondolo. It was an hour after sunset and a primrose sky faded into emerald green heights wherein a few timorous stars scintillated.

With a graceful gesture, motioning his visitor to an easy chair, he clapped his hands twice, and, genie-like, an old woman sprang out of the shadow of the vine. Intuition or custom had informed her of the master's need. She placed a tray holding two glasses and a chianti flask on the little wooden table, and, without a word, disappeared. " I hear, Signor Neville, that you are an artist—but rumour is quite unnecessary, for who would come to this place except to paint ! "

He laughed lightly, his fine jewelled hand steadily holding the flask while the ruby liquid flowed into his guest's glass.

"And if you'll forgive my curiosity," he added, smiling across the table, "for we have little but curiosity to sustain us here—I'd like to learn where all the paintings of this infinitesimal place go to!"

"Without disparaging Chioggia," replied Peter, "I should say the refuse heap."

He raised his glass and drank. To his surprise it was not the ever-popular chianti, but a time-mellowed vintage of rare flavour. Perhaps his pleasure and surprise were reflected in his face, for the old doctor, who had been watching with some anxiety, beamed as the crucial moment passed.

"Ah!" he said, gently, as though he had made a request. "You approve, signore?"

"I see, signor dottore, you are a connoisseur. I feel grateful to that cracked skull!" He raised the glass again to his lips.

The doctor in his boyish glee half rose from his chair. "Per Dio! Is it not good? You have not had anything like it at your hotel? No, of course not, it is a vintage which I—" then, apologetically, seating himself, "Forgive me for this boasting. Your pleasure excited me."

Peter laughed. What a dear old man he was, with his wrinkled eyes and his excitable boyish gestures.

"If your medicine, signor dottore, is one half as good as this wine, then Chioggia is fortunate."

"Ah, my dear young man, it is not! There is no medicine for old age or lovesickness. Those are the only illnesses here. Your glass—I have a large cellar, do not fear."

The sky was darkening now. The stars brightened

and winked through the swaying cypress trees. The dome of the night slowly changed from a bronze to deep azure ; a few bats circled in and out of the pergola roof where the fire-flies flitted like capricious stars. Beyond the gardens, the houses lay huddled in black silhouette against the west. Over them, mysterious in its undefined height, rose the square Campanile, a dream-tower in a land of shadows.

They talked of art, of books, of life and death in these houses of the poor, and touched far shores of former travels. The old dottore knew many a story drawn from the comedy and tragedy of that brooding Campanile ; he unfolded Ursula Bossi's history.

There was a silence after this, in which they slowly smoked in the verbena-scented darkness of the loggia. The night was alive around them. Little cries, stirrings, the whir of wings, the croak of frogs, came and went on the warm air. Then abruptly the silence was broken.

" Signor Dottore ! " a voice cried.

It came through the darkness, and only a footstep indicated the direction. The two men turned, peering towards the door behind. There stood a woman, indistinct in the deep shadow of the pergola, save for a patchwork of moonlight penetrating the vine-roof, which fell in macabre design upon her white dress.

Peter sprang to his feet. It was Lucia ! His instinct told him though he could not see. But her voice ! That one cry, " Signor Dottore ! " low, sweet, stirred him into response, his whole body quivering through his nerves, which were as strings swept by the music of her call. Such a voice could belong to no other. It did not surprise him. Now he heard it, there was a confirmation of what he should have known, that her beauty was not a separate thing. of face or figure or movement, it was herself. It was all one, visible in the light of her eyes, the sweetness of her red mouth, the fresh bloom of her cheeks, and the young lustre of her hair. The laughter that had imprisoned his fancy on that memorable afternoon as he sat by the harbour and watched the boat whence it came, was in this call through the darkness.

He recollected now that it was her voice that had first captivated him, her presence had only confirmed the magnetism it exerted over his senses. And now again he was to hear her, first, and thrill with the music of her voice. The dottore, too, had risen and took a step into the darkness of the loggia.

" Why—it's Lucia ! Cara, this is a surprise. Come ! join us. I will get you a chair," cried the dottore, taking her by the hand and leading her forward into the open space where the moonlight flooded the loggia. Then, suddenly aware that he had a duty to perform—

" Scusi ! scusi !" he cried, turning from one to the other, as his two guests stood silent for an embarrassed moment. " This is Signor Neville who has honoured me this evening."

He bowed towards Peter. " Allow me to present, Signore, la signorina Lucia Delfino."

On the far side of the small table Peter bowed stiffly. He felt absurdly self-conscious, although he knew she could not be aware of the constant thought in his mind these last few days. Now, as he sat opposite to her, the moonlight lent its lustre to her eyes and hair, as the night had given its mystery to her voice. Brown-eyed he thought she was, though in the darkness he could not be sure, so deep was their fire, so lovely the light that shone in them. Her thin black eyebrows, traced by the hand of Nature in unerring mood, arched as she spoke, emphasising the whiteness of her brow. The rose that gleamed on festa days amid her black tresses was absent, but to-night that note of crimson was on her lips, so gentle in smiling, so alluring to watch.

She sat, one little brown hand resting in her lap, the other toying with the green jewel that lay on the throat carrying the flower of her face from its full-bosomed bed. In her smile there was drowsiness too, despite the vivacity of her eyes and the vivid gleam of her small white teeth. The curve of wrist and elbow companioned the impeccable beauty of the head. Young and happy and glowing, this child of the lagoons was as much a creature of the warm sunlight as of the enchanting moon.

For a space the dottore talked, while they sat in conscious appraisement of each other. Lucia, for her part, fought the turbulence within that bade her look long, feeding the sight-hunger of these last days. Again she felt possessed by his virility, by the alert poise of his neat head, the strength of his face. He was a creature born to run, dance and sing, the song of youth in all his limbs, in the square breadth of his shoulders, and the supple poise of his body. She noticed yet again the strong brown hand, sensitive but masterful, as she had noticed it on that first day, closed on the bowl of his pipe. Now that he was speaking she took courage from the calm of his voice, though she dare not yet venture on the encounter of his eyes.

"Father sent me, signor dottore, to ask if you'll come in to-morrow night," she said, her eyes downcast, her hand still toying with the jewel at her neck.

"Ha! He wants revenge after his defeat! Per Bacco! he was surprised, Lucia!"

The dottore slapped his thigh and laughed boyishly.

"Cara, I'll come, or your poor father will fret himself into a fever." He waved his hand towards Peter.

"Signore, you will permit me to take you to Signor Delfino's? He is a man of rare hospitality—isn't he, Lucia?"

"The signore will be very welcome. My father thinks greatly of the Inglesi," she responded, smiling at Peter.

For the first time their eyes met in a level glance. A flush stole up into her cheeks, and her eyes fell again. She could hear her heart beating within.

"That will be a pleasure, signorina," said Peter. More he could not.

The dottore talked when silence fell between them. Nothing of Lucia's confusion escaped him, nothing of the young Englishman's spasmodic geniality. Dear young people, how interesting they made the world! For all his seventy years he loved romance. This well set-up young Englishman pleased him, pleased him more for his sensitiveness to Lucia's attraction, his eager and ill-disguised rapture over her beauty.

And she, dear child, could no more hold the light of admiration from her eyes than she could control the blushing of her pretty cheeks, and the shy downward cast of her head as she responded with ' Sì ' and ' No ' to his equally hesitating syllables. They called him, the old dottore, a matchmaker. È vero! He was! He loved lovers and took joy from their pangs. He who loved birds and flowers and sunsets, who knew every naked little toddler of the streets, who gave his philosophy of life to old men, his shrewd advice to old women, all of them his children as much as they were his patients— why should he not help young lovers? Per Dio! Were they not the hope of Life?

Thus it was, as they rose to go, he furthered the plot.

"The signorina goes down the Corso—" he said, meaningly, looking at the young man.

" May I see you home, signorina ? " ventured Peter, thus encouraged. She did not reply, but he read assent in her eyes. The dottore accompanied them to his door. Cordially he bade his guest return. Gently he kissed Lucia.

" Buona notte, cara mia ! " he cried, waving his hand.

" Goodnight, Signore Dottore," said Peter.

The old dottore withdrew from the calle, and closed his door, almost. Was it an afterthought, or a desire to see the stars, that caused him to open it again and peer out ? Whatever it was he saw what did not surprise him. Their way down the Corso, at the turn of the Calle, was to the left. They went to the right, where the Corso ran to the Tower Gate, to the Pontelungo and the fields towards Brondolo. The dottore sighed and closed his door. " Eh, la bellina ! " he muttered, shooting the bolt.

And the way of it had been simple. Given a warm night of May wherein the stars jewelled its velvet depth, a silence that follows the heat of day, when the dews are falling, and youth is desirous of the company of youth, then somehow words will be found to suit the purpose, a way be taken to feed desire. First they see the moon, rising undimmed in a fulness from which the stars shrink timidly, save one, bold in attendance. Chimneys and roofs glimmer white to the edge, where walls and streets are engulfed in deep shadow. There is a distant glimpse, toward the Tower Gate, of masts and rigging, black-fretted against the sky, where the boats lie huddled along the Canale della Madonna. The Signore has seen the view from the Pontelungo, across the lagoon to the western hills ? Bella vista ! Then, as he confesses not, surprised and enraptured exclamation. Lucia turned, her eyes glowing in commendation of its beauty, her young hands raised and clasped in ecstasy before her.

"Take me," he says, and they turn, as the dottore saw. In silence they gain the gateway of the Torre, step into its shadowed arch, and are again in the moonlight beyond, crossing the small bridge, leaving on their right the acacia-lined Piazza Vescovile, in the shadow of the Duomo. The moonlight lay on the rococo marble of the balustrade, where the Madonna of the Fishermen rose ghostly under her cross-surmounted canopy.

They had now left the town, and followed the road past the cabbage plantations, until they gained the many-arched Pontelungo, the bridge joining the island-town with the mainland. Here they paused, leaning over the parapet. In all his wanderings Peter had never felt the hand of beauty rest upon his soul as in this moment of wonder. Eastward, they looked into the mauve depths of the night to where, beyond the intervening lagoon, shadowy Sottomarina rose on its sea-bound strip of land ; but westward lay the unfathomable enchantment.

Before them, league on league, stretched the mysterious lagoon. Afar, on the dim horizon, so faint that it might have been a phantasy of the night, a crimson land rose out of the vast expanse of water. That way had the sunset gone, leaving in its track a faint glow on the emerald reaches of the upper sky, which lay reflected in the lagoon, whose faithful mirror took each cloud and star upon its bosom. A light wind veined the luminous water, breaking it into a jewelled track of dancing moon-flecks. Above them, as they paused in wonder, the tranquil night rose in its measureless splendour. Only the ceaseless croak of frogs under the arches gave earthly reality to the vision.

Entranced, they leaned by the parapet, and then, having drunk deep of this beauty, they looked at each other. The wonder evoked in them lay in their eyes, so that, scarcely breathing, their hearts grew eloquent. His hand closed over hers as it lay on the parapet, diminutive and warm. She spoke no word on this, thrilled by his touch, so soft yet strongly compelling.

" Signorina ! " he called, more in thought than in voice, since words intruded on the silence that wrapped them round. But she heard him, responded.

" Signorino ! "

That was all, but he was grateful. Not a sound in the vast night, across the lagoon. Yet the whole night pulsated with their emotion. She smiled at him, then shyly—

" I do not know your name, signorino, I have forgotten. It is difficult for me."

" Let me teach you it, signorina," he responded, eagerly, his face drawn nearer to her, his eyes held by her beauty, by the whiteness of her brow, and the dark tresses rimmed with the stars of night beyond. He caught the gleam of her teeth.

" Sì."

" If you will teach me yours," he pleaded, and she nodded in assent.

" Peter Neville," he said slowly.

She pursed up her red lips, half-laughing, half-serious.

" Pee—tarr—how ? " she hesitated.

" Peter Neville " he prompted.

" Pee—tarr Nah—veel—bellissimo ! " she cried, happy as a child at her attempt to speak his name, her face aglow. He wanted to hold her to him, to feel her red lips on his, her hands about his neck, but he dare not. Instead he pressed her hand, which answered his.

" Now teach me yours," he urged, his eyes steady on hers. He could see the warm blood mounting to her cheeks again, confusion making her more lovely.

" It is simple," she said slowly, " Lucia Delfino."

To his ears it was all music, as soft as the campanile bells floating out across the lagoons at even.

" Loo-chee-a Del-feeno," he murmured ; then, " Bell-issimo ! "

They laughed together at this, laughed because of the joy in them, eager for expression.

" Lucia ! " he echoed. " In England it is ' Lucy '—and Lucy is not so beautiful as Lucia," he added, gallantly.

This time she did not laugh, but placed her other hand over his, her breath quickened by his words.

" Pee-tarr—in Italian, it's Pietro—but I like Pee-tarr," she confided. " Pee-tarr ! Pee-tarr !—it is *musica,*— like the bells."

Once again, in silent pause, they looked across the western lagoon. The horizon had vanished now in the dark tide of night. The emboldened stars glowed in the infinite heaven, stabbing the water with spears of light. A warm wind blew from the distance, the cypress trees on the mainland shook timidly and the stars danced through them as they stirred.

" We must go," said Lucia, but she did not move.

" Sì—but tell me first," he pleaded, as she turned to him questioningly, " if I may call you Lucia ? "

She hung her head, the long lashes hiding the light of her eyes. " Non lo so " she said, scarcely audible.

" Please," he persisted, pressing her hand. Then, hoarsely, " Lucia—I shall call you Lucia !—when we are alone. And you will call me Peter. Say it, say it !— Peter ! " he commanded.

" Pee-tarr ! " she obeyed, but her voice broke on the last syllable.

Scarcely knowing his act, he caught her hand fiercely to his lips. Over his bent head she saw him, tear-dimmed with joyful confusion.

" Lucia—bella Lucia " he murmured, raising his face.

She withdrew her hand, her gaze averted, her faultless profile set against the mellow moon.

" I must go ! It will be late when I am home."

They turned from the parapet hearing only the swirl of the incoming tide against the arches. There was not a living thing on the road into Chioggia, but beyond the Tower Gate they saw the lights of the cafés in the Corso. The enchanted hour was running out.

" Lucia—do you know when I first saw you ? "

" No ! "

" Down there," he said, pointing down the Corso, " on a bragozzo in the harbour."

" I saw you," she confessed, " I knew— "

" You knew ? " cried Peter.

" Sì," said Lucia, her merry eyes dancing. " You were with the signori and the signora, and did not wish to be there ! "

" You're a quick child ! "

She laughed delightedly. " I knew you saw me. You were staring so ! Dio mio ! you were so—so— " she hesitated, raising her brow.

" So what, Lucia ? "

" Inquisitive," she whispered, in mischievous mood.

" Was I ? Yes, I must have seemed rude."

" Sì ! I liked it, and I, too, saw you go."

" Saw me go ? " he asked, astonished.

" Sì, Pee-tar," she answered, like a child breathlessly telling its story. " I saw you all go—and oh, you did not want. You looked back and back, and then the molo shut you out ! "

" But, Lucia ! how could you see ? You weren't there, I looked for you all the time."

" Sì, sì—but I was ! I was behind the sail, just peeping

round, oh, ever so little. And I see you often with
Marco in the boat, as you go out of the harbour ! "

He looked at her, and loved her more than ever for her
child's frankness.

" We shall see each other often now ? " he asked, with
anxious voice.

" No, Peetar. It is not possible."

" Lucia— "

" No—not often. Perhaps—accidentally ! " she said,
quickly, a light in her eyes as she halted, her quick brain
planning.

" Sì— sì— ? " he urged, readily.

" Il Duomo—when I go there. No ! Don Emilio is
sharp. No. The Campanile—sì, sì !—in the belfry.
It is quiet there—bella vista ! " she said, and spread her
hand expressively to emphasise the expanse and wonder
of its view.

" But when ? "

She looked round cautiously. They were nearing her
home, and curious eyes watched them pass down the
arcaded Corso.

" Friday afternoon, perhaps—at five," she whispered.

" Va bene—I will come."

For a few moments she seemed to be thinking.

" What is it, Lucia ? " he asked, as they halted before
the outer door of the Palazzo Delfino.

" Perhaps it is better not—it would not be well if we— "
she said, hesitatingly.

He would not hear her fears. What could it matter,
and who should know even ?

" Friday—at five," he said decisively.

Many eyes were upon them now. The little group
sitting about the squeaking violin at the Café Mazzini
opposite : Antonio Salati the wag, and his wife the gossip,

taking in the baskets spread before their shop : the four girls, arms round each other's waist as they walked, singing and laughing back at the jerseyed lads lounging by the arcades ; many eyes were upon them.

Peter raised his hat and bowed, almost impersonally.

Lucia shook his hand, smiled formally, acting her part.

" Addio, signore " she said, her voice raised for the listeners.

" No, a rivederci, signorina ! " Peter responded, a pressure of her hand giving emphasis to his correction. She laughed, and then was gone. The iron-studded door banged. He was alone.

He walked on down the Corso. She had said " Addio " but had she meant it ? He had corrected her, " To meet again," but she had only smiled. Surely she would come. Friday. Three days yet, three days to wait and wonder. If she did not go then to the Campanile ! If she had meant Addio ! No, she had not meant it. It had been said for those about them. She would be there ! Friday ! Two more days yet, then they would meet again !

He walked on, desire debating with doubt. She would come, he told himself. But was he believing only because he wished to believe ? No ! He could see her face still, her eager beautiful eyes, her young body swaying as a reed in the current of her emotions.

At the Piazzetta Vigo, opposite his hotel, he halted, and looked towards the Porto with its sentinel lights. The steamer in the harbour swung a solitary lamp at its masthead. It was moored there till dawn, when it would take its cargo of cabbages and hens into Venice. He was restless in this warm night. Everything about him seemed breathing and alive. A lad on the molo was playing his mandoline, the girls on each side of him

laughing and chattering. They stopped when he began
to sing.

Sospira, cuore, che ragion tu hai
Aver l'amante e no vederlo mai.

The song drifted across the water, plaintive and soft.
" Sigh, heart of mine, thou hast good cause." Did that
lad know then ? Or was this the land of lovers where
everything that lived must sigh and love, so warm its
caress, so seductive its beauty.

Lucia ! He called her name in the still night, as if its
repetition gave him ease, even while it enchanted.

CHAPTER VII

ALL the next morning Peter Neville was at work down
by the Vena canal. The careless beauty of a sail cutting the arched outline of the Vigo bridge gave him
his subject. He worked with brown urchins about him,
who tumbled in and out of the canal in gay unconcern,
for the sun quickly dried the thin vests and pants in which
they were clad. But at noon he retreated when the sun
beat down upon the fondamenta and the heat drew out
the smell of fish, tar, slimy boats and the rubbish that
littered the quay or rotted in the canal. He had worked
to kill his obsession, yet nothing drove out of his mind the
memory of the previous evening. After lunch, he took
his siesta, but in the dim, shuttered room he turned and
turned ; then, impatiently, he threw open his shutters
and read an English newspaper.

How strangely remote seemed all the turmoil recorded
in its columns. It was a wet summer—of course ; there
had been a stormy scene in the House of Commons.
The Americans were arriving in great numbers in London.
London ! His mind wandered to the Green Park, with
its spaced seats, the long railings down Piccadilly, where
above the fringe of trees rose the roofs of clubs and flats.
Three o'clock in London ! The last gossip would be
leaving his club for the office. The typist would be
looking at her watch, wishing it was tea-time. The long

flat barges would be drifting down-tide across the grey front of Westminster.

Then, his mind wandered to Neville Court. His brother would be in the library overlooking the west lawn, with its large copper beech at the end of the terrace where the peacocks strutted. Sir Roderick would be lying with his feet up on the red leather couch, a dead cigar in the ash tray on the morocco stool, his face hidden by a silk handkerchief, a protection against flies. Suddenly, from the lawn, would come a shrill cry. Sir Roderick would stir, murmuring " Damn that bird ! " and then doze off again. For to-day was Thursday, and Neville's Bank was closed for the half-holiday. The town itself would be dead, except for the clanging and rattle of the trams, the shops all shuttered, the great market square empty, save for half-a-dozen hucksters haranguing the unemployable lounging around.

And Maud ? He could see Maud at this very moment. The car would be waiting at the door, with Timson standing by, awaiting his mistress. Presently she would come down the broad oak staircase and sweep across the hall with a soft rustle of silk. Annette would follow silently, to see that the parasol was not left. Now she was on the steps, briefly surveying the lawn, the wood beyond, the peacocks ceremoniously walking the flagged terrace. Down the steps now—a graceful picture, yes— her ladyship leaving the ancestral home, maid, chauffeur, peacocks, and Sir Roderick asleep in the library. The setting was indeed good, and she graced it. Now Timson swings open the door, her ladyship enters. Annette's hand holds forward the parasol ; now she is seated. The door closes, Timson walks round the front of the car, seats himself, cautiously lets in the clutch. There is a quiet crunch of gravel, and a little gift of blue vapour for

Annette watching by the lowest step. Her ladyship is gone to pay an afternoon call.

In Peter's mind the contrast presented itself. Here he lay, on his bed in the hot afternoon, his window open to the turquoise lagoon glistening along its miles to Venice. No June leafiness so familiar to his boyhood, but the wide brilliant sky, the rich colour and the fierce sunlight. So, too, the human contrast. Maud, calm, purposeful, with her sense of dignity, her deliberate selection of setting, and Lucia, wayward, Nature's child, a quick darting creature of impulse. Could human nature show greater diversity ? He remembered Lucia's eyes as they gleamed last night on the bridge, luminous and soft as the darkening lagoon, timorous as evening stars, and yet so warm and eager in their vitality ; not, as he recollected, Maud's, so searching, impersonal and abashless.

He dozed a little after this, sleepy with the windless heat of the afternoon. Later he awoke to the soft calling of campanili bells around, as they pealed high in the air over the town and the waters. Six o'clock ! He had arranged to be with Marco in his boat. The lad had asked him to go sardine fishing on the lagoon, and promised to teach him much of the fisher's lore. There was nothing the faithful Marco would not do for his padrone, and whenever he was away from the signorino he was miserable.

Hastily Peter sprang from the bed, brushed his disordered hair, and ran down the stairs, and out across the piazzetta. Marco was waiting with his boat in the canal where it flowed under the Vigo bridge. His face lit up as Peter approached, his white teeth gleaming in welcome.

" The tide is out, signorino, it is just right," he cried, eagerly, rowing rapidly the moment Peter had jumped into the boat.

" Where are we going, Marco ? "

" To the *Valleselle di Sopra Vento*."

" It sounds beautiful—but where's that ? "

" Là ! signorino," cried the lad, raising one hand from the oar as he pointed northwards down the lagoon. "That is the *Valleselle di Sopra Vento* and there, beyond it, is the *Valleselle di Sotto Vento*, and down that side runs the *Canale di Perognola*."

Excitedly he continued his description, Peter not understanding, but letting the lecture proceed, for Marco was overjoyed at this opportunity of displaying wisdom to his padrone. Madonna! Hadn't he lived on these lagoons all his life, working, playing, splashing and shouting with half-a-dozen happy lads, learning bit by bit the fisherman's craft! Not a current, a canal or a wind but he knew it.

At that moment he was doing something mysterious and feverish. He had flung down his oars and rushed to the stern. A minute later Peter saw his object. A blue sail, patterned like a Chinese rug, rattled up the single mast, bellied and filled, taut with the breeze.

" Ecco ! " cried Marco, settling by the tiller as the boat sped forwards. They were running into the lagoon now, away from the Porto. The tide was out and they kept in the deep channels down which the steamers and boats traversed the great sheet of water. Marco's hand and tongue busily explained the devious routes, the great shallow banks, now barely covered by the receded tide. And as Marco talked, the wonder of this place grew with its marvellous fortune in the happy service of these tides.

For how narrowly was so much beauty preserved from disaster ! A change of currents, a greater refluence of these waters and the lagoons would be an evil swamp, Venice itself a fever-stricken city. Twice a day the sea

fed these shallow lagoons, pouring in over their shoals
from the Adriatic, through the three openings in the Lido.
This constant ebb and flow of the waters carried with it all
the refuse of Venice, preventing stagnation of the lagoon
waters. Through the four openings in that thin coastline,
the Porto, Lido, Malamocco and Chioggia, came the life-
giving sea. At high tide the whole surface of the lagoon
was water, a mirror of the sky for league on league ; at
low tide it became almost a vast mudbank, cut in innumer-
able channels running in all directions. These were kept
open naturally or artificially, the little channels, narrow
and shallow, branching into the innermost recesses of the
dead lagoon, and navigable by the smallest boats only.

Down the main channels of the lagoon flowed the boats
that trafficked on these waters. As they sailed softly
towards the *Valleselle di Sopra Vento* Peter saw innumer-
able boats, russet and crimson sailed, stained anew in the
sunset, and doubled in the reflective water. They were
mostly sailing down the wide channel which skirted the
low bank of the Lido towards Venice. Boats, laden with
produce, glided slowly by, propelled generally by two
rowers standing at their stations, their bodies swaying
forwards in the unforgettable rhythm of the gondolier.

Peter's boat was now passing one of the pali, those
white, black-headed posts, leaning together in groups of
three like drowning persons, which mark the navigable
channels and keep the boats off the shoals. For miles the
pali stretched in their converging parallels, the boats
sailing down the smooth tracks between them. These
pali were a part of the landscape, now black against the
crimson sunset, or catching the noon-day light, and
breaking the smooth water at their base.

" There's twenty thousand pali, signorino. See how
that water is furrowed ! It isn't the wind—it's the water

breaking on the mud banks, half an inch below, now the tide's out."

Marco, one hand on the tiller, with which he kept the sail taut, was now busy sorting out a long net, chattering all the time. He told Peter strange tales of the valli, or valleys, as they called these shallow stretches of the lagoon in which the netters worked. He told him what the workmen sang, driving the pali into the banks, as the hammer-weight was wound up and as it came down with a thud on the iron-bound end of the posts.

Suddenly Marco sprang up, his eyes ablaze, one hand wildly waving in the air. For a moment Peter thought an accident was impending. Then, fiercely, his voice ringing out across the still water, Marco sang the Song of the Pile Drivers. Not sang, chanted rather, now with passionate emphasis, now wheedling, as the pile was driven down. Per Bacco! it was an obstinate pile. His voice rose in stormy protest, his face quivering with angry expostulation.

> But what's wrong with it ?
> It is stubborn !
> And it must go now,
> Let it go now !
> Down to the deep,
> To the depths of the sea.
> And it will find there
> All its companions,
> Down in the caverns
> Horrid and gloomy,
> Down in the caverns,
> Grots full of horror !
> With these four blows,
> Give it him hot then !

He wailed out the last note, his hair flying, the sweat running down his face, lost in the passion of his recital ; then he flung himself back on his seat.

"Bravo! bravo!" cried Peter. Strange how that quiet shy boy could suddenly burst into such a flame of passion! He had made a wild picture, his lithe figure quivering against the emerald evening sky, his face dark with passion above the bright water. Now he sat in silence for a while, holding his sail to the wind.

"Ecco là! signorino, *la Laguna Morta!* The dead lagoon!" he cried, pointing to a great tract of water beyond the reach of the tides. Peter looked towards the mainland, over the crimson-stained waste below the sunset, now blazing fiercely on the Euganean Hills, black and sharp in outline. It was a strange territory, half swamp, half land, where earth and water strove for mastery. No boats sailed there, a silence brooded, broken only by the wild fowl whose haunt it was, who built their nests amid the wild growth of tamarisk and samphire and pale sea-lavender.

Beyond, where the land took solid shape, the evening glow fell upon the maize fields and the vineyards vanishing towards the foothills, where the great Venetian plain rose to the encircling Alps; this evening their serrated edges ran silver-lined under the bright sky.

Marco was now busy naming the arteries of the lagoon, which ran between the watersheds formed by the shoals. At high tide they saw nothing but a sheet of water one hundred square miles in expanse, now the shoals were but thinly veiled by furrowed water, or showed oozy shoulders green with sea-grass.

"Là! *Il Canale Curoman*—the way to Venice, signorino. Là! *Il Canale Poco Pesce*—the canal of few fish! Beyond, the *Valle della Dolcezza.*"

"*Valle della Dolcezza*—the valley of sweetness! Marco, that makes me want to go there!"

"No, signorino, it is an idle place. No fish, nothing

but sky and sea-holly. No boats go there. Ecco là! *Il Canale del Desiderio.*"

What a race of poets these simple folk were! Their very names heightened the romance of this strange sealand. Who would not sail to the Valley of Sweetness down that canal of Desire? He let Marco ramble on, the boy happily pouring out the poetry of his life on these lagoons.

"On the right, signorino, *il Canale di Perognola*! On the left—*la Valle del Brenta.*"

But left or right the view was as beautiful. The silver grey of early evening was on the water. They were running north now. A steamer, making for Venice, went by, tossing them in its wash. Marco grimaced, the resentment of true fishermen showing in his face against these monstrous tourist-laden boats. Close by, accompanying them, sailed a huge *trabaccolo*, with its great canary-coloured sails, and hull painted with broad red bands. Its deck was piled mast high with firewood, where moved half-a-dozen men, naked save for short white drawers bound with red sashes. Their muscular bodies, tanned with sun and wind, glowed in the evening light.

"From Istria, with firewood for Venice," explained Marco. They were nearing Pelestrina now, for the long backbone of the sea-wall gave place to the broadening strip of land where the village straggled down to the water's edge. The endless fringe of pink houses and white churches caught the evening sun, as also the brown limbs of the quick urchins splashing and shouting along the shore. On the mud flats to their left, the sea-mews fed in flocks, disturbed now and then by men and boys in boats, or wading thigh deep.

"Look, signorino, they're trawling. We'll begin now!" Marco lowered the sail, deftly turned his boat with one oar, and brought it broadside to one of the flats, cautiously keeping it from grounding. Here he dropped his anchor, let the boat swing slightly, then, satisfied, stood up, loosening his belt. A minute later, clad only in his orange shirt, whose tails barely covered his sturdy thighs, he hopped over the side, dragging with him one end of a fine net.

He was not alone, for the flat had quite a population of its own. All along the edge, where it deepened into the fairway, waded men and boys. Most of the latter were naked, their wet bodies glistening as they moved, the men clad only in shirts whose wet tails flapped about their brown legs.

And in that moment Peter realised what he had so much pondered, where the old Venetian masters, where Giorgione himself, had found their wonderful flesh tints. On the bodies of these men and boys glowed the rich bronze of Titian and Tintoret, of Bellini and Giorgione. Looking at these young Venetian fishers, moving in the warm glow of the evening, the green water throwing upwards on them its soft reflective light, Peter realised the full beauty of the human form. A rare combination, unknown elsewhere, had given to these fishers this radiant skin. Sea and sun had worked upon their limbs, in a soft climate whose gentleness had not spoilt the texture of the flesh, so that their bodies flamed as with an inward fire, flamed with the flesh tints of the old masters.

Lost in the wonder of his discovery he had forgotten Marco, who was now some yards distant, still pulling out his net and wading through the water.

" Signorino, will you help ? Take that end of the net, when it is all out, and wade up with me to the shallow."

Quickly Peter slipped off his trousers. The net was all out now. He gripped his end, and followed over the

side of the boat. The water was warm, and under him
the soft ooze gave slightly to his feet. Marco was walking
up the flat, leaving the deep channel behind. He called
to his padrone to do likewise ; in this way the fish would
be drawn in from the water and driven by the weighted
net on to the mud flat. Slowly they advanced, the water
first over their knees, now over their calves, until at last
they were but ankle deep. The sea-mews whirled and
cried overhead, anticipating some of the spoil.

With a final tug they brought up the net on to the
gleaming mud. Quickly, darting like a fish himself,
Marco doubled up to Peter, bringing up his end of the net
so that the fish were completely encircled. With a wild
cry he gave a final heave and brought the net high on the
mud bank.

" Look, signorino ! look ! " he cried, swooping down
with excitement. In the bottom lay a host of quivering
tiny fish of all colours and shapes.

" Hold it, signorino," he shouted, passing the end of
his net to Peter. He splashed recklessly through the
water to their boat, bringing back a basket into which the
sea-spoil was emptied.

" Ancora, ancora, signorino ! the tide is coming in
now ! " cried Marco, shaking out the net and plunging
once more towards the deep channel.

For an hour they toiled, walking through the warm
water. Above them the sky faded from rose to emerald,
the lagoon deepening into the purple horizon. An hour's
toil had filled but one basket with small fish, yet these
men and boys depended for their livelihood upon this
patient straining of the lagoons ; and there were days of
storm and a winter season when they could not work.
Once, as they waded some distance from their boat, they
came upon a solitary, mud-plastered hut, built high on

piles above the tide. From it a low palisading of wattled cane enclosed a sea-field. For some time Peter had watched the fishermen and their boys carefully wading along the enclosure.

" What are they doing, Marco ? " he asked.

" That's a valle, signorino. The fish are driven in there to spawn. In the Spring the men are here for days, keeping watch. Haven't you heard the tales of these valli, signorino ? "

Marco shivered in the warm air.

" Marco ! you're superstitious ! " laughed Peter.

" Dio mio, signorino, I don't fear anything that's seen, but in the *Valle dei Sette Morti*— "

" The Valley of the Seven Dead ! That's gruesome enough, Marco ! What's the story ? "

" Signorino, you may laugh, but—Madonna Santissima ! "

At that moment the incautious Marco, full of nis story, stepped into a sea-hole wetting his shirt to the shoulder. Throwing away his end of the net, he gave a loud whoop and plunged himself into the water, striking out for the boat. Peter followed, hauling in the net.

In the boat Marco had stripped himself and was wringing out his shirt, which he tied to the sail-jib to dry. Then, like an eager child, he squatted by the basket, shaking it as he examined the mass of horned, clawed and shelled fish within.

" Ecco qui ! We'll have *frutta di mare* to-morrow, signorino ! " he said, his face gleaming with anticipation, for what Chioggiotto did not love the famous dish ?

" Good, Marco—but what of that story of the *Valley of the Seven Dead* ? "

The lad drew in the anchor, raised the sail, and let the boat drift out into the channel before replying. They had the evening breeze to carry them home down the sea-lane. Overhead, the sky was still light in the highest reaches, but, below, the night folded them in its purple cloak. In this dim light, gliding over the lagoon, their sail rising shadowy with the darkness, they skirted the Littorale, festooned with the lights of houses along its shore. Then, in the warm placid night, Marco began his gruesome stories, stories bequeathed from generation to generation of lagoon fishers.

It was dark when the heaving of their boat told them they were crossing the open Porto to Chioggia. Over them rose the unfathomable Italian night, soft and diaphanous, for the moon was veiled in a cloud. Marco was singing. He had never been so happy as on this night with his padrone. The signorino had chosen him for his servant, and he walked proudly among his friends.

And then, to crown this evening, the signorino made a wonderful suggestion. He would buy a boat so that he and Marco could go sailing whenever they wished! It would be a swift boat with a great sail, and he, Marco, would handle it for the signorino. Per Dio! that would be a day of glory.

"We'll go to the squeri—I know them all, signorino!" cried Marco, his eyes lit with excitement, one hand gesticulating as he talked. Peter had seen the squeri, the boat building yards sloping down the side of the canal, whence all day long came a noise of argument, sawing and hammering, as the builders worked, pitch-blackened, with rolled up trousers and loose shirts. There would be renown for Marco in taking a rich client to buy a boat. Peter decided to let him have the full honour.

"I'll leave it in your hands, Marco," he said.

"Va bene! va bene, signorino," responded Marco, solemn with pride and importance.

A minute later they had gained the calm of the harbour.

CHAPTER VIII

IF Signor Delfino had been less occupied on the evening preceding Lucia's assignation, he might have noticed in her manner something to arouse suspicion. But on this evening he was engrossed in a far more serious matter than the wayward moods of a girl. Opposite to him, as throughout the years of their friendship, sat Galuppi. The candles were lit in their sconces; the small table, on which they shed their light from either side, bore the chequered board. At odd intervals a white hand descended from the gloom into the soft light, hovered a moment over an ivory piece, moved it, paused thoughtfully, and withdrew again into the darkness.

In response to his particular invitation, sent by Lucia on that memorable evening, the dottore had come, full of fight, to repeat his former triumph. They had been playing for two hours that night; two hours of intense concentration, of silence broken only by " Ah ! " or a less exclamatory " Sì ! " as a piece moved and the battle was more involved, the fighters more wary.

The old fleetmaster leaned back in his chair. The wooden clock on the wall by the open chimney-place struck ten. Delfino broke the silence.

" What say you, dottore, to a glass of wine ? " he asked.

" Ah, that's a good suggestion. The fact is, my friend, one can think about a move until the obvious step is lost."

103

Delfino laughed. His chair scraped on the boarded floor as he eased himself and peered down the room.

" Lucia ! " he cried, " the dottore will have a glass of wine, and I with him."

At the far end of the room, all in shadow except for a circle of light wherein she sat, Lucia bent over a large pillow on her knee. She was hard at work with nimble fingers making the point lace for which the district was famous. For an hour she had knotted the short spindles weighting the cotton strands. It was a craft she had learned from childhood, first from her mother, then from old Bianca. But patterns and tuition were ever forthcoming. Every woman, seated on a low stool in the shady threshold of her house, worked at this with busy fingers as she gossiped, raising her voice above the babel of scampering children.

Now, as her father spoke, Lucia stopped, her hands suspended, her face flushed with bending over the work-pillow. She had been singing to herself, singing not loud enough to disturb the players at the other end of the room, but sufficiently to voice the happiness that welled up from within her. That morning she had risen singing. Even Bianca, accustomed to her ways, had noticed it.

" Why, Lucia, you sound happy as a nightingale ! " she said, brushing her young mistress's hair. In a long battle of dispossession by the growing Lucia, she had retained this right.

" And why not, Bianca ? Doesn't the sun shine and isn't life good in June ? Oh, Bianca, I am happy ! I don't know why. I could run and sing and kiss everyone for sheer joy. Isn't it strange, just to get up feeling like that ! "

She shook her young body as she stood, lightly clad, while Bianca brushed out her long dark tresses, falling like a black torrent down each white shoulder to her knees.

"Santa Madonna! That's what being young is. It's a sad day when one needs a reason to laugh. There, cara, that's done. Why, there's the signore calling. He's wanting his breakfast, I know."

The good old creature hurried off, giving Lucia an opportunity to admire herself in the mirror. She flung back her tresses, folding her arms over her bosom, and said seriously to the mirror, "You are a silly girl, Lucia Delfino." And then suddenly the happy face was blurred to her sight, and she stood confused, the laughter checked within her. She must not think such things as she was thinking.

But she was singing again as she dressed, and came down radiant, giving her father a happy little kiss on his brow, so that he noticed her radiant health, and exclaimed, "Lucia, you seem to have found a fortune this morning!"

Now, as her father called, she laid aside the pillow and crossed to a table in an alcove, still bearing traces of a faded fresco of arrow-pierced San Sebastian. On the table she found two Venetian glasses and a long-necked chianti-flask, left by the thoughtful Bianca on retiring for the night.

"Here you are, father," said Lucia, carrying them on a tray to the players' table. "You've been two hours and not spoken a word. I think chess players are most unsociable people."

The dottore raised his handsome old head, removing the spectacles he wore when his predicament was grave. His eyes smiled benignly on her.

"And you, my little Lucia, have never ceased singing for two hours, though whether to distract me or your father, I can't say," he replied.

"You heard me?—I thought you couldn't. I'm so sorry, dottore."

"No, no, Lucia—it didn't trouble us," added the dottore. "I like to hear you so happy. But I couldn't hear a word you sang, so I don't know the reason."

Her father was carefully pouring out the wine down the long neck, his head bent forward over the glasses; otherwise he might have seen the slight confusion discernible on Lucia's face, dim above the candles. But the eagle-eyed dottore saw it, and he thought he knew; which reminded him of something, but he waited until the glasses were filled and Lucia had turned to fetch the biscuit barrel.

"Ah, my friend," said Delfino, raising his glass, and holding it so that the light glowed through the clear red liquid, "It is at these moments, in the midst of a strenuous game, that I like wine best."

"For my part," responded the dottore, "the moment that brings me a good wine is always the best!"

He drank, pursed his lips with the after-silence of the connoisseur, and then, lowering his glass to the table, looked across at his host.

"The other evening," he began slowly, "I had quite an interesting visitor—an artist, though that's not a unique qualification here. He's a young Englishman of about twenty-five, Neville by name. I found him very interesting. He belongs to a banking family but doesn't care much for the business himself. What interested me most was his personality. There was something about the young fellow that attracted me. I think you'd like him."

"Then bring him along, dottore. I like young people any time, providing they don't talk about themselves too much."

The dottore laughed boyishly, and moved his glass with his extended finger across the polished table.

"Ah—now that's just why I like young people. You and I, and other old fellows don't talk about ourselves. Why? Because we think we are interesting, and hold masses of art and wisdom if we deign to reveal ourselves. Now a young man, an intelligent young man, is always anxious to show it, if he's not shy. He must be brilliant wherever he goes. You might as well expect a firefly to flit without sparkling."

"And did your young friend sparkle?"

"He was most illuminating until—"

Lucia, who listened intently, had perforce to approach with the biscuits. The dottore placed his hand on her arm and smiled across at his friend.

"Until Lucia here totally extinguished him! His abashment recalled that passage—you know it—"

"My dear dottore, I never know those passages, not being a man of learning like yourself. But go on, please, I enjoy even when I can't understand you."

"Of course you know it. It's from our Dante—

> Ch'a tutte mie virtù fu posto un peso
> Subitamente sì, ch'io caddi in terra
> Per una luce, che nel cuor percosse.
>
> For on all my powers was set a weight so suddenly
> that I fell to earth because of a light that struck upon
> the heart.

And here was the light!" cried the dottore, playfully pulling Lucia's arm, while she, in a confusion as great as that described by the poet, knew not which way to turn.

"Ah, I can believe it," laughed Delfino, putting his arm about his daughter's waist and drawing her down on to his knee. "When I was a young fellow I could never open my mouth in front of a pretty girl."

" Now, Lucia, we are not going to believe that, are we ? " cried the dottore. Mischief gleamed in his eyes. " Why, I remember when your father— "

" Dottore, I forbid you ! If Lucia hears, she'll never cease teasing me."

Lucia clapped her hands excitedly. In that moment of animation, touched softly by the candle light, the dottore thought he had never seen her look more beautiful.

" Tell me ! You must tell me ! "

The dottore shook his head.

" No, perhaps it is not fair to an old friend," he confessed.

" But this young fellow—he's an artist you say, not a poet, I hope ! " asked Delfino, turning the subject.

" Why hope, father ? "

" Because, Lucia mia, every English poet who came to our Italy seems to have misbehaved himself. There was the Lord Byron at Venice, there— "

" Ah ! You are learned enough, old friend, to know all the scandal of literature ! " laughed Galuppi.

" No, not that, but— "

" È vero ! If Byron and Shelley had not had their liaisons ; if the young Keats had not died in Rome, if our own divine poet, Dante, had not languished for Beatrice, how much do you think the world would know of its poets ? It cares little for their work, it reads with gusto of their frailties or mishaps. Why," cried the dottore, warming to his subject, " I know nothing of Milton, and little of Shakespeare, the great poets of the Inglesi, but I know they could not get on with their wives ! "

" You must bring this young fellow to see me—is he staying here for any time ? " asked Delfino.

"Yes, he's at the hotel on the Piazzetta. I will ask him to lunch to-morrow—won't you join us?"

"I'm going to Venice to-morrow. Bring him in to supper in the evening. Does he speak Italian, for I'm no linguist, as you know, dottore?"

"Sufficient to make himself understood. He's been in Italy three years now, travelling about. I imagine he is a young man of good family. His hands are well bred."

As he said this he thought momentarily of Paolo's coarse strong hands. Had he known, Lucia had the same vivid thought.

"That may be the result of idleness," said Delfino. "I don't like lily-handed youngsters myself. A young horse should be sweated into condition."

"I've no doubt about his condition, my friend." replied the dottore, as his glass was filled for the second time. "In fact, it was his superb physique that first made me notice the young man. He glows with vitality, you feel it the moment you meet him."

"Well, I suppose that's the quality of Youth. Our glowing days are over, dottore!"

Delfino laughed good humouredly. He had been listening and watching intently, despite his easy manner. A certain tension in Lucia as she sat on his knee had not passed unnoticed. Youth being youth, he knew the way of its sudden flame, kindled without preparation, and soon consuming the senses. If the dottore had been attracted, and his words betrayed an almost hypnotic fascination, it was very probable that Lucia had been attracted even more.

Strange too, but none the less true, that a foreigner always possessed some kind of hypnotism over a girl. In his long life he had often seen women lose their heads over these foreigners, who had appeared and departed fitfully, often leaving perturbed waters in their wake. So Lucia had fallen under the spell.

Looking at her as she sat there, assuming a deliberate indifference to their conversation, which emphasised her real interest, his chance thought gave place to certainty. He must see this young man, and know the extent of this unwanted disturbing influence. That his plans for Lucia were not approved, he had already learned from her sullen responses to his suggestion, from her reluctance to take advantage of those meetings with Paolo that he had made easy. Deeply as he loved Lucia, the parent in him would not brood any disobedience. He knew what was best for her, and, since it happened to be also what was best for him, he felt encouraged by circumstances. Not for a moment did he give pause to consider whether his interests were feeding his will.

" Bring the young man in, dottore. It will be a change for Lucia," said Delfino again. " We'll have a little supper together. And now—what about our game ? Shall we go on ? "

Galuppi assented, and Lucia slipped from her father's knee, taking away the flask and glasses. Before the play began, she bade them good-night and went up to her room. Downstairs, the two adversaries bent over the board. Midnight, struck by the bells down the Corso, did not disturb them ; the candles burnt lower and lower.

But in the room above, Lucia was also awake. She had been a whole hour undressing that night. In a magazine she had read a new way of doing the hair, as it was now a fashion with the great ladies in Rome. Patiently she puzzled over the instructions, her arms aching, her eyes straining in side glances at the mirror. Would he like her so? In this wrap, or in this? Or with the large earrings, an heirloom from her great-grandmother who had been so beautiful in those days of masked balls in extravagant Venice, before the grim shadow of Napoleon had fallen upon the pageants and coquetry.

Then, from between the tissue paper where Bianca had so carefully folded it, she took the new dress. It had been made in Venice a month ago, but she had not yet worn it. The first occasion was to be at the festa, a fortnight hence, when all Chioggia would be en fête, the women in their bright cotton dresses, wearing the local *tonda*, the white veil with which they covered their faces. The men would be gay in white, with red sashes round their waists. There would be shows down the Corso, and in the Piazza acrobats and sword-swallowers.

The men's choirs then came in by boat from all the lagoon villages, from Malamocco and Pelestrina, from San Pietro and Brondolo. At night, outside the lantern-festooned cafés, they would stand up and sing in grand competition with each other. All day long the crowded canals had been a veritable forest with the thick concourse of masts, and now, by night, each one swung a coloured lantern, so that the canal was like a fairy chain, reflected in the still water below. From the harbour happy parties sailed out towards the Porto, singing in unison.

Then, on the molo, as the boats went out into the night, they would begin that century-old custom of singing in response across the water, the men's voices loud and clear out of the distance, the women's voices on the molo sweet and low, but carried in the still night air an incredible way, so that the song was heard and answered by those out of sight, rowing on the calm sea beyond the Porto.

No Chioggiote was absent on that great day of June when they honoured their patron saints, Felice and Fortunato. No girl allowed the occasion to pass without a new dress wherewith to draw the admiring glances of the clumsy lads, laughing in noisy groups, or hovering shyly about their charmers.

This new dress was for that festa, but could it be kept now ? To-morrow night he was coming to her home, and she must look her best in such a setting. For her it would be a gala night. Why, then, should she not wear this dress ?

With quick hands she shook it out and passed it over her head. It rustled down over her slim figure, opening like a lily out of its green sheath. Now her deft fingers fastened the hooks at her waist, and in a thrill of pleasure she flounced it out with a swaying of her supple figure, like a bird preening its feathers.

A little cry of ecstasy escaped her when she caught the vision in her mirror. Was this radiant creature in the shining green dress the humble Lucia ? This way and that she turned, raising her long white arms so that she seemed a graceful swan gliding on a green pool, snowy-bosomed and dark-eyed. A catch of song escaped her happy lips.

> In dove xestù stà che ti è sta tanto,
> O delicato fior del paradiso ?
>
> Where hast thou been so long away
> O fairest flower of paradise ?

The dress just covered her knees, emphasising with its cool green the rosy bronze of her legs, tanned with walking and splashing barefoot along the summer sea. Surveying herself, and lost in her happy dream, the midnight bells of the Campanile broke on her ears abruptly. Santa

Madonna! what a silly little thing she was! Why, to-morrow it would be all so ordinary. To-morrow! Would she go to the Campanile? And if she did?

Gravely she advanced to the mirror, curtsied and said, " How doo yoo doo, Meester Nahvelli? "

And, stiffening her soft young figure, she held up her head coldly, replying " How doo yoo doo, Mees Delfeeno? "

Then with a little cry of delight at her mimicry, she flung herself on the bed, laughing because she knew the tears were so near. But the thought of her crumpled dress brought her back to earth. She got up, carefully smoothed it out with her hands, and when she had taken it off, replaced it gently in the tissue paper.

Two minutes later the moonlight flung its latticed pattern on the tessellated floor.

CHAPTER IX

FRIDAY was a day of intense heat, not a breeze touched the unbroken surface of the lagoon. Marco and his master rowed out, as had become their custom, to the spot opposite the Littorale where Peter began his swim. The water was so warm that even swimming was an effort. The sea seemed overpowered with the heat, heaving in lazy undulation. For a long time the swimmer floated on his back, his face turned to the cloudless blue sky, which in its zenith was bleached around the sun. A large sailing boat made for the Porto, its great russet sails sagging in the still air. Marco saw it first, on the bright horizon, and his trained eye recognised its native build.

" Signorino ! There's the *San Giorgio*—it's from the fleet ! " he called, " that means a good haul ! "

Peter rolled over on to his side, but could see nothing from the water.

" Then the fleet's coming back ? "

" No, signorino. It's at the mouth of the Piave probably. If the shoal's moving they'll follow it. They send the catch home. Paolo Finghetti's been lucky again."

He said it with no joy, and watched the nearing boat in silence.

" Come along, Marco, I'll swim in now. You must be roasted there."

With a slow over-arm crawl, he thrashed his way towards

the Littorale. As soon as Marco had grounded his boat, he cast off his light clothes and plunged in. Ten minutes later he joined his master, bronzed in the sun. As Peter lay there he had been thinking. Marco's tone, more than his words, had fired a train of thought. The name of Finghetti seemed to cloud Marco's constitutional happiness. Was there an old family feud?

For a few minutes he watched the dozing lad as he lay, the brine beaded on his strong back, his wet hair fallen over his hands on which he rested his buried face. Peter waited until Marco turned over, in order to see his expression as he questioned him. A curious thought flashed through the mind of the elder.

"How old is Finghetti?—he seems young to have charge of the fleet, Marco."

"Sì, signorino, but he is clever. The Signor Delfino knows that. He's twenty-six, but at sea he's a hundred. Per Bacco! there's no man can handle a boat with Paolo Finghetti."

It was not jealousy of the fisherman, then. The tribute was genuine and ungrudging. Marco dozed again. Peter waited a few minutes. He must try another way.

"Marco!"

"Signorino?" The lad turned his face to him.

"Have you ever been in love?"

Alarm and suspicion crossed the lad's face, then, in a moment, he laughed, as if embarrassed.

"No," he said, quietly, plucking a blade of sea grass, which he chewed while beating the sand with his legs.

He cast a mischievous look at Peter, as if amused at his daring.

"Have you, signorino?"

Peter laughed. "Why often, Marco, I am seldom anything else."

" I know," agreed Marco, in a quiet voice, twisting the grass with his hand. It was Peter's turn to feel embarrassed.

" You know ? " he cried, raising himself.

" Sì, signorino," responded the unperturbed lad.

" But how do you know—and with whom ? " he asked, uneasy.

" You're often thinking about the signorina, and then you don't hear me talking."

" What signorina ? " cried Peter, now thoroughly alarmed.

" La bella signorina—that Paolo Finghetti will marry ! " he said fiercely. He was no longer chewing the grass, his face set, as he stared at the sea before him. There was a ring of hatred in his voice.

" Marco ! " said Peter, " you love her yourself ! "

The boy shook his head and looked dumbly at his padrone, but his eyes belied him.

" Forgive me, Marco—I didn't— "

Marco had suddenly lowered his face to his hands and was sobbing like a child. There was no restraint in his emotion, such as an English lad would have attempted. He gave himself freely to his tears. Peter watched his bowed figure shaking in its emotion. He knew it was useless to intervene, and waited for the storm to subside. Marco lay still for a few moments.

" I'm very silly, signorino," he said at last, wiping the tears off his face with the back of his hand.

" I had not guessed it was so," replied Peter, not looking at him. " I understand now why you dislike Paolo."

" It's not that, signorino," cried Marco, quickly. " It's not because of me—it's you, signorino, I'm afraid for ! "

" Afraid !—for me ? What do you mean, Marco ? " Peter sat up now. The lad at his side had risen to his feet and stood before him, his voice husky with emotion. There was a sudden revelation of another Marco altogether, such as he had seen for a few moments during the chanting of the pile-drivers' song—a Marco of action, of intense passion.

"He hates you, signorino. He will harm you! He'll plan evil for you. Paolo Finghetti walks in the shadow. I watch him always. I know how he looks, what he thinks, all he plans, Dio mio!" Marco shook his hand above his head, his whole attitude fiercely aggressive.

"But, Marco!—he doesn't even know me. And if he does, why should he hate me?"

The lad dropped to his knees on the sand, and looked with troubled eyes straight into those of his padrone.

"Know, signorino? He knows everything, every step you have taken in Chioggia, every person you've spoken to. He has eyes everywhere, those that fear him, and those that want his favour."

"But what is there to know, Marco, I've never crossed this fellow's path. What's he to do with me?"

"Signorino!"

There was a note of reproach in Marco's voice. The lad fell back on to the sand, and stared out across the sea. Peter saw he had hurt him in some manner.

"Marco—what is it? You're thinking something you don't say. Why should this man watch me?"

Marco did not reply for a time. He looked at the boat making for the Porto. It was near now. They could see the men under the big sail as it luffed.

"Signorino," he said, at last, in a quiet voice, his eyes still on the boat, "you love la bella signorina, even as I do. For me it is useless, I know that. Signor Delfino is rich. He would strike me for my insolence. I have only dreamed my dream, that's all. La bella does not know, and if she did, she would not care—why should she look at a poor fisherman's son ? It's my madness, but no one knows. They can't laugh at Marco, not even la bella ! "

There was a catch in the boy's throat. As he spoke, he sifted the sand through his fingers.

" But with you, signorino, it is not so. You are rich, of the nobili, and though Signor Delfino would not like it, it is for the signorina to say, though he may be angered."

Peter stared at the lad ; for the moment he was a solemn man, talking to another, no longer in the relationship of servant and master, fisher-lad and gentleman.

" Marco, you're an extraordinary boy ! How long have you known this—this feeling I have ? "

" From the beginning," said Marco, quietly.

" Why, I've only been here a few weeks. I've only met the signorina once. She doesn't know herself, nobody does ! "

" Scusi, signorino, but that's not so. I know, Paolo knows—and the signorina herself."

Peter stared at the lad, so self-assured in his answer.

" You're guessing, Marco—you're imagining all this ! It's quite impossible. You say ' from the beginning '— from what beginning ? "

He broke into a derisive laugh, but the lad was not perturbed. He threw back his hair with a jerk of his head, and looked boldly at his padrone.

" From the time when you first saw the signorina on the *San Giorgio* in the harbour."

A look of amazement leapt to the man's face.

" How do you know that ? " he asked, confession in his question.

" You told me, signorino."

" I ! "

" Sì—when you asked all those questions about the

boat, the night you came to the trattoria. When the signorina came in to dance—I knew then who it was—why you had come back to Chioggia to paint. As she passed you I saw it all—so ! "

He moved his upraised hand in a level line before him. Jove ! and he had been so careful, so discreet in his questions to this shy lad seated at his table !

" Did the others see this ? "

" No, only one."

" Who ? "

" Paolo Finghetti."

" Was he there ? "

" Yes. He was seated in the room and looking out of the window on to the yard. Our table was almost under it, and I saw him looking at you, curious, I expect. But when the signorina came in and began to dance, he watched her all the time. He lost her once, and I saw him searching the dancers as they came by. You were doing the same thing, signorino, and he saw you, and when you found the signorina your eyes told him what you were seeking. I looked up and saw him watching you. His eyes were never off us after that. He sat in the dark like a cat. The next day he asked me who you were, how long you'd been here and what you were doing. He knows everything, signorino. They say he reads the weather like that. He knows where the shoals are. His woman said he had second-sight. It is so, he is evil. He walks with his back to the sun ! "

Peter laughed at this, but there was a forced note in his voice. He slapped Marco's brown shoulder.

" Marco, you're a very imaginative lad, and you'd give me the shivers if I believed all you say. Still, I'm glad you've told me. But don't go and challenge Finghetti to mortal combat because he's dared to look at me ! "

He laughed again, but the boy did not answer to his mirth. Marco saw it was not wholly natural, and was a little hurt by his padrone's lightness.

"Scusi, signorino—but I thought you should know and take care. If you think I'm wrong—"

"I don't think that, Marco, and I appreciate your anxiety. But we've a saying 'There's nothing bad but thinking makes it so!' Why, look at this sun and this gorgeous sky. There's nothing can go wrong in a place like this!"

Peter rubbed off the sand that clung to his body. The warm air on his skin filled him with exultation in his health and happiness.

"Anyhow, Marco, our psychic friend won't know what we've been doing in his absence!"

He took a handful of sand and let it trickle down Marco's spine, who was bent forward with his head between his knees, his arms round his ankles.

"He will, signorino."

"Very well. And what will he know then?" called Peter, now exercising with imaginary dumb-bells.

"That you met the signorina on Wednesday and went with her to the Pontelungo."

Peter stopped suddenly in his action.

"Do you know that! Well, perhaps you saw us!"

"No, signorino, I did not, but all on the fondamenta yesterday knew you'd met the signorina at the Signor Dottore Galuppi's, that you went to the Pontelungo, where you stayed till it was dark, and that you saw the signorina home."

"Really, I shall soon think Chioggia's a hotbed of scandal!" cried Peter, unable to keep a note of anger out of his voice.

"It's a small place, with many women at their doors,

signorino. They mean no harm but they cause it, per Dio ! "

" Then Marco, if that's so, it means I must not see the signorina," cried Peter. " I can't have her name thrown to the scandal-mongers."

Marco raised his head, rubbing his hands through his matted hair, dry now.

" That is wise, signorino," he said gravely.

Peter made a short sprint along the sands. How good it was to race along naked under the blue sky. Nothing could depress him this morning, not even their conversation. He turned back when he had run two hundred yards. What a lad he was, running about like this ! Suddenly, he heard Marco calling.

" Signorino ! Signorino ! Presto ! Presto ! "

Marco's arms were signalling wildly, as he ran towards the boat.

" What is it ? " panted his master, gaining on him.

" Look ! There's someone on the murazzi ! "

Peter looked. A diminutive figure was approaching along the breakwater. Hastily they slipped into their shirts, laughing like schoolboys at the predicament from which they had just escaped.

The figure on the skyline at each step began to assume a definite shape. From the distance it had appeared to be the confused form of an old woman, shuffling and bent, her movements retarded by loose shabby garments. Nearer, the hatless wanderer was seen to be a man, bent and leaning heavily on a stick. There was something peculiar and arresting in his gait for one apparently so derelict. His bowed head was covered with long white hair, falling upon the shoulders, he had a curious confidence of step on that narrow ledge of the sea-wall. Looking neither to the left nor right, almost unconscious.

E

it seemed, of the world about him, he moved along the ledge, his stick well advanced, one hand raised before him as if about to touch something he expected to find. Across his shoulder, Peter could see a strap that was attached to a large basket swinging at his side. He was a fisherman probably, with line and bait, setting out on his pastime. But the keen eyes of Marco recognised the trespasser in their domain.

"It's *Il Ciéco*—the blind man of Pelestrina. He's going down to the Forte to collect alms of the men there."

"How marvellously he walks on that ledge! Is he quite blind?"

"Sì, signorino, quite. He was born blind, but he sees more than we do."

"What do you mean?"

"He can read the future and knows the meaning of the stars. Everybody knows Il Ciéco di Pelestrina. He told them when the campanile of Santa Maria would fall. And it fell to the hour, signorino."

Peter was about to exclaim "Rubbish!" He had once that morning laughed at the superstitions that were the birthright of all these people.

"He has what you call second sight—is he a fortune-teller then?" asked Peter.

"Sì," responded Marco, quietly, still suspicious that his padrone might be laughing at him.

"Then we'll have our fortunes told," said Peter, gaily. "Call him!"

Marco watched the nearing figure. It approached without hesitation along the sea-wall.

"There is no need, signorino," he said. "He will see us in a minute."

"But you said he was blind?"

"Sì, he is, but he will see us."

Peter made no comment. It was useless to argue with Marco when in one of these dogged moods. They watched the blind man coming in silence, standing motionless by their boat. The old fellow was clad in a faded blue shirt, without a collar. His feet were bare and the ragged ends of his trousers flapped about his skinny ankles. Long exposure to the sun and wind had set its mark on his lined face, but age had added dignity to the natural beauty of the leonine head. The only sinister touch in his appearance was the extended hand. It seemed blackened with age and moved claw-like, with tenuous fingers, in the air, as though it were imbued with a life of its own, seeking for something the blind sight could not find.

His path along the sea-wall lay a hundred yards from the watchers by the boat. Peter had an impulse to call, out of friendliness, to that pathetic lone figure on the sky line, but curiosity to learn if Marco's prophecy would be fulfilled restrained him. When he had passed by them, as, of course, he would, Peter determined to call and give him something. It was terrible to be blind in such a world as this, to move amid such beauty in vain.

Waiting there, with not a sound in the still hot noon, save for the tap-tap of the blind man's stick on the wall, Peter experienced a curious threat of foreboding. There was something brooding in the stillness of the air, in the calm beauty of the day. His heart had quickened in its beating, and the silence seemed interminable as he watched the moving figure. An irresistible impulse to call out, to shatter the growing spell overcame him, but it was checked by the blind man, for he had halted now, and stood still as a statue on the sea-wall, his stick no longer tapping, his outstretched hand motionless in the air.

Peter heard the blood drumming in his ears, heard Marco's short, stertorous breathing as he stood, one hand resting on the gunwale of the boat. There seemed no life in the world as they watched there, the idle sea at their feet, the long empty shore, the withered effigy, the cloudless sky, the still air, all quiescent in the hush of noon.

Then the blind man turned. The tapping of his stick sounded again. He was not following the wall, he was feeling with his stick for a way down to the shore. He was coming directly towards them! As he gained the shore, picking his way cautiously over the boulders, Peter grew certain that the old fellow was not wholly blind. Probably he was a fraudulent old beggar who had imposed upon the people, willing at all times to recognise begging as a legitimate means of livelihood.

" Buon' giorno, signori ! "

The old man had halted about a dozen yards distant, his head raised as he addressed them. Despite Peter's conviction, the voice startled him with its calm assurance. Before any acknowledgment of the greeting could be made, the beggar advanced, stick to the fore, the bony hand clawing the air. Involuntarily Peter drew back. There was something sinister in this noonday apparition, something unfathomable.

" Will the signore help the blind ? "

The beggar had addressed both of them at first, now he was speaking only to him, to the padrone. Then, of course, the fellow was not blind, or how did he select him for alms ?

" Pity the blind, signore ! The rich Inglesi are always kind to the poor blind."

Peter started and looked in amazement at Marco. The lad smiled as if pitying his astonishment. Peter spoke, forcing his words.

" How did you know I was English, if you are blind ? "
he asked.

The tenuous hand made a movement in the air

" I see all things, signore, being blind."

The man's voice was calm, the voice of one self-
possessed. There was dignity in it, as in his appearance.
Peter realised, as he saw the filmed eyes of the man, that
he was no impostor, and, looking on the face, its native
nobility belied his suspicions.

" May I tell the signore his fortune ? " he asked.

The young man laughed, having no belief in such
charlatanry. As for Marco, he was as solemn as an owl,
his keen eyes watching closely. Peter had a whim to
humour the old man so that he could earn his money.

" No, thank you, but my friend here would like to hear
his."

In an instant Marco had started back, his eyes flashing,
his whole body alert, as if for flight or defence.

" No ! no ! signorino," he cried, vehemently.

Peter laughed at his ridiculous alarm.

" Why, Marco, whatever's the matter ? Are you afraid
of your fortune ? "

The sullen expression came over the lad's face, as when
he spoke of Finghetti. He cast his head down before
replying, almost inaudibly.

" I'm not afraid, signorino, but we should not know
these things. Send him away ! "

Peter would have laughed, had not the boy been so
serious, for there was almost terror in his manner. Perhaps a folk superstition frightened him. He turned to
the blind man.

" Well, you can tell me my fortune, then. I expect
you'll make it quite pleasant. Do you want my hand ? "

He held out his hand towards the beggar. Marco had

retreated still further, but his curiosity would not let him go out of hearing.

" No, signore—but may I touch your face ? "

He raised his bony hand, from which Peter started involuntarily. Then, annoyed at his own foolishness before the observant Marco, he lifted his face for the fortune-teller to touch. The claw-like hand hovered over his brow, one finger lightly touching his eyebrows and nose. Then it travelled unerringly round his face, from temple to temple, sweeping his eyelids as it passed over.

The hand fell again, and there was a long pause, the old man neither moving nor speaking, the hand held before his face, as if he were trying to read something in the air.

" Well ? " asked Peter, at length.

" Will the signore give me something he has—something he carries with him ? "

Peter removed the gold signet ring from his finger. It had been his father's and was engraved with the Neville crest.

" Will that do ? "

" Grazie, signore."

There was silence again. Peter looked from the beggar to the youth, whose eyes were big with curiosity, his breathing heavy with suspense. Evidently Marco was a believer in the occult. A judge could not have commanded more reverence for his words. Would the old fellow never speak, or was he cautiously concocting his guess-work ? At last !

" Signore," he said, returning the ring to its owner, and trailing his staff lightly on the sand, " there is much I do not see clearly, but one thing is near and not to be confused—a death—a violent death."

So the business was the same the world over, thought

Peter. There was surely a long journey and a wedding somewhere about, but he kept silent, thereby encouraging the old charlatan.

" It is not your death, signore, though very near to you. It will change many things, but the chief thing it will not change, because you will fight hard for it."

How cautious the old fellow was ! Thus far he had only committed himself to one fact, a death, which might be anybody's, and must be somebody's !

Again a long pause, the inspiration seemed reluctant. The outstretched hand fell to the beggar's side. He no longer fidgetted with his stick. Everything was so quiet that they could hear the soft lapping of the water on the sand.

" Well," asked Peter, after a patient wait, " isn't there a long journey ? "

" It will need that, signore," responded the old man quietly, again relapsing into silence.

" But is that all ? "

" That is all, signore."

Peter turned impatiently. He was not even a clever humbug.

" Marco," he said, derisively, " let him have a try with you. I'm no good."

The beggar raised his hand, as if commanding attention.

" I am sorry the signore does not believe me," he said with quiet dignity. Something in the blind man's manner reproached the Englishman.

" Oh, it isn't that—but there isn't much to believe, is there ? " asked Peter, more genially.

" There can be no more than the truth itself, signore. I might say much if you want much said. It might please, but it would not inform you."

There was an air of finality in his words, as well as sense. " Well, you're frank," agreed Peter, commendingly, putting his hand into his pocket. As he did this, the old man stepped forward and unerringly took hold of Marco's open shirt collar. The bony claw had fastened on it before the lad could escape, and he stood, motionless with fear, his eyes wide in alarm, his body bent back. So might a scared rabbit flinch in the clutch of a stoat. Peter watched the strange scene, fascinated with the aspect of the actors ; the blind beggar calm and eagle-faced, the boy, his eyes dilated with terror. They were vivid objects in the bright noon ; so might a hawk and its prey hover in a serene sky.

The hand relaxed its grip, but Marco did not move, transfixed with fear. The old man passed his hand rapidly before his own eyes, then let it fall to his side and turned away. Not a word came from his lips. He seemed to wait for his dismissal from Peter.

" Well ? "

The blind man did not appear to hear. He stood as if in a dream.

" What do you see ? " pressed Peter.

The old head lifted.

" Nothing, signore."

" Nothing ? " asked Peter, disappointed again.

" Nothing—to speak of."

Marco found his voice now.

" Don't ask, signorino, don't ask ! He has seen something ! Santa Madonna ! È terribile ! terribile ! " he cried hoarsely, " Send him away ! "

The old man's expression did not change. Like a statue he halted there in the glaring sunlight.

" He will serve you faithfully, signore," he said. Then, as Peter gave him some money—

" Thank you, thank you, signore, buon' giorno ! "

He bowed his acknowledgment with grave and sur-
prising dignity. Again his stick began its curiously
sensitive action ; without hesitation he turned and moved
in the direction of the sea-wall. They watched him go,
slowly but confidently. His cautious feet stepped surely
across the boulders, up to the ridge of the wall, where he
turned in the direction of the Forte. Tap-tap, went his
stick before him, the outstretched hand clawing the empty
air. Slowly he moved along the skyline, a clear-cut,
grotesque figure against the bright sky. They watched
him until he grew small on the horizon.

The bathers climbed into their boat, and in silence
Marco rowed for a time. His face was still solemn, and
even to Peter, who ridiculed superstition, the day seemed
to have lost its gladness. With an effort he began to talk,
chaffing Marco.

" I don't see why you're so miserable, Marco," he said,
lightly, " I had nothing but a death, and you got an excellent testimonial—and it's the only part I believe ! "

" Signorino," he answered gravely, " You may not
believe but Il Ciéco knows. It is because he knows he
would not tell me."

" But why, Marco ? "

" Because it was not good that he saw for me. I read
that in his face. È terribile ! terribile ! "

" Oh, nonsense, Marco ! " cried Peter, forcing gaiety
into his voice, " The old humbug's hypnotised us !
We'll have a drink to his confusion when we reach the
molo."

" Grazie, signorino," responded Marco, but there was
no joy in his voice. He rowed on, in silence.

CHAPTER X

THE afternoon seemed interminable. After his siesta Peter wrote letters, one to his sister Susan and one to Roderick, who had required his signature to some documents connected with shares in Neville's Bank. To Susan he briefly narrated his occupation in the last few weeks but withheld any reference to the real influence that had drawn him to Chioggia. He had just finished writing when the servant brought up to his room a letter. It was from Dr. Galuppi inviting him to go with him to Signor Delfino's for supper at eight o'clock. Singular that this information should come at such an hour! At five o'clock he would meet Lucia, at eight o'clock her father; and if at five o'clock he had not met Lucia, then most certainly he would do so at eight. There was consolation in that thought, for all day he had tormented himself with the idea that Lucia would not go to the Campanile.

Their first meeting had been in the evening, when the setting sun had touched the shadowy world with its golden wand. In that romantic setting they had played their parts, irresponsible actors stirred by an impulse they had not analysed. Since then she must have thought often of that meeting, have recalled his words, have wondered at his eagerness. What had her judgment been? Had she thought him too eager, had he frightened her? Yet she

had not shown any sign of fright, or even of annoyance.
He had certainly insisted on meeting her at their rendez-
vous, but the place had been suggested and named by her.
Perhaps she was now alarmed at her boldness and would
not go to the Campanile. Well, he would see her in the
evening, nevertheless, and tease her privately with breaking faith.

He scribbled a note of acceptance to the dottore,
changed his clothes and went out. The Corso was quite
deserted, except for a noisy donkey-cart, the animal belled
and tasselled, which carried empty syphon bottles away
from the hotel. The chairs outside the cafés were in
orderly rows, in readiness for the patrons of the evening.
The steamer from Venice lay moored in the harbour. It
would go in an hour, taking the tourists back to the city.
Peter found the dottore's house door wide open. A cat
and dog lay in the shadow in the entrance hall. Not
wishing to be detained by the dottore, he quietly entered,
left the note on the small table, and tip-toed out undetected.

A clock down the Corso chimed the half-hour. Over
his head, as he walked, the green shutters on the upper
story of a house opened; the sleeping houses were
waking up. As soon as it grew dark, from all those windows would pour forth an assortment of noises such as
only an Italian town can produce. Mandolines would be
twanged, and black-haired women would lean out,
holding a public conversation with the occupants of the
windows across the street.

Below, outside the wine-shop, a dozen men would play
draughts, arguing with the vehemence of a race that never
came to blows; defiant children going to bed would add
protests to the noise; the gelati vendor would come
ringing his bell as he wheeled into the street his ice-cream
barrow, lit with an oil flare, that lured small boys like

moths to try with their *soldi* the luck of the roulette wheel, whose favouring spin gave them two ices for the price of one. And there would rise, amid the babel, the smell of fish, of garlic and decayed vegetables, mingling with the heat radiating from the sun-baked walls of the houses.

Peter had often laughed to see dismayed tourists hurriedly escaping from the trap into which their search for the picturesque had led them. Smelly ? Well, yes, for those who specialised in smells, who seemed to invade Italy for the excitement of detecting them, those who, insensible to their own native smells, or deliberately avoiding their location, seemed to derive a queer pleasure from their horror at finding what they sought ! But half-past four in the day, while productive of smells, offered few distractions of noise. It was still a sleeping town. Even the fat old woman dozed as she sat amid her fruit baskets, while an urchin extracted a handful of nuts.

The far end of the narrow street led Peter back into the Corso. A dozen yards along this, and he had gained the large open square, the Campo, at the side of the Duomo. There was not a living thing in the big stony quadrangle. A man lay asleep on the steps of the small church of the Baptistry, on the right. In the shadow, along the whole length of the left side of the Campo, stood the cathedral, in which Peter had never yet been, for, contrary to custom, it was sometimes locked, owing to the fear that its valuable reliquaries might be stolen.

But the most commanding edifice in this open Campo was the great tower of the Campanile, rising from the far end. In a land of campanili, those splendid, graceful landmarks of the Venetian landscape, it feared no rival. The campanile of St. Marks, ascended by thousands of pilgrims, might be higher, more renowned ; the angel-crowned pyramid of San Giorgio, dominating the view from Venice's chief quay, might stand more picturesquely silhouetted above the grey and silver of the ship-laden lagoon ; but loyal Chioggiotti, who knew their own beloved Campanile from every aspect, would concede nothing of its equality in age and grace. It was the most familiar and beloved object of their daily lives.

The fleet, beating up from the south, saw it long before the silver line of the land. Ships making for the Porto saw it rise, towering above the campanili of the surrounding lagoon villages. In the sudden squalls, its grim dark form leapt forth into the lightning-flooded sky. In sunshine, it proudly revealed every line of its ancient architecture, the light streaming into its open arches, where, far above the city, swung the bells, blessed and named in honour of the protecting saints.

Above those open arches ran the stone balustrade, on whose encircling gallery stood tourists, diminutive as puppets, while they looked down from their eyrie on the great sheet of silver water and green land. At sunrise its cupola was the first to herald the coming of the sun as he rose from his Adriatic bed, the sea-mists lifting in welcome, the awakened East at his back ; and, at even, the last to signal across the flood of night to the crimson Euganean hills and all the western splendour of the day's death.

Crossing the Campo, Peter pushed open the small wooden door at the base of the great brick tower. He had feared that it might be locked and he would have to knock until a slumbering and moody sacristan had been aroused. Fortune favoured him thus much.

Inside the tower he stood as if in the gloom of a deep well. A long vent in each wall admitted a feeble blade of light into a room that was obviously used by the ringers, whose bell-ropes, with their tasselled ends, hung looped on wall-hooks. In a corner of this wooden chamber he found a small door. Through it, he looked up an opening in which his unaccustomed sight at first could see nothing. Presently, less handicapped by his sudden entry from the glare of the day into the darkness of the tower, he discerned a flight of stone steps narrowly winding above him. Obviously it ascended the Campanile. The door swung to behind, and he began his ascent.

It was a strange and eerie experience. At intervals, as he slowly rounded the tower, the worn steps were feebly lit from the interstices in the walls. For more than four hundred years the feet of dead men had trodden these stairs, going, who knew, on what mission—to hang flags for victories, to look for the coming of enemies, to watch for a delayed argosy. The centuries of the dead echoed back from these steps. Now, he panted up them, vigorous with life, eager with love, to a meeting.

It was a toilful ascent, but he was nearing the end. He could see the light, a white disk, as in a funnel, cut by the black shape of the bells. Should he not have waited for her below? Perhaps she would expect him there, and go away disappointed. He hesitated on the steps, decided he would finish the ascent and then return. A few more minutes, and, breathless, he had gained the small inner gallery that surrounded the base of the enormous bells, swung from giant beams crossing the tower. It was light here, for wide arches, open to the sky, were just above. But there was no exit, no way out to a gallery. Baffled he surveyed the narrow ledge on which he stood. On the far side a flimsy wooden ladder was propped up against the wall. Above it, he found an opening in the roof; then there was a chamber above the bells, and access to the outer gallery must be from that.

He walked towards the ladder when a sound made

him start. Up there, in the height and the silence, it was almost inhuman. Breathlessly he listened. There followed a hurrying of feet, echoing over the boarded floor above him ; then, as if out of heaven itself, came a voice.

" Pee-tar ! "

There, in the opening of the floor above him, by the end of the ladder, stood Lucia, peering down into the gloom where he stood. His heart leapt at the sound, his hand trembled on the ladder as he prepared to mount, a strange exhilaration in his blood.

" Lucia ! " he called, with eager steps running up the shaking ladder until he had passed through the opening on to the floor.

He found himself in a bare room above the belfry, lit by the sunlight pouring in through the open doorway that gave access to the balcony encircling the outside of the Campanile. In this doorway stood Lucia, astounded now at her own audacity, all her doubts assailing her anew. But a few moments afterwards, as he stood before her, his breathing heavy with the long ascent, she soon forgot her fears in the pleasure of this meeting. Her eyes smiled an eager welcome to him, and when he had impulsively stretched out his hands her own had instinctively fled to them, thrilling in his firm grasp.

" Lucia, I thought perhaps you were below. Have you been here long ? "

" Half-an-hour ! " she laughed, and then, seeing she had betrayed her own anticipation, she blushed.

" If I had known I'd have been earlier—but I was not sure you'd come."

" Nor I," she said, hanging her head.

He made no response, but only pressed her hands. Then, withdrawing them as if suddenly conscious of what she had done, she stepped out on to the balcony.

" Look ! " she said, " isn't it beautiful from here ? "

Side by side they surveyed the world far below them. Up here, in the hot sunlight, not a sound came to them. The air was still, the red-roofed town below seemed like a child's play-box. The doorway was on the south side, and before them stretched the flat green lands beyond the Pontelungo, that ran towards Brondolo and the mainland. Their own island of Chioggia rested apart, as if floating on the lagoon, held only to the earth by the long bridge where they had paused on that memorable evening. On their left, beyond the long strip of Sottomarina, rose the blue and purple Adriatic, its far horizon broken with the shadowy outline of Dalmatia ; on their right, the broad expanse of the lagoon, veined with the passing of boats, shone like a mirror of the sky.

She named all the places for him, her small brown hand pointing and emphasising, her beautiful face animated with the things she told him. Then they moved round the balcony, now looking east, now north, over the whole length of the town. It seemed a herring bone with its long central Corso and the branching side streets. He told her this, and she laughed delightedly, so that in the ecstasy of the sound he made her hand captive again. Beyond the town the great lagoon ran north to the hazy horizon bounded by Venice.

In the stony Campo immediately below them a black speck moved out of the shadow of the Duomo.

" That's Padre Emilio—he's going to Luigi's for his game of draughts and his glass of wine," said Lucia, as they watched the black object from their still height. The priest moved like a fly across a sheet of brown paper and disappeared in a toy house.

" Isn't it strange ? " said Peter, philosophically.

" How ? "

Her voice sounded like that of a bird, of a bird that calls at evening across English lawns.

" That you and I should be up here, and that the world should be so far off down there. I don't feel that we belong to it, do you ? "

" Let's pretend we don't," she replied.

He raised his head, and looked at her, pausing before he spoke, to admire the flawless beauty of her profile, crowned with her black hair looped in the familiar red band.

" Could you be happy here—alone with me ? " he asked, his words almost whispered. She did not reply, but a slight quiver of her hand told him she had heard. It rested in his on the warm stone balustrade. With her left hand she began picking the mortar in the chinks between the crumbling stone rail, secured with lead binders. He watched her thin beautiful finger, olive brown with its long pink nail. Then, recalling his question—

" Could you ? " he asked, leaning forward so that he could see her eyes. She looked at him frankly, without moving her face.

" Si," she said, quietly, looking back into his eyes.

A senseless, useless question he knew. Yet it pleased him to hear this answer, stirred him, so that his lips parted, and she wondered whether something had alarmed him, for he released her hand, and stood upright in the space between the campanile wall and the balustrade ; unconsciously she too stood up, and turned, facing him. Then she heard a cry on his lips, and the next moment he had drawn her into his arms, his eyes bright above hers, and so near that she could see nothing else but the flame in them.

" Lucia ! " he cried, rapturously. Their lips met ; in the silence of the sky they knew only the beating of their hearts.

Through the long moment neither the world below, nor the bright day over them, obtruded with any knowledge of place or time. They had each other, now all they knew or asked of life. Slowly he released her; the world rushed in upon them again, and the knowledge of it found her shy, so that she rested in his arms, her face buried against his breast. A little alarmed now at his unruly impulse, he knew not what to say, how to break this silence with suitable words. Something beyond the power of speech had sought expression in that swift act of their kiss; now something expressed could find no name in words. The town asleep below them, the wide expanse of sea and still lagoon, the very air itself, belonged to a dead world, so pitifully dead in contrast with this beating of their hearts, this exultancy in their blood; yet to the world they must return, pilgrims from ecstasy.

She raised her head and looked unwaveringly up into his eyes. With relief he saw in them the sparkle of merriment, and, emboldened, he laughed back.

" Have you been kissed before ? " he asked frankly.

Her eyes never wavered, the light in them leapt anew.

" Often ! " she said, and then laughed softly as his arms tightened about her.

Then he had taken it all too seriously ? His anxiety gave place to light happiness and he laughed with her.

" And you, Pee-tar ? " she asked, her eyes full of reproach now.

" Never before," he said, his face belying him. Then, as Lucia pouted her lips in disbelief—"so near to heaven!" he added.

Confession made, and having forgiven each other, they kissed again. Two birds flashed by in happy flight; even as they, their hearts took wing in the bright air, so far away was the world. He called her by name and smoothed back the hair from her lovely brow. About his neck caressing hands lingered. The sun fell from its height to give the shadows growth, the town below stirred and creaked. Eastwards the sea darkened and the horizon lapsed into dusk. All this beauty swept towards night, unseen of them. Sufficient the presence of each other, sufficient the enchanted hour that gave them so much to feel with their senses, to see with their eyes, and so little to say, except in the eloquence of each long exchange of admiration.

It was a little thing that brought them back to the visible world, a russet sail on the mauve horizon, leading a host whose wings glimmered, moth-like, in the dusk under the faint glow of the scimitar moon.

" Look !—are those boats ? " he asked Lucia, and her experienced eyes knew in a minute the meaning of that sign in the East.

" It's the fleet ! They're coming home," she cried, after a quick glance to the horizon. " That's the *San Giovanni* leading. They must have had a great catch to come so soon. The town will be noisy to-night."

They watched the slim shapes stealing along to the Porto. A level light from the west suddenly caught them in its crimson track, and their sails drank up the glow of the sunset. The *San Giovanni* was now clearly visible, her full sail spread in the evening breeze. Peter recalled the vessel as he had seen it on that morning when it sailed with the fleet and Marco had been so gloomy. Marco's troubled face came back to him, and with it, his words about Finghetti.

" This means the new fleetmaster is in luck," he said, watching Lucia's face, wondering if he would find corroboration of Marco's belief. He saw her thin hands press firmly on the balustrade until the expelled blood left them whitened. She continued gazing seawards as she spoke, her voice even but controlled.

"Yes—he has been lucky. My father will be glad," she answered. Then, with a suggestion of alarm in her voice as she turned to him. "I must go, it is so late! I had forgotten the time."

He took her hand again, detaining her.

"Lucia—we'll come here again—to-morrow?"

She shook her head, and attempted to withdraw her hand. Instinctively he felt she had changed since they had seen the fleet. Then Marco was right. That boat on the horizon seemed as an ill-omened messenger. This sudden change from gaiety to apprehension could not be mistaken. This swift hurrying away was associated with those homing sails. When she spoke to him her voice had lost its girlish note, its joyousness.

"No—I mustn't come here again. My father would be angry. We shall meet to-night—let me go, Peetar!"

But he did not move out of her way, and she was compelled to meet his searching eyes.

"Lucia," he asked, quietly, "is it your father only who would be angry?"

She turned her face away. It looked pale against the crimson sky, and even more beautiful in its pallor.

"Tell me, Lucia mia!" he commanded.

She met his question with another.

"Why do you ask me? Please, I must go!"

His hand fell from the balustrade, and she was free to pass, but something in his eyes held her. He seemed hurt.

"Oh, please—I don't know—I— " Tears gave a new beauty to her eyes as she faltered. His own pain made him pitiless.

"Is it Paolo Finghetti?" he asked grimly.

" Sì," she whispered, almost breathlessly.

" Do you love him ? " he pursued, his calm face belying the hammering of his heart. Her reply was almost inaudible as she bent her head.

" No."

He took a step nearer to her, his hands trembling now with suppressed emotion.

" Lucia ! you know I— "

His next words were drowned in a sudden clamour that burst upon them. It came like a thunderclap in that still sky. The tower shook with the outcry of the great bells just below them. A sudden flight of pigeons from the arches gave life to the molested heavens. Above the tumult he heard Lucia call " It's the Vesper bells. We must go or we shall be locked in ! "

One bell was tolling now, but it filled the Campanile with uproar, and they were deafened as they descended through the floor to the belfry. Even Peter felt a tremor when the massive bell swung outwards past him as he descended the frail ladder, into the deep gloom below. When he gained the floor Lucia's hand sought his arm and it trembled.

" It will be better lower," he said, leading down the first flight of steps, so dark that he had to feel cautiously with a testing foot.

" Yes—but we should have gone before," she said.

" How long do they ring ? "

" Ten minutes."

The answer relieved him. He had been wondering if they would be locked in. Such a mishap would be very unfortunate. He reproached himself with detaining her. Turning and turning they descended. A narrow window opening on a blood-red western sky marked half the descent. It was on the last flight that he suddenly understood Lucia's real anxiety. They would be seen by the ringers.

He paused on the stairs until she was close to him. One more turn and they would gain the doorway leading to the floor. He could hear the chafing of the ropes as they rose and fell through their guiders.

"Lucia! Say you were showing me the Campanile," he whispered. She understood at once.

"Sì," she answered eagerly.

As he opened the door, two men on the ringers' floor stared at them in surprise. One was gowned, his biretta tilted back on his brow. Peter recognised Padre Emilio. The other stood in the deep gloom, but there was something familiar about the figure.

"Signorino!"

The voice was Marco's, raised in surprise, as his hands moved with the swaying rope.

"Marco! What, are you a ringer?"

Peter tried to put a careless note into his voice, but he felt he had failed, and saw the astonishment on the lad's face as Lucia came out of the door. The Padre saw her, and with a disengaged hand raised his biretta.

"Buona sera, signorina," he said politely.

"Buona sera, Padre," she responded, and then paused.

The silence was intolerable to Peter. Marco, still ringing mechanically, watched them with enquiring eyes.

"Signorina Delfino has been showing me your famous Campanile. It is magnificent!" said Peter, addressing the beaming priest.

"Sì, signore. È magnifico! But we did not know you were up there. Did we frighten you, signorina?"

He smiled at her, no longer curious about their presence in the belfry. Marco had remained silent. What was the boy thinking?

" I didn't know you were a ringer, Marco," the young man repeated.

" I help the Padre," he replied, still ringing. Again Peter saw the sullen look. It was a Marco different from the eager, smiling lad he knew. For some reason he now seemed angry, and was almost rude in his curt reply. Perhaps he was still upset by the fortune-teller on the shore.

They bade the ringers good evening and went out into the open Campo. Above them, the peaceful sky glowed with the sunset. Lucia said nothing as they crossed to the Corso, and he was the first to speak.

" Lucia, are you angry ? "

" No."

" Then why are you so silent ? "

She looked at him with large reproachful eyes.

" We have been very foolish," she said slowly.

But he would not agree. It had been a wonderful afternoon. Surely she would not let a little incident upset her so. Another time they must meet each other earlier.

" No—never ! Peetar, they will talk."

" Who ?—why should they ? " he pleaded.

" Marco and the Padre—they will laugh together now."

" I can answer for Marco—he will not talk for our sakes." And then the absurdity of it struck him. " Lucia! why should they talk ? Can't we meet like any human creatures ? We shall meet again to-night, we must meet often in this small place."

" Yes—but not alone. I hardly know you."

" Lucia ! " He was hurt and he meant his voice to reveal it. She turned and her eyes softened as he called her name.

" I did not mean— " She raised her eyes to his and a flame glowed in them. " Oh, Peetar, why have we met ? "

She put out a hand which rested lightly on his arm for a brief space, then, apprehensively withdrew it. Only her fear prevented him crushing her in his arms, reckless of all around. Actually he said nothing, but walked on in silence at her side, until they reached her door. Even then they hardly spoke in parting ; her face flushed as she bowed in response to his raised hat. Strangely agitated, he walked on to his hotel.

In the privacy of his room, as he changed, he reviewed the whole of their brief acquaintance. How and where would it end ? What was his intention, and, indeed, why was he here in Chioggia at all ? It was singular that from the beginning of this wayward adventure he had never asked himself that.

Seated on the bed, in his shirt sleeves, he sat staring before him, looking out through the open window on the cool shadowed lagoon, seeing nothing. His suspended shoes hung from his hands as he sat and stared in the semi-darkness. Out of that silence came no answer ; his reason stumbled and grew quiescent, for he saw only the face of Lucia, now bright with laughter, now pensive, but ever alluring. To what end ? He knew not ; whether he drifted or stepped deliberately, her spell was upon him, and being the subject he could not rebel. It would need a stroke of Fate to shatter the spell, something more powerful than the will, something not controlled by his own nature.

A clock in the town, striking eight, broke through his reverie. He started, and hurriedly completed dressing.

CHAPTER XI

I

THE *San Giovanni* sailing homewards in the sunset, with a full spread of her main-sail, combined beauty and pride. She was a bragozzo that had always carried the master of the fleet, as her pennant flag denoted. Built at Chioggia, she knew the Adriatic waters well. Her colours were familiar on the deep sea and on the lagoons, from the mouth of the Piave to Rovigno and Ancona. Her painted prow had cut the sea lanes on days when the water was a blue mirror of the sky, or when mountainous seas had carried it skywards, before plunging it down into troughs of wind-flogged water. On this particular evening of calm beauty, when all the softness of the summer day lingered in the serene sky, she rode towards the familiar Porto as if conscious of a mission well fulfilled. One might have said that she preened herself in the pleasure of her own well-being, since ships seem to have a conscious life of their own.

Certainly the human voices, calling across her littered deck, shared the spirit of gaiety. Tousle-headed men and lads, stripped to the waist, laughed and slapped each other's brown shoulders, and overhauled the smelly nets covering the deck. They were homeward bound, with a great haul, and therefore a glad welcome in the town, and their homecoming was appropriate for the most joyous festival of the year, celebrated on the eleventh of June, when every man, woman and child, together with a host of visitors from the surrounding places, would pay honour to their patrons, San Felice and San Fortunato.

On that great day there would be food and drink in plenty, with a procession of children from the Duomo, with the girls in gala dresses. Then all the boats along the Vena would be festooned with coloured lanterns; in the Piazzetta the choral societies would compete, and the Sindaco, or Mayor, make a powerful oration in honour of the winners. Not a fisherman missed this great festival, and however distant the fleet, he contrived somehow to be back for this day of feasting and reunion. Now they would be home with a good catch, with money in their pockets, and a ready welcome from the women.

Many a child, many a lad and lass, counted the days to the Festa. It was in the thought of these singing youths, at work on the nets. There would be a present for the beautiful Lucrezia, or the lovely Isabella, and perhaps she would walk with one of them from the Duomo, down to the Piazzetta where, if Fate favoured, she might allow herself to be rowed out on the lagoon while she sang happily under the swinging lanterns. Per Dio! it would be a great day!

Another dreamer stood apart, near the prow of the homing vessel. In the dusk he looked immense, an immovable colossus, brawny-shouldered and heavy limbed. It was Paolo Finghetti, proud as a man can be proud when conscious of his absolute supremacy. He was bringing home the fleet with such a catch as had not been known for ten years. He had struck the shoal off Rovigno, taken heavy toll, and sent a laden ship speeding to Venice. The next day, when scarcely the nets had been drawn, he hurried his fleet north, as if inspired. A Venetian trawler, surrounded by boats, like a cock in the farmyard, steered south past them, but Paolo heeded them not, and scowled when the skipper suggested they were ignoring obvious advice. In the waters deserted by the Venetians, almost at the mouth of the Piave, he found a new shoal, followed it through a night and a day, and then drew a great haul within the limit of breaking his nets. A second boat dispatched to the Fishmarket on the Rialto had set all tongues wagging. Young Paolo Finghetti had answered the old men who shook their heads and raised their hands at Delfino's folly !

Well might Paolo stand boldly at the prow of his boat. Chioggia, black there against the crimson and green sky, would hold him in honour, particularly the Signor Delfino. Yet above all, he sought approval from the one first in his thoughts, not only because essential to his ambitions, but also because her elusive beauty filled him with the zest of the hunter. Every rebuke of her eyes, each disdainful pout of her red young mouth, the birdlike wildness of her movements, flaunting almost, aroused his blood to the conquest. He would net that proud scornful creature, even as he netted his shoals. He had offered her love, which she had laughed at ; since passion put no spell upon her, as with other women he had known, then he would use the cunning born of ambition.

Nearing the Porto, his eyes swept the familiar skyline, past the Forte and the church of San Domenico, over Sottomarina and its houses, until the dominant pile of the Campanile held his gaze. It towered above the confusion of the town, clear-cut against the cool green of the upper sky, and, as he watched, the sound of its bells came over the evening waters. They would be preparing supper in the houses now. He wondered what Lucia was doing, how she had spent the hot day, whether she had heard of his good fortune, and if so, with what thoughts.

A light flashed green through the purple dusk over the sea, it was the lantern on the Littorale-end of the Porto. He watched expectantly to the left, and found the green light of the shoal buoy. In half-an-hour they would be in lagoon waters.

Walking from the prow, he gave orders for a slackened sail ; the straggling fleet crowded around him out of the dusk, then, shepherding his flock, he led them down the tortuous sea-lane into the Porto.

Peter Neville, leaving his room, heard the noise of their approach, the calling from the molo, the rattling of pulley blocks, and the creaking of main-mast runners as the great sails fell. Out of his window, a forest of masts crowded the dim sky. So the fleet was home. He watched the pageant, mysterious in the failing light as it passed to the Canal, then, suddenly conscious of the time, hurried out of the room into the noisy Corso.

II

The Signor Dottore Galuppi, for all his seventy years, was not indifferent to the pleasures of food. He had enjoyed the simple but perfect supper of his host, Delfino. The wine was excellent, a fine-flavoured Asti Spumante, brought cool from a deep cellar. From the soup to the early peaches, all had been of the best, and the spaghetti-al-sugo had been specially notable, so much so that he had broken his stern rule never to repeat a dish. It was a rule made, not in the interests of the digestion, but of the palate, which, as a gourmet of long experience, he well knew should never be robbed of anxious expectation.

" And you tell us, my dear signore, that the smells of
Chioggia do not distress you ! I always thought English-
men had inconveniently sensitive noses ? "

The dottore paused in the peeling of his peach, bending
his fine head in between the candles as he peered into
Peter's eyes.

" Together with conveniently long purses ! " laughed
Delfino, at the head of the table.

" Ah, signori, I have reversed tradition," replied Peter,
" I have an inconveniently sensitive purse and a conveniently long nose, which smells nothing ! "

He turned to Lucia, radiant in her evening gown and
glowing with the excitement of the occasion. She talked
very little, but that was because she loved to hear him talk,
anxious that her father should admire, as she admired,
this attractive young guest of theirs. He was making a
good impression. She knew that by the manner in which
her father addressed him, by the laughter that rang
round the table. Since the afternoon she had been full
of absurd fears and doubts. Once she had almost taken
the dottore into her confidence and told him everything.
He would understand, she felt, as perhaps her own father
could not understand.

Signor Delfino certainly lacked nothing as a genial host.
At the first sight of his guest he agreed with his old friend,
Galuppi, and understood the reason of his daughter's
infatuation. Young girls could not withstand this quiet
force of a foreign personality. Signor Delfino saw
quickly that little was to be gained by open opposition. It
might avail him more to win the young man's confidence.

So he was attentive and attracted the intruder with his
singular air. He told stories of the fishing, of the artists
who had visited the port, of his own early experience of
London, when an apprentice on a Genoese cargo-boat.

Supper finished, they moved out to the loggia opening from the dining-room, and raised over the small garden leading to the canal beyond. The air was still warm. The deep shadow of the house lay across the garden, at whose foot three cypresses stood sharply defined in the moonlight. They could hear voices on the boats down the canal, with the rattle of winches and banging of boxes.

"They're unloading already," said Delfino, listening to the noise along the fondamenta.

"To-morrow morning you must go to the fish market," said the dottore to Peter, who had been looking furtively at Lucia seated beside him. How silent she had been all the evening!

"If the smell is not too much," added Lucia, "for I confess that it keeps me away."

"That, my dear child, is as it should be," laughed the dottore, "for you would distract them just when they should be busy."

Signor Delfino smoked quietly awhile, saying little. Secretly he was consumed with anxiety to go down the canal and hear everything about this haul, how they had fared, how Finghetti had managed it. The sounds coming to him now, out of the night, called to the fleetmaster. But he knew his duty as host.

"Lucia," he said at length, after a discussion between the dottore and the young man, upon local songs, "I think we'd like to hear you sing."

"Ah, excellent! This is the hour of nightingales," declared the dottore, dramatically waving his hand to the night overhead. "Signor Neville, we have with us one of the hopes of Venetia!"

"Dottore! You dreadful exaggerator!" complained Lucia.

"We have a famous *maestro*, Signor Zambra—"

"I heard him recently, at Count Casmiri's, I believe?" interjected Peter.

"Ah, then you know him! He is a connoisseur, you'll grant me? The *maestro* told me that of all his pupils—and he has all Venetia to choose from—the one he most—"

"Now, dottore," interrupted Delfino, "I am not going to let you turn my little girl's head—or prepare such disappointment for Signor Neville. Cara Lucia, fetch the mandolin and we'll give them some boat songs, if you'll let an old frog croak with you."

Lucia returned with the mandolin, which her father examined critically. First he tried the strings with his thumb, head bent to one side. Next the instrument was firmly gripped between his knees, the left hand stretched out to the keys, as he tuned with precision. This process completed to his satisfaction, he drew forward his chair, crossed one leg, swept a thumb over the strings so that their vibrant notes filled the dark night, then, with a preparatory wave of the hand, addressed his daughter.

"Now, Lucia mia, I am ready."

Their programme must have been practised of old. They began with a Venetian lullaby, slow, with an exaggerated pianissimo that became inaudible, suddenly swelling into a sustained note, then dying again like a gust of wind gone by. Now it was a Venetian air, old, so old that the listeners moved in a medieval garden; here smiled the scarlet Cardinal, there bowed the Doge. A laughing silken lady lowered her black mask, taking the gallant's hand in the processional measure. Those stars, shaking through the cypress, had seen them, had heard, centuries gone, this toccata of Galuppi's, seen this grace of maiden limbs, this sweep of hand and neck; for Lucia was dancing now, her slim ankles and quick feet threading the traceless pattern of an old-world dance.

Then, like a threat of thunder in a summer heaven, a heavy hand smote the strings, the sinuous body paused, the head stiffened proudly, a hand rose in declamation. She was singing, singing to the lilt of the muted instrument. Peter, his blood quick with the exhilaration of her beauty, leaned forward, scarcely breathing. What she sang he knew not, nor cared, only that it was something, somehow, allowing no comparison. Her young voice rose effortless, the night seeming to listen, glad to answer through its depth with far echoes. Now she was returning, from what Elysian garden he knew not, dropping as the lark drops, in sudden rushes, poised intermittently, trilling with quivering body, then dropping again, until that final perfect descent to the waiting earth, and the following silence.

Peter leaned back. He dared not look at her, the spell of song still upon her as she stood ; he watched a glimmering star and wondered at its distant agitation. The dottore sat alert, smiling in the pleasure of the moment. Delfino had not lowered his suspended hand, as if listening for the last pulse of the eddying sound. Then silence complete.

" There—can she not sing, Signor Neville ? " asked the proud father, uncrossing his legs as he lifted the mandolin. " And the young lady rebels each time she goes to Venice for her lesson ! "

Peter did not answer. He could only smile into Lucia's eyes, his agitation robbing him of words. Perhaps she saw all he could not say, for she glanced abruptly away.

" Dottore ! " she cried, sitting suddenly on his knee, one arm around his neck. " I believe you'd have been asleep in one minute ! "

" Carissima ! and who wouldn't ? When you sing those lullabies I could go off like an infant ! "

Peter found words now ; poor, silly inadequate things.

" I—I have never heard such singing—nor such songs, signorina. I think I know now the meaning of *bel canto*."

He turned to Delfino with these last words, but his host had risen and was peering over the loggia into the dark garden.

" Who's there ? " he called, listening.

" Paolo—can I come up ? " answered a voice.

Instantly the night grew alert. Lucia slipped from the dottore's knee, standing still, her face turned to the garden, where a giant figure moved out of the shadow into bright moonlight. Peter, startled by the voice, began to wonder why their evening seemed to have clouded. He did not know this man, who had just as much right, nay, even more right than he had there. Yet he resented his intrusion, particularly now, an interloper out of the darkness.

Delfino, still leaning over the balcony, waved his hand joyously—

" Welcome, my Paolo !—come up !—come up ! "

He turned from the balcony. " Now we shall hear all about the catch," he exclaimed jubilantly. " I knew Paolo was a born fleetmaster ! Was I not right, eh, dottore ! eh, Lucia ? "

He rubbed his hands ecstatically, looking to them for ready confirmation, but without waiting for their response, he hurried into the dining-room, leaving the three standing, hiding their perturbation. They heard his boisterous welcome within, the happy noise of his laughter, the quick eager questions of the old man, the slow few words of the young one.

Peter, alert as though something menacing drew near, knew the pleasure of the night was shattered. An absurd, unwarrantable feeling of enmity grew within him. He was going to dislike this Paolo ; they would be antagonists. He now began to understand Marco's change when Paolo's name arose. Perhaps it was Marco's antipathy acting now. He must dispel it.

As for Lucia, the joy had suddenly been crushed out of her evening. She had sung as never before, sung in sheer happiness of heart, telling her love in song, as she had never dared to tell it in words. His awed silence told her she had succeeded ; when he had looked at her, wordless in his emotion, the swift intuition of their love had caught them up in its rapture. And now a shadow had fallen on their song-laden garden ; it was as if a knife had dropped from a cloudless sky, sinister at their feet, a warning, a challenge.

Delfino threw back the inner window and stepped on to the loggia.

" This is a happy night ! " he cried. " It calls for the best our cellar can produce. Ah, allow me, Signor Neville —this is my dear Paolo Finghetti, who has brought our fleet in so grandly to-day. Paolo ! this is Signor Neville, my English guest."

Peter moved, conscious that he was watched alertly. The two men shook hands, firmly, quietly, level glance meeting level glance. What saw each there ? Certainly nothing to be read without intuitive prompting. Peter saw how just was the old fleetmaster's faith in this resolute strength. Here was a man of heroic figure, made for hard contests with Nature, for the unending warfare with the elements ; a man to lead, drive, or oppose men as occasion called. And what Paolo saw, none might divine. Certainly no change in his face, or flicker of his eye, revealed an inner thought. Perhaps he had no thought at all, too conscious of his triumph, of Delfino's loud welcome.

Their host had disappeared indoors, seeking that ultimate bottle. The dottore broke the awkward silence, as they stood there in the semi-darkness.

" Well—I hear you've had a record catch," he said.

Paolo grinned, and Peter noticed the power of his jaw, the long firm set of his animal teeth.

" You didn't expect me back so soon as this, eh ? "

The reply was to the dottore, but also it seemed for Lucia, for he glanced at her as he spoke, and the young man heard a boast in it, or thought he heard.

Lucia laughed at him. " Perhaps San Felice hurried you home for the Festa," she said, alluding to the saint, in whose honour the festival was almost due.

" I shall believe Santa Lucia prayed for us," he answered, a more gentle note in his voice as he looked at her. Her reply was checked by the entrance of Delfino, old Bianca following with a tray, bottle and glasses. He declaimed while she set it on the small table.

" Per Dio !—what a catch ! At the Piave mouth, too ! Per Bacco ! It's the young fellows who have all the luck, eh, dottore ? "

The cork popped.

" And, I might add, all the love too ! Eh ? " he laughed, holding up a glass to the neck, too happy and intent to require an answer.

He filled the fine glasses, placing them in a row along the table.

" Now, Signor Neville, dottore, Lucia—let us drink ! " he called, raising his glass dramatically, and throwing out his chest. " To our Paolo—and the good catch ! " He bowed to Finghetti, who stood embarrassed, fingering his glass, the centre of their circle.

" Many such catches, Paolo mio," said Delfino, when he had sipped the golden wine.

" Sì ! " cried the dottore, " and my wishes are no less sincere, because this wine is the best I've tasted for many a day ! My good friend supplies a good reward. Non è vero ? "

He threw back his head and contemplated the half-empty glass. Then he turned excitedly in the glow of the connoisseur, " Non è vero, Signor Neville ? "

Peter laughed. " I am a fortunate guest at a fortunate moment," he responded. Lucia drank silently. Paolo crossed to her, his clumsy hand grasping the glass which he raised slowly.

" To the voice of the nightingale," he said, and some-how, what should have been the act of a gallant was a fulsome, clumsy compliment.

" Grazie, Paolo—I did not know you were listening."

Was there a sting in it ? Peter thought so, and caught the dottore's eye for a moment. But it was too subtle for the fleetmaster, and her father was engrossed in replenishing the glasses.

They had resumed their chairs now, and Paolo answered Delfino's quick questions. Undoubtedly it had been a triumph. Moreover, the Ancona fleet had been encountered and outwitted, for he had got to the wind-ward of them, spread his nets, and monopolised the fishing ground. Frustrated, they had gone home.

Encouraged by the approbation and the wine, he began to be dogmatic. Twice he contradicted the old fleetmaster, who hid his annoyance. They were going to be the largest and best fleet in the Adriatic ! It was time things were done. Chioggia had been losing its supremacy for years. The whole fleet was thoroughly out of date !

" How ? " interrupted Delfino, this criticism of his régime rankling.

" The day of the trabaccolo and the bragozzo is dead. We must have motor auxiliaries."

" God forbid ! " ejaculated the dottore, with vehemence.

" Noisy, spitting things ! You'll spoil the lagoons. Look at Venice—the place is a nightmare with their pop-pop-popping ! The steamboats were bad enough—but these abominations ! What say you, Signor Neville ? "

The dottore looked to him for strong support.

" As an artist I should deplore any change," agreed Peter, " the sails of Venice have been famous for centuries."

" Our beautiful sails," sighed the poet in old Delfino. " Yes—they are very lovely, our sails of sunset. I do not think fishing could ever be the same without our sails. I would like to go before they go," he sighed.

" It's no use being sentimental," continued Finghetti, in his deep voice. " If the signore here'll forgive me, we can't live on artists. We never have done. They've generally done nothing but interrupt our— "

" Paolo—our guest, our guest, please ! " said Delfino, a little of the old dictator sounding now. It sobered the triumphant Finghetti.

" I know—but I'm only speaking my mind ! "

" Certainly," intercepted Peter, " I quite understand."

" Ah, then I'll be plain," continued Finghetti, pushing back his glass on the table, and planting wide his legs, as he rested a hand on each knee.

" Over at Rovigno they've made up their minds to go ahead. There's no silly sentiment there. They've no artists or tourists who'll raise their hands in horror. They've got a great marine museum, they've a fleet of motor-boats, and they're fitted with acetylene flares for night fishing."

" Acetylene flares ! " echoed the horrified dottore.

" And what can they do with acetylene flares ?—why not oil lamps to look for the fish ! " said Delfino, an old fisherman's contempt in his voice.

Paolo sat back, crossing one leg over another. Then he placed a hand in each jacket pocket, and surveyed the company with an air of superior intelligence.

" You see, you don't know anything about it ! "

There was a flash in the eyes of old Delfino. Peter caught it, and saw the fire that had not burnt low yet in the old fellow. Lucia put a soothing hand on his arm. His body was suddenly tense.

" I know nothing about it ! Per Dio ! What was I doing at sea for forty years before you were born ? "

" Nothing about acetylene flares," asserted Paolo Finghetti, doggedly, in no way rebuked.

" I don't think I want to know," murmured the dottore, looking hard at his glass. " It sounds a monstrous contraption."

" Fishing's fishing," said Finghetti, suddenly. " They're getting tremendous hauls."

" How ? " asked Delfino fiercely.

" Now that you'll listen, I'll tell you. They go out at night. The flare is under a cowl at the stern. It attracts and dazzles the fish, who follow the boats as they make for the shore. Behind them sweep the nets, closing in, and when the lights go out and they try to get back, it's too late. I met some of their fellows. They are making fortunes out of sardine fishing while we're looking for shoals. You can't afford to be out of date. We must fit motors ! "

Ignoring Delfino, who all this time had sat with his head slightly bent forward, his eagle eyes fixed on the speaker, Finghetti filled up his glass and emptied it, gulping noisily. Peter found himself hating this hulking fellow, not only for his indifference to the beauty he would shatter, but also for the manner in which he approved the change.

Delfino, deeply shocked, slowly shook his head. He had felt the truth of it. Yes, there was no denying progress. But at what cost!

"My beautiful sails—the skill of the sailor—what will come of all this? A thousand years our sails have taken the dawn and the sunset, and now you say they must go!"

The dottore rose, placing a hand on the shoulder of his old friend.

"Delfino—I feel grateful for these seventy years. These lads,"—he waved his hand in the direction of Finghetti, "belong to another age. I would not if I could! Take away the peace of our lagoons and the sails of our boats, and what is left us?"

Finghetti laughed, his whole body stirred with derision of this weak sentiment.

"Money, dottore, money! What's the good of pretty boats for artists?"—again the sneer, thought Peter— "if the villages are starving. One day they'll build a great port down this coast, with wharves and coaling stations and—"

Delfino sprang to his feet.

"Enough! Paolo! Enough! I believe you'd like to see it! Our beautiful Venetia, is it nothing? They have ruined Venice with their dastardly steamboats, their swishing motor boats, their raucous *serenate*. Every palazzo and hotel, every—"

"And they're making money," interrupted Paolo, doggedly. "But I see you're all romantic. Well, keep your romance, what you can of it. I'm going to make money. You can buy romance any day of the week."

The dottore listened to this outburst with sorrow on his lined face.

"My friends—I feel we are losing romance now. This

beautiful night; the music, the wine, such as only la bella Italia can give—shall we forget these?"

He spread his hands, appealingly. Paolo knew he had gone too far. Delfino, who during Finghetti's tirade had paced the loggia excitedly, sat down again.

"Come," he said, "we'll not let Paolo frighten us. Young men will never understand these things, my dear dottore!" He smiled at Peter, somewhat pathetically. "I know you artists are our allies," he said, "and I trust you will have cause for many years to come. Lucia! let us have another song. Let us sing *Me trago sul balcon*, and make Paolo wonder what our maidens will sing about when there are no more sails going seawards."

"Sì, Lucia mía, sing!" urged Paolo. "I'll have to go in a minute, but I'll wait for that."

"Don't let me keep you," retorted Lucia. "You would leave us nothing to sing about."

"Lucia—now that's unfair. I could hear you sing all night."

"Maybe, Paolo, but you won't."

The dottore clapped his hands.

"Now, children, no quarrelling! Ah—I could always cry a little when I hear that!" he sighed, as Delfino played the opening bars.

Lucia stood forth and sang, her young voice rising in the warm night, her shadowy hair gemmed with the bright stars of the velvet canopy behind her. In ecstasy, the old dottore swayed to the rhythm, and perhaps it was pure sentiment that finally caused him to wipe his eyes.

> *Me trago sul balcon, vedo Venezia,*
> *E vedo lo mio ben che fa partenza;*
> *Me trago sul balcon, vedo lo mare,*
> *E vedo lo mio ben a navegare.*

Sia benedetto l'albaro e l'antena,
La barca del mio ben e chi la mena ;
E chi la mena e la sa ben menare ;
La barca del mio ben sa navegare.

Venice I see from my window above,
I see the dear one that I love
Set sail and seaward go.
Now blessings on the yards and mast,
My love's aboard, the sheet is fast,
Set sail and seaward go !

When the last note had died in the listening night, Paolo rose.

" I must return—they're still unloading. Good-night, Signor Neville," he said bowing. " When do you go ? "

There was a slight pause. Was there an emphasis on the last word. Perhaps not. Peter returned the bow.

" I have only come recently, and Chioggia is too attractive to think of going yet," he replied, smiling.

" Why, of course," added the dottore, " and Signor Neville must paint—while there's anything left to paint ! "

They all laughed.

" I've aroused powerful enemies, I see," said Paolo. " But at least I will make some atonement. We are having a serenata on board the *San Giovanni* on the Festa night. You will all come ! Marinetti and his daughter will sing, and we'll watch the fireworks from the sea. Is that agreed ? "

" Sì, Paolo, sì ! " cried Delfino, heartily. " We will all come, and the signore shall learn how we can play as well as work. It will be a great night—a great night ! " he repeated, following Paolo through to the dining-room as he left.

When Delfino returned he made but one allusion to the departed guest.

" Our beautiful sails ! Dottore, they must not take

those ! Ah, these young men ! What they will throw to progress ! Yet Paolo is right. I admit it. He knows. It is we who find it so hard to change, for we know what we shall lose." He sighed absently, and then, recovering, —" Now, gentlemen, your glasses ! "

Lucia went to her father's side.

" I must bid the signori good night, padre mio," she said, kissing him, and a minute later had left them to their cigars and gossip under the starlit night.

A clock struck one as the dottore walked homewards with Peter along the Corso, still bright with the cafés, whose patrons sat around the small tables, drinking and talking, now their work on the fondamenta was finished. Voices were loud and spirits high. Paolo Finghetti had brought home a great catch. There would be money for the Festa on Thursday. A clever lad, Paolo !

CHAPTER XII

MADRE PAPPINI was the first to realise that something of the utmost importance was about to happen. At seven o'clock in the morning she had pulled the last basket of onions out of her cavernous shop in the Calle Mazzini, thus completing the array of stock on the pavement. There she would sit on a little wooden chair watching her baskets, and working at her lace-pillow, for the whole of the day. Towards noon, her crimson face grew redder under the reflection of the awning that she drew, which protected her fruits from the sun but not from the flies, who almost obscured them at times.

There was one period in the day when the chair was empty and the baskets unguarded. You might have helped yourself freely, from one-thirty to three-thirty ; Madre Pappini was having her siesta, and not all the commerce in the world would have kept her from slumber in the shuttered room upstairs. Her stock-in-trade was safe, however, for the simple reason that everyone was doing likewise ; any thief might have taken all he wished, in return for his extraordinary exertion. Chioggia lived industriously from six to nearly noon, and vivaciously from seven to well beyond midnight. Mid-day was a stagnant backwash in the life of Chioggia.

Thus came Madre Pappini to be astir well before seven in the morning. She was, in fact, nearly into the middle of the tenth row of her lacework when the unusual noise caused her to look up the street. The unusual noise was the sound of boots on the flags. In places where the community, through the long summer, lives barefoot or straw-sandalled, boots create a singular noise.

Looking up from her work, she had further cause for surprise. There, coming towards her, was Marco, known to her from the age when he had played naked among the cats and fish baskets, a fat brown baby with a wonderful smile for men, animals or food. She knew Marco's mother, a thin worried little woman who spent her days packing fish or mending nets while her husband lounged all day on the balustrade of a canal bridge, when it was warm enough, or slept on the shady steps of the Duomo when it was too hot, and fishing required too much exertion.

Marco she liked, for he was a willing lad, and always had a gay jest for her. But Marco this morning she hardly knew. He was marvellously arrayed in a manner that foretold an event of importance. He was wearing a clean shirt of a vivid lilac hue, wide open at his brown neck. With this he wore a broad-brimmed felt hat, under which his dark eyes gleamed with earnest pride, for he looked, and knew it, handsome as an artist's model should look. Further distinction was gained with a pair of light brown linen trousers, gathered in at the waist like a shirt by a thin black belt. But surpassing all, he wore boots, with patent toes and light grey felt tops! Only twice before had he worn them, and they pinched him terribly. Those occasions had been the funeral of his grandmother, and the wedding of his sister.

He seemed a little self-conscious as he approached Madre Pappini, and would have passed her without speaking, but her curiosity was not to go unrelieved.

" Good morning, Marco ! " she called, not stopping

her busy fingers. " It's a bright lad you are to-day. Is it a wedding that you're for ? Madonna ! but you do look fine ! If I was the bride I'd want to change my man ! "

He paused and laughed, a little embarrassed, but pleased with her compliments.

" You shouldn't have been born so quick then, Madre Pappini, and have given me the chance ! " He moved to go.

" But whose wedding is it ? " she asked.

" Nobody's ! I'm not going to a wedding."

" And who's died—that I haven't heard of it ? " she queried, choosing the only alternative.

" No one I know," replied Marco, starting away again.

" Ah, then it's to Venice you're going ! Now you might call at— "

" I'm not going to Venice," retorted the lad, pulling a sleeve so as to show the blue enamel cuff-link.

" No ? " cried the old woman, tucking away a wisp of hair. " Well, if it weren't the wrong end of the day, I'd say it was a little signorina you were off to see."

" Then you'd be wrong again, Madre Pappini."

" Oh—well, it's something special ! "

" It is," agreed Marco, gravely. He would have to tell the old woman. " I'm going to buy a yacht ! "

Mother Pappini dropped her thread spindles.

" A yacht ! Santa Maria ! " she exclaimed, with a sly smile. " Ah—you think me an old fool, Marco. It's the Signorino Neville you're going to meet. Sì ! that is it. And he's going to buy a yacht ? "

Marco scowled slightly.

" No ! I'm buying it—for the signorino," he corrected her.

" Sì—sì. I hear he's very kind to you. There's some use in being the friend of a rich Inglese. It's no use being the friend of poor people. They can't help, if they want. You're a lucky lad, Marco. I'm sure he's a very pleasant young gentleman to work for."

" He asks me for all he wants," said Marco, expanding with importance. " The signorino wants a yacht, so he asked me to buy it. I am now going to the squero to fetch the yacht I ordered Mollinari to build last week."

" There! Then I'm sure it's a great day for you, Marco ! " asserted the old lady, duly impressed.

" It is, Madre Pappini. It will be the best yacht in Chioggia—at the Festa too."

" Perhaps the signorino will let me come aboard it ? "

" Perhaps," agreed Marco ; then teasingly, " If you won't capsize it ! "

Madre Pappini clapped her hands in enjoyment of the jest.

" Oibò ! you rude boy ! " she cried. " Be gone ! "

By this time shutters on each side of the street had been thrown open, and heads in various disarray appeared in the black spaces. Many wondering eyes followed the disappearing Marco. Then a chattering broke out until the street seemed a gallery of monkeys, with Madre Pappini presiding at her baskets, by the right of weight and wisdom.

Marco, on his way to the shipyards, felt no violation of his conscience in the magnification of a simple sailing boat into a yacht. In Marco's eyes all boats owned by gentlemen, who did not use them to obtain a living, were yachts. His elaborate attire this morning proclaimed the solemn importance of the occasion. He was to receive the boat to-day, and, if approving, duly take it out of the squero, christen it, and make the maiden trial on the sea. The signorino had entrusted all this to him, having agreed to join him at the molo at ten o'clock.

After escaping from Madre Pappini, whose inquisitiveness had not altogether displeased him, for she would proclaim to all the importance of his task, he did not go direct to the shipbuilding yard on the San Domenico canal. He turned aside and entered the great Duomo.

Within, he paused for a moment, peering down the long marble floor towards the High Altar, dim in the greyness of the interior, one cold shaft of light from the lunette tipping the ebony and silver crucifix. Crossing himself, he advanced down the nave, hat in hand. Then kneeling on the steps, he contemplated awhile the beautiful altar, built of veined marble with carven intaglios of agate and lapis-lazuli. After a short prayer he rose, passing the high canopied pulpit, and walked on tiptoe towards the Chapel of Saints Felice and Fortunato, the patrons of the city. Here, with bowed head, he prayed long and earnestly on behalf of his padrone, seeking every blessing on one who was so dear to him. And in his prayers came the name of Lucia Delfino, since the signorino's happiness could not be fulfilled without her.

He was not alone at this altar. A woman, her lined face lifted anxiously, knelt at the other end of the predella, still as a statue. She had sorrow written on her brow, and Marco, glancing, saw that her lips never moved, as though she had ceased to plead, if not to hope. With boyish sympathy he forgot his own mission for a moment, wondering what had drawn her aside at this hour. Perhaps she was deserted, or sought a man-child, as Sarah of old. Whatever the reason, necessity made her oblivious of the lad kneeling only a few yards distant. He rose and left her, still immovable, the cold light striking the upturned brow, bloodless lips and patient eyes of that white face, framed sharply in straight black hair.

One more prayer, this time before the wood statue of

San Rocco, the special patron of all who sought the sea. He would guard their boat, leading it into safe waters, and to still anchorage; and because Marco prayed so earnestly, all his young heart outpoured on behalf of his dear padrone, would not all be well with the signorino? San Rocco would grant his request; his patron saint was not deaf to the plea of a fisherlad in whose heart no evil dwelt, who was merely thoughtless at times, and so joyous in life that he sometimes forgot the eternal in the ecstasy of the transient.

These prayers said, with a simple eloquence aided by faith and desire, Marco stepped out of the grey silence into the sunshine and noise of the Corso. Here the world was astir. Donkey carts clattered under the Tower Gate with garden produce for the shops. He greeted half-a-dozen friends stripped to the waist, working on board the boats lined up in the Canale della Madonna. But he did not stop, despite their curiosity at his appearance, and the shower of questions that followed him as he turned towards the San Domenico Canal.

Crossing a bridge over the canal, the poetry of the scene held him for a minute as he looked down through a veritable forest of masts, gaudy with folded sails of orange, crimson, brown and yellow, so that the blue sky seemed like an artist's palette smeared with loose colours. Shouting, hammering, and the rattle of winches sounded along the fondamenta, crowded with fishermen and fisher-women carrying hampers of shining fish towards the Public Market. Everybody was good-humoured this morning and worked merrily. Such a catch meant a great Festa in two days time. Per Dio! Paolo Finghetti knew his job! For the fifth time a sweating, half-naked sailor, his trousers rolled up over his knees, told a group of women, busily packing fish in crates, how Finghetti had outwitted the wily men of Ancona.

Marco left the shouting and laughter behind. He had crossed to the San Domenico canal now and could see the squero, where their boat was berthed. Mollinari, the boat builder, ran to meet him. His greeting had a degree of respect as well as of familiarity. Marco was a powerful patron these days. The rich signorino had money to spend, on Marco's advice.

" Buon' giorno ! " he cried, sharing the lad's carefully suppressed excitement. Through a litter of shavings, logs and pitch-pans, Marco followed him to the boat, tilted towards the canal.

It was a slim craft. The signorino did not want to wait, so they had worked upon a boat half-constructed. Speed was in every line of her.

" There ! " exclaimed the old fellow, proudly, displaying his arms as if to embrace his work. Then, seeing three black curly heads along the gunwale—" Hi ! you scamps ! Get out of there ! Subitissimo ! "

The brown urchins, naked as they were born, slipped like lean rats over the side to the ground, and ran splashing into the canal, whence they shouted rude remarks at the old man.

Marco, regarding the finished boat in all its splendour, repressed a desire to dance.

" Sì !—sì ! " he said, solemnly, a little concerned about his boots on the pitchy ground.

The old man knocked the props away, preparatory to launching. This done, they pushed the boat down the mud slope until it breasted the water. Marco hopped over the stern before the last push sent it clear of the sloping bank. Completely entranced with his work, old Mollinari stood, arms akimbo, watching the craft as Marco manipulated it with one oar over the stern, which he wriggled in the water so that it acted as a propeller.

" Santa Maria ! Bellissima davvéro ! Can I not build boats, Marco ? " he called, thirsting for praise.

" Sì—so far she's good. We'll know when we get the sails on."

" What will the signorino call her, Marco ? "

" I don't know. I do not ask the signore his business," replied Marco, resenting the old man's interest in his padrone. Then, conscious of his abrupt reply, " I'll bring her back to-night and you shall see her rigged."

" Bene, Marco ! Eh, but she will be a beauty ! I have spared nothing ! "

He watched Marco paddle her down the canal, sighed, and turned to the upturned boats being pitched by his men, a fearsome crew, embroiled in the dense smoke of the pitch-pans, their bare legs black to the thighs, covered with mud and pitch. Dirty open shirts revealed on each tanned chest a chain with pendent charm.

Marco was now half-way down the canal. It was a solemn procession. Everyone stopped work on the boats to watch him. They all knew it was the signorino's boat, built to the order of Marco. They hailed him, proud of his acquaintance, and he responded gravely. As soon as he passed, a babel broke out of questions, surmises, criticisms.

But the triumph was nothing compared with what was to come later. They should see then ! His signorino would have the finest boat on the lagoons.

Marco's yacht, as he had grandiloquently named it, was in reality a small topo, one of those popular boats of the sardine-fishers and market-gardeners that make such a common sight and yet such a pageant of beauty on the lagoons. At dawn and even they spread their gorgeously coloured sails as they flitted in intricate, swerving designs across the shallows and along the channels of the lagoons or lay crowded together, their vivid wings folded like alighting butterflies, along the quays. To the experienced eye they possessed fine distinctions. Peter had often been puzzled by Marco's infallible identification of a Chioggian boat, however distant.

" How do you know, is it the colour ? " he asked, one day.

" No, signorino—not that. I will tell you. Look at those topi. Do you notice anything peculiar ? "

Peter examined them critically as they drifted by, low boats, with a great spread of orange and crimson sail that stained the reflective lagoon beneath them. They were market gardeners' boats, sailing towards Venice, their decks bright with coloured piles of tomatoes, pumpkins, peaches and crates of fowls. Like all Venetian topi, they had the singular sail-formation that surprises the stranger, and yet leaves him without realisation of the cause. Built without keels, for the navigation of the shallow waters, they were steadied by large rudders and, thus weighted at the stern, rose in the bows, a fact Peter had observed.

But it was some other unusual feature, which disturbed him even while it baffled detection. Then, as Marco spoke, he saw, in a flash, their true originality. Unlike all boats elsewhere, these vessels of Venetia carried their larger sail at the stern, the smaller forward. And there were other singularities to be observed. He was fascinated by their curious, toy-like weathercocks of fretted woodwork, fitted to the masthead, and filled in with bright-coloured bunting. The deep force of legend and superstition often added the fantastic figure of a *gobbo*— the hunchback who brings good luck. Endless too were the designs of these vivid sails. The sea-going boats, such as the bragozzi of Delfino, having no figure-work on their great sails found expression for the love of decoration in gaudily painted bows, with flying figures of Fame, in a swirl of drapery and blowing trumpets, or of saints on prancing chargers.

The topi reserved their adornment for the sails: religious sentiment and the love of flamboyant design were freely expressed. Many an hour, Peter lay in a boat lazily watching the topi drift by, sketching the patterns and figures of their sails. On grounds of red, blue, orange or green, painted in strange geometrical designs or brightly striped, they sometimes aspired to high pictorial art in the upper triangle, cutting the sky. There a crude St. George slew a cruder lion, the one scarlet, the other ink-black. St. Sebastian, that human pincushion of the faithful, collected arrows, smiling withal; or Titian unwillingly inspired a Madonna, in an Assumption out of perspective.

But all these things were common to the Venetian waters. Marco's infallible clue escaped him.

"Marco, I give it up. I don't see how you know."

The boy laughed, showing a row of white teeth, his eyes dancing with delight in his knowledge.

"Look, signorino—and you'll always know afterwards. Look at those sails, and then look at the masts! Do you see now?"

Peter examined them, critically and steadily, still unenlightened.

Marco threw up his hands in exclamation, then came from the stern, gesticulating.

"Look, signorino—the yards of the sails are both on the same side of their masts! All the Chioggian boats are like that."

He laughed in great glee, and resumed his position at the tiller, proud of his display of erudition.

The boat Marco was now taking down the canal, this bright June morning, had no sails. The two masts stood gaunt as lightning-stripped trees. Ah! he had a great secret and surprise for the signorino! The more disappointed his look, when the boat reached the molo, where he would be waiting, the greater would be Marco's ultimate triumph. He was speculating upon this when a voice from the fondamenta hailed him. It was Paolo Finghetti calling to him.

Marco paused with the oar, and turned in the direction of the call. Finghetti, his hands in his pockets, stood near a bragozzo which had been emptying its freight. He wore a blue and white striped jersey, with blue cotton trousers.

" Buon' giorno, Marco—what's that you've got ? "

Marco thought it was a quite unnecessary question, since the fellow had eyes in his head, but Finghetti was not a man to be ignored.

" A new topo," said the lad, paddling again.

" Whose is it ? "

" Signor Neville's," responded Marco curtly. In another minute he would be past and out of range.

Finghetti spat in the water, shifted his weight from one leg to the other, stared hard, and then called—

" What's he want with a topo ? "

Marco had a swift retort on his lips, but checked it. He would have to live in Chioggia when his padrone had left. Finghetti was a man to be feared.

" I've not asked him. It's no business of mine," he cried, suppressing " or yours," content with his slight deviation from the truth.

" Well, see he doesn't drown himself ! " came the sneer, followed by a laugh as the great fellow turned away.

Yes, it was war between him and his padrone.

Finghetti could not disguise his feeling. He would warn the signorino again.

At the end of the canal he turned the boat deftly into the harbour and looked immediately for his master. Yes, he was there. Marco waved excitedly, and paddled vigorously until he had brought the boat alongside the molo.

" Eccomi ! " he cried, eagerly searching Neville's face.

" So this is the boat—but there are no sails to it ! "

" No, signorino," said Marco, complacently.

" But we need sails ? "

" Si."

" Well—haven't you ordered any ? "

Marco's face was blank.

" Jump in, signorino," he said, ignoring the question, and shifting his oar.

Realising that Marco was reserving something, Peter jumped into the boat, and the lad immediately began that rhythmic sway, the familiar sway of the gondolier, bending forward on the long oar, making such a silhouette against the bright horizon and above the smooth water as the centuries have known. The boat sped on, its direction cleverly manipulated by Marco's single oar. Curious how that lad, rowing only on the one side, sent the boat creeping sideways, as a dog walks. Peter had tried often and failed, despite his Oxford days, when his punting had been immaculate. This was a different motion, familiar to generations of the Venetians. He now saw that their boat, unlike the gondola, was equipped with a forcola, or rowing fork on both sides, so that the oarsman could remain faithful to custom and row forwards, seeing his course in front.

Still, however that might be, this was a sailing boat, not a rowing boat, and it had no sails, a need emphasised by the two gaunt masts. There was some good reason, of course, which Marco was determined he should not learn yet ; and, from experience, Peter knew that Marco could be as dogged as a mule. The lad, in grave silence, was rowing him to their bathing place.

They crossed the open Porto, rose and fell as they entered the Adriatic, and turned north towards the Littorale. But Marco did not turn inwards at the point opposite their accustomed strip of beach, he rowed on steadily. When Peter looked at him, questioningly, a slow smile grew over his brown face and his dark eyes danced with suppressed excitement.

" Marco, I insist on knowing what you are doing ! Are you abducting me ? "

The lad pouted his red lips and then burst into wild laughter before his baffled padrone.

" Signorino, I will tell you now ! We are going for the sails ! "

" But where ? " asked Peter, well knowing there was no village for several miles up the lonely Littorale.

" Là ! " cried the lad, pointing to the barren shore a quarter of a mile along the murazzi. Peter stared, more deeply puzzled, while Marco shook in mirth. But not another word would he say until he had driven the boat aground. He leapt out and ran eagerly up the beach.

" Marco," said Peter, panting after him, " I shall think you're mad in a minute. What are you doing ? "

At this the lad fell all his length in the sand and rolled like a dog in his enjoyment ; then to his padrone, who stood over him—

" Signorino, I said we were going for the sails. Ecco ! they are here ! " he said dramatically, beating the sand with his palms.

" Here ? " echoed Peter.

"Sì—but I will explain. Only half a boat is built at the squero. A good boat is what its sails make it. It is not many who can cut a sail. I can, signorino. My father taught me, as you shall behold. They send for him at Venice. Bah! they can't build boats, and they can't cut sails at Venice. It is Chioggia that makes the boats."

Marco stood up, proudly declaiming. Then pointing to their boat—"That is a good boat—but the part that matters most is my work, signorino," he said, gravely. He stooped and lifted a heavy boulder, placing it a few feet distant. Peter's wonder grew.

"I have cut our sails myself, I have sewn them also. And, signorino! I have painted them!"

Peter stared at the excited lad.

"Painted them!"

"Sì. That too, is not known to all. My father taught me that, as you shall see, signorino."

He then fell on to his knees, and with vigorous hands began to scoop out the sand, dog-like, on the spot where he had removed the stone. In a minute he was tugging at something in the bottom of the pit he had dug. Then, with a last heave, he pulled forth a large bundle of cloth, which he gravely placed at his side, returning to his delving until he had produced a similar packet. Breathless, he rose to his feet, flung back the long hair from his flushed brow, and cried, triumphantly—

"Signorino! Our sails!"

This said, he capered in the high enjoyment of his little joke, the air noisy with his mirth.

"But, Marco—" asked Peter, when his merriment had somewhat subsided, "why all this mystery—why have you buried the sails out here?"

Marco raised his hand, authoritatively commanding attention.

" You shall hear, Signor Neville," he replied, gravely.

He thereupon related how he had borrowed a good sail and brought it to this beach, where it had been stretched out. The sail-cloth was now unwound, laid over the original, carefully measured, and cut strip by strip, with overlapping to allow for sewing. The strips were then numbered and rolled up.

" That completed the first morning's work, Signorino. I took the strips back to Chioggia and all that night my mother and father and myself and young Pietro sewed them."

" Splendid ! " cried Peter. " I shall feel confidence in our sails, knowing they are home-made."

Marco bowed solemnly, then waved his hand as before.

" You have not heard all, signorino. That is but part. There is the design and the colour. These are important."

They were indeed. Venice was not Venice without her coloured sails, the lagoons without its pageant. Day after day he was held by the enchantment of these sails, with their crimsons and oranges, blues and russets, changing in light and shadow, glowing or dull, in colours that had given Titian and Tintoretto their immortal palettes.

" It is an art known to my father, signorino. I have helped him often. These are my first sails, and you shall judge."

He stooped and unrolled them reverently, until there spread across the sand a glowing sheet of colour. It began at the bottom edge, in a deep russet, paling to gold and slowly merging upwards to bright orange. Two-thirds up, there was a sudden, daring break in the colour. A bright blue band crossed the sail, like the line on a butterfly's wing, and above it, a sea-green triangle completed the sail-tip. It was on this triangle that Marco had wrought his masterpiece. A crimson lion, rampant, with lashing tail, paws fiercely extended, raised its noble head, the fire of courage and defiance glaring from the eye.

Peter, amazed, stared at the gorgeous spread of sail; a sunset seemed to have sunk in the sand. Marco stood silently by, somewhat paler now in the intensity of the great moment.

And then, in a flash, Peter saw the significance of that lion. It was not the ever familiar lion of St. Mark, symbol of puissant Venice, it was—

" Marco—you dear lad—that lion's the— "

It was as if a burst of sunlight had struck the boy's face

" The lion of the Inglesi ! " he said, his voice quivering, his young face uplifted towards his padrone.

Peter, stirred by the boy's emotion, and a sudden thought of home, smiled at him mistily.

" Marco—I shall never forget this day—and your tribute."

" The signorino is pleased ? "

But the exile could not answer, and looked aside. Then, recovering himself—

" It is beautiful—molto bella ! " he emphasised. " You are a great artist. We shall have the most beautiful sails on the lagoons."

Marco was now unrolling the smaller jib sail, russet-coloured. He spread it out at the side of the other, and then stood back and surveyed his handiwork.

" What I want to know, Marco, is, where have you got your colours from—what is it ? "

" Ah," said the youth, looking very wise, " that is our secret, signorino ! "

" Which I may not know ! "

Delighted with his secret knowledge, the lad threw back

his head and laughed, giving his thigh a sharp slap, then clicking his fingers high in the air.

" Signorino, I will tell you, padrone mio. Look ! "

He unscrewed a paper parcel, retrieved from the sand hole, and spread out its contents, which consisted of a large sponge stained with mixed colour, and four small wooden boxes. Each of these held a different coloured powder, red, blue, orange and green.

" So those are your paint boxes ! And where are the brushes ? "

" There is none, signorino. We use the sponge."

Peter examined the boxes comprising Marco's wonder-working palette. It was not paint they held, but a kind of coloured earth, something like the reddle used for marking sheep. These crude colours had been mixed with water, and roughly applied with the big sponge.

" But won't the sails run when they get wet ? " he asked.

The lad shook his head vigorously.

" The colours have been made fast, signorino. The sails were dipped four times in the sea and left on the sands to dry. They will never run now. Let's fasten them on," he added, eagerly folding them in readiness for carrying.

An hour later, sweating in the hot sun, they had fastened the sails to the yards. With a loud cry of delight, Marco hoisted the mainsail, which lifted with a rattle of its running hoops on the mast. The russet and orange cloud spread out in glory, flaming in the bright noon. The shallow water under the gunwale was stained with quivering gold, orange and blue.

" Signorino ! Signorino ! Per Dio ! she is beautiful ! " shouted Marco, filled with the ecstasy of the artist, as the sail bellied with the light breath of the noon, and quivered like a thing waking to life. Turning his glowing eyes to his padrone—

" What shall we call her, signorino, what shall we call her ? " he asked excitedly. Then to survey his triumph fully, he leaped over into the shallow water.

There was a cry of dismay. The excited lad had forgotten his own personal glory. The glossy boots and new trousers disappeared in a foot of sea water. For a moment he was a pitiful figure, but the occasion was too great to mar with a personal incident. He waded to the sand and then removed his ruined splendour.

" They have always hurt me, signorino." he said, ruefully, holding the wet boots in his hand. " I'm quicker on my feet without them," he added, rolling his trousers up his sturdy brown legs. The next moment he was exclaiming with delight upon the beautiful boat, his disaster forgotten in this great triumph.

Peter followed him, and looked critically at their new plaything. Yes, she was a beautiful creature, flaming there like an arrogant peacock.

" Signorino—what shall we call her ? " asked Marco.

" Call her, Marco ? Now I never thought of that. Yes, what shall we call her ? "

Marco was silent. It was a solemn occasion. He puckered his brow. Suddenly inspiration came.

" Signorino—*San Giorgio*!" he exclaimed, triumphantly. " Your patron saint ! "

Peter shook his head.

" No, Marco— we've a lion on the sail, Giorgio was a dragon slayer. Actually he was a disreputable merchant from Cappadocia, I believe."

" Then *San Pietro*—your own patron saint."

" No, that wouldn't be in good taste. I'll call her *San Marco*, I think, since Marco made her."

The lad laughed at this. "There are dozens of *San Marcos*, and it must be something quite distinct."

"I suppose, if it's to be a saint, ladies are included? Well, I've got it. I vote for *Santa Lucia* !"

But Marco's face was shadowed instantly. He looked at his master with narrowed eyes.

"No, signorino—not that, it would not be wise. There would be talk in the Porto."

Peter accepted the reproof.

"Very well. We'll be really original, and give the saints the slip. We'll call it *Cela va sans dire* !"

"Sì ?" queried Marco, "Is that an English lady ?"

Peter laughed happily, and slapped the lad's shoulder.

"It's French, Marco, for ' It goes without saying.' "

"Ah ! Va bene ! Va bene ! " cried Marco, his eyes glistening with the joke. *Selavasandir* ! Sì—they shall see it go ! Ha ! "

He kicked the sand around him, anticipating the awe his display of cryptic knowledge in the name would entail among the lads of the Porto. "*Selavasandir* ! " he repeated, stolidly, memorising it. Another repetition was checked by something cutting the sky above the horizon. Peter saw a sudden shadowing of his face, a parting of the lips as he drew breath hardly. Following Marco's gaze he found a small sailing boat, turning now and making for the shore. It had a sea-green sail, tipped with white. Whoever was handling it was a master. The white foam leapt at its prow as it came speeding under the breeze.

"Do you know the boat ? " asked Peter.

"Sì " the reply was almost hissed.

"Whose is it ? "

"Paolo Finghetti's."

There was another silence. They watched the sea-green sail, its white top gleaming as it swayed under the breeze and passed from shadow into sunlight. It was nearer now.

" He has come to spy," said Marco, the old hatred in his voice. " Let us go, signorino."

" What is there to see—why should he come ? It's just a coincidence, Marco, let him come."

" Signorino, there's always a coincidence with Paolo Finghetti. I've known it before. He comes to spy on us. He has watched us come here. He saw me go down the canal with the boat. He wanted to know, and I would not tell him. He is never baulked, so he has come."

With an impatient shrug, Peter was about to chide Marco for his ridiculous suspicions, when something left him staring speechlessly out towards the boat. It had turned, tacking as it came coastwise, and the starboard was now visible. The great sail flared in the sun, below it sat two diminutive figures, their heads level with the yard-arm. One was Finghetti, the other—

His heart thudded within him. It was a woman, every line of her body dearly familiar. Then the boat veered, obscuring her, and the sail filling, it leapt southward under the strong breeze.

CHAPTER XIII

I

LUCIA, skipping up and down the fondamenta that morning, had a word or a swift retort for every lad who gave her a jocular greeting. To protect herself from the sun, she wore a vivid lemon silk shawl over her black hair, which fell in a tasselled fringe to each side of her vivid green blouse. She was a fisherman's daughter this morning, for whereas Marco, to celebrate an occasion, had departed from custom, and gone painfully if brightly shod, Lucia in turn, to celebrate the fleet's return, had gone forth unshod. Not without protest from Bianca, who, scolding, sought to impress upon her wayward charge that, while it had been quite permissible for a run-about girl to discard shoes and stockings, a growing young lady, a gentildonna, could not be seen bare-legged in the thoroughfares. Whereupon the uncontrollable Lucia had defied and kissed her as usual.

" I may one day be a prima-donna, Bianca mia, but never a gentildonna ! I am a fisherman's daughter." She raised her skirt revealing two sturdy brown legs as far as the knees.

" Look, Bianca !—why should I be ashamed of them ? They're brown and well-shaped."

Bianca raised her hands despairingly.

" Every woman on the fondamenta," continued

Lucia, now revealing her knees in growing self-satisfaction, " will be barelegged to-day. I should look an
oddity."

Thus Lucia again asserted her freedom. And that she
did not look an oddity, the admiring eyes of the lads,
unloading the bragozzi, told her. They popped up
eagerly over the gunwales at her approach, with " Morning
signorina ! " or " Nice day, signorina," or, the more bold
and familiar, just said " Eh, Lucia ! " softly, and gazed
devotedly. Yes, as her father had remarked overnight,
she did not hasten work along the canal.

From boat to boat she went, gossiping. The *San
Sebastian* had lost its cat overboard, the *Santa Theresa*
had lost her nets in the heavy haul, the skipper of the
Santa Elena had gone to get married this very morning,
while fortune beamed on him.

Luigi Spinelli, alert and smiling, observed Lucia. He
was a striking figure in his red vest, collarless and
revealing a broad brown chest. He watched her hungrily,
while she chatted with him. Poor Luigi ! it was the
desire of the moth for the star, yet he found some pleasure
in his impossible passion.

" Where's Marco ? " she asked him.

" He's not been with us. Marco's in luck with his
signorino."

" And who's that ? " she asked archly, though she knew.

" Signor Nevilli. Marco's just gone by with the
signorino's new boat. Eh !—and he was proud too ! "
said Luigi, enviously. Then almost whispering, timid
at his audacity—" Lucia, won't you let me take you in
my boat at the Festa ? "

" Perhaps so, Luigi—we'll see," she answered, " but
Marco will be angry. He'll want me to go in his padrone's
boat, I'm sure."

" Sì," agreed Luigi, dolefully, " and the signorino too. They say he loves you."

Lucia lifted her head swiftly, like a bird.

" You are as impudent as ever, Luigi Spinelli ! " she said, and sped away, a little flame of anger in each cheek. He watched her slim bronzed ankles skip over the ropes. Hurrying on, she was suddenly aware of Paolo Finghetti looming above her. He saw the crimson in her cheek, the fire in her eyes. He did not know what had happened to flutter this lovely swift bird that had almost blundered into his arms. The raised head of Spinelli beyond suggested a reason. He would deal with the brazen lad later. Meanwhile—

" Lucia—where are you flying to ? You nearly knocked me down."

" As if anyone could ! " she retorted, staring up at his great shoulders and massive head.

" I'm going out to try a jib sail I've got for the Festa. Come with me, Lucia ! " he urged.

Any other time her refusal would have been prompt and final. But she was angry. What Luigi was saying, all might soon be saying. It frightened her, for the moment, to think that those Campanile meetings might be known. Had Marco been talking ? She remembered his surprise when they had descended that evening into the ringers' room. But Marco surely would be silent for his padrone's sake.

She was conscious that Luigi was still watching her from his boat. She would refute his surmise on the spot. To Paolo's astonishment she assented.

He helped her to descend and his eyes watched her firm ankles and brown legs ravishingly as she tripped down the rungs of the steel ladder into the boat. Satisfied that Luigi had seen her, she seated herself near the tiller, while

Paolo cleverly worked himself out from a veritable net of cordage tethering the bragozzi to the quay. Now that she was aboard, self-annoyance possessed her. To give the lie to silly gossip and that boy's suggestion, she had run into Paolo's hands. He was exhibiting her all down the canal, a smile of satisfaction on his big, weather-bronzed face. The more they were seen together the stronger his claim would be.

She had flouted him shamelessly for weeks. Well, he was a patient and sure player of the game. No prize had yet escaped him. Now that he had her, he would reveal the Paolo men followed and women obeyed. On land he knew he was a clumsy, heavy-limbed creature. He had never sought to be otherwise, having a complete contempt of sleek, soft-handed men, such as that Inglese, with his drawing-room tricks and his picturesque neatness. Bah ! he was a man, not a mannikin ; a smasher of heads if they got in the way.

" Where are we going ? " asked Lucia, lightly. Having entrapped herself she would show no annoyance. Her question came easily, in a tone of complete indifference.

" Out of the Porto awhile," he answered. He had taken the oars now, and his massive chest bent towards her, the muscles playing under his thin vest. " I want to try this new jib sail. You're not limited to an hour, Lucia ? " he asked.

" No," she answered. If he had said " to a day " she would have assented as indifferently. And she was in the hands of a skilful sailor, a man of immense strength. Looking at him now, she could admire his heroic pro-portions, but it raised no other feelings in her. So might she have regarded a Michael Angelo statue come to life.

They had crossed the harbour and had emerged from the shelter of the molo. The boat danced as it struck th waves in the sea-channel. Paolo raised his mainsail, and came astern, seating himself by her side at the tiller.

"Lucia," he said, with a softer light in his eyes, "this is the first time you've been in my boat."

She laughed lightly. Perhaps the fellow really was in love with her. He had suddenly lost all his arrogance. A slight pity for his impossible passion stirred in her, but he blundered in the moment of his advantage, for his hand had seized upon hers, hot, clumsy and forceful. It was the hand of the animal stirring in him. Its grasping strength filled her with revolt. She threw it off, fiercely. Her dark eyes glinted and struck his amorous, ridiculous gaze.

"And it will be the last, if you're going to behave like this!" she retorted.

"Lucia mia, you know I— "

"And you know I don't!" she said, vehemently, cutting him short and lifting her head angrily.

Per Dio! what a wild cat to tame. The lust of the chase filled him.

"I do know, Lucia mia, but I want you as I have never wanted anything before. I can wait. Paolo Finghetti is a patient man, he is not to be turned aside."

A sudden luffing of the boat checked him. The prow lifted, and they swerved to larboard as he kept the boat's head against the wind blowing south.

"I came for a sail—not to see you make yourself ridiculous!" cried Lucia.

She had the satisfaction of seeing an angry flush in his cheek. The sensuous grasp of his heavy hand still burned her own.

He made no retort, but stood up, gazing out over the jib-boom towards the north horizon. The sea around them lay motionless as a lake, save for a slow unbroken undulation. The noon was stifling, and not a breath of air caught the listless sail now they were on the open sea. To their left, the long white strand of the Littorale blazed in the sunlight, a thin barrier between the burnished lagoon and the darker Adriatic. East and West, the sky and sea imperceptibly merged in the pearly heat haze. Paolo was staring northwards into the leaden horizon. After a long silence he looked down at her.

" There's a squall coming. We must run in soon," he said still gazing forwards, his voice sounding loud in the muffled noonday. The water lapped the boat's side idly.

" I don't mind a breeze," answered Lucia, with continued indifference. " Let's run up the Littorale a little way."

He did not answer but sat down again, after raising the mainsail to its full spread, and began to tack. The sail flapped lazily as they turned, seeking the wind, scarcely sufficient to belly it. For half-an-hour they beat northwards. On the port side, Paolo's watchful eye, which had been regarding the blackening north horizon with growing anxiety, caught the gaunt line of a bare masthead cutting the skyline of the Littorale. Whose boat was that ? With the pretence of examining the jib he went forward. On his feet he could clearly see the coast line. Two figures stood beside the beached vessel. His surmise was correct. It was Marco, with Neville and the new boat.

Without a word or sign, he made his way back to the stern. The north horizon had grown dark in the last few minutes and the wind had risen threateningly. He brought the boat about, to run south before the squall should be upon them. As the sail swung over, Lucia changed to the opposite side, and for a moment the line of the Littorale was in her vision.

" Look !—who's that ? " she asked.

Paolo's face attempted to mask the annoyance of this discovery, but he was a clumsy actor. She looked again, and this time knew why his face had clouded at her question. If she had had any doubt of the identity of those distant figures, she was made wholly certain by Paolo's marked annoyance.

" That's Marco and Signor Neville—oughtn't we to warn them ? " she asked, looking at him directly.

" Surely they'll see for themselves ? "

" Marco's only a boy, and the signore doesn't know— "

" You're very concerned about the signore," he growled, still keeping his southern course. She ignored his sneer, and her eyes met his defiantly.

" We must go and tell them ! " she said.

He laughed at her, as he might have laughed at a wayward child, and kept his course.

" Do you hear ! " she cried, shrilly.

" I'm master of this boat," he said insolently, knowing she was his prisoner.

Lucia moved forward beyond the mast. He watched her dully, wondering what she was going to do. At the bow she turned to face him, her eyes blazing with anger.

" Then I'll not stay in it ! " she shouted.

A quick action of her hands discarded the shawl on her head, and with a live step she sprang on to the bow. Finghetti leapt to his feet and scrambled forwards, but in the same moment she stood briefly poised against the sky, beautiful in the defiant lines of her figure, and then leapt.

Paolo Finghetti reached the bow, to see her come up from her dive and strike out for the shore, with the confidence of one accustomed to the sea.

" Cristo ! " he blasphemed, racing back to the tiller, to put the boat around. The perspiration beaded his brow, he stared dazedly at the dark head rising and falling in the sea. And then, an oath escaping his lips, he kept the boat on its course. Let her swim to him! He would not be made a fool of, and ⁓me following after like a cowed dog! Paolo Finghetti was not to be used in that fashion!

He watched her, swimming easily between him and the coast, yet it was with no hope that she might call to him. He knew her spirit would never allow that, she would sink first. There was no danger, however, she was a fearless swimmer, though her short skirt must be hampering her. Per Dio! he was sure now! So the gossips had been right. It was that cursed Inglese. Well, he would deal with him, swiftly. Only a foreign fool would have crossed his path. None other had dared.

Meditating his revenge, and still running south, he kept a watchful eye on the diminishing swimmer, until he saw her rise to her feet in the surf, and the two men went running towards her. Satisfied that she was safe, he crowded on more sail and ran under the freshening breeze towards the Porto.

II

Had Venus risen from the waves, or, as in Botticelli's vision—floated, zephyr-borne, through the surf towards them, Marco and Peter could not have been more amazed. On the lonely strand, three miles from the Porto, with a desolate sea before them, the apparition veritably sprang from the wave. And when that slim figure, with saturated garments emphasising every line of graceful maidenhood, came forward under their astonished eyes, they could not immediately recognise the mermaiden.

Marco was the first to identify the vision.

" Signorina ! " he exclaimed. " Santa Madonna, is it you ? "

The breathless swimmer raised her hands and then, embarrassed at her appearance, folded them across her bosom.

Peter splashed forward to help her out.

" Lucia—where have you come from—what is the matter ? " he cried, oblivious of his revelation of their intimacy before the observant Marco. They had seen Finghetti's sail turn southward. Was it credible that she had—

She was speaking now, and as she reached the sand sank down on to it, drawing the wet skirt over her bronzed knees.

" The storm," she panted, " Look ! You must not stop ! "

She pointed to the north horizon, now black and closer, with loose white thunderclouds in the higher heavens.

" I thought you hadn't noticed," she continued, " so I came to warn you."

" But why like this, Lucia mia—where have you come from ? " cried Peter.

She looked at him steadily and then pointed out to sea. A dark sail was speeding south.

" Finghetti ? " asked Marco, with fierceness.

" Yes—he would not come to warn you—so I came alone," she said simply. And then, her mission in mind, she sprang up. " Quick ! The squall is coming. You must not stay ! " she cried, hurrying towards the boat, which Marco was already making shipshape.

" But you can't go like this—in your wet clothes," remonstrated Peter. He took off his blazer.

" No," she said, refusing it. " We'll all be wet in a few minutes."

She pointed to the sky, which had lost its brilliance.

A dark haze slowly shut out the sunlight. The sea was blackening from the north, the light withdrawing like a tide. The noise of the surf grew more and more thunderous as they pushed off. They could no longer follow the gleaming Littorale where it stretched northwards, for it had now been engulfed by the coming storm. The gulls, wheeling low, cried plaintively as they passed overhead. The beauty had suddenly gone out of the day. A shining blue sea had lost its light and had changed to a cold, sullen grey, and the sun was obscured by great cloudbanks.

While Peter and Lucia sat in the stern, as Marco manipulated the sail, there was a strange and sudden commotion in the air about them. The silence was harshly broken, and Marco, suddenly lowering the sail, shouted something, but they never heard him. There was a whirring in the heavens above them, a seething around, a sudden leap of the boat that made her shiver from bow to stern, and the next second the squall engulfed them. They rose, somehow, out of the sudden night, water streaming leeward from every spar and rope. Saturated, they crouched in a pool of water swishing about them with every movement.

In that immersion the oars had gone overboard. Marco's hand was bleeding, cut with the line of the jibsail that had wrenched him, sprawling, forward. Under them, a wild sea soared skywards, bearing them to an incredible height where they hung poised as on the pinnacle of the world. The next moment it fell away beneath their hull, and they were hurled down into the trough of the sea.

In the ensuing minutes they ran with the storm, rainlashed and buffeted. After the first onslaught, the violence had somewhat abated, leaving a choppy, foam-whitened sea. They could hear again the boom of the surge along the Littorale, and before them, as they rose on a wave-crest, they saw the storm ahead swallow up the sunlit day in its wild sweep southwards. They had survived the worst for a while, but behind there gathered the full force of the storm.

Swiftly they sped towards the green flash of the shoal buoy. Once through that narrow channel, between the shoal and the breakwater running down from Forte Caroman, they would be safe in the mouth of the Porto, with the calmer lagoon beyond. It was a desperate attempt, but to run before the storm was impossible in their open boat. The lull in the wind had ceased, and under the shrill gusts that struck them no small craft could hope to avoid capsizing. Often they were carried high to the crest of a towering wave, whence they looked down on a dark seething world.

As they turned for the Porto, a flash of lightning lit the sky and was quiveringly mirrored on the leaden-gleaming sea ; afar, momentarily, they saw the dark campanile of the Duomo against the bleached sky, like a stern finger reproaching the tumult of heaven. The long coast line of the Littorale flared into being, a grey foam-washed strip between the glaring water on each side. From the height of their wave they saw a sudden illumination of glimmering lagoon, steel-grey under the storm. But nearer, in amazement, Marco and Peter had seen Finghetti's boat in a deep sea-trough where it rolled perilously.

Its proximity was dangerous, for the sea-channel into the Porto was narrow. On Finghetti's port lay the shoal, and once aground, nothing could save him ; on their own side lay the submerged rocks, whose merciless teeth had for centuries been Chioggia's best defence, and its gravest danger to her own sailors.

Wind-whipped and wave-driven, they must take the channel or perish, and half of that channel would be held by Finghetti. With a masterly and rapid lift of his sail, Marco brought his boat half about, gave her head to the wind for a fraction of a minute, and then was driven by the impetuosity of the storm towards the channel. He turned exultingly to Peter, but suddenly, from a smile of triumph, his face changed to a look of horror, and an oath half-despairing, half-accusing, left his lips.

"Santo Dio!" he cried, "He'll murder us! Dio santo!"

Then it was that Peter saw, what a few seconds before had been seen by Marco. Finghetti, too, had taken the channel, taken it with a full sail on a running sea! He rode now twelve feet above them, and when the wave behind fell away he would come down upon them unless— But destruction waited for them on those rocks; better the desperate chance of shooting the shoal ahead. With a full sea it might be accomplished, if not—

Peter heard the lad's wild curse above the wind and the surge of the water. Another flash of lightning rimmed them in its wild glare, then darkness, and the lash of the rain, and a thunder-riven sky. Onward they raced through the black tornado—to destruction or deliverance. The next moment an overtaking wave hurled them skywards. The two men stared at each other with blanched faces, breathing hard in the face of their fate. With a cry of fear, Lucia's arms were around Peter's neck, her eyes closed as he held her chill rain-lashed face to his. And in the moment of peril it was not fear but strange happiness he knew.

III

Finghetti had seen them in that wave-lifted moment as they made for the channel. His instinct told him to run further south to Porto Fossone, but the sudden vision of their boat moved him to passionate hatred. They were there together, the three of them who flouted him. In blind passion he brought round his boat, recklessly abandoned to his hate. He would run them down, anything to avenge this insult! In his obsession he had no thought of consequences. His own death was not worth a moment's consideration. Revenge! To the fury of the storm he added the fury of his flouted passion. Revenge!

Cursing, half-sobbing in his delirium of hate, he crowded more sail on the mast. He would sink them or drive them on the reef, and run triumphant to his end. As the sea lifted him and he saw the doomed boat, he gave an exultant cry, ere the falling wall of water bore him down upon them.

But man is a plaything of the storm, and may not oppose its will or command his fate. In that black swirl of water, under the blinding lash of the rain, Finghetti saw nothing as he was hurled down; he could only cling blindly, cursing as he lay, eyes shut, wave-drenched, hurrying to his triumphant destruction. The sea broke over him, there was a thunder of falling water. The frail craft shook and lifted her prow as if leaping from the thing that tortured her, but in the act was seized anew, for a gust struck her and snapped the mast, carrying overboard her sail.

In that moment Finghetti knew the storm had tricked him. Straight before him was no dark wall of water, no doomed vessel, but a white combing of shattered waves where they struck the reef, now burying it, now pouring down precipitously to meet the renewed attack of their successors. A curse, half-choked in the terror of that sight, then the broken, water-logged boat raced with him on to the teeth of the storm. A malignant lightning flash lit him to his doom.

IV

In that last leap skywards of their boat, Marco had found a swift hope. The great flood of water carried them, perilously poised, in its swift race through darkness, towards the shoal. It gathered volume as it ran, massing and speeding under the force of the wind. The two men saw the shoal fade down beneath, saw a sudden flowering of the sea that carried them, as it foamed on its shallowing course, then darkened as it deepened in the channel beyond. Behind them broke a white seething of the water receding over the shoal.

They had ridden it and were safe across the storm barrier ! The agitated lagoon lay in its leaden waste before them, and whitened where it splashed the granite wall of the molo.

They did not speak. Their consciousness of shared knowledge, even more than the spell of their passed danger, held them silent. They had all seen Finghetti, divined his purpose. They looked back and saw nothing emerge. The majesty of Death awed their hearts.

But when Marco had brought the boat to the molo and the long suspense was ended, he leapt excitedly to his feet, eyes flaming with their knowledge.

" He tried to kill us ! Santo Dio ! you saw, signorino ? He ran us down ! Signorina, he wanted to murder us ! And he is dead himself, dead himself ! "

He laughed hysterically, clasping his hands, and they

saw not sorrow but joy on his transformed face. It was as if he had triumphed in the deadly combat, and his face, wet and wind-whipped, was radiant with hate. Again he shouted, standing exultantly by the mast, a wild figure with his sodden garments and sea-drenched hair.

" He is dead, and he would have killed us ! " he exclaimed, searching their faces, as if bewildered by their cold silence.

" Marco ! " cried Peter sternly, " you must not say such things ! Be quiet ! " he commanded, for the lad was laughing hysterically again, clicking his fingers as if in ecstasy. Lucia gave him a frightened glance, and clung to Peter in a fit of sobbing.

" Don't let him say it ! He must not say it ! I would not have him dead ! " she cried, her wild eyes searching Peter's face, her hands gripping his shoulders. " He cannot be dead—he will come yet ! Say he will come yet ? " she pleaded.

And again Marco broke into that wild exultant laughter. " È morto ! Madonna ! È morto ! " he cried.

Peter turned on him angrily.

" Are you mad ? Be silent !—do you hear !—not another word ! Get out of the boat ! "

The lad looked at his padrone, sobered by the sudden anger of the man who had never before spoken in this fashion. His face fell, shamed.

" Sì, signorino—scusi, scusi."

He made the boat fast to the iron ring, and as he clambered up on to the molo, running figures loomed out of the storm, excitedly calling, marvelling at these who had been miraculously delivered from the raging sea.

CHAPTER XIV

THE wine shops and the cafés were crowded that night. A hundred times they repeated the story, changing and challenging its details. Three separate accounts provided the original versions, multiplied and embellished as they progressed along the Corso, through the byways, into the dark wineshops where black-hatted men sat drinking in the yellow lamp-light.

The first version, championed as the most authentic, came via the kitchen of the Signor Neville's hotel. Maria, the chambermaid, had carried downstairs the signore's wet clothes, and, waiting for them outside his bedroom, had heard him, as he stripped, telling the story of their escape to the padrone of the hotel, who constantly interrupted in order to express to the Santa Madonna his amazement.

That extra-mural version, conveyed by the round-eyed maid to Elizabetta, the cook, had, in turn, duly improved, been passed to her dissolute husband, who called for the scraps that were the perquisites of his industrious wife. He, in turn, found glory in the wineshop that knew him better than his home. Like the eddies of a disturbed pool, his story went out in all directions, carried by eager inheritors to other wineshops, where it encountered the ripple of incoming versions, one of which came from no less a source than Marco.

" He swears he is dead ! " exclaimed Antonio, black-eyed and black moustached, with dramatic emphasis. " But he would say no more. There is something he knows. Per Dio, he knows, but he will not say ! "

The third version provided the great sensation. It brought the shy Luigi a night of renown. The first revelation of his detective gift was made at the *Trattoria del Sole*. It was regarded as so truly astounding that he was taken off and exhibited by proud sponsors at the Café Vittorio Emanuele, whose clientele was gathered from circles of some importance. Even the Sindaco sometimes took his siroppo at the café.

" Signori ! " exclaimed his sponsors, bringing up the shy Luigi, flushed with the fame that had come so swiftly. " Listen, signori, listen to Luigi here ! "

The lad was bidden to seat himself, by no less a person than the Postmaster.

" And what is the story, my lad ? Is Finghetti drowned, do you know that ? " asked the Postmaster, from the midst of the crowded circle about his table. But before Luigi could find his tongue, an excited voice cried out from the dark fringe of the assembly—

" Signore—he's dead ! I've just come from the Porto. The boat's been washed up ! "

Babel broke out on this. There was a stirring and chattering as the crowd opened up to allow this sensational messenger to present himself. Luigi and his sponsors, wholly eclipsed, were swallowed up in the veering spectators. It was known that watchers from Forte Caroman, and the lighthouse at Forte San Felice, had been searching the shore since the storm had abated, as suddenly as it had risen. Both the Littorale and the shoreline of Sotto-marina had been searched.

The man told his story to the gaping crowd. Paolo

Finghetti's boat had been washed ashore, bottom up, its bow stoved in, the mast and sail gone.

" But Finghetti—did they find him ? "

" No, signore. It will be some days yet."

Chattering broke forth again. A hot argument grew about the time in which the sea gives up its dead. The older men recounted their experiences in this matter. A few of the younger provoked derision by suggesting Finghetti might not be dead. Who had ever escaped the reef in such a storm ? Finghetti was a marvellous man, but what was a man's strength compared with a boat's ? And the bow was staved in. Ecco !

As this argument subsided, Luigi's displaced sponsors made another bid for publicity. They wedged their way to the table where the Postmaster presided.

" Signore," they called, " Luigi's here ! "

The Postmaster assumed his official air at once. He must hold this large audience.

" Eh ! Luigi ?—where is the lad ? " he cried, peering over the rim of his glasses, and as Luigi was pushed forward—" Ah, Luigi !—what do you know ? "

" Nothing, signore, nothing— "

" Nothing ! " exclaimed the Postmaster, critically. " Nothing ! Come, this is no time for nothing ! Do you know anything at all ? "

" Sì, signore," stammered Luigi.

" Then tell us at once. Why do you hesitate so ? "

" Only this, signore—I saw the Signorina Delfino go with Finghetti in his boat."

" And what of that, my lad ? Why shouldn't the signorina go in his boat. Doesn't everyone know she's ' promised ' to Finghetti. Eh ? "

The Postmaster looked for approval of his magisterial

manner. Every eye was on the nervous Luigi, playing with his leather belt.

" Sì, signore—but they didn't come back together."

" Of course they didn't—the signorina's saved, thanks to Our Lady. That requires no great intelligence ! " rapped the Postmaster, swelling before these stupid fisherfolk.

" No, signore, but— " began one of the sponsors.

" How did the signorina— " began another.

The Postmaster saw his blunder, and hastened to retrieve himself, before the crowd had realised the significance of Luigi's tale. He raised his hand authoritatively.

" One at a time, please. I must hear all the evidence," he directed. " Now, Luigi. If the signorina went out in Finghetti's boat, and returned safely in the Signor Neville's, she must have changed, eh ? Isn't it so ? "

The assembly gave a long sigh of excitement, impressed by this clever cross-examination.

" That's so, signore. That's what I— "

" Sì—sì—but *where* did the signorina change boats ? Do you know that ? " pressed the Postmaster. There was a deep silence at this vital question.

" No, signore. Perhaps— "

" There can be no ' perhaps ' in so serious a situation. Did the boats go out together ? "

" No, signore—I only saw Finghetti's go."

" I saw Marco go an hour before," cried a voice in the crowd. The excitement was now high.

" Then," said the Postmaster solemnly, " the boats encountered each other somewhere, and the signorina changed boats ! That raises a serious question."

An outburst of muttered comment followed this observation. The Postmaster let it run awhile, then—

"It is a serious matter. One, I think, for the polizia."

The polizia! Ah! There was a mystery. Yes! It was true Finghetti was drowned, his boat wrecked. But it was not all. As the signore had remarked, there was a mystery. In some way the signorina had changed boats. She had left Finghetti's boat for—

And then someone mentioned what all knew. The signorina did not love Finghetti. It was Signor Neville, the Inglese, she loved. They had been meeting in the Campanile. And now poor Finghetti was dead, and she was saved—in the foreign signore's boat. Ha! there was a mystery! They had no liking for Finghetti. But the dead command sympathy. He was now the 'povero signorino.' He was brave, he had brought them a great haul; their imagination endowed him with many virtues. Yes, there was a mystery. The Postmaster spoke truth. As he stood up now in their midst he commanded a reverent silence.

"Signori," he said, gravely, endowing them with the grace of gentility, thereby increasing the weight of his authorisation, "It is a matter for the polizia. Let us go. Luigi shall make his statement to them."

Again there was an outburst of chattering and gesticulating. Everyone had something to say about the 'povero signorino.' They would never see such a man again. Who could handle a boat like him? And his strength! That day at Ancona, for instance; or when he had thrown a man head-first across the gunwale on to the fondamenta! Per Dio! Men like Paolo Finghetti were not born every day. And now he was dead. Who would handle the fleet, who would outwit those scoundrels from Ancona?

Thus lamenting, they streamed after the Postmaster

and the shaking Luigi, and the now retiring sponsors, on their way to the polizia.

They were seen by the Signor Pretore, who stiffly returned the profound bow of the Postmaster, as he entered with Luigi, leaving the crowd to stand outside, waiting and whispering as it speculated on the drama being enacted behind those windows. Through them, they could see the gleaming bald head of the Signor Pretore under the hanging lamp. That gentleman showed no surprise. He almost made the Postmaster feel his errand was useless. Yet, actually, he had only just crossed from the café where he spent the most useful part of his life, listening to gossip which told him more than all his underlings.

When he saw the crowd at the far end of the Corso, following at a reverent distance behind the Postmaster and the boy Luigi, immediately he knew it was an official moment, one of those opportunities of glory all too rare in his eventless life.

" We thank you, signore," he said, addressing the now subdued Postmaster as though he were a public meeting. " We were not unaware of these circumstances, we assure you. But no detail is unimportant in so serious a case. My clerk will take Luigi Spinelli's deposition, which he must then sign."

Beads of perspiration stood on Luigi's brow. Terror of the unknown processes of the law seized him.

" I can't write, signore ! " he cried, seeing a means of escape.

" You can make your mark, which will be witnessed," responded the Pretore curtly. " Repeat your statement to the clerk, and only tell him what you can swear to."

The wretched lad was motioned to a desk, where a hunchback on a high stool slowly wrote in a fly-blown ledger.

It was at this unforgettable moment in Luigi Spinelli's life that Lucia faced her father, in the dark sitting-room whose west window looked out over their cypress-bordered garden and the masts in the canal beyond. Four candles burned in the candelabra on the centre table, throwing a light that only served to give life to the heavy shadows of that panelled room. It served also to show the rich beauty of Lucia as she faced her father, her face set and white against the dark wall, her eyes blazing, her young body quivering in this moment, long dreaded, long postponed, and now resolutely faced.

Delfino had not been at home when Peter and Marco had brought back the distraught, sea-drenched Lucia. He had gone that morning to look at his market garden down at Brondolo, and it was not until he arrived at a shop in the Corso, where he deposited a crate of fowls, after a drive through the blinding thunderstorm from which he had had to shelter, that he heard of his daughter's danger. It was only half of the story he heard then, which, after his first anxiety was allayed, aroused him to anger at her indiscretion. For he was only told how the Signor Neville had battled with the storm, and miraculously shot the shoal and gained the Porto. The shopkeeper had heard only the first instalment of a story that was destined to thrill Chioggia for a week.

Delfino showed no sign of anger to his informant, but drove rapidly on, his wrath increasing as he drew nearer home. The distressed Bianca ran to meet him, as the horse and cart clattered into the cortile, and the introduction of Marco in the story somewhat mitigated his wrath. Still, this folly must stop. He was not going to allow her name to be gossiped adown the Corso. He had planned her future with Paolo. This attractive young foreigner must be warned off and the encouragement he received promptly stopped.

He waited until the dinner hour approached, by which time his anger had somewhat abated, leaving his resolution the stronger by cool reason.

" Is Lucia coming down to dinner ? " he asked, having restrained himself from going up to his daughter's room, where she lay in bed, amenable to Bianca's solicitude.

" Sì, signore," said Bianca, " the poor child is getting up now. Santa Madonna ! What a will she has ! There she lies in bed, like a rose on a white wall. Anyone might think she's enjoyed it, though her teeth did chatter as I undressed the half-drowned child ! "

When Lucia entered the room her father showed no sign of his anger. He looked at her anxiously after he had kissed her, all severity fading from his eyes, now affectionately resting on her fresh beauty, which, as Bianca had said, seemed rose-like and sweeter for the storm under which it had bowed. But as he drew her aside into the window-seat, he unburdened his mind, proceeding deliberately to his purpose.

" Lucia mia, you can't know how foolish you've been these days. I blame myself somewhat. I can't be both mother and father to you, so you've had a liberty which is not good for a young girl. Now all that I say to you is for your good. There'll be gossip after to-day, perhaps malicious gossip. There must be no more fuel for it. I shall speak to Signor Neville, and you must not see him again."

His arm was around her as he said this, and he felt her body stiffen. He ignored the sign.

" I shall announce your betrothal at once."

" To whom ? " she asked, looking directly into his eyes.

" To Paolo, Lucia."

She sprang to her feet, confronting him.

" You cannot ! " she cried, " He is dead—I hope he is dead ! "

There was an exultant note in her voice as it struck the ears of her astonished father. He raised his hand, commandingly.

" Lucia ! What do you say ?—you are crazed, child. Paolo dead !—what do you mean ? "

" His boat was smashed on the reef after he had tried to murder us ! " cried Lucia, with set face in which her eyes glowed with inward fire.

Delfino rose to his feet, but gripped her arms tightly, as he scrutinised her.

" Paolo !—what was he doing there ? You were in Neville's boat ! Why was Paolo there ? Where is Paolo ? Tell me—or is this hysteria ? "

Perhaps it was, for she laughed then, satirically, he thought. Could this girl, exulting in her horrible story, be Lucia ? She was still dazed with her experience. He should have waited before speaking of this matter.

" Lucia mia—you are not well yet. Go and lie down, my child. We'll talk of this later— " he said, holding her more gently. But she fended him off, standing back, a bold white figure against the age-blackened oakwork.

" No—we will talk of it now ! " she cried, huskily. " You shall know, since no one has told you, what kind of a man your Paolo is, what sort of creature you would sacrifice your daughter to, for the sake of your pride and ambition."

" Lucia ! "

" Yes, I am saying all I think ! It *is* pride, it *is* ambition. You've known his dirty life, his discarded women, his disowned bastards, his— "

" Lucia, I forbid you ! I will not— "

" You shall ! We need not keep silence about this, you and I. The Corso knows it, you know it, I know it. Need we pretend, we two ? You want him to run your fleet, to join with his boats and make yourself master of the Adriatic—at the cost of my life ! That's your ambition ! Well, it's ended ! Paolo Finghetti took me out this morning. The storm gathered, and we saw a boat beached that would have been in danger. I wanted to warn them, but your Paolo wouldn't because he knew whose boat it was, and wanted them drowned ! So I left him— "

" Left him ? " asked Delfino, hoarsely, his face pallid before the fury of this transformed woman.

" I leapt overboard and swam to them—and Paolo Finghetti never changed course ! We only saw him once again, when we made for the channel. He knows that channel in a fierce sea, as you know it. So he deliberately ran for us, knowing we'd strike the shoal, even if he struck the reef himself. That's his hate of us, his love of me. But we rode the shoal and that black-hearted scoundrel struck the reef. You must find a new fleetmaster, my father. The sea has delivered me ! "

Her voice rang on these last wild words, so that he marvelled at the pale, slim fury before him, ruthless from the sea as Medea of old. Looking at her, changed from a gentle girl into a woman inspired with love and hate, he suddenly realised the gulf her passion had made between them. Even so, his brain could not believe this was an awakening ; it was only a temporary obsession, an hysterical outburst, partly imagined, an exaggeration of her fears. But whatever its cause, he was not one to tolerate revolt against his will.

" Lucia," he said stonily, " when you're aware of what you've said you'll regret this frenzy. Not another word,

I pray you ! Go to your room, you are in no fit condition to leave it."

Her only retort was to laugh, such laughter as he had never heard before, defiant, cynical. It was while she laughed thus, erect against the wall, her piercing eyes meeting his, that Bianca tapped on the door, opened it, and announced the Signor Pretore. For a moment he halted on the dark threshold, conscious of intrusion, then, hat in hand, he advanced.

" Signor Delfino, I pray you forgive this haste ! Ah, good evening, signorina," he cried, bowing to Lucia. " May I offer my congratulations on your miraculous escape ? "

He fidgeted, conscious of a strange atmosphere.

" Will you not be seated " asked Delfino, in a voice that revealed nothing of his emotion.

The Pretore sat down and straightway explained his mission. He was distressed at troubling them at such a moment, when perhaps the signorina still suffered from the shock. But duty, yes, at all times duty ; they would appreciate what had compelled him. It was necessary to clear up a point of the utmost importance. Would the signorina—ah, he regretted the necessity—be gracious enough to answer a question or two ? The poor Signor Finghetti's boat had been washed ashore—povero diavolo, he was loved of all. So strong, so brave, and ah ! what a fisherman !

He paused in his recital, partly to admire the tact with which he was performing his difficult mission, partly in surprise at the unechoing wall against which his solemn news fell. No ejaculation, no lament came from the pale signorina's lips at this news of her lover's sad end. Then, perhaps, rumour did not lie ? Per Dio ! he must pursue this.

" The boy, Luigi Spinelli, tells me, signorina, that you left the harbour in Signor Finghetti's boat ? "

" Yes."

" I understand that, after your distressing experience, you returned safely to harbour, Our Lady be praised ! "

" I am here," said Lucia without expression.

" Ah, it is so, we are indeed gratified to see you safe again. We all rejoice in your deliverance, And we owe much to Signor Nevilli and Marco Migone, I believe ? "

Poor little man, how he fumbled and skirmished round his point. Lucia anticipated his subsequent question, which he had prefaced so awkwardly.

" You wish to know, signore, how it was I went out with Paolo Finghetti, yet returned with Signor Neville ? "

" That is a point, my dear signorina, a point we must—"

" My father can tell you. Ask him ! "

Delfino and his daughter exchanged a swift look.

" Yes, I can explain that," he said, addressing the Pretore.

Briefly he told him how Neville and Marco had been seen by his daughter and warned of the storm approaching. He made no mention of the incident aboard Finghetti's boat.

" Grazie, signore, grazie, but excuse me if I do not clearly understand. The signorina returned with Signor Neville ? "

Lucia cast a pitying smile at her father's failure to cheat the scandal scented by the little Pretore. How like a weasel the fellow was, with his shifty eyes and pointed ears !

" What do you wish to know, signore ? " said Lucia calmly. " Is it why I left Finghetti's boat for the other ? I left it because Paolo Finghetti would not go to warn them. So I swam to them. That's the reason."

" Signor Pretore," began Delfino, in a voice of distress,

"I pray you make no mention of this! My daughter is somewhat overwrought. We should hate a scandal—especially now the poor fellow is dead."

"Signor Delfino, I am a man of the world, which means I can perform my painful duty with discretion. But it is a point that must arise in the evidence at the—"

He was checked by a tap on the door, after which Bianca entered, giving her message straightway.

"Signor Nevilli is below. He wants to know how Lucia is," she said, in her abrupt manner.

The Pretore raised his hands in delight.

"This is most fortunate, Signor Delfino, most fortunate! May I see him?"

For the moment Delfino hesitated.

"I don't see that he can tell you any more than my daughter has told us," he argued.

"That is so, quite so," assented the Pretore, half bowing to Lucia, to dispel any suggestion of suspicion of her story, "but all evidence is valuable, especially corroborative evidence—the process of the law, my dear signore!" he added blandly.

"Very well," agreed Delfino. He motioned to Bianca who went out.

When Peter entered he did not see the Pretore in the dark room. He greeted Delfino, who stood by the door, then Lucia, who moved towards him. Peter smiled at Delfino as he saw her.

"I'm easy now, signore—I had wondered if the shock had been too much for the signorina. She was wonderful!" he said, his eyes falling upon her in undisguised admiration.

Delfino ignored the remark.

"This is the Signor Pretore, Signor Neville. He will ask you a few questions."

The little man hopped out of the shadow, his eyes glistening, his face sallow in the candle light, so that he looked more like a blackbird than a man, with his dark clothes, his long yellow nose and beady eyes.

" I regret the necessity," began the Pretore, " but the law, signore, compels me to fulfil my duty, my often unpleasant duty. I will only enquire of one thing. Did you see Paolo Finghetti at any time to-day ? "

" Yes."

" Ah—when ? " The Pretore seemed to dart the question, bird-like.

"When he tried to— " Peter hesitated, his eyes seeking Lucia's, but he read no instruction there ; and then he caught a glimpse of Delfino's long face, silvered head, and narrowed eyes, learning at once that he knew all. A second's contact with that eagle eye instructed him.

" —enter the channel," finished Peter. His quick brain was telling him at that moment that he must find Marco and stop his mouth before the Pretore had him in his clutch.

" Povero signorino ! " lamented the Pretore, " povero signorino ! You saw him go to his doom, signore ? " he asked, tearfully.

" Doom ? " echoed Peter, looking hard at the little man.

The Pretore raised his hands, dropped them expressively and sighed heavily.

" You have not heard, signore ? His boat has been washed ashore. We must wait for the body," he said, mournfully.

And then Peter laughed, to the horror of the Pretore and the astonishment of Delfino and his daughter.

" You needn't wait long for the body, Signor Pretore, it has already returned to Chioggia ! " he said.

The Pretore gazed at him, wide-eyed.

" I do not understand you," he stammered.

" Paolo Finghetti came from Brondolo a few minutes
since—all the Corso is seething with excitement and is
running to meet him."

Peter turned to the east window, and pointed down to
the Corso below, with people hurrying by.

" Look ! " he cried, " you can see how the news has
spread."

They all turned to the window in silent amazement.
But Lucia Delfino did not look, and Peter saw her blanched
face, the despair in her eyes.

" You are not well yet—this has been a terrible experience," he said sympathetically, going to her side.
She put out a hand to him almost blindly, which he would
have taken but that she withdrew it again ; the two men
at the window had turned.

" We shall have Paolo here in a minute," said Delfino.
" He will have a marvellous story. I wonder how he
escaped that sea ! "

The Pretore smirked at Lucia.

" Ah," he exclaimed, omnisciently, " there is a special
providence looks after lovers. Eh ! And now I will go,
since all ends happily and there is nothing for me to do."

With bows and exclamations and wise glances, he
fluttered away. Peter prepared to follow, but Delfino
detained him.

" Lucia," he said, " tell Bianca to serve dinner—I
will be with you when I have had a few minutes' talk
with Signor Neville."

She hesitated, but his stern eyes challenged hers.
After the news of Paolo's return she felt crushed in the
spirit, and her revolt was exhausted. She bade Peter
' Buona notte,' and left the room. Delfino waited until
the door had closed after her. His strained manner fore-

warned Peter of his object. He resolved to say no word that would inculpate Lucia, but he was not going to be frightened off the ground by an angry father.

After a long silence, during which Delfino paced the room, he suddenly halted and stood with face and hair illumined above the candles.

"Signor Neville," he said, in a calm voice, "I am going to speak to you very frankly. What I shall say will be said in my capacity of father, but I hope you may see it also as from one who would be your friend. I am an old man, with a very young daughter. It is the custom in our country for the parents to arrange matches for their children, such as are suitable and likely to prove happy in experience. You may know that for my daughter Lucia I have a thought of betrothing her to Paolo Finghetti, the master of my fleet?"

He peered over the candles, leaning with his finger-tips on the table. Two pin-points of light glinted in his dark eyes; Peter saw in that face the long impress of an indomitable nature.

"I have heard something of this, Signor Delfino," said Peter, himself steady in voice. Delfino made a quick gesture with his hand.

"Then, my friend, you will understand my concern. My daughter Lucia has a romantic mind, which is not unnatural in an inexperienced girl of twenty. She has set her will against this match. She is strengthened in this opposition by yourself!"

"By me?" asked Peter, wondering how much Delfino knew.

"I will be frank. When a young man, a handsome young man, pleasantly mannered, well-bred—for these are your attributes, signore, makes himself agreeable to a young lady, and, with that pleasantry, has the attraction which foreign birth curiously exerts, it is difficult for her not to feel honoured. From that feeling passion may grow. I hear of an incident to-day which reveals it. Possibly that revelation stirred a revengeful instinct in Finghetti. It was natural."

" You call murder natural ? " asked Peter, grimly.

Delfino's eyes looked across at him steadily.

" That's an ugly word, Signor Neville."

" I use it deliberately—and am one of three."

" Very well. I will not argue. Let me make my point. You are a young man, of good family, I presume. You are English and will have responsibilities in England, as I have here. Are you sure you could meet those responsibilities by a foreign marriage ? It presents grave difficulties."

" Marriage ? " asked Peter. The word sounded strange to his ears. " You must think our—our relationship has been very intimate."

" No. Perhaps you've never thought of it. That is what I wish you to realise—that my daughter may be led to think in this manner. To-night, for the first time in her life, she has openly challenged me. Had you not come into her life she would have accepted the plans I made. This revolt dates from your advent. She spurns one marriage because she is beginning to desire another— which I absolutely forbid, signore ! "

His fist descended on the table and there was a ring of passion in his voice, which had been even and quietly incisive.

For the first time Peter felt uneasy. Delfino had very cleverly forced him into an unpleasant position. To declare that he had no serious intention was to stamp himself as a philanderer. Also, it was shirking his part to Lucia. She was making a fight against this monstrous design of Delfino's.

His hesitation, his difficulty was read by the elder man, watching him over the wavering candle flames, as an agreement in his views.

" I think, Signor Neville, you cannot regard it as unreasonable when I ask you not to see my daughter again."

Assured that he had made his point clear, he was wholly unprepared for the young man's retort.

" But I do, Signor Delfino, and I can give no such promise ! " said Peter, his pride, rather than reason, speaking the words. " Surely it is for your daughter to end our acquaintance, if she wishes ? "

Delfino ignored the question.

" My daughter will obey *my* wishes. I am sorry you oppose me. There is nothing more to be said. I will wish you good-night, signore."

A minute later, Peter found himself in the Corso. Incredible the dignity of the old fellow ! He had been dismissed like a schoolboy, and moreover, had felt like a schoolboy during every one of those unpleasant minutes. What an old autocrat ! The dignity of age was unfair, tyrannous. It had closed his mouth against all kinds of things he had to say, all manner of crushing retorts. The old villain was going to sell his daughter to that scoundrel !

A sudden memory of Lucia's face when she learned Paolo was alive stirred him to sudden fury. He would go back and denounce the old tyrant, and expose his callous mercenary mind.

But he did not go back, instead he looked moodily up and down the Corso. The people were seated at the cafés. What had become of Paolo and his escort ? He had expected him at Delfino's. Now, there was no sign of him. Curious, he would have enquired of some of the gossips at their coffee-tables, but he could not be heard asking about Finghetti. So he walked on, under the darkening sky, towards the molo.

The withdrawal of the storm had left a sky singularly calm and clear. There was in the air a freshness and quietude, so that the world around seemed to have that quickened consciousness known to the human body after severe trial. The night, ascending from the cold green and purple of the north horizon, to a sapphire belt wherein the evening star sparkled coldly, was domed with a diaphanous blue veil through which the far-off constellations glimmered. To this ethereal beauty, the lagoon held up its calm face, no furrows of the angry day remaining, receiving from the sunset sky its legacy. It lay quiescent, league on league of deepening colour, stretching northwards, where the night enfolded it, though of life it gave a shadowy sign, where a solitary sail, now crimson, now black, veered in the level light from the west.

Peter crossed the small Piazzetta, ascended the steps and paused on the arch of the Vigo bridge, resting his arms on its balustrade, while he gazed northwards down the lagoon. To his right lay the Porto, the ripples of the incoming waves detecting somewhere the rising moon. It was calm enough, now, beyond that bar where Death had beckoned through the storm; neither sea nor sky gave a sign of the dark noonday fury. Only the faint fret of a subsiding sea along the Littorale broke the evening hush.

The night deepened, but although he watched its changing beauty, he gave it no thought. Delfino's face was in his mind, Delfino's words in his ears. The sense of them troubled him, stirring self-questionings that would not be dismissed. The old man had brought him face to face with the reality of the situation. Where was he drifting in this pleasant affair with Lucia? He had come to Chioggia, for what? The honest question demanded an answer, demanded it with Delfino's voice.

At twenty-five he had not escaped the driving of the impetuous appetite of youth. But he was no prisoner of the senses. Confronted with the finding of a reason for his presence in Chioggia, he knew Lucia supplied it. Beyond that he had never given it thought; in the origin it had been no enticement of the usual vulgar affair. And yet, if it were not that, what was it? When Delfino had said ' marriage ' he had felt a shock. Somehow that had never occurred to him. Yet, morally regarded, what else could his attentions portend? He had sought her deliberately, once chance had shown him the prize.

Yes, old Delfino had shaken him. Loving Lucia was one thing. Sacrificing his nationality, or transporting Lucia from hers, was another. Would Lucia in England, under grey skies, in sombre dress, be Lucia? Did she not rather stand for all that was radiant, happy, and free in this place of the lagoons, for the passionate-coloured Venetian spirit, that elsewhere could not live?

Also Delfino had shaken his self-satisfaction. A man of ' responsibilities in England ! ' he had said. Well, actually, he had none. Roderick had those, and thinking of it he felt slightly ashamed. For three years he had wandered pleasantly, playing the dilettante. His art had been an excuse, not a justification. He could not deceive himself in that. ' Responsibilities in England '—confound the old fellow ! He hadn't shot his arrow in the air. Yes, had he any right to be a perturbing factor in this girl's life unless— Again and again he came back to Delfino's view, and the bitterness of it was that the old man's view served his monstrous purpose. God forbid that sweet child to be sacrificed to a ferocious bear like Paolo Finghetti !

Thus pondering, the Italian night deepened about him until the lagoon lay silvered under the unfathomable sable heaven. Finally, he arrived at a decision to leave Chioggia. His presence, as Delfino said, was provocative. Then the next moment he resolved to go to Lucia, avow his love and put her to the supreme test ; but he feared for himself and her. Her father, her homeland, these were sacred ties, nor could he foresee an untroubled aftermath. Had he been twenty-one the future had occasioned no thought. Twenty-five, with less heat in the blood, and more sense in the head, told him the heart was a rash thing of itself.

It was completely dark when, at last, he left the Vigo bridge. The moon had been hidden by a bank of cloud. He did not go to his hotel, for his mind, after its mental strife, was too active for sleep. Descending the steps, he walked slowly along the Vena canal, filled with the dim outlines of the boats. From some of them gleamed a light, a yellow square in the black landscape, but most were in complete darkness. A mandolin sounded distantly from an upper window in one of the narrow streets, cutting through from the canal to the Corso.

Several times he stumbled against the hawsers made fast from the boats. The darkness was heavier than he had anticipated, but for safety's sake he kept well away from the edge of the canal, in the shadow of the houses.

Once, he was startled by a swift scurrying at his feet. It was a cat, disturbed at her meal of a phosphorescent fish's head. And again, he thought he heard the sound of feet behind him, not the clear steps of the shod foot, but the soft pat-pat of the naked sole on the flags. Swiftly turning he saw nothing, and walked on, impatient with his nerviness.

There was something eerie about this canal, so full of

life and yet so motionless. The intermittent brightening of the moon, as it climbed through the cloudbank, gave momentary vistas of black masts and rigging, massed like a wintry forest, along the Vena. He decided to turn at the next calle, and cut through to the lighted Corso, where the gossips would be sitting at their tables. He would have an ice and keep his ears open for any news of Finghetti's adventure.

Thinking this, he suddenly halted, involuntarily, flinging himself back on his heel, seized by an instinct forceful and immediate. He heard something sing past his head, and then sound softly but distinctly against the wall on his right. It had not the known whirr of a night beetle, and it had seemed larger.

He searched the dim wall. At that moment a racing cloud cleared the moon, and what he saw caused his heart to thud. There, in the door-post of a house, horizontally held by the force of the impact, was a long knife, its tip buried to the depth of half-an-inch! Seizing it, Peter pulled it out. It was a wooden-handled fish-knife, with a sharp nine-inch blade, such as he had seen the women use, as they worked, opening the fish, along the canal.

He looked round hastily in every direction but there was no sign of any living thing; only the croaking of frogs broke the silence.

With quickened heart he walked on, grasping the knife, and turned up the next calle. Only one hand could have thrown that knife, for only one in Chioggia could have desired to throw it.

He had almost traversed the calle, and was about to step out of the deep shadow of the narrow way into the Corso, when he heard a woman's voice far-off down the street, call out shrilly.

"Buona sera, Signor Finghetti!" said the voice.

" Santa Madonna ! it's wonderful to be seeing you in the flesh ! "

Halting in the shadow, Peter looked back. He had recognised the voice of Madre Pappini, whom he had painted. She stood there, in a flood of light from her doorway, dragging in one of her fruit baskets. Finghetti had been caught in that sudden shaft of light and been recognised jubilantly by the old crone. Restraining a curse, Finghetti shook off his ecstatic discoverer, and hastily disappeared in the shadows.

Peter strode on, grateful for the security of the Corso, Finghetti's message still in his hand. The feud was declared. He would not leave Chioggia now, and let the scoundrel think he had been frightened away.

CHAPTER XV

I

MARCO was an early caller at the hotel the next morning, so early that he had to wait on the molo before he could see his padrone, who had not yet come down to breakfast. He spent the time overhauling the *Celavasansdire*, whose mystic name filled him with the pride of the cognoscente. The boat was not damaged by its fierce sea-baptism. It had remained, overnight, made fast to the iron ring to which it had been tethered when they ran in from the storm. Marco raised the sail, for it to dry in the warm air, baled out the water, and washed off the sand which the sweeping seas had deposited. He was still working when his padrone hailed him from the quay above. The lad threw back a glad greeting and clambered up the iron ladder.

" Signorino, I've been waiting for you," he said, looking around, although they were alone on the outer wall of the harbour. He drew closer to his master, as if afraid the wind might betray him.

" Finghetti—you've seen him ? " anticipated Peter.

" Not that, signorino. I saw the signorina this morning. She sends a message."

Surprised, Peter stared at the lad.

" From Lucia—what did she say ? " he asked.

Again Marco looked around him.

" She will be in the Duomo at five o'clock to-day. The signorina begs you to go. She will be in the chapel of Santi Felice and Fortunato."

" Was she distressed, Marco ? "

" Sì, signorino, I think she's been crying," he said, simply, adding—" Will you go, signorino ? "

" Certainly."

" But not afterwards ? " cried Marco, earnestly.

" What do you mean ? "

" Signorino—these meetings will bring trouble to us all. I heard the talk at the tables last night. My father heard Finghetti vow he'd kill you."

" So ? Well, he did his best, quickly."

Marco regarded him with a puzzled frown, grieved that his master took these warnings so lightly.

" He threw a long knife at me on the Vena last night. It buried itself in a door-frame instead of my heart," explained Peter.

Marco's face set.

" You will give it me, signorino ? " he said, thickly, his dark eyes glowing.

" No—why ? "

" I will swear a vendetta ! He has challenged us. Per Dio ! It is good ! Give me the knife. He shall receive it, signorino ! "

Peter looked at the boy's grim face. This was a transformed Marco. Had he ever known this boy, really ? But he laughed to dispel the intensity.

" No, Marco, you must not be so romantic. This is not a book nor the Middle Ages. I will return it myself."

" You, signorino ? " cried the astonished lad.

" Yes, but more graciously than you propose. I shall send it back with my compliments, and suggest he should practise a little to avoid future mistakes."

Marco stood stupefied. So they were the mad English, and his padrone was no different. Eh! What a race!

Peter smiled at the speechless astonishment of the lad, watched the sulphurous burning of his eyes, troubled with the surges of passion, and then questioned him about Finghetti. The latter, said the lad, had been carried south, clinging to his wreckage. Off Porto Fossone, some three miles from Sottomarina, he had been sighted by a ship carrying stone from Istria, as it made for the Porto. They had thrown him a line, brought him alongside and dragged the half-drowned man aboard. His exhaustion was only temporary, and a few hours later he set out from Fossone, and walked to Chioggia, still in his wet clothes. The astounded Chioggiotti had fêted him everywhere he went, which had not been far, for at ten o'clock, having worked his way but half down the crowded Corso, after an orgy in the *Trattoria del Buon Pesce*, he had apparently gone home drunk.

" So that was why his aim was unsteady ! " commented Peter. But Marco would not accept his levity.

" Signorino," he cried, " he'll kill us all in his rage, as he tried to yesterday. He knows everything now. The signorina shouldn't have left him like that."

" It was for our sakes, Marco, don't forget. But I will be on my guard. Now, let's run out and spread this wonderful sail of yours."

" Through the Porto ? " queried Marco.

" Why not ?—I should think we can pass it in any weather now ! " laughed his master, descending the ladder boyishly.

Marco followed, marvelling at this strange padrone of his, to whom love, storms and vendettas seemed all in the day's play.

Running out of the harbour, Peter's thoughts returned

to Lucia's message. What could she want? Only something urgent would have caused her to employ Marco. She knew he was aware of their intimacy, but she gave no sign to him of that knowledge. Perhaps she had heard of Finghetti's drunken threat and wished to warn him—or, and his heart sank a little at the surmise, had she succumbed to her father's will? Would this summons be for his dismissal? Last night he would have accepted it philosophically, but this morning, with the sunshine, all his ardour returned.

Marco had now cleared the harbour, and under the morning breeze the full sail spread itself gorgeously, staining the reflective water with quivering patches of blue and orange. They were heading for the Porto, but they were not destined to reach it. Marco's quick eye had seen a gesticulating figure running down to the point of the molo. The voice was lost in the breeze, but the arms telegraphed to them frenziedly. Peter recognised one of the hotel waiters, in that evening-dress which was also their morning, and, for aught he had seen, their only dress, for in the morning they swept the rooms in it, in the afternoons cleaned the silver, and at night, bearing signs of both these labours, served dinner in it.

Marco looked at Peter for instruction, bringing the boat half round. The waiter was still waving excitedly.

" Whatever does the fellow want? " said Peter, aloud. " We'd better run in, Marco, or he'll swim and ruin that suit."

They turned and made for the harbour again. As soon as they were within hail they heard the fellow cry, " Telegramma, signore! " A disbelief in telegrams in such a world-forgotten place made Peter suspect a letter, misplaced in the morning's post. Gaining the ladder, he climbed up. Yes, the fellow was right. It was a telegram. Inserting a finger, he opened it and read, Marco waiting below, the waiter attending by him.

And it was Marco who saw the change in his face, the absence in his eyes, and heard a strange, strained voice speaking to him.

"We—can't go out now, Marco," his padrone said, quietly.

And then Peter looked at the radiant sky, looked at the scintillating lagoon across its laughing miles, where the sails hovered like butterflies born for the bliss of this June day. This bright world was no longer his. Nine words on a flimsy sheet exiled him from it, nine words that ran—

Come at once. Roderick killed accident. Funeral Saturday. Maud.

He folded the slip of paper, stood a long moment in thought, and then said to the lad below—

"Furl the sail, Marco. I have bad news. I shall want you," and went along the molo towards the hotel.

The next two hours saw a stirring of the stagnant life of the hotel. The signore was calling for time-tables, bills, laundry, and such sundries as are preparatory to rapid departure. But rapid departure in Italy, Peter found, was regarded as a form of insanity. In Chioggia itself, it was almost an impossibility. A long and nerve-stretching examination of time-tables left him with various probabilities, for all the tables were old ones, and the connections in them highly speculative. As if aware of its enchantment, Chioggia did not make escape easy. Boats left for Venice at three and six in the afternoon. Trains left Venice, with continental connections via Paris, at eleven that evening or six-fifty the following morning.

It was Thursday. Poor Roderick's funeral was fixed

for Saturday. Maud's wire had been despatched on Wednesday afternoon. Further search revealed that both connections from Venice arrived in London at four o'clock on Saturday afternoon. He would then be three hours from Neville Court, Meltonhamshire, and would be too late. He decided the best thing was to get to Venice, and there find whether to depart by the night train or the early morning express; perhaps a few hours could be saved somewhere, in flight from Paris to London.

The dismay on Marco's face was reflected throughout the hotel. The sun had fallen out of the sky for the lad, who ran about on his padrone's business, scarcely able to keep back the hot tears that threatened whenever he thought of the calamity. His life had been a wonderful thing since the signore's coming. There had been days of boating, bathing and fishing. He had had many a jolly meal with his padrone on those outings on the sunny lagoons, or along the sandy lido. And with the signore went all the prestige that had been his and had given him importance in the eyes of others.

His wages had been generous, too, and there were all the perquisites that had rewarded his service—the black velour hat from the expensive shop in the Piazzo San Marco at Venice, where the Inglesi bought their things, of the highest quality if of the highest price. He wore that hat on Sundays and kept it in a paper bag in the intervals.

Then there were those cigarettes—English cigarettes! His mind rapidly ran through his acquisitions. White flannel trousers, a fountain pen that had belonged to a Signor Waterman, a fancy leather belt, and a marvellous yellow knitted waistcoat. This the signore had given him for the winter, but that was a long time to wait, so he had worn it one Sunday, and perspired in pride. Moreover, he had worn it inside-out, in order to display the magic words " Selfridge, London." that he found on the collar label.

But it was not of these things, memories of happy days, that he thought deepest. Superficially they were in his mind, which had a child's simple delight in its pleasures. Less clearly, dumbly, he was thinking of the signorino himself. Sorrow that came to his padrone was his also. In his fervent devotion he would have protected him from every trial, even, had the need arisen, as he would have given his life for him. The name of the dead signore conveyed nothing to him, except that as a brother his death hurt his padrone, and took him away from the place he had grown to love. Leaving it would hurt ; perhaps leaving him, Marco, would trouble him a little, at least he liked to think so ; and perhaps, harder than either of these, would be the leaving of the signorina. And at that thought of Lucia, he remembered his message of the early morning—how far away that seemed now ! Had the signorino forgotten, and would it be possible for him to go now ?

When he had finished packing a parcel, he ran up to Peter's room, tapped and entered.

" Signorino," he said, as his master looked up from a box, " Will you be able to go now to the Duomo ? "

No, he had not forgotten, for he answered straight-way—

" Yes, Marco. I'll have just an hour. I'm catching the six o'clock boat."

Marco put down his parcel, lingered, and glanced round the littered room. Once he turned to go, then hesitated, and spoke.

" Signorino—I'll go to Venice with you and look after the things," he said, dolefully.

Peter turned and saw the abject lad standing by the door.

"No, Marco, thanks—you needn't do that."

"But I—I—want to, signorino," he cried, in a strangled voice, and then rushed from the room to hide his emotion, no longer controllable.

II

The human heart is not so much the prey of Time as of feeling. It will live unchanged through long dateless days of happiness, slip idly through the uneventful years, scarcely conscious of its sure approach to the invisible event that ends its pilgrimage. But its received impressions, its clearest memories, these will be the events not of years, or days even. A few hours, impressing themselves with the burden of their joy or sorrow, will stand vivid as a ruin in a placid evening sky, where the sheep stray through meadows that once were the streets of a forgotten city.

Lucia, in the brief march of twelve hours, found herself sundered from the years that had brought her to womanhood. Yesterday all those years were as an hour, happy, inconsequential, imperceptibly succeeding each other through the slow growth of experience. Most marked had been that thrill of a new-born emotion, when she had stood with the strange young Englishman watching the sunset from the Pontelungo. That sunset had been as none other, the crimsoned water, the golden air, the music of speech, the communicable thrill of his touch, had made that experience something wholly unrelated to life as she had known it.

But even then, though she knew it not, the magic of Youth touched all its colours with the gold of romance. It was a dream, an interval from life, not an awakening to a fuller knowledge of it. This had come later, in these last few hours, stern with their hard reality. It was as though the storm had been only the prototype of the conflict within her, a forerunner shattering the peace of the world, as the storm of her father's clashing purpose had shattered the sunny security of her own world.

From that storm she had emerged a woman, and looked back over but a brief span of eventful hours to a girl's life and the make-believe landscape of youth.

Life now stood revealed to her, and many strange things bore new meaning. Poor Ursula Bossi and her fate! It had been a story stirring the imagination and pity of childhood. Now, that mad leap from the Campanile spoke of the despair culminating in her desperate act. It was an act no longer spectacular to Lucia, it stood forth as a memorial of anguish suffered and forgotten, anguish she could now understand. For she loved, and she hated, the height greater for the depth. Life and all its glowing joy stood ranged with Peter, this Peter she scarcely knew in the sense of experience, but wholly knew in the strong impulse of intuition.

Never had Finghetti stirred her interest. At least, he had remained a nonentity, or, at most, the puppet of her father's will. Obedience and custom might have claimed her, as it had claimed others. Now, she was in revolt, fighting for all that life offered her. She was no longer a pawn in the game. She stood in open conflict with her father's will, in open hatred with his choice, and, knowing the man whose blood ran in her veins, she knew she had thrown down a gage that would be taken up.

She had seen all that in her father's eyes during dinner, after the first sharp conflict of their wills. She knew he was the more implacable for his silence, for his omission of any reference to the scene between them. When he had joined her after Neville's departure he had vouchsafed no word. She saw his astonishment and chagrin at Finghetti's non-appearance, while he waited through the evening to hear the story of his escape. And later, when Finghetti did appear, bemused, alternately bragging and whining, Delfino sat in stony silence while he poured out his story. Nothing in her father's manner, her father's face, betrayed his thoughts to Lucia.

"You are unnerved, Paolo," he said sternly, when Finghetti began to curse Neville and Marco. "Go home and rest. Do not repeat those words to anyone."

Finghetti glared at this.

"Repeat them!" he echoed, in his thick voice, as he stood, his hands gripping the chair back. "Repeat them! I've been saying it all night all over Chioggia! What do you think I am? D'you think I let men laugh in my face? If so, you don't know Paolo Finghetti! I give him twenty-four hours to clear out of Chioggia, or I'll break every bone in his body! If I see him to-night I'll—"

"Be quiet, Paolo! You're demented," snapped Delfino, rising and facing the younger man. "You will not say another word! Sit down and be silent while I talk to you."

The lifelong air of command sobered Finghetti. He collapsed clumsily into a chair. Delfino regarded him a few seconds contemptuously, and then looked at his daughter, white-faced, as she paused by the door.

"You are going, Lucia? Good-night!" he said, and the question was a command. Its sudden decision checked the outburst on her own lips, but her eyes spoke to him, spoke all her contempt as they travelled from the dissolute figure sitting collapsed in the chair to Delfino's own eagle gaze. And to her surprise, his eyes wavered before her own, so that she forewent her advantage, saying simply, " Good-night, father ! " and quickly left the room.

There was silence for a space, while Delfino surveyed the man in the chair. Then, standing before him, erect in the dignity of his age, he spoke, quietly but in tones not to be ignored

" Finghetti, you have come to my house to-night in a condition I allow no man to enter it. It is not the first time I have resented your manner. The other night, in the presence of the Signor Dottore and a guest you talked with an arrogance that—"

" You old men won't learn," muttered Finghetti, leering.

" Be quiet ! If it weren't your condition that talks, and not yourself, I'd turn you out. You are trying all my patience. I've made you master of my fleet but not of my house."

" An' whose gain's that ? "

" Both—if you keep your head. I know that," said Delfino curtly. " Now listen. Before you came here to-night, I had a visit from Neville. He thinks what Lucia thinks, what Marco— "

" An' what's that ? " growled Finghetti. " If I'd been here when that damned— "

Delfino ignored him.

" They all say you tried to sink them in the channel."

" And you believe them, of course ? " sneered Finghetti, slowly rising to his feet, and standing immense in the dark room. " Well, think so if you like. I'm going. I'm going out to look for that soft-handed Inglese. He'll leave Chioggia to-morrow, if he can. And when he's gone I'll ask you to complete your bargain. It's time that wild-cat girl knew her master."

The door slammed behind his great bulk, and echoed

down the dark room, where the candle flames bent and flared under the sudden draught. The old man watched them until they burned steadily, ringed with yellow light. He stood motionless in the silence that followed, his fine thin hands gripping the back of a chair giving him support. But there was no silence in his mind, no steadiness as of those candles. 'Complete your bargain' that shouting braggart had said. Had ambition led him to this, to insults in his own house, to defiance from his only child? 'Her master'—this gross threatening clown, ruler of his fleet, ruler of his house, ruler of his daughter? All this to defeat his rivals at Ancona?

He stared at the black tracery of masts beyond his window, beautiful in the moonlight. They were creatures of his life. Ships, ships, ships; they were not false, as flesh and blood were false. They served the master-hand, they were power and beauty and wealth, but they were obedient to the will that ruled them. Yes, he must not forget that. Ships were his life.

These young people could not understand. Later they would. The wonder of their legacy would change them, and they would know he had been right. But they were young, headstrong. He must not let anger at their foolishness master him, and defeat the noble heritage he had planned for them. Paolo was a born sailor, the rest belonged to youth, would pass with it. And the wildness in Lucia, that too would go. He must be patient, bending her slowly to his purpose, leading her to see his wisdom. They were young, these two, so full of the headstrong impulses of youth. Yes, he must be patient, there was so much at stake.

He stared out into the night, dreaming over the beauty of the boats, his hands gripping the chair, his body motionless as he schooled himself in his task. " I must be patient with them," he reiterated, " they are young. It will come right with patience ! " And as he stood, watching his beloved masts, he fell into a dream in which all passed as he would have it pass. And ever there glowed in it the glory of his fleet.

III

When Lucia, following her father's command, had left the room, she had not directly gone up to bed. Perturbed by the state of Finghetti, and knowing the temper of her father, she had lingered in the corridor, fearful of what might ensue. But she had not waited long when the door had opened below her, and Finghetti's angry voice filled the house. She heard his threat against Peter, heard the door slam as he lurched out, and then hastily sought the front corridor, from the window of which she saw him emerge into the Corso, stand hesitatingly for a few seconds, and then slouch away across the road and disappear in the darkness of an alley leading through to the Vena. He was probably going to sleep the night on his boat, which knew him better than the house now kept for him by a deaf old aunt, who served him in a condition of terror, and only lived in ease during his absence at sea.

Lucia could not sleep that night. The events of the momentous day had left her mind in a distraught condition. It had not been due to the terrible fight with the storm ; that had not unnerved so much as fatigued her, for, a sailor's daughter, she had known other storms, though none in which she had endured such personal peril. The scene with her father, the tense strain that had ensued when Peter came, and she knew they would soon be facing each other defiantly, while her own fate was debated, these events had worn her.

But more than these, the advent of Finghetti, half-drunk and threatening, and on his departure swearing vengeance against the man she loved, who probably moved ignorant of the danger encompassing him—this last trial of the crowded day left her unnerved, with a feverish brain figuring dread possibilities.

Once, she rose from her bed and sought the coolness of the window seat, overlooking the silent garden, black and white in the shadow and moonlight, with the distant Campanile silhouetted against the sky, stolid and enduring.

One clear necessity was in her mind. She must warn Peter at once. Every hour he was in jeopardy. Probably Finghetti would wake on the morrow sobered, but not changed in his purpose. She knew him too well to think that he was a man to forget a deep insult.

She realised, now, that she had been foolish to flout him as she had done with that headstrong desertion of his boat. She should have cajoled him, not have inflamed his suspicion and jealousy. And yet, sooner or later, he would have been awakened to the reality of her love for the Englishman. The crisis had come sooner than she had anticipated, that was all.

Her thought of Peter's safety suggested several ways in which he might be warned. She dare not leave it until the Festa, two days ahead. By then Finghetti might have found some means of striking, and it would be a means that provided no accusing clue. He had deliberately, openly, attempted their destruction off the Porto ; but there was no evidence, only conjecture in regard of his foul intention then. He would be too wary to arouse open suspicion. The blow would probably come from some agent of his purpose, from one of those desperadoes who infest every port, whom Finghetti often employed on his boats, holding them in terror of his temper.

Lucia decided she would seek the aid of the Dottore, imploring him to go immediately to Peter. But the kindly Dottore might doubt the reality of the danger, and, moreover, she would expose the nature of her affection. It was then that she thought of Marco. He would be about early in the morning, as she had often seen him. He, surely, would see Peter during the day, and could go to him without attracting attention. Yes, Marco was her best agent in this matter. He would realise the nature of the peril threatening his beloved master. He knew, also, the intimacy between them.

To divert suspicion, and to carry out her purpose, Lucia went early next morning to Mass at the Duomo, where happy chance found Marco. Returning home with an easier mind, she kept in the house all day until the hour appointed for their meeting.

Shortly before five o'clock, fastening about her brow the *tonda*, that native headpiece of white muslin worn by the native women of Chioggia, which is at once a protection from the sun and, if need be, a complete veil for the face, Lucia set forth to the cathedral.

As she had hoped, it was empty, and only the north door, standing in shadow in the deserted stony Campo, was unlocked. Fortune favoured her, for she had seen the caretaker fast asleep just inside the doorway of the Church of San Martino, across the Campo, where he kept vigil during the afternoon for tip-distributing tourists, who might wish to see the Duomo or ascend the Campanile.

Within the cathedral doorway, she paused in the cool grey light, her heart palpitating, while she looked down the broad open floor of the nave, towards the magnificent High Altar and the choir stalls of carven wood. Then, swiftly, she crossed to the chapel of Saints Felice and Fortunato, and there waited in that richly ornamented place, panelled with the work of eighteenth-century Venetian masters, glowing in the dim light that filtered through.

Falling to her knees before the altar, tawdrily decked with tinsel ornaments and heavy with half-burnt candles, she tried to pray, seeking some kind of guidance or peace in the confusion of her mind; but the words would not come, for her thoughts were elsewhere. She was listening acutely for the sound of a step, and when she heard it, sprang to her feet, crossed the chapel and looked eagerly across the nave. The far door, in opening, had shown a space of the brilliant day outside, had closed again, and beside it in the dim light stood a man. As he moved towards her, anxiety gave place to joy. It was Peter.

Hastily she drew back into the retreat of the chapel, embarrassed now by the foolishness of her apprehension. What was there to fear? Her forebodings of the previous night seemed chimerical in this happy Italian day.

He had seen her, and, smiling, paused on the threshold of the chapel.

" Lucia ! " he called.

She did not move from her position at the end of the altar steps, nor did she look into his face at once, but only when he stood near her did she throw back the tonda. Then it was she raised her face, her dark eyes luminous with arrested tears.

" Lucia—you have heard ? " he asked, surprised that the news of his going had reached her.

" Peetar—I must see you ! I sent Marco because you are in danger. Paolo last night quarrelled with my father. He was drunk, but he said what was in his mind. He left our house swearing revenge on you. Peetar, I know Paolo—he will carry it out ! "

Impulsively she put forth her hands and he took them,

folding them about his neck, looking down into her face, pale and nun-like, framed thus in the white veil.

" Lucia mia—I have news for you. I—I'm going, dearest," he said, quietly.

She looked steadily into his eyes and he was aware of a swift flash of reproach in her own.

" Going—you are afraid of Paolo ? " she asked, firmly.

" Afraid of Paolo ? "

He laughed at that, holding her to him.

" Carissima, is that what you think of me ? Listen ! Last night he tried to kill me. He threw a knife in the darkness. I pulled it out of a doorpost. I have saved it. One day Finghetti will receive it back from me ! "

" Santa Madonna ! " gasped Lucia. Then, her face upturned, her eyes beseeching him—" Peetar," she pleaded, " he will kill you, he means it ! You must not send back the knife. Dio mio ! What will happen ! What will happen ! "

He smoothed her face with his hands, and then drew her to him.

" Listen, Lucia. I am going away, at once— "

" Peetar ! "

" Lucia, I must. My brother's dead, they've sent for me."

He saw the first blindness in her eyes, then the realisation and the pain. He pressed his lips to hers, half-stifling the cry she made. Her arms were about him, holding him convulsively. Suddenly she threw back her head, resolute.

" When—do you go ? "

" Now, Lucia. The evening boat."

Another cry, from the depth of her being, and in her eyes despair appealing through the tears that gathered.

" Peetar ! I will go with you ! I won't stay ! I

daren't stay! It will be death here without you! Take me with you! Peetar! Take me away!"

She pleaded, she sobbed, abandoned to her emotion, her head buried on his chest, her body shaking as he held her in the stillness of that dim place. The old masters looked down upon them. From the altar the waxen, passionless face of the Madonna stared vacantly through the gloom.

"Lucia! Lucia mia! It's impossible, my dear child."

"No—no!" she sobbed, "I will go! I will go!"

He let her tears fall, waiting while her distress subsided. Then he raised her face, held it, quivering, between his hands, and talked to her tenderly, firmly, while she mistily gazed at him, vainly attempting to control the convulsive sobs that broke from her.

"Lucia mia, have you thought what going with me would mean? There is your father, would you leave him without word or warning? I'm going to England, where you would not know a soul, where you couldn't understand a word they said to you. I can't take you away like this. What would they say here, when it was known? One day you'd want to come back, and you couldn't. I'm older than you, Lucia, I must think of these things for you."

But she would not heed his words. Her cry was "Take me, Peetar, take me!" and then as she failed to prevail upon him, in a tempest of tears she implored him.

"I won't have Finghetti. They'll force me and I'll kill myself! I won't have him! I won't have him! Take me away from them, Peetar," she cried.

In vain he tried to soothe her, to reassure her. Blind terror seemed to have seized this half delirious girl clinging to him. Her cries echoed from the high roof and the resounding walls of the small chapel. What had he done, he asked himself in that passionate moment, what blind impetus of youth had caused him to play with this poor child's love ? He had not foreseen the depth of passion he had so thoughtlessly stirred, the bonds he had placed upon her. What had been romance to him, was reality to her, and all the selfishness of his quest stood naked before him in the anguish of that moment.

Yet God knew, in his innermost heart he had not willed to play with her love. She had been such a creature of joy, of beauty, in this vivid, colourful land. Like a flower he had taken her, as might a passing wind, fitfully enamoured of the beauty it swayed in the morning meadows. Could he leave her so, bowed and broken by his zest ? Never had she seemed so desirable as in this grief, this self-abandonment in her faith of him. Yet, stronger than emotion, spoke reason. Life was inexorable in its judgment, irrevocable in its acts. He knew that, he knew the impossibility of her desire, the deeper folly that would be his in acquiescence.

"Lucia, my child, Lucia ! I must go soon, and you must be brave and let them see nothing of this. Later you'll know it could not be as you wish now, and you'll not think me unkind—will you, Lucia, will you ? " he asked, seeking reassurance himself.

"No, Peetar, no," she choked. "You will come back, soon ? "

Her eyes burned his as she asked this, so that he might not avoid her gaze, dismiss her question. God ! what had he done to light such fires ! His face shadowed with the struggle of that moment, and courage failed him. He could not strike her this blow and leave her without hope of the future, now all that she clung to.

"I will come back," he said, in a voice that he hardly

knew for his own. "Now, Lucia mia, I must go. Good-bye, Lucia. Carissima mia, good-bye."

He gathered her to him, his lips on hers, as they clung in the communion of that intense agonising rapture. Then abruptly, blindly, he took her arms from his neck, looked breathlessly at her tear-suffused face as they stood in that moment of silent renunciation, and so went from her, hurrying into the pitiless glare of the unheeding day.

She heard him go, heard his feet cross the flagged nave, echoing fainter and fainter, heard the shrill screech of the iron hinges as the door swung back, the full heavy sound of its closing, the following silence, and then knew the emptiness, the sundered space that wrapped her round.

For a long pause she stood there, immobile, head thrown back, eyes closed, breathing hard as she strove to make credible the cruel knowledge of her brain. And then, her will surrendering to the surge within her bosom, she collapsed on the altar steps, hands interlocked, head bowed in her arms, as she moaned to the Madonna, Mother of Sorrows, Queen of Holy Love.

How long she lay there, pleading, praying, she knew not, but the coldness of the stone steps struck through her dress. The unbroken silence soothed her, the calm face of the Madonna reigned serene beyond all human grief.

Rising to her feet, she slowly left the chapel, paused in the empty nave of the cathedral, wiping her tearful face, and calling to her mind some form of ordered thoughts. He was gone. That heavy door had shut him out with the day, had closed on the familiar loved figure of her young lover.

Quietly, like a shadow moving amid shadows, she crossed the wide floor, stood irresolutely by the door for a space, and then, with quick determined hands, opened it and stepped out into the sunny Campo. He was leaving by the evening boat, at six o'clock. She would watch it carry him away into the distance. Quickly she crossed the stony space, until she had reached the shadow of the Campanile. Its door was unlocked. She entered into the coolness and silence of the ringers' room, and then began the long winding ascent. With what a different heart she had climbed this dark way on other occasions ! Then, it had been to a wonderful meeting, now it was for a sorrowful parting. This place was hallowed with their love, the silent understanding witness of their happiness. Alone, of all Chioggia, it seemed to know the trouble of her heart.

Breathless, she had gained the empty room over the belfry. Would she be in time ? A cool breeze greeted her as she stepped on to the balcony, and hurried round it to the south side. There, statue-like, she halted, disappointment chilling her heart. In her anxiety she had forgotten that the quay could not be seen because of the overshadowing houses fronting the harbour. But beyond the molo all the great lagoon stretched northwards to Venice, side by side with the dark Adriatic, divided from it by the long line of the Littorale di Pelestrina. There lay the Porto, through which they had been swept from death to life, there ran the shore to which she had swum to warn him of the storm. Was it only yesterday, or years ago ?

Searching the lagoon, she could see no boat, only a few sailing vessels putting out from Porto Secco, probably going to join the sardine fishers on the mud flats on each side of the deep channel. He had not left yet, perhaps now he stood on the deck, leaning over the rail, saying farewell to those who would gather round him. Marco would be there, and the padrone of the hotel, the waiters, perhaps, and the maids, for they adored the signore ; and she, who more than all had the right to be there, must watch distantly.

As she thought this, a shrill sound floated thinly to her ears in that high tower. It was the boat's syren, sounding before the hawsers were cast off. Again! She heard the hoarse note die thinly away, and the silence, and low sigh of the wind about her platform followed. With lips parted, her troubled eyes held those northern waters, held them until the dark stumpy boat crept up above the nestling house-roofs, on to the emerald sheet beyond. She could see the broad paddle boxes, the funnel, smoke-plumed, the light canvas awning over the saloon deck, and the opalescent track left by the receding vessel as it moved up that emerald waste, beyond the purple band of the sea channel, beyond the turquoise belt, to the wind-veined, glistening water that bore it, mile on sundering mile, to Venice.

Now it seemed motionless, yet diminished steadily, now it danced, a black mote amid the myriad scintillations of the water, and now it faded into the haze where the horizon called it to its invisible bourn.

He was gone—gone from her vision and her life. No longer could she see that boat threshing the lucent waters, nor the sky, nor the cramped red roofs of the houses even. In the silence and the solitude her eyes saw nothing of the sorrowful world below. Her head was between her arms, cold cheek to the cool balustrade, and the only sound in that high heaven was the sound of human grief, of a girl sobbing as only the heart of youth can know.

CHAPTER XVI

I

IN the cold grey morning light a black gondola rested in the small canal running along the side of the Hotel Danieli at Venice. It waited by a small stone platform under the side-door of the hotel. As the gondolier stood on his *poppa*, a black-suited servant in noiseless felt slippers came out and deposited a portmanteau in the gondola. A minute later two figures emerged, one entering the low-roofed cabin, the other seating himself in the small chair nearer the prow. Silently the gondola glided down the narrow waterway, under the arch of a white stone bridge, then out into the broad lagoon that fronted the flagged Riva degli Schiavoni.

Before them rose the island church of San Giorgio ; on the left, lost in the early dawn, ran the hazy line of the Lido. A number of boats were clustered off the entrance to the Guidecca ; a white steam yacht that sailed for Triest, a giant trabaccolo from Istria or Fiume, with its fantastic rigging, a Glasgow tramp steamer, and a swarm of pleasure boats, reefed and anchored, stretching towards the Customs House and the great pile of the Church of Santa Maria della Salute, rising upon her marble steps at the entrance to the Grand Canal.

The gondolier swung round his boat when clear of the small opening and headed for the Grand Canal. On their right now, glimmered the pink and grey of the Doges' Palace, its columned tiers perhaps lovelier in this cold light of morning than in the blaze of noon or the silver of night. Next, they passed the Piazzetta leading to the great Piazza and San Marco itself. A few minutes later they were in the Grand Canal, silent and beautiful, for the steamers were not yet running, the palaces folded up in sleep, the water unruffled by any passing craft.

Peter had bidden the gondolier to follow the Canal, and make no short cut this last time. Could it really be that he was leaving all this, that beyond this beauty and calm he was bound for a scene of tragedy? The House of Desdemona, secretive behind its arabesque windows and balcony: the retiring Accademia, swept by behind them. Under the low flat Ponte di Ferro, past the Palazzo Rezzonico, with a thought of Browning: the Palazzo Giustiniani, with a thought of Wagner: and the Palazzo Mocenigo, with a thought of Byron, they journeyed, the faded splendour of Venice receding behind them, until the light lessened as they shot under the high arch of the Ponte di Rialto.

The silence was broken beyond this. Along the public quay clustered the boats from the Littorale, which had come overnight with fruit and vegetables, now being noisily sold in the fruit market. Further down, there was a babel of voices from the fish market, but silence folded them in again as they followed the canal winding towards the station. Once in that station, gloomy, noisy, dirty, Peter knew that romance was dead. There, Europe began, with its office hours and time-tables, its formal manners and stiff collars.

Marco, the faithful silent Marco, carried his signorino's portmanteau down the platform to the waiting train. Nothing could prevent the rendering of this final service to his padrone. He had insisted on taking the boat from Chioggia. When Peter decided to catch the early morning train, Marco asked the time.

" I'll be at the hotel at five, signorino," he said, in a quiet determined voice.

" But you must sleep somewhere ! "

" Si—I'll find a boat I know at the Rialto."

" Nonsense, Marco—you'll stay here," said Peter, and thus it was Marco slept in splendour at the Hotel Danieli, a thing to be oft related later at Chioggia. Not slept, however, there was no sleep for Marco. He lay and waited for the dreaded hour, and saw the dawn come across the lagoon, touching the campanile of San Giorgio opposite, even as Peter had seen it nearly two months ago, after that restless night on the eve of his adventure.

Marco, standing now on the platform, knew this was the end of all. When Peter had taken a corner seat, he descended to the platform and stood by the boy, watching the other travellers choosing their seats. A motley crowd , American women, veiled and experienced, a few English , deliberate and silent : Jews, familiars of many capitals, polyglot nomads of the earth. A dapper young man from Bucharest contested a seat with a fat Greek from Athens, speaking atrocious French which disguised their resentment. But Peter, though watching, had no thought of these. He knew that in a few moments he would have to say farewell to the silent boy at his side, and they would have to be short decisive words in order to carry the lad through his trial. Yet it was Marco who spoke first, following to the last in the service of his padrone.

" I will take care of the boat, signorino, until you come back."

Peter had forgotten the *Celavasansdire*. A happy inspiration leapt to his mind.

"Marco," he said, "I want you to have the *Celava-sansdire* for yourself."

He had expected a gleam of happiness on Marco's face, but to his surprise the shadow deepened. The lad looked at him mutely, inwardly struggling with a thought that wounded him.

"Marco, you'd like it—it would be of use to you, wouldn't it?" asked Peter, searching for his trouble.

"Yes, signorino—but—" Marco turned his face away.

"But what, Marco?"

Marco looked at him blindly. Rebellious tears glistened in his eyes.

"Signorino, you're not coming back again!" he called in a strangled voice, swift to read the meaning of the gift.

"Nonsense, Marco, of course I am!" replied Peter, as lightly as he could. For the second time his dread of a scene had committed him to a promise. He had promised Lucia, now Marco.

"It's the Festa to-day, signorino, when we should have gone out."

"You must still go out and take the signorina with you. Tell her I wish it. I'll think of you on the lagoon to-night."

"Sì, signorino," said Marco, mirthlessly.

The carriage doors were being slammed to. It was the end now. Peter grasped the lad's hand, holding it firmly. His voice was almost stern with determination to brace up the quivering lad, and himself.

"Marco, take care of the signorina for my sake. Write to me, tell me everything you do."

Marco raised a face of misery to him.

"Signorino—you will come back? You'll come back soon?" he pleaded in the misery of his heart, as if ignoring his padrone's request.

" Sì, Marco—I'll come back as soon as possible."

Marco's eyes changed, and glittered suddenly with fierce resolution.

" I'll guard the signorina till you come—soon, signorino, soon ! "

The boy's voice broke on the word. Peter could not see his face, which was lowered as if examining the ground. The platform was emptied now, a porter shouted excitedly at them.

" Addio, Marco ! " said Peter, forcing his voice.

" A rivederci, signorino ! "

The next moment, as the compartment door slammed behind him, the train drew heavily out. Peter leaned through the window, smiled cheerfully at Marco, waving his hand. And the lad smiled back, smiled while tears ran down his brown cheeks, mistily seeing the hateful train taking his padrone away. The day of the Festa !

" Madonna santissima ! " he sobbed, abandoned to his grief now he was alone.

II

It is singular how the sense of sight changes our world and renders futile the other senses clinging to the past. A few hours ago Peter had seen the lagoons, the houses of Chioggia, the faces of Lucia and Marco, and now, although memory clung to these, how far away they were ! Had that life been lived one hour or one hundred years ago ? That unhappy lad's ' A rivederci ' was still in his ears, but the world to which he belonged had vanished.

Peter looked at the swarthy Greek and the little Roumanian seated opposite ; ancient Athens and gay Bucharest were known to them, as to-morrow perhaps Paris or London. The world was full of cities and streets and houses, of men and women living their lives of struggle and hope, unconscious for the most part of life filling other streets and houses. Custom and distance split up the vast flood of humanity, united only in its birth-spring and its death-plunge. One man laughed in his chair in a Roman house, while another met death in a New York Avenue, or a child found birth in a London attic. This compartment, this train drawing to Milan, had gathered a few of the threads in the strand of Life, soon to be frayed by the winds of Chance.

As they ran through the brightening morning, past Padua, in early mist, and Verona in clear sunlight, Peter was still in Chioggia, Chioggia dancing in his mind alternately with Neville Court; Lucia and Marco with Roderick and Maud. Others looked in on that meditation. His mother, in her slip of a house on the hill top at Melton- ham; Parsons, bald, spectacled, discreet Parsons at the Bank, drawing clients aside, murmuring, subdued; Susie, sane, practical, ever doing something, organising amid the consternation; and Finghetti, hearing the gossip about his departure. The dottore would be sad about it, and Delfino—well, he would feel it was not unfortunate.

The Greek opposite was eating a lemon. Mother Pappini and her fruit baskets, she too would hear and regret. He had friends there, and the children—' Where is the Signore ? ' they would be asking. Inghilterra, they would be told. Strange, far, wonderful ; and that was his home, where he was known and had his friends. And Lucia knew nothing of his new familiar life, lonely, crying and praying for his return.

The attendant passed down the car. First service of lunch in the dining car ! Peter went forwards, seating himself by the plate-glass window, beyond which the vineyards of Lombardy slipped by, the vines festooned from pole to pole. When would he come this way again, and with what purpose ?

Twice the waiter asked his choice of soup. Yes— *Ministrone.*

He had promised, twice, both Lucia and Marco. Was he glad ? No, this was the end. Life began now. Dreams cannot last for ever, the facts of life break in upon them. There was the Bank at Meltonham, the Bank, with morning coat and black tie, clerks in rows, and Parsons tapping on the Chief's door ;—lagoon fishing, sunbathing, the feud with Finghetti, Lucia on the Campanile balcony, Marco with his laughter, his superstition. Lord ! what a jumble. No, not a jumble, these two worlds did not meet or mix. He was in the other one now, it claimed him, it was a real world.

Real ? Well, no, silly perhaps, in its organised falseness, its alienation from Nature, its imprisonment of the spirit. But it held men, from birth to death, and to them, other worlds, such as Chioggia, were holiday worlds. He had made the holiday world his real one, that was his trouble. He had forgotten the life he had escaped from. Well, it claimed him back now.

Yet he had promised to escape it again, had promised Lucia. Time would relieve him of that. And Lucia ? The dream had gone but Lucia remained. Had he played with Lucia. No, he had really loved her. Had ?

He left the dining-car, and walked down the swaying train to his compartment. He was ill at ease. Lucia. There was a tangle there. Time and distance might straighten it out. She too might learn something from Time. He would know, for Marco would write—often first ; then occasionally, then—

That detestable Greek had closed the window. He

sat perspiring, rolling his eyes, like a Pekinese's, lemon-sucking, demonstratively smelly and noisy. There was no need for closed windows, they were in a station. Peter opened it, leaned out, and then drew back with a start. Marco and his superstitions, that lad and his world, flashed back, with a sunlit stretch of sand bleached between sea and sea-wall. By the door of the station restaurant, stood an old man, tin-mug in hand, breast-plated, with the appeal ' Il Ciéco.'

The blind man ! Marco's ' È terribile ! ' The train moved, and he sank back into his seat recalling vividly, particularly—*but one thing is near and not to be confused —a death—a violent death.*

Peter heard his own mocking question ; there would be a long journey, surely ? And that claw-like hand had assented, with the weak voice. *It will need that, signore.*

Peter laughed, then, to himself. It had indeed been a dream world. Well, Marco should feel at ease, the prophecy was worked out. Had Marco recollected ? He must remind him when he wrote. His faith in the prophet deserved that commendation. But perhaps the lad would feel disappointed. He had been so certain he was the centre of the drama. And the drama had not been enacted in their world at all !

Thus he rehearsed his days, journeying from the scenes of his recollections. Darkness came on as they roared through the Alpine valleys, shattered the silence of the lonely peaks, threw racing yellow reflections upon the bordering lakes, and saw the low clouds combed with black firs, dense in moonlight.

CHAPTER XVII

FATE was perverse, even to the minute details. A midsummer Channel gale had made flight from Paris inadvisable. Their boat was half-an-hour late at Dover, and it was six o'clock in the evening of Saturday when he stood under the gloomy span of St. Pancras Station. Roderick had been buried that afternoon at two o'clock, so the butler's voice had told him over the telephone. Peter had rung up from his club, where he had expended two hours' interval, between train connections, in a hot bath. He had insisted that Lady Neville should not be brought to the telephone, but asked for the car to meet the nine o'clock train at Meltonham.

" And, Grieve, I shall want the car to take me to my mother's house later. I'll sleep there," he said to the butler.

" Very good, sir. I will tell her ladyship."

Dear old Grieve ! It was good to hear his steady articulation again. There was much to be said for the English.

And for England also, he thought later, when the train had shaken off a hideous medley of slum backs, blackened factories, gasometers, self-conscious villas with over-preened gardens, and new suburbs, red coated and spaced like soldiers. It had been raining, of course ; the summer had been disappointing in this land of confirmed weather

251

optimists. In the evening light, long pools in the flooded meadows shone with the reflection of fleecy clouds or glowed golden from the west where the storm-grey sky was stabbed with crimson.

Meadows of England, shining in the rain.

Yes, the poet Flecker could see and sing that, new from exile. How luscious the green was, and could all Italy show such trees ? They had the skeleton Lombardy poplar, and the melodramatic cypress, that Noah's ark tree of the theatrical landscape, but they had no vast spreading elms, no sturdy oaks such as these. They were not trees, they were institutions ! The very winds of history had fondled them.

He watched the rolling counties, sweeping from valley to hill-top, ribboned with roads, dotted with farmsteads, or suddenly revealing a cluster of age-brown houses huddled about a grey church spire. And he knew of the long grass, the tall elms and the irregular, weather-greened tombstones in that garden of Time where the birds kept evensong.

Lovingly, Peter's eyes followed the loose pattern of furrowed field, of waving green wheat, and hawthorn-bordered pastures. Never before had he seen them so entrancing as in this level light of eventide. The landscape was so full of calm, of the sense of living things, of Nature's richness, of man's long care and the low sky's amorous tears.

It was twilight when they ran into Meltonham station. He paused for a minute on the long covered platform, surveying the familiar scene. He wondered if the same red-faced old collector would be sitting in the ticket-office at the top of the stairs. Suddenly, as he wondered, a voice called " Peter ! " He swung round, startled, yet glad to be recognised.

" Susie ! " he cried, joyfully, as he saw a slim figure
swathed in black. Taking her in his arms, he kissed her.
" But you shouldn't have come ! How well you look,
Susie, and you've grown, old girl ! "

" Not stouter ? " she asked, with a smile of alarm.

" As if you cared ! " he laughed, walking up the platform.

Neither made any reference to the event that brought
them together. They were in the car, shut in by the
chauffeur, and moving out of the station before he alluded
to Roderick.

" Jove ! " he exclaimed, looking out of the window,
" it's good to see old Meltonham again, although I hate
it when I'm in it." Then, abruptly, " How's Maud ? "
he asked.

She told him then all he wanted to know. Roderick
had been thrown from his horse just outside the gates of
his home. He had ridden out to his agent's house, down
the main road, and was returning when an overtaking car
had caused his horse to plunge and slip on the tarmac.
Death had been instantaneous, his neck was broken.
The coroner had absolved the motorists from all blame.
Treacherous tarmac, just after a storm, had been re-
sponsible.

" Poor old Roderick ! Maud's frightfully upset, of
course ? " he asked when Susie had finished her story.

" Yes—but she's wonderful. You know Maud's absolute self-control. Not a shriek, not a tear, when they
brought in poor Roderick. She's seen to everything all
through, without a quiver of the lip. It's now she'll pay
for it. There's a crust all over Maud, but she's a volcano
underneath."

" And mother ? " he asked, a little perturbed by Susan's
unflinching diagnosis of his sister-in-law.

" The old dear's marvellous. I took her home before coming for you. She wondered when she'd see you."

" Oh—of course, she hasn't had my wire yet, she would be at the funeral. I'm sleeping there."

Susan raised her voice in surprise.

" At Cliff House ? "

" Yes," he answered.

Now why should Susie be surprised ? It was his home. He lived there, not at Neville Court.

" Maud's expecting you at the Court to-night," said Susan.

" I told Grieve I should go home."

Susan straightened her skirt. There was a silence, and Peter was very conscious of it, while he looked out of the car. They were crossing the river now, its crescent curve cold in the fading twilight. Susan put a small black-gloved hand on his arm and looked directly into his eyes.

" Peter, I'm going to say what you'll think is a dreadful thing ! "

Peter laughed, for Susan was always famous for being outspoken and original.

" That's nothing new, Susie, is it ? " he asked, but there was no answering mirth in her eyes. They were very keen.

" Peter ! Maud means to marry you ! "

She sat back, straight and stiff, with an air of " There ! I've said it," but also with determination to stand by it.

" Susan ! " exploded Peter.

" You're shocked ? "

" I am ! " exclaimed her brother. " Good heavens, Susie, whatever will you say next ? And poor Roderick only buried to-day ! "

He looked at her bewildered by her frankness, and there was something beside surprise at her statement. He had a vivid recollection of that encounter at the breakfast table at Danieli's. He could not forget how Maud had looked at him that morning.

" Susie, my dear girl, you really mustn't say such preposterous things ! It's unfair to Maud ! " he cried, and something of his own alarm crept into his voice. If he had hoped to reprove Susan he failed utterly, for she stood firm on her ground and faced him.

" Peter, why shouldn't I say what I think to you ? You are concerned, it's you that— "

" Susie, I won't listen to such raving," he protested, but Susan ignored his annoyance and interrupted him.

" Maud's talking of you assuming your responsibilities," she continued, seeing him start at the word, " and by those she means the Bank, Ronnie, the Court, and herself. They're all one to Maud. It's the Neville institution that she's determined to consolidate."

Peter lowered the saloon window to let in a little air.

" Susie, I don't know how you think I'm going to face Maud," he said angrily, " with all this nonsense poured into my ears. It's monstrous of you, at a time like this."

" Would it be monstrous at any other time ? "

" Why, yes—but now particularly, with Roderick scarcely— "

" —buried," said Susan, decisively. " Oh, yes, I know all that. Do I generally talk nonsense, Peter ? "

" No."

" Isn't it better you should know where you are, right from the very beginning ? "

" Susie, you never have liked Maud," he protested.

" That's true, but it's nothing to do with it. Maud's one of those women one does not like, one admires her."

They were passing through the country now, the last suburbs of Meltonham having been shaken off. Neville

Court stood on the brow of a wooded hill overlooking the
distant river, and Meltonham itself, ranged on the opposite
hillside, ten miles distant. Peter looked out on the
hedgerows, not wishing to encounter his sister's eyes.

"Well," said Susan, with an air of finality, "you can't
say I haven't warned you, Peter."

"Thanks, I suppose you think I need it," he retorted.

"I do. Peter, you old dear, you flatter yourself you're
one of those strong, silent men who shut up designing
women in boxes, and you're nothing of the kind. You're
always in a tangle with some woman simply because
you're too nice and kind-hearted to be fierce. I'm sure,
for instance, that you've been in some tangle at Chioggia."

An answering flame burned in his cheek, more in anger
than confession. His sister saw it, and knew her prophecy
was correct. His outburst alone had told her that.

"Susan, I don't think you know how objectionable it is
for a brother to sit and hear his maiden sister talking in
this fashion," he cried, indignantly.

Susan put a slim hand over his own.

"Now, Peter, you're beginning to talk just like poor
Roderick! I've never known an advocate of sex-eman-
cipation who extended it to his own sister. Peter, old
thing, do you realise we're almost quarrelling?"

"I'm sorry, Susie, but really!"

"Well, I'll say no more—now," she added, retrieving
her right. "I'll let you think the rest! Meanwhile
remember that I'm a doctor, and my diagnosis is not
confined to ills of the body."

For the remainder of the journey, as Susan suggested, he
did think. That was where Susan was so horribly right, as
Roderick had often found to his annoyance. Peter saw,
more clearly than ever, all the significance of that unforgettable breakfast at Danieli's, of the night before at Count

Casmiri's, and, later, in the gondola. Maud had a way with men, a masterful way, as Susan said. Roderick had been her devoted slave. Could Maud dispense with a slave ? Frankly, he was sure she could not. Resolutely he was determined he would not be enslaved.

They were breasting the long hill now, elm-bordered, at the farther end of which they passed the lodge, with tall massive wrought-iron gates, the family crest of the dolphin on their pillars. Poor Maud, how grossly unkind was all this thought about her ! She had suffered a fearful blow, and Susan had denied her sympathy just because she faced her trouble so splendidly.

The tyres crunched as they left the tarmac and mounted the gravel. On their left, behind its row of elm trees stood the church ; on the right, the paddock where, as boys he and Roderick had chased and bridled their ponies ; an inquisitive donkey now came up to the gate and brayed at them. In front, the road suddenly ended, giving access to a steep, rutted ravine that dipped to the fields and the nestling village. The car swerved off to the right, and instantly they saw the broad flat expanse of Neville Court, square and straight-windowed in the Queen Anne style, approached by a circular drive surrounding the green lawn with its central statue-fountain of Hercules. There, to the left, catching the light of evening, ran the raised terraced lawn, with its lion-guarded steps and background of yews and thick woods.

The chauffeur descended from the car. Grieve simultaneously appeared, silhouetted in the expanse of open doorway.

" Good evening, Grieve ! " said Peter, as he stepped in.

" Good evening, sir. I hope you have had a comfortable journey, sir," he responded, quietly.

Tactful Grieve ! On any other occasion he would have

said ' pleasant ' journey, but this was a mission of mourning, and Grieve was a man of the appropriate word.

" Her ladyship is in the drawing-room, sir," he said,
as Peter hesitated and turned to Susan.

" You go up to Maud—I'll finish my letters, Peter," she
instructed him, disappearing in the library.

He ascended the broad, shallow, oak stairs, treading
silently on the thick, pile carpet ; at the turn, between the
two stained glass windows, richer with the sunset flooding
them, he passed the Kneller portrait of an early Neville,
delicate hand on sword, lace-wristed and wigged, the
Neville nose defying the disguise of fashion. Momentarily, Peter looked down into the hall, where once, as a
boy, he had dropped a ripe pear on Grieve's bald head,
and gone supperless to bed. Grieve's cranium was shining there now, reflective under the chandelier as he stood
beside the armoured figure, winding the Chippendale
grandfather-clock.

On the landing, Peter halted before the dark mahogany
door leading into the drawing-room, one hand on the
ivory handle, his restless eyes surveying the floor with
its leopard skin, the Empire gilt couch, and the
ormulu table under the leaded gothic windows, glazed
with the familiar dolphin. Had he been frank with
himself, he would have admitted he was nervous at the
moment. Actually he persuaded himself that the occasion
was trying : after all, one's brother did not die every day.
He wondered exactly how Maud would look and act,
what he should say for the best. Then, turning the
handle, he opened the door.

The drawing-room had at one time been the picture
gallery. It was long and high. Its six large windows,
replete with wooden shutters that folded back into the side
frames, panelled with gilt and white enamel, looked out

high over lawns and falling woods to the strip of the river afar, which now caught the sunset and gleamed like a bar of gold across the grey horizon. The room was in darkness save for a veined alabaster lamp standing on an occasional table near the Queen Anne fireplace. In the gloom it marked out a glowing circle where its light fell upon one end of a lounge, in black and crimson silk damask, a Persian rug on the parquetry floor, and a table littered with books, magazines and a small bronze.

Outside that circle of light, investing the gloom with mystery, there was a faint gleam of gilt from the rows of portraits on the north wall, and the ghostly outline of the heavy white marble mantelpiece, which a foolish ancestor had imported from Italy in the belief that it was the work of Canova.

That isle of light, far across the surrounding darkness, blinded Peter for the moment. Standing on the threshold, he knew the voice that called him.

" Peter—I heard the car. How tired you must be ! "

It was then that he saw Maud, indistinct in the shadow. She had risen, dressed in black, of course, with a glimmer of light on her face and neck. Simultaneously another figure rose, and, as Peter came down the room, he saw the clerical collar and recognised the face of young Mr. Trivett, the vicar of the near village.

" Maud—I'm distressed at being so late," said Peter, and, as Maud lifted up her face, when his hands had taken hers, he realised as a brother-in-law of one bereaved, it was his duty to kiss her, which he did decorously. Before he could say anything more, Mr. Trivett began to bleat his way out.

" I must really go now," he said, having exchanged greeting with Peter. " It will be such a comfort to Lady Neville to have you here. She has been wonderful !

wonderful! Mr. Neville. We are all so distressed. We were all so fond of dear Sir Roderick. It is a comfort to know Lady Neville will have you by her. We have all done what we can, but, alas, it is so little. It was such a shock, Lady Neville has been so wonderful! Good night! Good night! I will call again soon, if I may, Lady Neville. You have been very brave to-day!"

Poor little Trivett, he was so young and nervous! The door seemed a mile away, his words sounded so futile and feeble. All three of them knew it. What could one say on such an occasion?

Peter escorted him to the door, the little fellow still talking, terrified of the silence that would engulf his trite remarks. On the landing itself, as he said ' Good night ' again, he assured Peter that Lady Neville had been so wonderful. At the angle of the stairs, he called ' Good night ' once more to the courteously waiting Peter, this time with a Christian cheerfulness forced into the farewell.

"Poor Mr. Trivett!" exclaimed Lady Neville, as Peter seated himself at her side. "He has been so kind, but he is a bore. I had to ask him to stay to dinner. I wonder how such a timid man got married, and to such a nice woman too. Cigarette, Peter?" She held out a silver box to him, which he declined.

"Do you mind if I do—I suppose a widow can? Widow! What a hateful word! I never thought I should be that."

All the time she was talking, Peter found himself marvelling. He had pictured Maud in many moods, statuesquely grief-stricken, noble in black, a study of Christian fortitude, severe and restrained, but never had he imagined her in this mood—feverish. For she talked inconsequently, incessantly. She told him of Roderick, all he had said on the fatal morning, what he had eaten, how he had called to her through the morning-room window as she arranged some roses, how he had been brought back, of Grieve's self-control, of Ronnie's sobs and Nannie's hysterics. All of which Peter wished to hear, but not in such extraordinary detail.

Then followed the whole funeral procession ; what Mr. Trivett had said, what the Duke of Bowater had said, for he had come to the service, poor man, despite his gout and the house-party at the Towers. And Colonel Brent, the Duke's faithful echo, who always proposed the vote of thanks to his Grace at functions in Meltonham, thereby earning the allusion to ' my gallant friend, Colonel Brent '—he was present, and actually dropped a tear as he leaned over the grave, for Roddy and he had hunted, and sat at the Petty Sessions together. ' The Colonel says he's fathered him from a boy.' Yes, and there was Parsons, from the Bank, with the clerks, and the members of the Home Hunt, and the Chairman and Members of the District Council, and the Mayor and the Town Clerk of Meltonham. Old Lady Canton had driven over from Canton Hall, for she'd been at poor Roddy's baptism, and couldn't think of missing his funeral. Poor Roddy was so respected. The tenants had all—

And then it was that Peter did a thing which shocked and surprised him. He yawned, discreetly, in the gloom, and was only brought to a sense of the gravity of the occasion by an intimation of tears in Maud's voice. She was off now on a recital of all Roderick had done, of his immense grasp of affairs, of the vast responsibilities that devolved on her, the maintenance of the traditions, the administration of the estate, the Bank, poor little Ronnie, fatherless in his infancy. Suddenly, with a gesture that startled Peter, her hands had caught the lapels of his coat, and she had slipped down, with head buried, crying on his breast.

Peter, with an inborn dread of scenes, could not deal with the situation. Was this reaction after the long strain? Never had he imagined Maud distraught; she had always been so self-possessed. Whatever it was, grief or hysteria, or both, he knew that he felt an utter fool, sitting back, with a crying woman in his arms, incapable of word or act. He would have sat imprisoned there, dumbly, for an hour, if Susan had not entered the room at that moment. Half-way down the floor she paused in surprise, and Peter caught her expression as he turned a distressed face towards her.

" It's Maud," he said, with bathos, " it's been too much for her. She's been wonderful! wonderful! "

Strange how that nervous little Trivett's expression came to his lips. Why did not Susan say something sympathetic, or do something? She looked positively hostile, he thought. Maud lifted her face, raising herself from him, and looked beseechingly into his eyes.

" Peter, you'll look after us? There's all Roddy's affairs, and the Bank, and poor little Ronnie—and me! We've no one else to help us. You'll stay and look after us, Peter? There's the Bank, until Ronnie grows up, and there's no one but you."

" Yes, Maud, certainly! I'll do everything, don't you worry at all, my dear," he heard himself say. " I'll take over all Roderick's affairs. Leave it to me, Maud. Ronnie shan't suffer, nor you Maud, I'll see to that."

There was a grateful sob from Lady Neville, as she straightened herself in her corner of the lounge, while Peter adjusted his collar.

" I simply had to have a little cry to someone," explained Lady Neville. " It's silly, I know, but I've been all alone until you came, Peter."

" Of course, Maud, of course. You've been wonderful," he assented.

And then it was he saw Susie, standing with her face above the glow of the lamp, her eyes bright as they turned on him. He was sure she was laughing.

With an angry tilt of his head, he stood up and said he must be going.

CHAPTER XVIII

THE dowager Lady Neville, to whom the car was now taking her long-absent son, the younger and the favourite, lived in a slip of a house on the highest point of the terrace that surmounted a wooded amphitheatre of dwellings known as The Circus. There was a precise distinction about this locality. Not only was it the choicest residential situation in Meltonham, it was a preserve in which the local aristocracy, more of business than blood, hid itself away in the recesses of that ducal hillside. For the particular distinction of residence in The Circus came from the ducal possession. There were three ways into it, gated, crested, and marked ' Private.' The Bowater unicorn, surmounted by a coronet, greeted you at either end of the top entrances to the amphitheatre, or at the bottom, where it launched itself into the valley and the estate became slightly confused with the vulgar town. The lower end, consequently, had not the exclusive recommendation of the higher terraces furrowing the steep hillside.

It was indeed a natural social ladder, whose highest elevation was watched over by the Duke's residence, The Castle. Not that His Grace ever lived there. The town held it on a nine-hundred and ninety-nine years' lease, which assured The Circus that while the Castle might never belong to the Duke it nevertheless remained his.

The town had converted the vast galleried place into a museum, stocked with some treasures, and much rubbish bequeathed by dead townsfolk.

It stood on a bold rocky eminence of some hundred and fifty feet, the broad valley and the curving river at its base, a noble colonnaded edifice of the heavy Italian style, built in the seventeenth century. It marked the site of an earlier Norman castle, destroyed by the town in riot, wherein Queen Isabella had carried on an amour with Mortimer, Earl of March, in the fourteenth century. The place certainly seemed well adapted for this favourite diversion of history, for the rock was honeycombed with secret entrances and exits. But Mortimer went to the nest once too often. The hole in which he was trapped by the young Edward III., who disapproved of his mother's flightiness, was still religiously preserved as the most notable relic of a town rather proud of its amorous reputation.

In one sense, The Circus, thus dominated by its castle on the eastern extremity, was well named. Once in it, without a very clear conception of its topography, you went round and round. It was composed of a number of circuses, crescents and bisecting roads roaming the steep concavity. They were all named after members of the old ducal family, but the naming was designed, in peculiarly English fashion, to add confusion rather than direction to the place.

It was felt by the inhabitants, doubtless as Hereward the Wake had felt in the security of his marshes, or the old Venetians in the bewildering maze of the lagoons, that this complexity added to their seclusion, as indeed it did. You might brave the ducal gates, ignoring their ' Private ' warning, since you were calling upon the ducal tenants, but your real exclusion from the circles of the choice was soon demonstrated. You were hopelessly engulfed in

the curving, precipitous channels that deposited you **in**
circuses, which you circumnavigated in feverish search,
only to bɔ projected through a long crescent intersecting
yet another circus.

It is true, all the houses had names, but they all scorned
numbers. Their garden gates, set in high walls, forbade
intimacy with those remote dwellings behind. Stray
persons from the town wandered awe-struck along these
bosky galleries of the select. By a natural process, they
sank lower and lower through this superior world until
they were ejected at the lower gate, into the vulgar valley
filled with the rattle of trams and the smoke of mean
streets.

Sometimes they would halt, and cling pitifully to the
palisadings that surrounded the green lawns, where the
elect played tennis, walled in at the pit of that amphitheatre by rows of elms and poplars and sycamores,
scarcely screening the spaced villas. But the knowledge
of unworthiness soon drove on the intruding strangers ;
they descended slowly but surely to the gate that ejected
them from the forbidden paradise.

Cliff House, the home of Lady Neville after her son had
succeeded to the title and married, commanded a magnificent prospect of the river valley and the ranges of hills
beyond. On a fine day, from the upper drawing-room
windows, the dowager Lady Neville could see the far hill
and its wooded crest where Neville Court, her former
home, kept watch over the valley. Immediately below
her, The Circus lay out on the hillside. She was in the
centre of the curving top terrace and could look down on
the winding roads, roofs and gardens falling to the shaded
tennis lawns. To the south, this amphitheatre opened
into the flat landscape where a part of Meltonham lay
under its smoke pall.

There was something Italian about Cliff House, and it was conveniently if curiously situated. Its main entrance at the back, looked on the public road, close to the heart of the town itself. Its front, commanding the prospect of The Circus caught the southern and western sun. As a house it was peculiar. It was tall and narrow, room mounting over room, the slim staircase running through from back to front. Its kitchens belonged to an age when servants were scarcely human beings, their days confined to dungeons, their nights to attics. Modern necessity, and scarcity, had demanded the sacrifice of the back part of the house to the servants.

Thus it happened that, for the chief inhabitants, Cliff House had only a front, a tall, sunny, much-windowed face, continentalised with green folding shutters and sun-blinds. There was a small flagged terrace and a rockery, gay with mosses and flowers, which fell to a diminutive lawn that scarcely warranted the summery sound of a lawn-mower. The dining-room was on a level with this terrace and the narrow hall ; the drawing-room overran both on the first floor. This was Lady Neville's chief abode. Here she passed her days, gave her At Homes and tea parties, sewed, read and watched the sun setting over the opposite ridge of the horse-shoe crescent.

It was in this room, delicate with gilt-framed water-colours, light chintz and turquoise carpet, that she awaited Peter, her baby, as he still remained in her fond fancy. Death had violently robbed her of husband and eldest son, Death which had hovered so long in her presence without advancing, as if fully conscious that she would not trouble to elude him.

Olivia Neville was still a striking woman at sixty-five, despite twenty years of invalidism. She had gone out of the life of the world from that time when the birth of

the twins had wrecked her health with its pangs.
The needs of these young lives, as well as those of her
husband, caused her to fight desperately for a measure of
activity, but her last physical effort collapsed with the death
of Sir James in an Atlantic shipwreck. Her children
were still children to her, they were her world, complete
save for such friends as called and brought news of the
wider life they came from.

Looking at her now, as she waited, a flush of expectation in her cheeks, you would not have surmised the
invalid or the woman of her years and trials. Something
of the early beauty that Sargent had captured in his
portrait of her, still remained. There were the same
plentiful loops of hair, scarcely silvered yet. Her blue
eyes retained their vivacity, even if their sparkle was less
lustrous, and, to the envy and wonder of all, her skin and
complexion had a girlish texture and colouring that contradicted the lines left by the years.

She had no secret in this respect, save perhaps the rigid
milk diet to which she had been reduced for long years,
and the kind humorous outlook on life, translating the
zest she felt into her eyes and expression. For her mind
was still young and adventurous. People called her a
charming old lady, but she was something more than that.
Lady Neville was a vivacious old lady, if one might use
the word ' old ' of one whose heart was perennially young.
It was characteristic that she had nicknamed the sedate
Roderick ' Grandfather,' it was more characteristic that
she had a nickname of her own, an incredible nickname
save to those intimate with its fantastic origin.

Milk and fish had been her diet for years, fish to an
extent that had caused Peter, chaffingly, to declare she
was a veritable pelican. This avenue of mirth speedily
led to an amazing and endearing sobriquet. Who can

explain such things ? It is part of the exclusiveness of life that our best humour is not translatable. The richest jokes spring from personality, not situation, from the fantastic perversion of one mind intimate with the idiosyncrasies of another's. Lady Neville had a slight double chin. Peter was mirthful about it, patted it play-fully when he kissed her, attributed it with mock gravity to the consumption of much fish. It was a pelican's pouch. Thus step by fantastic step, her ridiculous son christened her. She was to him, in the intimacy of their humour, the Pelican Pouch.

To-night she would see Peter again after an interval of three years, three long years during which she had uttered no word of impatience at his long absence, conscious that youth must live its own life, that age too often inflicts its chains of affection on the young spirit.

She had been up to Peter's room. There were flowers on his dressing-table, the clock was wound up and ticking at his bedside, a hot-water bottle was in the bed, to make doubly sure that it was aired. His old bath-gown had been found by the equally excited Agnes, the house-keeper, who had once been his ' Nannie,' and his slippers taken out of the tissue paper in which they had been stored. The room awaited its long-absent owner.

The car had not come to a standstill before the door opened and the expectant Agnes beamed on the step.

" Well, Agnes," he cried, bounding up the steps into the vestibule, " here we are ! "

" Oh, Mr. Peter ! " was all she could say, confusedly obstructing the chauffeur bringing in his bag. Then, in an agitated voice—" Her ladyship's in the drawing-room, sir. She sat up for you."

" Good ! I'll go up," he replied, eagerly, and mounted the narrow staircase, bursting boyishly into the drawing-room. Lady Neville got up and went towards him, arms outstretched.

" Peter, my dear boy ! "

He put his arms about her and kissed her.

" Well, here I am again—why, you've not altered one little bit, mother ! "

He held her away from him, surveying her critically, grey hair, blue eyes, smiling at him as she returned his scrutiny.

" How brown you are, Peter—but you're no fatter," she said, returning to her old anxiety through all his boyhood.

He laughed and patted her under the chin.

" And the Pelican Pouch is the same ! "

" You silly boy !—I was hoping you'd forgotten that nonsense."

She drew him down to her side on the lounge, a trim, dignified figure from whose face the pink and white had not been banished by age. He noted her resolute beauty and was stirred to pride in her.

" Mother—you're an amazing old thing," he exclaimed, admiration in his voice. " Now tell me all about yourself, you wrote such short little letters to me."

" A boy doesn't want bothering with his mother's letters when he's travelling."

" And all those letters were really about one thing ! "

" How, Peter ? "

" The solemn precaution always to wear woollens next to the skin ! " he laughed gaily. " You silly old Pelican Pouch, as if one wanted to wear anything in that climate ! "

" Well, dear, I know how careless you are," she said. " You've seen Maud and Susie ? " she asked, changing the subject.

" Yes—poor Maud ! She seems very upset, mother.

And you ? I know you never show anything, but it was you I was thinking of all the time coming."

Her hands, holding his own in her lap, tightened and he saw tears filling her eyes.

" Poor Roderick," she said softly, " to go like that too. It seems our way, Peter. Your father, now Roddy— "

She checked her reminiscences and he saw the courageous uplifting of her head. She was a woman who never looked back or lived in the past.

" Peter, I'm so glad you're here. Maud will need you very much. There's the Bank, until Ronnie grows up it will all fall on you. Poor little Ronnie, I think that's what troubles Maud most. I know you will do all you can for them ? "

He gave a reassuring pressure to her hands.

" Of course, mother. I realise I must settle down now. I've had a good time," he said, a note of resignation in his voice, which Lady Neville detected.

" And, Peter, dear, I'm glad you're home for another reason."

She hesitated then, and he looked at her, something in her eyes causing his heart to jump.

" Mother—you're all right ? " he asked, quickly.

She did not answer him directly, and vague fears immediately filled his mind.

" Susan's not said anything ? " she asked. " But she's not had time yet," she continued, seeing he had not been told. " Now don't be alarmed. It may be nothing. They don't know yet. Susan wants Sir Malcolm Lane to see me, but I thought I'd wait until she'd spoken to you. Now dear, I'm going to bed. Peter, my dear boy, it is good to have you again ! "

He helped her up and kissed her, but the gladness of this union had faded. She saw it immediately.

" Now don't worry, dear. Perhaps it is nothing," she said.

" But mother—what's the matter, what is it ? " he asked.

She put her hand to her side, saying quietly, " It may be something—here. Now good-night, dear boy."

" No, mother, I'll take you up to your room."

She laughed, holding up an admonishing finger.

" No ! your mother's not a feeble old thing yet ! " she said, as he followed her to the door and on to the staircase. He watched her go up the stairs, gracefully, without even a supporting hand on the banister. On her landing she paused, looked over at him, and smiled.

" Good night, Peter."

" Good night, Lady Pelican Pouch ! " he responded, with mock gravity.

" You absurd child ! " she called. " You're not a bit better ! " and with a wave of the hand she was gone.

He stood for a moment, listening as she talked to Annette her maid, then he returned to the drawing-room. But he did not sit down. He was too agitated by many things. Lucia in Chioggia, Maud at Neville Court, and now here, his mother. Was there anything wrong with her ? She was not a woman to complain, hypochondria had never been her weakness. She had always spoken contemptuously of those women who inhabited hydropathic establishments and luxurious health resorts, complaining of imaginary ills while they were pampered, preying on their solicitous husbands and relations. There must be something really wrong.

Something—that was all she had said. He knew what that meant. A growth. His mind jumped to the worst. It was the scourge of age, every paper was full of the menace, its ravages baffled science. Cancer, could it be that ? But his mind, which conceived this menace, fought desperately against the idea. His mother, no, not his mother. It was too terrible to think of. Dear, lovely old creature, surely hideous things like that would not touch her? Was he becoming distraught? After all, he had been under a strain these last three days. He must keep himself sternly in hand. To-morrow he would see Susie. It was silly to torture himself like this, probably without real need.

Going to one of the windows, he pulled the heavy velvet curtains apart and raised the blind. Before him, under the clear moonlight, lay the dark amphitheatre of The Circus, a few lamps steadily burning on its terraces, or from the uncurtained windows of the houses. Below, across the valley, he saw the distant cluster of lights marking the railway sidings. Home!—Meltonham sleeping there in the darkness under the high moon. Strange, that same moon would be shining on the sea and the lagoons around Chioggia! With a start he recollected this was the final night of the Festa. The boats along the Vena would be festooned with gay lanterns, and little singing parties would be on the molo, dancing, or gliding softly in their boats on the smooth silver bosom of the lagoon.

It was nearly twelve o'clock. What was Lucia doing now, where was she, with whom? He wondered if she was happy, if she had enjoyed the Festa. His mind was back there, on the molo, along the Corso, seeing Lucia's eyes, hearing Marco's " Sì, signorino."

Then he came back to Meltonham, to the darkness of this hillside, to his home. This dreaming must end. Deliberately he drew down the blind, as though shutting out the vision. All that was ended now. He was home, he was committed to serious responsibilities, others depended upon him. He had given his promise.

Switching off the light, he went slowly up to his room.

CHAPTER XIX

I

In the following four weeks Peter Neville had little time for introspection. He was denied the opportunity of brooding over the past, either to regret or to desire it again. He was immersed in a multitude of business details. There was Roderick's Will, his estate, the cease-less conferences with his solicitors, with the agent, with his co-directors at the Bank, and also with Maud, who never allowed a day to pass without their meeting. If he neglected to go out to the Court, for which he read reproach in her eyes, or heard it in her voice over the telephone, she called at the Bank, and, once in his room, she was difficult to get rid of. Lady Neville worried Peter, because somehow she always frustrated his desperate retention of liberty. All his objections, counter-appointments, counter-acts, vanished before her forceful appeals.

She was strongly armed, of course. There was always the ghost of Roderick, or the helplessness of Ronnie, or, in a final resort, her own helplessness. Yet, if he was sure of one thing, it was that Maud was never helpless. Her sure efficiency amazed him. He encountered it at every point, in Roderick's Will, modified by codicils that seemed to have come literally from Maud, in the adminis-tration of the estate, for he discovered that the agent had merely executed her wishes, dressing them in Sir Roderick's authority. Had Roderick realised this himself? Peter was sure he had not. Nowhere could he find the pure Roderick, except in the worship of system, the methodical care of detail.

Not even in the Bank had Maud's overshadowing influence been absent. On the banking side she had truly no jurisdiction because she had no knowledge, but her strength was always betrayed in the clear recognition of her limitations. She never battered a closed door. Lady Neville had entered the Bank far more adroitly than ever she could have done through the managerial channel. She had started the welfare idea for the employees. They had a luncheon room, a sports ground, a literary club, an orchestra, and anything else that Maud's fertile brain could think of.

Thus, in an effective, indirect way Mr. Bentley, who had given Lady Neville much valued assistance in her welfare work, became chief cashier, although Sir Roderick was never certain that Bentley had been the best choice. Young Jones, Sir Roderick's secretary, he too was a protegé. He often consulted Lady Neville, as secretary of the staff tennis club, and little that Sir Roderick planned was unknown, and much that Lady Neville had desired was accepted by Sir Roderick as a sensible suggestion of young Jones. For Maud never attempted anything unreasonable. Her agents found her commands not difficult; Sir Roderick was never conscious of force or even insistence.

Peter had realised all this. Her method with him was wholly different, as also her aim was wholly different. She had worked for power hitherto, ever seeking to make the devoted Roderick the unconscious agent of her will, fostering his amiable vanity of strong-mindedness.

There was nothing she desired of Peter except himself.
Roderick's death had united her determination to consolidate her position with her dormant desire. She had never
known Peter intimately, but she knew that she had loved
him to the point of passion, from that memorable day
when Roderick had taken her down to Eights Week at
Oxford, where the dark-haired, fresh-coloured undergraduate had greeted them at the station.

His superb youthfulness, the careless grace of his manhood, had set her dreaming. He stirred her as Roderick
never had, and the power of it was the deeper for the
indifference he displayed to her disguised ardour. The
scarcely hidden disdain whipped her desire, his indifference struck her as an affront, yet made her more
subject to his magnetism. The meeting in Italy, after a
long separation, told her that instinct had not fooled her.
His appeal had grown with his own development. She
had been secretly afraid of herself during that brief
sojourn at Venice, and the wisdom of their parting had
made tolerable the agony of it. She would not wound
Roderick, for she loved him and admired him for his
poise, his surety. But her love for him was a different
thing from that she had buried in her consciousness,
where Peter held mastery. One represented the mind,
the character, the whole personality that told her she was
a fortunate woman to have found such a husband. What
was the other ?

She could discover no more than that he was the man,
the completion of her nature. He stirred her in a manner that alarmed her. Reason, custom, reserve, these
forces, undeniably sane, were swept aside when he was
present. She would have gone out into the wilderness
with him and found it paradise. His voice, the set of his
shoulders, the warmth of his hand, the fall of his hair,

they had a preposterous power with her senses, and she knew that even her eyes betrayed her, outraging her will. Susan's face had revealed that, and Peter's nervous hostility warned her. Side by side with her sure determination ran a mood of panic ; she was frightened by the forces using her, shrinking from the boldness with which she was impelled on her quest.

One Tuesday morning Peter had ushered her out of his private room, after a conference that almost brought them naked to each other's eyes. After some details connected with the probate and Ronnie's interests, they had discussed a clause of the will in which Roderick had fixed the income to be retained by her in the event of re-marriage. It was generous, revealing a progressive attitude that seemed foreign to Roderick's nature.

" Dear Roderick—that was so characteristic of him," declared Lady Neville, " —though I shall never take advantage of it."

Peter made no answer, knowing they were both aware how uncharacteristic it really was. The spirit of mischief in him would not be silenced.

" Never ? " he asked, calmly, looking up from the document on his desk. She met his gaze awkwardly.

" No—never," she reiterated, but her eyes belied her and the voice lacked resolution.

A few minutes later, after declining an invitation to lunch owing to an engagement at the Shire Club, he ushered her out to the waiting car. When Parsons entered the room, Peter was standing with his face to the window, watching the car wind round the memorial statue of the Queen, until it was lost in the vortex of traffic. That uncanny Susan was right. The poor woman was in love with him !

Should he pity her ? She had admirable qualities,

she was a remarkable woman; and beautiful. He started. If he once began to pity her he would be defeated. Maud needed no pity. He would find himself in need of it if he was not cautious. Peter looked at his watch. He had to meet Sir Malcolm Lane at two-thirty. On Susan's advice they had summoned him from London. His sister had not been at all satisfied by their mother's doctor. In consultation with her he had confessed himself baffled.

"What do you think it is, frankly?" Peter had asked him, as he cogitated. But he had obtained no answer that was definite. It might be serious, or might not. If it was the beginning of a serious formation then it would be wise to have an authoritative opinion. So they had called in Sir Malcolm Lane, who was coming down from London with Susan.

II

Three times in the space of a few minutes Peter left the silence of the drawing-room and went out on to the landing, listening for the voices in his mother's room. Not that they would tell him anything, if they had been audible, but the anxiety to learn the truth made him restless. They were holding their examination, Sir Malcolm, their own doctor and Susie, and all the time he was thinking of his poor mother. She had been so calm through these awful weeks as the menace grew nearer. At first, owing to her bright demeanour, her cheerful courage, he had disbelieved Susie's fears, raised two days after his return, but soon he found that Lady Neville was thinking of him more than herself. He threw the responsibility on Susan, who found her mother willing to see the specialist.

"After all, Peter," his mother had said, "if what

we all fear is right, I've had a good long life, I can't complain."

"What do we fear, mother? I don't think there's anything wrong—not really wrong. Just look at you! I heard you playing Chopin this morning, *con spirito*," he cried, forcing himself into cheerfulness.

Lady Neville smiled at him, calmly.

"Peter dear—it was to hide the pain."

"Mother!" He was at her side in a moment, taking her thin hand in his. This was her first confession.

"Then you've been suffering all the time?"

She ran her hand over his hair as he knelt at the side of her chair, one arm round her.

"Not much, Peter," she replied simply.

To lighten his heart he gave her chin a playful pat.

"You brave little Pelican Pouch!"

She laughed at this, and they had remained thus in silence for a few moments, heavy with thought. And even then her mind was not on herself.

"You've worried me, Peter," she said at length.

"I, mother? How?"

"You're unhappy," she responded, looking shrewdly at him.

"Now what makes you imagine that?" he cried, trying to cover his surprise with a gay denial.

"There's something on your mind, dear. I've seen you go off into a long day-dream when you've been talking. And, sometimes, you sit without saying a word."

"Poor Pelican Pouch—have I neglected you?" asked Peter, still attempting to mask his uneasiness.

"No, not that, Peter. There is something, isn't there?"

He returned her look, but he had not the courage to lie to those loving clear eyes. He turned his head aside.

" Well, you'll tell me when you want to, Peter.   I think I know what makes a young man like that," she said quietly.

That had been a week ago.   So he had not buried his feelings as he had imagined !   The image of Lucia would not be dismissed.   His mother had seen something of the struggle.   But then she was curiously clairvoyant.   As a child he had often been dismayed by the things she knew, although he had so painfully concealed them.   Susie had remarked on that.

Peter went back into the drawing-room.   He stood moodily looking down on the little lawn.   Illness of any kind mentally depressed him.   He had not the sort of courage that could endure the sight of suffering, he would rather feel pain than be asked to watch it in others whom he was unable to alleviate.

His eyes wandered over the lawn and the rockery, where the visiting gardener was transferring some lobelias from pots, then he followed the climbing of the creeper where its running tendrils wound about the string trellis on the long wall.   At that moment he heard a car coming along the road below, briefly visible as it ascended the curve ere it was lost again beyond the trees.

In that car sat Sir John Coate, his crutches propped up at his side.   The body had deserted the field, but not the brain that still dominated the enormous business he had built up.   The white-faced young student of engineering, who had dreamed dreams in Essen, was now the millionaire owner of the great works whose name was known in every continent.   If you took a train from Cape Town up into the veldt, or left Moscow for the lonely Steppes, or sought Pekin, it was in a Coate train, along Coate rails that you probably went.   He had a passion for conquest.   In the Middle Ages he would have gone crusading and have driven the Turk from his strongholds, or, for the love of adventure, he would have hired his sword to a prince, if he had not dethroned him.

The Coate tentacles were everywhere, South America, China, India, Russia and Egypt; by rails, bridges, docks or ships, the name of Coate crept in.

At sixty, while investigating a line they had built in the Argentine, Sir John was involved in an accident that robbed him of a leg. Now he would retire, they thought; but on his return the great works, eating into the green fields about Meltonham, spread forth over three hundred more acres. The less active body somehow sustained the more active mind. The old lion still had his dreams of conquest, he bent four stalwart sons to his purpose, renouncing with fury one who had fooled with music. He had written an opera. An opera! Jingling things! What was that compared with a bridge, or a great locomotive eating up the miles?

His sons groaned, his fellow directors watched with amazement. At six-thirty every morning the Coate car drew up to the gates of the works. He celebrated his seventieth birthday by opening a new workshop, gleeful as a child with a fresh toy, when he heard the rumble and clangour as it stirred into life at his bidding.

Peter knew him, from brief brusque meetings. Coates banked with them and were clients not to be disregarded. One morning he had seen Sir John, who had called at the Bank. Peter had gone out to him, as he sat in his chair.

" A bad job this, Neville," he said. " I'd have given your brother a long lease. Suppose you're putting your neck in the collar? Time you did something. Hope you're less rutted than Sir Roderick—can't run a business on tradition these days! There's only one way now. It's the age of amalgamation. That's where we've beaten 'em. Grow, buy, manufacture wholesale, sell retail, cut out the middleman, no man can stand up to a machine like that ! Banks are going the same way. The family idea's dead, Neville ! Dig yourself in with a big concern, or you'll be starved out. Sir Roderick couldn't see it. Thought the name of Neville was enough. 'Tisn't ! I'll have to change if you don't. Coates wants a universal bank, your method of clearing cheques through other banks is a nuisance. You want branches like Coate's everywhere ! Think about it. Come up and see me sometime. Morning, Neville ! "

He was gone, having jerked out his advice. There was a threat in it too, as well as sense. He was right. The day of the family bank was dead. Amalgamation was the new law of survival. Peter went back to his room vaguely troubled. Sir John had only given rough voice to his own belief.

The scream of the car through its crescendo of gears, as it ascended the hill, made Peter think of the masterful old fellow. Lady Neville had something of that unbowed spirit, in a very different nature.

The sudden opening of the door broke his reverie. It was Sir Malcolm Lane, followed by their own doctor and Susan. Sir Malcolm advanced to the centre of the room, confidence in every line of his elegant figure.

With a strong forefinger and thumb, he took a pair of pince-nez off his nose, holding them poised in front of him as he spoke.

" Now, Mr. Neville, your vigil's at an end," he said, smiling, as he pulled out his watch. " Will you be so good as to have the car ready, I have ten minutes before my train to town ? "

" It's waiting for you now, Sir Malcolm."

" Thank you."

The great surgeon sat down, as though time and trains

were ordered for his needs. There was no visible haste. He displayed the perfect mastery of the moment.

"You will be disappointed when I say we have learned little. There is a growth, but of its nature we can only surmise. The symptoms are too primary yet, which is fortunate if an operation, an experimental operation, Mr. Neville—is decided upon."

"What might it be?" asked Peter, breaking the subsequent silence.

Sir Malcolm displayed his hands.

"We can only surmise. Cancer perhaps, or a tumour, more probably the latter."

"Would an operation cure her?"

Sir Malcolm smiled, as though a boy were questioning his schoolmaster.

"That is the question always addressed to us. We can promise nothing, but we can hope, reasonably. How old is Lady Neville?"

"Sixty-five."

"H'm. There is a great risk I think this is a matter for Lady Neville to decide. She may not value life so greatly, or she may be tenacious."

"And if she decides against—what does it mean?"

The surgeon glanced round at Susan and the doctor.

"Miss Neville can explain. It would mean a period, long or short, of considerable suffering, until the climax. I think you must ask Lady Neville to decide."

He rose and buttoned his morning coat, replacing the pince-nez, indicating the discussion was ended.

"I will show you down, Sir Malcolm," said Peter, opening the door. The surgeon shook hands with Susan and the doctor.

"If my mother decides—you would operate, Sir Malcolm?" asked Peter, following him down the stairs.

" If you wish, Mr. Neville."

" Thank you," said Peter, pausing in the hall, in an embarrassing moment while he took out some notes. It seemed a horrible mercenary termination of a solemn affair.

" Your fee, Sir Malcolm, thank you."

The famous surgeon took the notes, counted them deliberately, and placed them in a wallet in his breast pocket. So far as he was concerned Peter had been unnecessarily sensitive. But then, it was a daily occurrence in the life of this man.

The house-keeper handed him his hat, gloves and attaché case. With a final ' Good afternoon,' Sir Malcolm had passed through the door to the waiting car.

In the drawing-room Peter found Susan and the doctor, in animated conversation. Susan saw his solemn face as he entered.

" Peter, you look as if you had already buried mother ! " she cried ; " cheer up, you should show a little confidence in us."

Her cheerful voice annoyed Peter. Was this just ' a case ' to her ?

" It's a horrible thing—poor mother ! " he exclaimed. " Who's going to break the news ? "

" Oh, she knows—she made Sir Malcolm tell her every symptom, as well as a full explanation of the operation. He didn't like it, but she made him talk."

" Lady Neville is a most extraordinary woman," said the doctor. He rubbed his chubby hands together, and then scratched his bald head. " I have the greatest faith in her pulling through, if she wished. She's a very remarkable woman. There, but I must go now ! You'll want to talk it over. We must let Sir Malcolm know as soon as possible."

When he had left them, Peter stood moodily by the window. Susan rang for tea.

" Mother'll be down in a minute. We'll have tea, Peter."

" Poor old Pelican Pouch ! " was all he said, flinging himself down in a chair.

Susan stood over him, blew out a cloud of smoke from her cigarette, and then scolded.

" Peter, you miserable pessimist, I'll not allow you to go on like this ! It's bad for the patient, and it's so useless."

Her brother's eyes fixed on her for a moment.

" Susan—I don't think you're a woman at all ! " he cried indignantly.

" I'm not, I'm a doctor for the present. You'll look cheerful when mother comes in, or you'll be sent out without any tea ! "

The door opened as she spoke, and Lady Neville halted on the threshold.

" Have the wise men gone—may I come in ? " she asked, a smile hovering over her lovely features.

Peter sprang up and brought her across the room to her chair, where he squatted on a footstool.

The old lady arranged her skirt with great care and surveyed the tea tray as the maid brought it in. Only when the door closed again, did she speak of the thing in all their minds.

" Well, children, what's it to be ? " she asked, calmly.

" Mother—Sir Malcolm says it's for you to decide," answered Susan.

" We don't want you to suffer, mother—that's all that matters. Sir Malcolm doesn't think the operation would mean— " said Peter.

Lady Neville's hand ran over her son's, and she gave him a mother's smile as he looked up at her.

" My dear, suffering doesn't matter much, at sixty-five," she said. " It is the young who suffer most, they fight so hard for life. I shall have the operation. If it fails, perhaps I shan't know anything about it and it will be a happy release. The other way's too long, I should be such an unpleasant nuisance to everybody."

" Mother, you mustn't think we— " began Peter.

" There's nothing, mother, we wouldn't—" started Susan simultaneously.

Lady Neville checked them both.

" Now, dear, let's have tea, and we'll not talk about it— again."

Her hand lifted the silver teapot, while Susan watched her through a mist that gathered.

CHAPTER XX

THE room that had been Sir Roderick's at the bank over-looked the open Market-place. It had a clear view, save for one obstruction, which always irritated and annoyed him—not that he had ever lacked loyalty. No one who saw him stiffen and look severe whenever the National Anthem was played, could doubt that. His annoyance was directed against the civic authorities and the sculptor, who had combined to obstruct his view with the memorial of the Great Queen. For there, solid and immense, the old queen looked out across the Market-place, her capacious back resolutely turned on Sir Roderick, her still more capacious front dominating the busy scene.

Before her august eyes, in a brilliant line, bordering the open market, ran the awning-covered stalls of the fruiterers. Her Majesty, year after year, contemplated the spoils of Empire, whether they were juicy Maltese oranges, best Canadian Pippins, or ripe bananas from the Barbadoes. In due season other fruits, pineapples and pomegranates, added to the brilliant symbols of Empire. Sir Roderick was not so much distressed by Her Majesty's constant contemplation of the fruit stalls, as by the incessant insults from the congregation of ice-cream barrows and chip-potato stalls that perpetuated such gross *lèse majesté*. For they crowded up to the very

287

railings with which a cautious sculptor had protected the plinth of his work.

The citizens had shown their devotion to Her Majesty's memory by a scene of tremendous animation at the unveiling ceremony, performed by the Duke of Bowater. Sir Roderick had been a boy then, but he had not forgotten the occasion, rendered memorable by his own presence with his father in the select enclosure, where the local notabilities witnessed the ceremony. Thus guarded and exalted amid the perspiring mob, to the sound of cheers from thousands of throats, to the concerted braying of bands broadcasting the never hilarious Anthem, they had seen the Duke of Bowater pull the cord which denuded the statue of its shroud. As it fell, a hush descended over the assembly; it may have been the hush of awe, of reverence, of loyalty, but most probably, as those who analysed their feelings afterwards thought, it was the hush of dismay.

She had been a wonderful queen, had lived and reigned an obstinate time. She had given a name to her era and snubs to her ministers, but was it fair to perpetuate her memory so—robustly? Even the sun cast a malicious glance, emphasising the imperial rotundity, and the laws of perspective aggravated the aspect of that crowned head fading heavenwards, and almost shut off from loyal eyes by the tremendous central girth ballooning the unfortunate lady.

But the lustre of the occasion could not be diminished by any suspicion of criticism. The Duke pronounced it a noble work to commemorate a noble life. The Mayor, perspiring beneath his triangular hat and gilded with his chain of office, lamented Her Majesty, in terms that suggested a heavy personal loss, which the Sheriff, in a similar hat, claimed to share, judging from the aggressive

'Hear! Hears' that punctuated His Worship's excursion
in simulated grief. And when the Mayor had thanked
the Duke, and the Duke had thanked the Mayor, and his
gallant friend, Colonel Brent, who had seconded the vote,
and the school-children had sung their songs, the Veterans
performed their salute, and the Press photographers taken
their shots, all the notabilities adjourned to the civic tea
in the Town Hall.

Three days later, the first ice-cream vendor took up
his location by the railings.

A week later, Her Majesty was surrounded by a cooling
fringe. A spell of cold weather produced another
encroachment. The fried fish and chip stalls brought
their vinegary aroma within range of the royal nostrils.
A fortnight later, a " Loyal Citizen " wrote to the *Meltonham Times*, pointing out that the Wednesday and
Saturday cheap china and pot markets were still held on
their usual site—where the authorities had located the
statue ! But the Queen resolutely turned her back on the
medley of pot-tapping, ice-cream vending, and fish and
chip frying, and steadily contemplated the orange and
banana stalls.

Sir Roderick could also turn his back on the vulgar
litter, but not the windows of his room. He grumbled
to the Mayor, to the Duke, but these gentlemen, having
enjoyed the remote occasion, had no further interest in
the Queen, moreover, the pot market would not be put
out by a statue, which in a way was an enlarged signboard
of their trade.

The head clerk hinted to Peter that it had worn Sir
Roderick's nerves. It certainly did not wear Peter's, to
him the busy area was a source of continuous interest.
Often when Parsons entered the room he observed that the
Managing Director was not at his desk but staring out of

the window. For Peter the scene was variegated with life. Hucksters took up their pitches from time to time, haranguing the crowd of wastrels into buying watches, boots, jewels or pills. The knowledge of crowd psychology displayed by them was amazing.

Also, he derived amusement from the hypnotism of school-boys by the ice-cream barrows. It was to their credit that they were clean, gay concerns, with their gaudily painted sides, often depicting Neapolitan scenes, their bright-striped awnings, and the dark-faced Italian vendors, immaculate with large white sleeves. They were all members of one family, he learned, who sat behind these ice-barrels, shallow glasses and piles of wafer and cornet biscuits. The name Lazzarini on the barrows brought back a memory of Italy, and an old lady, evidently the mother, who occasionally presided, with vivid kerchief on her head, and heavy gold earrings, reminded him of Mother Pappini.

Watching her one morning, while his mind was running upon Sir John Coate's talk about amalgamation, he was suddenly aware of another figure that had joined the old woman. For a few seconds his heart bounded, for the head, profile, dark hair and crimson mouth, as the girl turned to speak, created the illusion of Lucia ! It was a momentary illusion, which faded when the Italian girl revealed her full face, as she laughed and chatted with the old woman, probably her mother. But the disturbance created within him did not subside. Lucia ! Lucia in Meltonham ! Lucia near him ! His mind played with the idea, finding pleasure in the absurdity.

" Excuse me, sir,"—it was Parson's voice breaking in on him again. " Will you sign this credit note for Mr. Walsh ? "

Peter walked to his desk, and sat down to sign the slip Parsons had placed on his desk.

" *Banca Commerciale Italiana* " he read aloud, on the order. The note of surprise at this coincidence of ideas sounded in his voice.

" Yes, sir," commented Parsons, " Mr. Walsh says he leaves for Venice to-morrow."

" Venice ! " Peter almost shouted the word. Parsons hid his surprise at the Chief's exclamation. The latter, conscious of aroused interest, signed the draft in silence and then passed it to his clerk, saying lightly—

" Lucky Mr. Walsh ! Venice is a delightful place, Parsons."

" I believe so, sir," agreed the urbane Parsons, withdrawing.

Alone Peter sat on at his desk. The girl at the barrow —Venice—Chioggia—Lucia. And here he was, imprisoned in Neville's Bank, Meltonham, brought back to bondage by a trick of Fate. Life was a queer thing. He looked down at his well-creased, striped trousers, at the black morning coat, at his white cuffs, correctly emerging. On that hook hung his tall hat, symbol of the Chief of Neville's Bank. His grandfather had worn such a hat, his father and Sir Roderick too. Now he wore one, as would his son also—his son ! No, that was wrong, young Sir Ronald inherited—the hat and the business. He was only a trustee in Ronnie's interest. Eighteen years or more would pass before Ronnie could inherit the Bank and the hat. Eighteen years, here, in Meltonham,—was that his sentence ?

His son ! What an extraordinary idea that seemed ! And yet why was it ? It was the way of humanity, and unhappiness dogged all who frustrated its design. Marriage, of course. Well, that was a thing of youth. It was a graceful, spontaneous thing in youth, an idyll. Only yesterday he had presented one of the young clerks with a wedding present from his colleagues. The lad had coloured, a frank, clean-looking, bright-eyed lad with all the urge of manhood in him. He would have sturdy little beggars to carry on his youth as it lapsed.

Lucia ! What dark eyes his children would have ! And if they had Lucia's laugh ! The Italian children were so marvellous ; perhaps theirs would inherit that lustrous vivacity from their mother.

The clock on his mantelpiece began to strike. It roused him from his reveries. Good Heavens ! What nonsense was he thinking ? Nonsense ? Yes, nonsense !

The faint chime ceased. Twelve. Noon in Italy ! He would be on the Littorale now, with Marco, having bathed, and lying naked in the sun while they dried. Space, air, sunshine, the blue sky and the lazy sea, surely that was living ! And those velvet nights when the earth seemed to sigh in its happy languor, when the air was acute with voices or hidden music, or Lucia singing as on that evening in the Palazzo Delfino.

He would write to her. He had been silent for a month now, and what might she be thinking ? Crossing to the door, he turned the key, to prevent interruption. Then, seated at his desk, he took up a pen. But the words would not come, or rather, the proper form of them. For a long time he put nothing to paper ; then, quickly, the sentences gathered as he began to tell her of his life in Meltonham.

CHAPTER XXI

THE first Sunday in August was a perfect day. It made the English summer a reality instead of a myth obstinately believed in by a race of optimists. It was hot, so hot that Grieve erected the sun umbrella on the front lawn at Neville Court. A peacock reposed on the lowest branch of the copper beech tree, and not a bird-note broke the deep hush into which Nature had fallen. All the ground-floor windows of Neville Court were thrown open, revealing the backs of Chippendale chairs, small tables with pot-pourri bowls, and a large Ming vase. The creeper which covered the whole front of the house was just beginning to turn golden, but the blue wistaria running along the terrace balustrade was radiant, challenging the blue depths of the cloudless sky.

Four o'clock struck lazily in the church tower, hidden behind the row of elms ; a disturbed peacock, in the region of the walled kitchen-garden, screeched with annoyance. It was answered by its friend in the shady copper beech, who stretched himself, spreading fanwise a gorgeous tail, that for once was matched by the flowers and borders of the sunny garden set in an elaborate design of lozenges, diamonds and circles. As the last echo of the hour died, Lady Neville emerged from the house, crossed the terrace, descended the steps and walked leisurely on the lawn to the wicker chair and cushions prepared by Grieve. The peacock watched her with a glittering eye, as a rival not to be taken lightly.

Grief and convention had reduced Lady Neville's customary lustre. She was a nocturne in black and white, that, with skilful touches of design, wherewith a Parisian modiste had made bereavement alluring, was not wholly at a disadvantage with her customary symphony in blue, her favourite and safest shade.

This afternoon she had skilfully relieved her attire with vivid notes of colour. Under one arm she carried an additional flamingo cushion that blazed in the sunlight. Over her head she bore a quite unnecessary parasol, souvenir of a spring at San Sebastian, in which the gay riot of Spanish life had been expressed. It seemed to have soaked up the radiance of those vine-clad hills, of rocky promontories gleaming through sunlit spray, of the rich gloom of clustered palms, of extravagant undergrowths of heliotrope and syringa blossom, of crescents of golden sand and reaches of ultramarine sky. Shut, and resting at her side, she knew the exact effect of its shrunken splendour against her sombre dress, of the parrot's head handle, stained and carved. Flamingo cushion and Spanish parasol, backed by the cool green of a beech-shaded lawn, herself cooler than all, that was a picture only August and impeccable taste could compose.

And to see her there, reclining on her cushions, a glow of gentle light about her under that garden sunshade, a jade-green novel between her white hands, with slim silken ankles, and glossily clad feet that seemed never to have known a creasing burden, Lady Neville was a creation, whether of nature or art, or both, that commanded admiration.

One feminine connoisseur had described her as ' sulphurous ' for he had alluded to her eyes, with their enormous pupils and the penumbra under the long lashes that gave them such mysterious depth. It was not sufficient to call her a beautiful woman ; she was more, she was as the iris compared with the lily, for she made simplicity appear sickly. There was an elaboration about her that stealthily fascinated.

Her reading was interrupted by a child's shout of joy as Ronnie, clad in a white sailor suit, outpaced his nursemaid in a scamper across the lawn. He had finished his afternoon's walk, which had included feeding the donkey in the paddock, and was en route for the nursery, a domain of white paint and fairy-tale frescoes, when he discovered his mother.

Lady Neville always regarded it as a testimony to her maternal character that the child preferred her to Nannie. She was no stranger to Ronnie or the nursery ; it was part of her order of things that Ronnie occupied the centre, and into that order came Peter. He represented masculine control, so essential to a boy's welfare, and the ultimate heritage of the Bank.

" For a few minutes, Ronnie—until Uncle Peter comes," she assented, laying aside her book, and dismissing the nursemaid.

The importance of Uncle Peter was emphasised by the cakestand carried out by Grieve, with its tiers of delectable things. Sir Ronald Neville would, at that moment, have bartered his heritage for the coloured miscellany of the first shelf.

" I don't think I'll wait any longer, Grieve. Mr. Neville may be unable to come," said Lady Neville. But with the appearance of the teapot came Peter, through the hall door, down the steps towards his sister-in-law.

" Forgive me, Maud. Phew ! this is a wonderful day ! " he cried, fanning himself with his straw hat before he deposited it under the wicker chair. " Ah—and how's Master Ronnie ? Won't you come and say ' How do you do ' to your poor old uncle ? "

Lady Neville laughed, giving her parasol a shake, much as the peacock ruffled his tail.

" Old ! Peter you make me nervous for myself ! Now doesn't this compensate for your beloved Italy ? "

" Almost," he agreed, taking Ronnie between his knees and slapping the child's legs. She noticed the perfect confidence they had in each other. It stirred her.

" It's too hot to have Ronnie clambering over you." She leaned forward and tinkled the bell on the table.

" No, Maud, let him stay."

" Please, mummie ! "

" No, dear, your tea is ready," she replied, and as Grieve appeared half across the lawn—" Let Grieve take you to Nannie, darling."

Tears welled up in the child's eyes, which looked upon the coveted cakestand. Peter saw and understood.

" Grieve shan't have you, shall he, old chap ? Let's ask mummie if you can have that big red cake before you go."

Lady Neville smiled indulgently.

" Very well, then you must go like a good boy, Ronnie."

The cake was seized and Peter swung him up, one leg over each shoulder, the free hand buried in his hair.

" Shall I take you ? " he asked the child.

" Right round the lawn ! " came the command.

The disregarded Grieve smiled at them as they set off. But the service did not end at the hall door. There was an imperative order to mount the stairs, which the willing horse obeyed.

Ere the complaisant uncle re-appeared, flushed of face, Lady Neville indulged in a day-dream. How nice it was to have a man about the house ! He got on so well with the child. She derived pleasure, too, from his well-groomed appearance, from his young strength. Ronnie needed a father, she mused ; ignoring her own need.

" Really, Peter, you'd spoil the child if you were together for long ! " was what she said when he returned. " One lump or two ? "

" Three ! I've a tremendous thirst after those stairs."

" Shall we talk business now, or after ? " she asked, when her questions about his mother were answered.

" Oh now, if you like—what do you think of the idea ? "

" Of amalgamation ? I don't know what to think. If it will be best for us all, for Ronnie, then I suppose it must be done, but I know nothing about such things."

She arched her shoulders—charming white shoulders they were—to emphasise her pitiful helplessness. What a cool fascinating picture she made, with her dark restless eyes and pale flawless features. He had often wondered about her coiffure, those alluring rings of hair that half-hid her ears, and crowned her brow. Was that a natural or assisted beauty she possessed ?

It was difficult to know, with Maud, where Nature ended and conscious art began. She did not trouble to hide the carmine on her lips, for she knew well enough her eyes and hair warranted that assumption of artifice. All her curves were Aubrey Beardsley curves, he noticed ; her finger nails, for instance, filberted and clipped to white points.

" —such things," she sighed again, giving her parasol a twist. Its gay flutter aroused him abruptly. He looked away.

"That's not what they think at the Bank, Maud—they've a tremendous admiration of your business instinct."

" Yes ?—it's nice to know one's admired for something ! "

" I think it would be best for us all," he continued.
" Old Coate's a far-sighted fellow, he sees the trend of
things. There's another aspect too. We should not be
so tied."

" Tied ? " Her voice took up the word with some
surprise.

" You see, it will be some years before Ronnie is of an
age to take it over—if he wants to."

" But he must, there's always been a Neville at the
Bank."

" Yes, but as old Coate says, that sort of thing counts
for nothing now. The personal element's at a discount
with these big organisations."

Lady Neville could not, would not see it. Neville's
stood for security, it was the basis of all trust in the Bank.
Then, with a note of impatience, she suddenly uncovered
the source of her opposition.

" I suppose you don't want to be tied ! " she suggested,
shaking herself slightly.

" Well, not altogether, though— " he began, apologetically.

" You want to go back to Italy ! " she continued,
petulantly.

" No—not at present, I— "

" We shall have to manage, Ronnie and I, in the hands
of solicitors."

He became alarmed at her mounting opposition, she
seemed hurt.

" I had no idea, Maud, you felt like this about the
amalgamation. Of course, if you don't want it, we'll
drop the idea."

It was a weak concession, he knew it was weak. He
should have stuck resolutely to his recommendation. But
there, she was a woman, his brother's widow, with a child.

" Oh, the amalgamation may be all for the best," she cried; " I don't oppose it. I know nothing about it. Only— "

She broke off, and played with the simple string of pearls lying on her bosom. She saw the surprise her contrariness evoked, and suddenly rose to her feet, the parasol opening over her with a click, hiding her face.

" Shall we walk round the garden ? " she asked.

But she could not play with him like that.

" Yes," he answered, " and we can continue our talk."

" Is there anything more to be said ? "

It was asked archly, but there was a sting intended, which he ignored.

" You didn't finish your sentence just now. You said ' Only '—only what ? " he insisted.

" Well, only that I was disappointed."

" In what way ? " he pursued. He knew well enough, but he was not going to let her embarrass him without retaliation. She did not answer at once, but studied a rose tree in late bloom.

" I thought I should have you near me. Perhaps I'm too anxious about Ronnie. If he had been a daughter it wouldn't have mattered so much. A boy without a father loses more, especially an only boy. You get on so well with Ronnie. Let's go through into the Avenue, it will be cool there."

He bent to unlatch the small iron gate that led into the woodland crowning the hill. The latch was rusty and he had to stoop to force it. At last it gave to his repeated pulling, and in the act his wallet fell out from an inside pocket, scattering half-a-dozen envelopes on the grass. Peter picked them up.

" Is that the lot ? " she asked, beyond the gate.

He halted, with the retrieved letters in his hand, and surveyed the ground.

" I think so," he said, coming through the gate.

Lady Neville lowered her parasol in the shade of the elm-avenue but her face was flushed. The postmark on the outside envelope in his hand had been *Chioggia-Venezia*. It might be an hotel bill. It might not. It might be anything. All she said was—

" How beautifully soft this turf is ! "

He looked at her, a little curious at this comment, and the sight of her commanding graceful carriage aroused a companion thought. How perfectly this setting suited her ! Old Roderick had not blundered. She would wear so well. Age gave more than it took from an admirable woman like Maud.

At this moment there was a sudden stiffening of her swan-like figure. She raised her head and drew back the arch of her neck, alertly offensive. Her whole demeanour was of one suffering an affront.

" What insolence ! " she exclaimed, in a cold voice.

The cause of her annoyance was a youth and girl at the far end of the glade. The dappled sunlight found them through the branches, as they lay almost buried in the bracken which they had crushed. This end of the wood was strictly private, the other end was thrown open to the public, whose festive noise sometimes penetrated as far as the grounds.

Sir Roderick had always disapproved of this liberty allowed " the masses," and his indignation rightly rose high after a public holiday, with its legacy of paper bags, bottles and cigarette ends. But his grandfather and father had permitted this vandalism. To stop it now would raise an outcry, and ridiculous letters in the local Press. So he had contented himself with building higher fences around the more private domain. Roderick's memory added a little to Maud's indignation at these trespassers. But when she had exclaimed " What insolence ! " it had not been wholly an observation of anger. It might have been disgust, or surprise.

That hatless youth, tousled-headed, with chestnut hair clouding his brow, had just kissed the girl. He was in the act of raising his face, and laughing half-insolently, half-shyly, with a gleam in his dark eyes and on the white small teeth, when Maud's cold eyes had detected the lovers. The girl, an apple-cheeked lass of the village, with a large rose pinned to her ample bosom, had taken off her hat, and lay supine in happy abandonment to her lover's caresses. There was nothing clumsy or incongruous in the picture they made in that sylvan scene. The healthy lad and the buxom girl on that summer evening appeared a perfectly natural sight in the landscape.

At their approach the lad merely stared at them, with the studious unconcern of a young colt looking over a fence at harmless mortals. The girl showed her embarrassment by turning her head to one side, revealing only a white neck and a pink ear under the folds of her black hair. The lad did not even remove his arm around her, on which he now raised himself as he lay at her side.

" Go and speak to them, Peter," cried Maud, averting her eyes. " They have no business in here ! "

A smile broke across Peter's face. He watched the lovers for a moment, and the lad in the bracken, misinterpreting its cause, smiled back confidently.

" They're doing no harm," replied Peter, and he caught a flash of Maud's luminous eyes as she turned to him in another outburst.

" I won't have these bacchanalia in the woods ! They're trespassing, too ! "

He laughed aloud this time. They were almost on a level with the culprits, the boy gazing into the embarrassed girl's face in amused unconcern.

" Bacchanalia ! Now, I think it's rather delightful ! There's something splendid in those young things, I like to see a fine lad kissing his girl. It's youth, Maud ! "

" It's disgusting ! " she retorted, with a tilt of her head.

He gave a deep ringing laugh this time. In her annoyance she would have liked to strike him ; as it was, she contented herself with a hard stare. But he was not to be shaken, he caught and challenged her look, until she was compelled to turn her head. A low laugh escaped her.

" Really, Peter, you are too absurd ! " she cried.

" Because I'm human ? "

They had passed the lovers, and turned into a side path. The lad's head had disappeared in the bracken.

" That's what I've often wondered," she queried— the illogical turn of the conversation caught him, and the puzzled expression of his eyes caused her to add " —if ever you are human, like that."

" What ? In wanting to kiss a pretty girl ? Of course I am ! "

It was her turn to laugh now, provokingly, he thought, as though she disbelieved him.

" So publicly ? " she cried, banteringly.

" Dash it, no ! A fellow— "

" Only in Italy, I suppose," she added, swiftly, her keen eyes watching the effect. He had coloured a little at her arch look, and she knew she had never loved him so much as in that moment of masculine disadvantage.

They had come out of the wood and were in sight of Neville Court again. Peter opened a wicket gate.

" You mustn't let your imagination run away with you, Maud," he said, somewhat severely.

" You're angry," she protested, her eyes dancing before his. " How illogical you men are ! When I'm angry with those people in my wood, you laugh at me, and when I suggest you express yourself similarly in Italy, you're annoyed. It was you who defended them ! "

She dropped her parasol then, and watched him pick it up. His mouth quivered as he restored it to her, and for a wild second she thought he was going to kiss her violently. She would have liked him to be violent, although she would have been very indignant afterwards. But the fateful moment passed, and with it, his emotion. There was defiance in his eyes as he encountered hers.

The first dinner-bell sounded across the lawns.

" We've timed it nicely," she commented, after the long pause.

" If you'll excuse me, I won't stay long after dinner. It's our last evening at home," he said, alluding to his mother's departure to the nursing home on the morrow.

" Of course, I quite understand," she replied.

They reached the house in silence, and while Lady Neville went to dress, Peter smoked a cigarette on the terrace. He felt like a man reprieved. But he resolved not to put his head into the lion's mouth too often.

He was waiting for Lady Neville in the library when she came down. Peter realised again, on her appearance, that she never dispensed with the asset of surprise. Mourning confined her to black, but she happened to be one of those women who can make a string of pearls rival the whole language of colour.

As she swept towards him, apologising for having kept him waiting, she gleamed, even as a pool is the brighter for its setting in the dark hills. Her long white arms, with those curiously Latin fingers, had a beauty so chaste, and yet so provocative to the sense of touch, that he understood how the legend of a woman's beauty may live founded on a detail. There were Duse's hands—Duse, born in a train midway 'twixt Chioggia and Venice, that had stirred D'Annunzio to ecstasy and creation, and had captured, with his adoration, that of Europe. The world had flocked to its theatres to see those hands.

Peter felt Maud's arms had a similar genius in their cool sinuous grace. As she seated herself at the table, how statuesquely they rose from the dark mahogany and the silver, so that while he was conscious of Maud mentally he was even more conscious of her physically. If Circe had beckoned him as she sat at her regal table, it would have been with such arms, ere he had been transmuted to the animal evoked in him. Yet there was nothing in Maud's demeanour, certainly nothing deliberate, that justified him in this emotion. Why was it she affected him so, whereas Lucia, of a beauty more dominant, made no such appeal to the self he mistrusted?

Over dessert she began to banter him about his life at Chioggia.

" I wonder how many broken hearts you left there," she laughed, a provoking light in her eyes.

He looked her frankly in the face.

" I suppose you think man's vanity imagines such chaos after his departure ? " he said, lightly. " I'm sure, Maud, you've been—are— " he emphasised, " —far more destructive than ever I was."

" Are ! What a flatterer you are ! "

" Do you feel flattered ? " he asked, regarding her without embarrassment.

He caught her then, and she was angry with herself at being naïve. She dropped her napkin aside and rose.

" Shall we have coffee on the terrace ? "

" If you'll excuse me, I'd rather go—the Pelican Pouch

will be waiting for me," he replied, with a smile, following her into the hall.

She stood on the steps, watching him get into his car. Why hadn't she let him forget himself that moment in the wood ; a movement, a look and he would have crushed her in his arms. Impossible, of course. Wasn't she a widow, a very new widow ? Had the recent strain unbalanced her ? No ! It had left her free to feel, to know all she always wanted, always stifled. It was folly to live in this artificial way, to pretend so much, to fence with words and looks.

She saw his hands on the steering wheel, brown masculine hands. If they held her ! She saw the forward tilt of his head, as he bent to switch on the motor. How she knew and loved that poise, since first she had seen him that far day at Oxford, as he closed their carriage door on the platform.

" Peter ! " she cried, in a stifled voice.

He thought he heard her call, above the opening throb of the engine, and looked up at her. She stood, one hand pressed to her bosom as it clenched a handkerchief. There was an extraordinary expression on her face, tense under some strain of thought or feeling.

" Maud—what's the— " he began, but she broke in upon him.

" Ronnie—when shall I tell Ronnie you'll be here ? " she asked, desperately, he thought. " He's always wanting you," she added, weakly.

" Ronnie ? Oh, perhaps Wednesday, Maud. I'll ring you up. Give him my love. Goodbye ! "

He let in the clutch, there was a crunch of gravel.

" Goodbye," she called, waited a minute until the car turned out at the gates, and then went in.

Coffee was waiting for her on the terrace, but she did

not go out to it at once. She went up to her boudoir, but when she had closed the door she stood in the centre of the room. What had she come there for ? The reflection in the mirror looked at her, impersonally she felt, as if surprised at this strange creature, standing so purposeless in the room.

Crossing to her desk, she idly turned over some old envelopes. The postmarks were not *Chioggia-Venezia*. A child on a rocking horse watched her out of a silver frame. She moved abruptly across the room, out on to the landing and opened another door at the end of the corridor. Stepping swiftly and silently in, she paused for a moment in the bright day-room of the nursery, then pushed open a door half ajar.

Everything in the child's bedroom seemed white, except the cover on the bed, gay with animals marching into the Ark. She bent over the bed. Ronnie was fast asleep on his side, one small hand over the coverlet, from which a yellow toy gosling had been released. Stooping, she kissed the soft hair of her son, and watched him a few moments, meditatively. There was a quiet step behind her, and Lady Neville turned to find the nurse had entered.

" He's sound asleep, Nannie," she whispered.

" Yes, my lady," smiled the young woman, hiding her observation of the tears in the other's eyes.

" Good-night, Nannie."

" Good-night, my lady."

The wondering nurse watched her glide out of the room.

In the corridor again, Lady Neville halted. A wild medley surged through her brain. She hurried on towards the staircase. How poor Roderick had loved his son ! His son ! Yes, his, as much as hers. What had she been thinking of, what folly had she been near to committing? Roderick's son's mother, Roderick's widow, scarcely two months yet! And this evening she had forgotten all but herself and Peter.

Peter! Standing there on the landing, hearing the sunset twitter of the birds outside, the ticking of the hall clock below, she tried to think she hated Peter, who made her such a traitor to memory, to decency.

Grieve, ascending to close the drawing-room shutters, drew aside to let his mistress pass, and as she went by he wondered at the pallor of her face, the firmness of her expression. Poor Lady Neville. This was a large lonely place to live in.

CHAPTER XXII

A SOMEWHAT agitated young man walked into the drawing-room at Cliff House, where his mother sat at a small table, under the light diffused from the pendent alabaster bowl. A small mahogany workbox, inlaid with ivory, once fashionable with our grandmothers, was open on the table, and around it lay numerous papers, photographs and queer old trinkets over which the dowager Lady Neville's hands hovered. She lay on a long couch, propped up with pillows, but no other sign of her illness was apparent. Her hair showed no lessening of a desire to look well, her complexion still retained its marvellous fresh colouring, so that those who saw her for the first time might reasonably have mistaken her for a woman in high health.

There was a brightness in her eye as she looked up on her son's entrance, and her delicate beauty, combined with the knowledge of what awaited her in the next few days, brought a surge of pity into the young man's heart.

" And how's Maud ? " she asked. " Did you tell her she was to bring Ronnie as soon as possible—after ? "

He bent over her, patted the pelican pouch playfully, and kissed her brow, before he sat down at her side.

" I know you'll never trust me to deliver a message, will you ? " he laughed, lifting one of her pillows. " But I really did remember this time, Lady Pelican Pouch.

They'll come and see you as soon as visitors are permitted."

" Do you know what I thought a few minutes ago ? "

There was an amused twinkle in her eye as she spoke.

" I thought it would be very economical of me to go now."

" My darling mother, whatever do you mean ? "

" Well, you see, you're all in mourning in readiness ! "

He caught her hand and pressed it. Two young lovers they might have been, so light was the spirit of joy between them.

" You're a wicked old Pelican Pouch to think such things. Now whatever have you got spread out here ? " he asked, surveying the littered table.

Her hands touched them lightly.

" Not much, but I want to tell you about them. First, those are the keys to my secretaire. You know all that's in there. But this is really my toy-box, and you'll see what a sentimental old thing you have for a mother."

Her thin fingers unwrapped a tissue covering, revealing a gold locket and chain, of old-fashioned design.

" This belonged to your great-grandmother who was Mistress of the Robes to poor Queen Caroline."

" And who was she, mother ? " he asked, taking the locket and chain.

Lady Neville raised her hands in mock horror.

" Peter—were you never taught history at school ? You must have heard of the famous trial ? "

" No ! " he laughed—" but then, we were always trying Queens—there's Mary Queen of Scots, Lady Jane Grey—"

" Peter, you're impossible ! Open the locket."

He inserted his thumb nail, and after some pressure it opened. Inside, set in ovals of twisted gold thread, with small satin mounts, were two faded coloured photographs. One was of a young lady, bound up in a very tight black bodice with a high collar. Her abundant hair, drawn severely from the brow, towered in a long diminishing coil on the summit of her head. The young gentleman opposite was no less singular. An enormous black scarf throttled the stiff linen collar. The face was clean shaven, but had long side-whiskers, and a plentiful lock of hair was drawn flat across the brow. The young buck had an alert, defiant look, as though caught in the act of fierce protest with the photographer.

"What a quaint couple!" he exclaimed, laughing gaily. "Who were they—the Mistress of the Robes and her spouse?"

"Peter! Don't you know? Look!"

"It's not you?" he asked, after a close study.

Lady Neville laughed delightedly.

"That's your father—we were taken at Vienna on our honeymoon."

Peter looked at them again, the fine features, the general air of confidence, the light of youth in their eyes.

"H'm—you're not a bad-looking pair. Jove, I'd no idea Dad was such a gay dog! No wonder he captured you!"

Lady Neville took the locket from him, regarded it for a long silent moment, sighed, and as she closed it—

"There—you can show that to your children some day—when you look as quaint to them as we do now."

She put it back into its tissue paper, and placed it in a corner of the workbox. One by one, the mementos of the past were opened, looked at wonderingly and laughed over, perhaps more gaily because there were tears in those quaint old relics of vanished happiness, when other lovers were young, and the morning of life seemed too bright ever to pass to sunset. There were yellowing cabinet photographs, stiff, strange costumed, and yet with eyes that were queerly familiar to those who looked at them across the years.

This group of a lady and gentleman, sedately poised in an old-fashioned brougham, for instance. That was old Todd, on the box, who had ridden Peter's grandfather's horse to victory at the Harbyshire Steeplechase; that boy in Eton jacket and school cap at the side of his father was Roderick, in his first year at a preparatory school; that little bundle hidden in her mother's arm, was Susan, and the other invisible something, swathed in long clothes, and held by a firm-featured nurse in sateen, was Peter !

There was a heavy gold bracelet, with a large ' O ' inscribed. Lady Neville put it on her wrist, looked at it and laughed.

" How taste changes ! I thought this was quite beautiful once. Your dear father gave it to me— " She hesitated a moment, and her voice changed tone, " when he knew you were coming, Peter."

The next object of their scrutiny was a square leather case. It opened to show the faded portrait of a striking young man in fancy costume.

" There ! I ought never to have kept that, Peter. It was my only secret from your father. That was Hugh Trafford. We first met in some amateur theatricals for the County Hospital. It was " Twelfth Night " we did, and I played Olivia—probably because my name was Olivia. He was Orsino, so handsome, with such a wonderful voice that I thought I was in love with him. I remember your father, who sat in the front, looking so jealous when Orsino was courting me, that I almost forgot my words in the fear that he'd make a scene. I was frivolous enough then to ask Hugh for a photograph of himself in the part—and at his request we exchanged. You see what he had inscribed opposite."

Peter read the inscription on the gold plate sunk in the crimson silk :

> *Make me a willow cabin at your gate,*
> *And call upon my soul within the house ;*
> *Write loyal cantos of contemned love,*
> *And sing them loud even in the dead of night ;*
> *Halloo your name to the reverberate hills,*
> *And make the babbling gossip of the air*
> *Cry out, ' Olivia ' !*

" Poor Hugh ! He told me I had broken his heart, which I couldn't believe, for every girl fell in love with him and he wouldn't have to remain unconsoled long. But he took it more to heart than I knew, until he wrote saying he had accepted a commission in the army, and was going out to the front because he could not live in happiness without me.

That was the time of the Afghan war. His poor mother came and begged me to accept him, to prevent his enlisting, but how could I ? So he went, and we heard he had won the D.S.O. Then, one day came the news of his death. Poor Mrs. Trafford never forgave me, I know, and for a long time after that I could not get Hugh out of my mind. I made myself more wretched by delaying the marriage with your father. I suppose I felt I ought to do penance of some kind, though I never gave Hugh the slightest encouragement after those theatricals. So you see how difficult it was for me to part with this memento of him."

Mother and son stared at the photograph for a while. Something of the glamour and the pathos of that old love affair seemed to rise before them. More than forty years ago ! The vivacious girl he had loved was now a fragile old lady in the valley of the shadow, and the eyes that had been so long closed in death still looked out from that record of their youth, with bold confidence in the promise of life. And suddenly, Peter felt the burden passion places on the human heart, and knew more than ever that lovers were only the playthings of Fate, even while they strove to command their desires and mould their futures.

" Mother," he said, breaking the silence, " isn't it strange how life might be so different ? Supposing you had married Hugh, I should not have been *I*, and—Lord, what a mystery it all is ! "

His mother sighed, closing the case, replacing it in the box.

" Yes, dear, it is," she assented, " and yet I am quite sure that we are guided aright, if only we follow instinct, and act really as the heart dictates."

" You believe that, mother ? " he asked.

" Emphatically !—every year I see the misery made by outside interference. Old people consider they are entitled to give the young advice. They're not, Peter, for they've no idea how intensely the young feel about things, and they should only speak when their advice is asked for."

" You're a revolutionary old Pelican Pouch ! "

Lady Neville smiled.

" And suppose," continued Peter, " I asked your advice—about marriage, for instance ? "

Lady Neville brought her hand smartly to the little table.

" I don't expect you will, Peter. You might tell me what you thought of doing, and if I knew you wanted my opinion I would give it."

She looked at him keenly, and then put out her hand on his arm.

" Peter, my dear, I've seen what's been troubling you ever since you came home," she said, quietly.

He looked at her, startled, as she said this.

" You've seen—seen what ? " he cried.

" Your heart's in Venice."

For a long second their eyes met, and he saw that denial was useless, though she had startled him with this deliberate knowledge, which he had not admitted to himself, because of the difficulties in which he would be involved.

" It's because of that, Peter," she said, after a pause, " this illness has worried me, I feel I've tied you."

" No, no, you haven't, my dear," he said, emphatically, so emphatically that she saw he was anxious to kill the truth for her sake. " If I've felt tied at all it is by the Bank, and Maud and Ronnie."

" Perhaps a little," she responded, " but they've no right to tie you. Nothing has any right to frustrate a man's full life."

" You think that, mother ? " he asked.

" Certainly, and if Maud thinks otherwise you may have to seem cruel to her, Peter."

With a quick turn of the head he betrayed his deep surprise at her remark. Wonderful old Pelican Pouch ! Did anything escape her eyes ?

" Has Susie been saying anything ? " he asked, suspiciously.

" Nothing, Peter, so don't scold Susan. I'm not blind, and poor Maud's not nearly such a good actress as she thinks. You mustn't let pity sacrifice your happiness. Altruism of that kind is never a success."

Her thin fingers picked up two other tissue packets and opened them. One contained a strand of yellow hair.

" That's from Susan's hair when she was three, and this was once your dearest possession."

" This ! "

He took the object in his fingers and examined it, incredulous. It was a large rubber ' comforter,' with an ivory ring, to which was attached a length of ribbon.

" When you had measles," explained Lady Neville, " we had a nurse, and the first thing she did was to take away that comforter, which was pinned to your night-gown. She said it was unhygienic and ridiculous for a child of three. I suppose it was, but you loved it dearly and made a terrible scene, so that they had to call me up into the nursery. I was as afraid of the nurse as you were, and gave way to her, and you thought I had deserted you. I brought the comforter away with me, and, like a fond foolish nother, cried in my room about it."

Peter put it in his mouth.

" Yum-yum," he crooned, and then taking it out— " What a wonderful age when the whole world seems destroyed because your ' comforter's ' gone ! "

Lady Neville wrapped up the treasures.

" There," she said, closing the box, " now you see what a sentimental old lady I am, storing all this rubbish. It's of no value, and you needn't keep it when I've gone."

He took her thin hand in his, and knelt down beside her couch.

" Mother, you mustn't talk like that. Sir Malcolm Lane's full of hope, so's Susie, so am I. We want you very much."

He kissed her then, raised one hand and patted her chin.

" Whatever should I do without this fine Pelican

Pouch ? " he asked, in a strained cheerful voice ; and for the first time he saw grief in her eyes as she smiled at him.

A few minutes afterwards Annette came for her, and when his mother had gone, Peter stood by the window, whose blind he had raised, looking down into the dark Circus, with its lights channelling the amphitheatre. So even the Pelican Pouch saw all was not well with him. Her advice had seemed almost revolutionary. Tied ! He had not used that word. It had been his mother's. Yes, he was tied, by the Bank, by the appeal of Maud for help, by his own pity for her, by his lack of ruthless resolution. Also by his love of the Pelican Pouch, though she urged him to live his own life. Did she give this advice, sacrificing her own feelings, because she had seen, in the experience of years, the futility of denying the heart's desire ?

Duty was exalted as a virtue. As he looked out into the night, down on to the houses of people he knew, there were many among them who were slaves to duty, because they were too weak to rebel and live their own lives. Himself, for instance. Candidly, he knew the Bank could prosper without him. Sir John Coate had told him that, in his wise blunt fashion. Ronnie's interests would be stronger for amalgamation, his own also, and Maud's. He wanted to return to Chioggia. He loved Lucia. He let duty tell him he ought to stay in Meltonham, to marry one of his own race, to be near his mother, and sister-in-law and nephew. Yet his own heart denied all this, and now with a suddenness that left him shaken, his mother had denied her claims, and those of all others, telling him to live his own life.

Turning from the window, he went to the mantel-piece, and, with one foot on the curb, drummed his fingers on the marble while he thought it out. Lucia! What was she doing now?

He took from his pocket the envelope whose postmark had been seen by Maud, and extracted the now familiar letter. It was four days old, written by Marco in a large deliberate hand, obviously a considerable task to its sender, and yet with an earnest note that more fluent writers might not have captured.

CARISSIMO PADRONE,

Your letter is very welcome to me. I have read it often. I can see the Signor in his English house, with the Signora, his mother, so glad to have him. The *Celavasansdire* is the swiftest boat on the laguna. They call it the Signorino's boat, though they know it is mine, and I am glad they call it so, for then I feel it may be the Signorino's again one day.

I have not seen the Signorina Delfino for three weeks. She is now living in Venice with her aunt, and studies with the Maestro. They say it is because she will not see Finghetti, who is very angry on the boats, and the men are more afraid of him. Perhaps this is because the Signorina is away, and perhaps because it is said the Signor Delfino has had quarrels with him. Last week they returned with a poor catch, and Finghetti was drunk for three days in his house so that no one dared go, and his aunt left it, and Signor Delfino went and they quarrelled a long time.

The fleet goes out to-morrow again. Some say that the Signore will go with it, but some think they gossip too much. I will tell you, Signorino, which be true. I have asked Bianca with care, as you instructed, but she knows nothing, whether your letter reached the Signorina or not. She would not say more, and was afraid.

Beppo Bensoni, my friend in Venezia, who knows the Signorina's aunt, gave me her address which is—Ca' Flora, Ponte Baratteri, Venezia. Finghetti will not employ me, but I am well contented by a gentleman, an Americano, who employs me to take him in the *Celavasansdire* which makes me the more sad though happy, for it is not you, Signorino, who sits in the stern and laughs with me.

I shall be glad when the poor Signora of your brother is

comforted, and you will wish to return. Also, I am sure, the Signorina, who was much in distress when you went, as all say along the fondamenta where they ask much of you.

From the Signore's lonely servant,

MARCO.

Dear old Marco, the boy's simple heart beat in every line. Lucia in Venice ! Perhaps that accounted for no answer to the long letter he had written that morning at the Bank. Had her father seen the postmark and withheld from forwarding it ? He had written a fortnight ago, which would be after the time of her going to Venice. But if she had not gone then, if she had received the letter ? Was she angry with him ? Perhaps she had decided to end the affair ?

In agitation he pondered these questions, now believing this, now hoping that. He decided to write again, care of Marco this time. His last letter had been guarded, without an expression of his love of her, it had gossiped pleasantly of his new life in Meltonham ; in so far as it had been so silent in one matter it had been an innocent capture for her father. But perhaps it had reached Lucia, and bitterly disappointed her with its trivialities, its careful silence on the one thing that was all to her.

With sudden resolution, Peter sat down at his mother's secretaire. In its drawers reposed those love relics of her own girlhood and courtship, which they had lingered over to-night. As he picked up a pen, his mother's phrase rang in his ears. " They've no right to tie you. Nothing has any right to frustrate a man's full life."

He wrote for an hour, as a lover writes, in language which, unsought and unknown to him, was that of the poet exalted by the intensity of passion. And this time he addressed it to Marco, entrusting the delivery to his faithful hands.

CHAPTER XXIII

I

ONE week later Peter Neville, seated at his desk in his private room at the Bank, tried to maintain an appearance of outward calm. Earlier in the morning he had met his sister and Sir Malcolm Lane at the station, and conveyed them to the nursing home. As Peter left the building he looked up at its white-curtained windows, reflecting how little the outside world knew of those grim encounters with watchful Death within. He had seen the matron, nerveless and with an assuring smile; Dr. Cane, the anaesthetist, humming cheerfully as he passed in the corridor; the red-cheeked nurses; Susie, calmer than all; Sir Malcolm attired and carrying himself like the best man at a wedding—all these about to battle for the life of the trustful creature who had parted from him with a brave air that reproved his own emotion.

Now he waited, waited through an interminable hour, his nerves strained, his mind incapable of concentration. The telephone rested on the table at his right hand. When it rang he would know the best, or worst. Susan had promised to telephone as soon as the operation had been performed. Meanwhile Parsons, quiet and soothing in his imperturbable manner, sought to occupy his mind with business. It had been a momentous week. There had been board meetings in London, conferences with the directors and managers of the great bank with whom they proposed to amalgamate. The task had been made easier by the ready acquiescence of Peter's co-trustees, and also, in a less agreeable manner, by Maud. She had deliberately retired from the field, taking upon herself the rôle of an ignored, ruined woman in the hands of unscrupulous men. Her cold assent, her monosyllabic replies, her air of studied indifference to points on which she was consulted, and her constant reference to " poor little Ronnie," had brought Peter to the verge of despair. She had the art of making him feel a low, black villain defrauding the helpless orphan and widow. It was useless to emphasise the fact that she would derive an increased income, and her son a safer inheritance. No, they were being robbed of Neville's Bank. Peter was betraying his ancestors.

Then blunt Sir John Coate tackled her. At Peter's request he sallied out to Neville Court and had a bad ten minutes in the library.

" Couldn't do anything with the woman, Neville ! She just looked at me with her great black eyes and let me talk. Wouldn't argue with me—took it all. It was like hitting a punch ball, you only sweated and moved the wind. She didn't even cry, or try to be ravishing, which are two of the extra business assets of women. I might have been the bailiff come to take possession. Phew ! Go ahead and let her mope ! The first quarter's income'll convince her."

But Peter had doubts about that. Her opposition was not based on the amalgamation, or the change of name. Everything she said or looked conveyed the charge of desertion. He was deserting them, and by ' them ' she meant Ronnie and herself, which actually meant herself. That was the point. He was getting free. As a director and trustee he would not be so tied to the life of Melton-ham. He might even travel for intervals.

" When are you leaving for Chioggia ? " she had asked, one morning, as he reported developments.

" Good heavens, Maud ! I don't know that I'll leave at all. There's a tremendous lot to do yet, besides which, there's mother, if she pulls through. Have you no conception of the work, the detail this amalgamation means ? "

" No—and it's all unnecessary," she retorted.

" It's for the best, Maud."

" Your best ! "

" Maud ! That's extremely unkind. You have no right to say it. It will be for the best for all of us."

She gave her head a quick lift, with the peacock survey and ruffle of her feathers which he knew so well.

" I shall miss this room—Roderick's room, and seeing Bentley about the clubs," she sighed, mournfully.

" But this room will remain as it is—you can come any time. Parsons will be here as general manager—he was Roderick's favourite. And why should you give up your welfare work ? "

" Everything will be swallowed up."

" You won't know there's any change—it's only the name. Believe me, Maud, it's essential. You know Sir John Coate threatened to transfer his account ? "

" I should imagine that man does nothing else but threaten," she complained, drawing on a black kid glove— " What will the new name be ? "

" The National Corporation of Provincial Banks," he said.

" No mention of Neville's ? "

" No."

She stood up, gathering her bag and umbrella to her.

" It seems to me we're to become nonentities. Neville's

once meant something. The very name commanded respect. Now I suppose we'll be part of the National Corporation of Provincial Banks—what a ridiculous stretched-out name ! and Neville's will mean nothing at all ! Ronnie's name may just as well be Robinson for all that matters."

" And mine," Peter could not help adding.

She showed him her absolute disapproval by allowing him to have the last word. As she went, he could not help noticing that she abdicated like a queen. Out of his room she passed, into the client's lobby, and handsome young heads and bald old ones bowed down before her as she swept by their desks. The Bank porter, with ' Neville's ' inscribed in gold on his frock-coat lapels conducted her to the main door, and also bowed. He would soon lose the magic name on his coat ; and those huge brass nameplates rounding the Doric pillars, they would also go. Thus swiftly she reviewed her descent from power, and as the chauffeur closed the door on her, the final loss presented itself. Peter would go too. And here perhaps was the real reason of it all, shrewd old Sir John Coate notwithstanding. All sacrificed for a low intrigue at Chioggia ! At that moment she hated him.

Such had been the scene two days before. The discreet Parsons had sensed the disapproval of her ladyship, and he hoped, when he succeeded to that room, his consummate tact would triumph. But Peter was the power now, and would be for many years, until the advent of young Sir Ronald. Parsons was never a man to oppose authority, wherever placed.

He was returning a private ledger when the telephone bell rang. He saw Peter's hand instantly seize the receiver, and discreetly retired from the room. On his return a few minutes later, he looked questioningly at his chief.

" No—Parsons, not yet," responded Peter ; " it was Sir John Coate. He's agreed to join the local directorate. I'm very glad, for it strengthens our hands considerably. I don't want the head office to overrule us too completely."

He had just spoken when the bell rang again.

" Don't go, Parsons," he called, hesitating a second, before taking off the receiver ; " this must be it."

It was Susan's voice in his ear. They had finished and all was well, so far. It was a tumour, not cancer. Sir Malcolm was very pleased with the operation. Lady Neville would be dazed with the anaesthetic until the evening. Sir Malcolm was leaving for town immediately after lunch.

" So, Peter, old thing, I don't think we'll be orphans. Sir Malcolm says the Pelican Pouch has a hundred-year-constitution. You can cash up with a light heart, though we've the next three days to pull through."

Susan rang off then. What a girl she was, he thought. Never a tremor in her voice, nor in her hand that morning, he was sure. In one way he would have felt happier if she had been less calm. Was Susan quite a woman, and wasn't she missing a great deal in life through this self-reliant efficiency of hers ?

Peter gave the news to Parsons, and then thought about lunch, which he was taking with Sir John. He would be glad when the next few hours were over and he was permitted to take a peep at Lady Neville. Wonderful old Pelican Pouch ! He felt very proud of her for behaving so well.

II

Peter Neville had scarcely observed the passing of the days, so hurried and full of developments were they, divided between his office, conferences in London, visits to the nursing home and, rarer, to Neville Court. With the end of August, Peter, having tea one afternoon in the library with Maud and Ronnie, became suddenly aware of the reddening creeper covering a wing of the house, where it flamed in the westering sun. A remark of Maud's, upon the dread of the dreary winter, turned his thoughts to the South and to his mother.

" I've been thinking of taking her to the Riviera for the Winter, as soon as she can travel," he said. " We're through with the amalgamation and I could leave for a time."

He thought she was going to ignore his remark, for she stared vacantly across the lawn, where Ronnie had gone to play with an Aberdeen terrier, but suddenly she turned her dark eyes on him, saying directly—

" Do you think you'd stay there ? "

The question was fiercely asked. His visit this afternoon had been to obtain her signature to some papers, in final settlement of the new arrangement. He had anticipated some trouble and to his surprise she had signed without comment, with none of the lamentations for the departed glory of Neville's, which had become so familiar to his ears. There had been a calmness, almost languor in her attitude, that recalled, in its atmospheric peace, one of those afternoons when, from the Bay of Naples, he had watched the lazy smoke cloud on Vesuvius, and the boatman had shaken his head in foreboding.

Her sudden question, addressed to him with a fierceness that scarcely smothered anger, was in the nature of a taunt. He resented the tone she employed, but he showed nothing of this. After all, they had come to the end of a difficult business and had avoided open rupture. It was worth a little patience with her now.

" Why don't you think I would stay there ? " he asked, lightly, leaning back in his chair. His smile and unperturbed manner, his self-possession, which at any other time attracted her, annoyed now, and a sudden desire to hurt him, to insult him, moved within her. Should he be allowed to make her suffer so, and sit smiling there, indifferent to her agony ? Never had his spell been stronger. His magnetism had a physical character this afternoon. She craved to see him in violent action, in rage, anything but this irritating self-possession.

She saw the lean brown hands, resting on the side of his chair, and wished they might seize her in anger or desire. The very strength she divined in his figure as he sat, one leg crossed over the other, roused her to deeper resentment of his indifference. Men had never treated her like this. She had seen their sensitiveness to her beauty, their deliberate behaviour, their sternly-guarded restraint in her presence. Her sovereignty had never been ignored in this fashion.

His question was not in her mind, for when she answered him she was voicing the bitterness of two months of struggle in her nature between loyalty to a memory and the unburied desire of her heart in that far day at Oxford. For three years now she had not admitted the knowledge, the cry in her heart. It had leapt up again at Venice this Spring, been crushed with duty and desperate self-deception. The summer had been for her a season of self-torture. Her fear to wound the devoted Roderick, oblivious of his own inadequacy, and happy in the thought of the veneration he inspired in the woman he loved, had driven her to hateful simulation of dead affection. And the mother reproached the traitoress for her treasonous knowledge.

But most devastating to self-respect and tranquillity, was the passionate resentment stirred by her imagination. Another woman in Chioggia was gaining all she might not have. That was the torture. Some peasant girl triumphed where she might not even attempt rivalry.

Genuine grief at Roderick's death gave her respite, but the struggle began again, intense, in the presence of Peter, with the possibilities of this new freedom. Her signature that afternoon had seemed like an assent to her death sentence, and his mention of the Riviera, with its suggestion of the South, of freedom, shattered her resolute calm. His " Why don't you think I would stay there ? " with its ease, its utter indifference to the struggle she was making, infuriated her.

" Stay ! " she sneered, " when you've scrapped Neville's for an adventure at Chioggia ? "

The sudden flaming of his face and the alertness of his whole body filled her with careless pleasure.

" Whatever do you mean, Maud ? " he asked, coldly.

" Well, the Bank was in your way, and it's gone. I don't expect your mother to hold you."

She did not hesitate. In her eyes he saw no desire to give or take mercy. They were face to face now.

" I can't accept that, Maud," he said, warmly. " It's a monstrous suggestion ! I've done my very best for Neville's. It was inevitable. Sir John— "

She interrupted him with a swift outburst, rising from her chair and crushing the thin lace handkerchief in her hands.

" Sir John ? You want me to believe it was Sir John's doing ? You might be honest and give your peasant girl the credit ! " she cried, reckless in her desire to wound.

He was on his feet now, facing her.

" I have a perfect right to live my own life, and I shall ! "

" And sacrifice ours ! That's a man all over, I suppose," she retorted bitterly.

" There is no question of sacrificing anybody. You have asked me to be honest. It is scarcely honest to accuse me in this manner."

She was losing self-control. Self-pity led her towards hysteria. Why didn't he let himself go. Her inability to wound him enraged her.

" I do accuse you," she cried. " My son's future has been sacrificed to your low intrigue ! "

She was frightened then, for his face changed under the lash of those words. His chair went back with a sharp kick of his leg, and, before she had realised his purpose, he had taken her in the vice of those brown hands, pinning her arms to her side, his white, tense face close to her own.

" You've asked me to be honest," he said, in a voice of passion. " I will be ! It isn't Neville's Bank you care about, nor your son's future ! You want me ! "

She was afraid now, desperately afraid. His passion frightened her, but, more than this, the open statement of the truth between them took all her courage. She half-closed her eyes.

" Don't, Peter—don't, please. Oh, Peter ! " she murmured.

He released her, his mouth quivering in the swift rage that shook him. She would have fallen, had he not been quick to catch her. She sank into his arms, her head falling back on his shoulder. Her nearness, the pallor of her brow, the collapse of her anger, filled him with momentary compassion, and he felt anew the long allurement of her exotic nature. A savage will to kiss her took

him, which her opening eyes divined. Her arms went
about his neck, but the action renewed his anger, and
deliberately he withdrew her hands, forcing her help-
lessly into a chair. For a moment he stood over her,
grim, quiveringly breathing, and then passed behind the
chair, where he paused.

" I shall ask Grieve to send your maid. I shall say you
are unwell. I'm very sorry this has happened."

That was all. She heard him cross the floor, open the
door, close it. Then silence. Through the window
came Ronnie's shrill cries. She thought she would
weep, but the tears did not come ; if only they had, she
might have known some relief for the loneliness and
despair that closed round her in the silent room.

CHAPTER XXIV

I

ON the journey back to Meltonham, Peter's mind was in a strange jumble. The distressing scene with Maud had unnerved him, following on top of the tension of the past few weeks. Lady Neville's illness, the endless negotiations at the Bank, the continuous sense of an approach to disaster in his relations with his sister-in-law, all these had contributed to the strain he had undergone, still heavier in a respect that he could not mention. There had been no word through all these weeks from Lucia. His second letter seemed to have met the fate of the first. Had she received it and ignored it ?

This storm had cleared the air a little. It had been long threatened. He and Maud had been wearing masks in each other's presence. They knew each other openly now. He was distressed by the scene between them, for her sake more than his. Her pride had suffered an irreparable injury, which he had sought to prevent. She had forced him to the point, and that terrible moment, when he had almost succumbed from the weakness that is in man's nature, had shown how desperately she was meeting his challenge. She would have taken and held him with that kiss, even though it sprang from transitory weakness combined with pity. Even now he pitied her.

Women of her nature suffered terribly, humiliation following upon futility.

Peter determined not to see her again before he left England, a resolution perhaps unnecessary, since she would avoid him for the sake of her own dignity. A recollection of that night in the gondola as they returned to the hotel from the Palazzo Casmiri, of Roderick's sure happiness, of Maud's bantering challenge to his manhood, showed that this day's scene was the culmination of a long silent battle in a woman's heart. More than ever had he reason for leaving England now. His very presence would be cruelty to Maud, whether she hated or cared for him.

As he entered the drawing-room at Cliff House, the nurse had just taken his mother's food into her room. Lady Neville had been back from the nursing home two days, and her vitality gave endless surprise and pleasure to those about her. She was tremendously proud of her achievement, and as Peter went into her bedroom this evening he thought she looked as delightfully vivacious as ever.

" Ah ! " he cried, jovially, trying to dismiss the memory of the past hour, " am I allowed to watch the Pelican Pouch at feeding time, nurse ? "

The nurse smiled, as she raised Lady Neville's pillows.

" If you will behave yourself, Mr. Neville. Last night you stayed half-an-hour too long. I shall deduct it to-night."

" Peter," said Lady Neville, with a note of triumph in her voice, " I walked round the room three times this afternoon ? I believe we forget the thrills babies have when they're first conscious of their legs. It's a tremendous adventure ! "

He caught the gleam of excitement in her blue eyes,

and he thought she looked at him critically. When the nurse had left the room she commanded him to sit down beside her.

"Peter," she said, "you look very worried."

"I!" he asked, trying to belie her accusation.

"Yes. Do you know, there's been something on your mind ever since you came home from Italy—even if you don't tell your old mother, she's not blind."

He tried to laugh then, but it was a poor performance, and to avoid her searching eyes he tucked in the sheets at the foot of the bed.

"You're a very imaginative old lady," he said, slowly.

"Very well, I am. Now, dear, go and get your dinner, you're ten minutes late. There's a letter waiting for you —nurse brought it up with mine—it's from Italy, I see."

He rose, and her sharp eyes were on him, brightening into a smile.

"Now, mother," he said, lightly, "what have you got in your mind?"

"Nothing—but suspicions."

He stooped and kissed her brow, and then, looking down at her face, wrinkled in a mischievous smile—

"You are a very alert old Pelican Pouch," he confessed.

"And you are a very bad actor. Now go and get your dinner, dear. I know you'll tell me all about it—but not before you want to. Men are all like that. Women always know what men want to tell them for such a long time before, and it's an awful effort to look surprised!"

Peter shook his head at her admonishingly, and ran downstairs. An envelope was propped against the mantelpiece clock. The postmark was Venice. It was not in Marco's writing. With a quickened heart he tore open the envelope. "*Peter adorato,*" it began. Swiftly he turned over the sheets to the back. It was signed " Lucia."

For a few seconds his brain could not control the sensation he felt and the lines conveyed nothing to him. Then more steadily he began to read, translating the pointed Italian.

Ca' Flora,
Ponte Baratteri,
Venezia.

Adorato Pietro,

I have read your letter again and again this hour in which Marco brought it to me, from Chioggia. Who is so cruel to us, mio carissimo Peter ? I have not seen your first letter to me. If so, how could I have been silent ? Indeed I am neither angry nor cold. Each morning and evening you are in my prayers, which are answered now, amor mio. I am here at my aunt's and study each day at Signor Zambra's. I am writing this in my room which looks down on to the narrow canal and the ponte crossing it. Sometimes I watch for you, for there are so many cross it on their way to the Piazza, but it has been all vain, you never crossed. A week ago I saw Marco crossing the ponte, and I left my window and hurried after him. When he told me he had received a letter from you I cried so much that he took me to a café, where he swore that you loved me, and that you had already written to me a letter which I have not received. I could not think it was so then, Peter. To-day, Marco brought your letter, which comes when I am so ugly, for I cried last night.

Tesoro mio, you say you will come to me, that you love me. When will you come ? Let it be soon, amor mio, and I will follow you wherever it may be, for without you there is no life, and with you I am in paradise. I kiss your letter, dear, dear words. They tell me that you love me, that you long for me, and I cannot read them again because of my tears, but I know them in my heart. Let it be soon, carissimo. To-night I shall sing to you, the song you loved that time at Chioggia— *Me trago sul balcon*, but I shall not look out of my balcony when I have sung. I shall imagine you are listening on the ponte below, and if I looked it would be an Americano, or an Inglese, who stays to listen.

Amor mio, write soon, come soon ! My father keeps me here with my aunt who is old and deaf, because I will not speak with Paolo Finghetti. My maestro tells me that one day I shall be a diva, but oh how he swears at me when I do not please him ; and oh, how I work ! You shall be proud of me, anima mia. I will write to-morrow. I kiss this happy letter winging to you.

LUCIA.

He turned from the window where he had read the letter through and through, surveying the table. Dinner ! who wanted dinner ? The maid, entering with a tray, saw nothing but the young master's back, as he stood humming *Me trago sul balcon*, and reported his demeanour to the cook.

" He's singing his I-talian again, that letter's done it, I know ! "

Cook sighed, incorrigibly romantic, despite one unfortunate experience from the cause of which she was separated.

" Poor lad, he's been gloomy-eyed ever since he came home. I told you he was love-sick."

" Lor," ventured the scullerymaid, " don't them Italians work 'emselves up. There's that Capocci man with the ice-cream barrer near the Queen's statue. He says to me one night— "

" That's enough, Lizzie. Take these dishes in the scullery ! " snapped the maid, and as she obeyed, turned indignantly to cook.

" There ! the impudence of that chit of a girl. Her imagination isn't fit to hear ! "

II

Towards the end of September, with the departing swallows, they went South, Lady Neville and maid, Susan and Peter. One of Lady Neville's friends had placed her small villa at Mentone at their disposal. The journey was made in short stages, first to London, where Peter completed his business while his mother rested or drove about leisurely shopping. In London Susan joined them, vigorous, hard-headed Susan. Hard-hearted too, Peter had come to believe her, but in the first five minutes of their meeting in the lounge of the Hotel Cecil, Susan shattered that conception of her character with a single unheralded sentence.

" When I come back in the Spring I'm getting married," she said.

Peter's cigarette fell out of his mouth at the shock. He sat upright on the settee at her side and looked incredulously into her calm face.

" You're what, Susan ? Married ! You ! " he exclaimed.

Susan pushed her hands down into her jersey pockets and looked at him calmly.

" I know you've never thought me human, and old Roddy thought me a freak, and probably you'll think it's business when I tell you I'm marrying a doctor—our House Surgeon."

" Susie, I'm delighted, old girl," cried Peter, slipping an arm round her shoulders and giving her a hug, despite the publicity. " I was afraid you were going to miss the divine coincidence."

" And what's that, romantic brother Peter ? "

" Being young and in love."

" Peter, you know absolutely nothing about science, it's not a coincidence, it's a biological impulse."

" Very well," he laughed, " I'm glad you've the impulse. Does the Pelican Pouch know ? "

" No—and it's very funny, Peter, but I dread telling

her. He's quite 'suitable' as they say in the vicarage, and all that, but I couldn't break the news abruptly to mother, and the abrupt style's the only one I have. Will you do it, Peter, you're such a diplomat?"

He had promised forthwith. Before they left, her destined partner in love and work was presented and approved. Susan, for all her bold individuality, had been singularly nervous throughout. It was a festive trio that reached Paris and left, after a week-end halt, for the Riviera. Once across the channel Peter breathed freely. The shadow of Maud had been upon him down to Dover. He had not seen her since that dreadful afternoon, nor heard from her. Once only he had spoken to her, over the telephone, naming the day of his departure. She had visited Lady Neville, but he was out at the time. When they would meet again perhaps the impression of their unhappy incident would be blurred. She might be actress enough to laugh at the affair, and impute the blame to him. He would accept that interpretation if it would soothe her wounded pride.

The unforgettable thrill of the South came back to Peter on the still evening when he looked out of the windows of their villa on the hillside. He flung back the lattice shutters, and before him lay the palm-fringed promenade and the sea. It was the old, old blue, fading on its horizon into the cloudless canopy whose depths it mirrored. The side of the house was in shadow now, but the walls radiated the heat, giving off that singular aroma of sun-baked plaster. All he saw and heard and smelt told him he was not far from that island in the lagoon. This was the warm hospitable South, where the night had such enchantment, such mystery in its depths, such meaning in its sounds.

They dined that evening in the open loggia facing the sea, while the dusk drew over it like a veil, and the cooler air brought out the perfume of the flowers. Peter was in high spirits throughout their meal, laughing and joking in the exhilaration of his beloved South. Lady Neville saw the sparkle in his eye and knew well its cause, but his joy was infectious, and they talked noisily until suddenly her son raised his hand. Down below them, on the road, hidden by the dense foliage, someone was playing a mandolin. The music grew out of the darkness as the player came towards them. It was one of those light, melodious airs, dear to the children of the sun. It died as the player departed on his way.

Unknown, he had left tumult in the heart of an unseen listener. That mandolin had given life to old memories, poignant with happiness. An hour ago Peter had written to Lucia, repeating all they had told each other these last few weeks, yet still striving for fresh expression ; and this time he had written something that put an end to his exile. He would be with her in a week. The poet which awakens in every lover had led him to be fanciful in that hour of reunion. He would stand on the ponte under the Ca' Flora at nine o'clock, and she was to sing *Me trago sul balcon*. When Lucia had finished she would look out this time and see, not an Americano or a strange Inglese, but Peter.

One week more ! That unseen player had passed like a herald of happiness.

Susan rose from her hammock chair and went indoors to fetch Lady Neville a wrap. Peter, who was squatting on the loggia steps at her feet, had turned silent and was deep in reverie. Something in his face told Lady Neville its nature. She put her hand to his shoulder, and paused before speaking.

" Peter—I hope you are going to be very happy. You have been so good to me, dear boy."

She wanted to say more, but the silence of the night seemed to say it. He turned his head as if to answer, then looked down again, and his hand, closing over hers, brought it to his lips.

CHAPTER XXV

THE Milan-Venice express had slipped by Desenzano as Peter sat at lunch in the restaurant car. Once again he caught a glimpse of the blue expanse of Garda, where Sirmione, beloved of Catullus, cut a narrow path into the wide head of the lake, with the villa-lined shore glimmering brightly along the foot of the barren mountains. Next the fortified and moated walls of Peschiera streamed by, turfed and peaceful in the sunny afternoon, a memorial of desperate days. They were nearing Verona now, and its very name brought back to Peter the touch of vanished romance. Its sound was music, its suggestion poetry. Here had Shakespeare's imagination winged, calling up the sad ghosts of those famous lovers ; here had his Two Gentlemen lingered. But Shakespeare had travelled farther along that route to the sovereign City, upon whose canals in a few hours another lover would hasten, as young, as eager, as the one who had gone with the dawn from a casement in Verona.

Now Vicenza is past. Can it be that this night he will stand in Venice, see the silent passing of a gondola, hear the drift of talk and music down the dark canals ? Yes, in a few hours the dream will be reality. Here is many-domed Padua aglow in the afternoon sun, its beauty rising from the plain before his eyes, much as it appeared to that learned young doctor also bound for Venice, how many hundred years ago ?

In the force of his excitement Peter Neville left his seat and walked along the corridor. Around, in those happy Autumn fields, the peasants were cropping the vines. Heavy ox-carts rolled leisurely along the white roads, bearing their luscious freight to the presses. Golden-limbed lads and lasses, bare-legged, open-throated, laughed and waved as the train roared by. Slowly the landscape changed its nature, growing flatter and greyer. They were drawing into Mestre, that dirty and outcast station which seems deliberately to depress the traveller, as if to heighten, by contrast, the enchantment that lies beyond the long low bridge crossing the dead lagoon, whose level miles of backwash are studded with gaunt telegraph poles, keeping many-isled Venice tethered to Italy.

They have crossed those two miles of desolate waste; there is a roar, and a darkening, as they enter the station. Two minutes later, in a gondola, his heart furiously beating with the wonder of it all, Peter drifted down the broad stream where history sleeps in a hundred palaces, whose balconies and windows still keep the form of the greatness they knew, in a city where only the tide is faithful. And yet, for him, this is a living Venice, where the ghosts of a thousand dead lovers cannot check the leap of the heart within him.

It was all planned with a certitude in curious contrast with their eagerness. Lucia was to sing her song while he listened below on the bridge. This time, when the last note of *Me trago sul balcon* had risen into the stillness of the night, she was to give action to the words and look out over her balcony. For this time it would be no Americano, no strange and curious Inglese who would stand listening on the bridge to that hidden voice in the house above the canal. It would be the one to whom she had sung in her loneliness, for whom she had prayed in her longing. There would be a glad cry of recognition, she would disappear from the window high above, and a minute later, in the black shadow of the house, the weeks of vigil would be all forgotten.

Peter changed and dined at his hotel; the day seemed reluctant to leave the golden sky. At nine o'clock he would be on the Ponte Baratteri; but the minutes dragged with leaden feet. He walked round the gay Piazza, and then sat at a table at Florian's, listening restlessly to the orchestra leaving his coffee untouched. Half-past eight! Once more he traversed the arcades, past the shop windows, scintillating with their coloured glassware and tourist-trumperies. A quarter to nine! Now he may go to the Ponte Baratteri.

As he passed under the dark clock-tower leading into the narrow Merceria he tried to be calm. He would know the house, her description was so explicit; when he stood on the ponte bridging the canal, it was the yellow house across on the right. The third window, with the iron-wrought balcony, was hers. He would identify it by a Persian rug thrown over the balcony.

It was quite dark now, a few yards, and he could see the steps of the Ponte Baratteri rising to its central arch. A yellow ray of light lay across it from an open fruit shop near to him. As he gained the first step of the bridge the clock over the arched gateway, through which he had passed from the Piazza, struck the hour with ruthless clangour. Breathlessly his eyes scanned the high front of the houses towering above the black canal. That was it!

One, two, three, he found the balcony. No, he was wrong. There was no light, no Persian carpet. His direction must be wrong. Feverishly he looked about, correcting his position. No, he was not wrong, the house was across on the right hand, it had a yellow front. There was the iron balcony, on the third floor, exactly as she had said. But the window was shuttered, there was no light, the house stood heavy and lifeless above the black water.

Peter leaned on the cool balustrade. He must think slowly, there was some error surely. A gondola slid silently under the bridge, bearing its freight of lovers. He watched the ripple of the water with a troubled brow. So detached was his mind, the touch of a hand on his sleeve caused him to start, and turn apprehensively.

" Signorino ! " said a soft voice at his side.

He recognised the tone immediately.

" Marco ! " he cried, gladly, peering into the familiar face of the lad who had bowed and stood, all smiles, before his beloved padrone.

" Signorino—welcome to Venice ! "

Peter seized the lad's hand, for Marco had become inarticulate with the joy of this meeting. He could only look and smile, happy as a dog finding its long-lost master.

" You didn't expect me yet in Chioggia—what are you doing here, Marco ? "

The lad became solemn at once, looking cautiously across the ponte and up at the houses. Then he drew nearer to Peter.

" Signorino, I come from the Signorina."

" Where is she ? "

" At Chioggia."

" Chioggia ! " cried Peter. " But I was to meet her here ! "

" Sì, that is why I am here, signorino. Let us move into the shadow, these houses have eyes."

Like two conspirators, they sought the black shadow by

the shops, walking slowly along the Merceria towards the Piazza.

" The Signorina sent for me this morning," began Marco, in a subdued voice. " Yesterday, her father quarrelled with Paolo Finghetti. I'll tell you all later, signorino. There have been scenes between them. Last evening the Signore was taken ill and the Signorina was sent for. She left at once, and this morning she begged me to meet you here in her place, for she could not let you know in time."

" She is well ? "

" Sì, signorino—but she is much distressed."

" And the Signore ? "

" He was better this morning. They nearly came to blows. There has been great trouble with the Fleet."

Marco told him all then, as they approached the Piazza. A fierce dispute with the Ancona boats had led to a fight. Finghetti had completely lost his head. His luck, too, had been out. Three expeditions had resulted in poor catches. Ashore he was continually drunk, and resented Delfino's supervision. The Ancona fight had ended in a lawsuit, and compensation had been claimed for a boat whose bows Finghetti had stoved in, and for damaged tackle. Delfino was ordered to pay for both. Marco thought the quarrel had been over the loss of the lawsuit. It was the Dottore who prevented them coming to blows, and old Delfino had a seizure later.

They had gained the open Piazza now, where a band was playing, and the lights blazed in the arcades, before which were grouped the crowded tables of the cafés. Peter led the way towards one of these.

" Let's sit here. I want to hear everything, Marco."

When the waiter had received his order, the lad narrated all he could remember since his padrone's departure.

" We're all so excited at your return, signorino. When I told them you were coming in a few days a little festa was suggested. We were coming out to meet you in decorated boats, but now I've had to tell them I don't know the day."

" When did you get here, Marco ? "

" A few hours ago—by the *Celavasansdire*. Your boat is here, signorino."

" My boat ?—why, it's yours now, Marco ! "

The lad shook his head solemnly.

" It will always be yours, signorino, when you are here."

A burst of applause around them, for the orchestra, interrupted their conversation. After a time it died down.

" Now tell me, Marco—when does the Signorina expect me ? "

For a few moments Marco did not answer. Peter read in his eyes at once a perturbing thought.

" What's the matter, Marco ? "

The lad looked at him directly, an earnest ring of appeal in his voice.

" Signorino—must you go on with this ? Scusi, I know I have no right to say this—but I'm afraid."

" Of what ? "

" Many things, signorino," muttered the lad.

" What are they ? I want to know."

" The poor Signorina—it will break her heart when you go again. Per Bacco ! It was terrible when you went, terrible for me. There was no sun in the sky, but for her it was night. All along the Corso we knew it. Finghetti knew it, and cursed you, so that none dared to speak your name when he was near."

There was genuine distress in the boy's voice. Peter leaned across the table putting his hand over Marco's as it lay there.

"Marco, you do not understand. When I leave again Lucia will go with me. She has promised me this."

The lad looked at him a little frightened, he thought.

"Well ? " asked Peter.

"But after—when you have grown tired, signorino, what will she do ? She loves you so, she does not think now. But her name will be—so ! " He dropped his hand from the table, towards the ground. " We do not forgive our women. We love thoughtlessly, but they pay. It is the way of men." He looked at his padrone, whose burning eyes checked him. " Scusi, signorino, you are angry," he said, quietly.

" No ! " The man's voice was like a command. " You do not understand, Marco."

The lad regarded him, puzzled, and then raised his shoulders.

" No ? You are a man, signorino. It is our way, our nature leads us. I understand that."

Then, feeling he had gone too far, he raised his hands appealingly. " But I talk wildly and you must be angry with me. Scusi ! "

" You talk sense, Marco," cried Peter, his eyes holding the lad's. " You regard me as I deserve to be regarded. You do me no injustice. But it is all different now, Marco. If the Signorina trusts herself to me it is as my wife that she leaves Chioggia."

The lad seemed hurt and humbled when he had said this, and turned his head away, avoiding Peter's eyes.

" Now, Marco, what is it ? Tell me ! "

But even as he spoke the lad could not face him.

" You should beat me for this, signorino. You will never be my friend again. I am a beast ! " he said, contritely.

He found it hard to understand, when his padrone

gripped his arm saying, " Marco, I think the more of you for it, and the Signorina, if she could know, would thank you."

They got up then from their table. The clock by the Merceria struck ten.

" Signorino, I have not told you all yet," said Marco, as they left the café. " The Signorina will be at the campanile at noon to-morrow—and the next day, till you come."

" To-morrow ! I must be there to-morrow, Marco."

" It is not possible, unless you leave by the early boat, signorino."

They were now at the corner of the Loggia, where the Campanile towered up into the moonlit heaven. A white light glimmered on the marbles and mosaics of the cathedral façade and the fairy fabric of its domes, statues, spires, Byzantine arches and pillars. Above the vast central door deeply sunk from the moonlight, the four bronze horses arched their proud necks and pawed the air, aloft on their pedestalled gallery. Nero and Constantine and Napoleon had commanded them, but tenacious Venice now held them, after much journeying. Strange that mortal eye this night could look on them, where once, on a day six hundred years ago, Petrarch, seated at the Doge's right hand, had viewed, from their flanks, the populace in the Piazza below, as the city celebrated its triumph over the Dalmatian pirates.

The wonder of that façade, the seat of dead majesty, always held Peter. Silently he turned down the Piazzetta, towards those columns between which the proud Republic hanged its traitors. The lagoon sparkled beyond the Molo. The white steamer for Trieste lay anchored off the Dogane. Close by it clustered a crowd of gondolas around the concert party holding a *serenata*.

" Where is your boat ? " asked Peter, as they came to the edge of the bright lagoon.

Marco pointed out towards the vast shape of Santa Maria della Salute, silhouetted against the sky.

" I have an idea, Marco," said Peter, at length, as they stood looking over the lagoon. " Let us sail down to Chioggia through the night—if you are willing ? "

" Sì, signorino ! " responded the lad eagerly. " It is a beautiful night. We can watch the dawn come up."

He licked his finger and held it up.

" Bene ! The wind blows south. Let us go, signorino."

" Very well. We'll have a gondola and take my bag from the hotel to our boat."

Later, as they crossed from the hotel towards the *Celavasansdire*, Peter recollected their last journey in a gondola together. He asked Marco if he remembered.

" Sì, signorino. In the grey dawn. It was all grey. Dio mio ! my heart was heavy then ! "

" And it's light now ? " laughed Peter, recovering happiness in the beauty of the night, " Eh, Marco ? " he asked. But the lad did not reply. " What's in your mind now—tell me ! " demanded Peter.

Marco shook his head slowly. " Nothing," he said, unconvincingly.

" That's not true, Marco. Tell me, what is it ? "

The lad could not avoid his command.

" If you must know, signorino, I feel we are going towards trouble."

Peter was about to upbraid the lad for his silly premonition, but he remembered his sensitiveness on the point.

" Trouble ! " he echoed, " who's going to make trouble ? "

" Finghetti."

The name fell like a shadow on their happiness. A moment later they had reached the *Celavasansdire* and response was unnecessary.

Peter never forgot that journey through moonlight. Like a path of silver shone the channel to Chioggia, marked by the white triple pali on each side, the Littorale low and dim on their left. Lone isles floated silently by, cypress sentinelled, still black shapes on the bright lagoon. From time to time the market-gardeners' topi, laden with produce for the early market at Venice, glided by, their moon-tipped sails shaking ghostly in the night breeze. But for the most part it was a voyage through silence and moonlight, with nothing save the soft lap-lap of water on their prow to tell them that this was an earthly journey, and not the enchanted passage of a dream.

They took turns to sleep and steer, but at the first saffron break of day over the Adriatic, Marco woke Peter. The world about them slowly changed as the moon sickened in the brightening sky. The windless dawn passed with feet of pearl over the opalescent water.

" Look signorino ! " called Marco, from the tiller.

Peter followed the direction of his hand. Ahead, in a haze of morning mist touched with the rose of the East, a low line of buildings gave substance to the enchanted vista.

It was Chioggia.

CHAPTER XXVI

I

THE town was already astir when the *Celavasansdire* ran into the harbour and moored up against the molo. To Peter, looking on that familiar sea-wall, on the white front of the hotel, the high arch of the Vigo bridge spanning the mouth of the Vena canal, it seemed as if he had never been away. There were a few who knew him, standing on the molo, and they ran forwards with glad cries of welcome. These brought out the waiters at the hotel, in their shirt sleeves as they prepared the breakfast tables. The voluble little fellow who had let him in and chatted with him on that memorable night when he had first seen Lucia dancing at the *Trattoria del Sole*, waved his arms excitedly, which brought the proprietor to a window above. He in turn filled the air with " Signor Nevilli !—Signor Nevilli ! Buon' giorno, signore ! " and then ran down and out on to the quay. Yes, he could have the same room. Was it not the signore's room whenever he wished ? Bella vista !

After these affectionate greetings, he got rid of them all and was alone in his room when Marco brought up his bag. The lad seemed unnaturally excited and his eyes were aflame.

" Did you see, signorino—did you see him ? He was there ! He saw ! He spat in the water ! Per Bacco ! He was there ! "

" Who ?   Who, Marco ?   What are you talking
about ? "

" Paolo Finghetti !   He was on the Vigo bridge ! "

" Well, he's every right to be there."

" Signorino, you will never believe me.   He means evil
to us.   It was in his face."

" Very well.   He'll get his chance, Marco, I've brought
his knife back."

Marco gave a gasp of incredulity.   The mad English !
Yes, they were mad, even his padrone.   He went off,
muttering to himself, his brow thunderous, his eyes
aflame.

Immediately after breakfast, Peter sought out the
Signor Dottore.   He found the old fellow, still in his
dressing-gown, seated at the breakfast table.   He sprang
up as Peter was shown in.

" My dear young man !   Eh, but this is wonderful !
So you've not forgotten us ?   Pray forgive me !—I was
late last night.   Delfino kept me—thought we should
never end the game.   Dio mio, what a game it was !
There !—I've kept you standing while I gabble.   Come,
you'll have coffee with me, and tell me of yourself ! "

" Thank you, dottore.   But first, how is Signor Delfino ? "

Galuppi sat back in his chair, pushed a plate and cup
away from him, and was professionally grave at once.

" Ah, Signor Neville, it is a sad business !   He is not ill
in the body as much as in the mind.   This Finghetti pest,
he is the source of it all.   Delfino sees he was wrong about
the fleet, wrong about poor little Lucia.   But he's too
proud to confess it.   Delfino has had nothing but quarrels,
the little Lucia nothing but tears.   It was a sad house,
and a sadder when he sent her away.   Signor Neville, if
an old man may be frank with a young one, I would say

that your going left sadness with us.   Poor child, she came
to confess and sob on this weather-beaten breast of mine
many a day.   And now, signorino, you behold a guilty
accomplice.   Yesterday, for a long hour, I was called upon
to admire your epistolary style—in extract form.   Eh, you
young people are poets, though perhaps I wrote letters
like that once—with no effect ! "

The old dottore laughed at the joke against himself, and
then beamed on his visitor.

" And now," he cried, putting a friendly hand on Peter's
arm, " what are we going to do ?   Lucia says I must talk
to her father.   I swear that is your task, though I'll aid
where I can.   But, as a dottore, I prohibit advances for
the present.   Poor Delfino must have peace for a time.
His seizure was not serious but another will be."

Peter thanked him gratefully.   The old fellow would
be a staunch ally.

" What do you advise me to do, dottore ? " he asked.

Dr. Antonio Galuppi peered over the top of his spectacles, as if in professional rumination.

" Eh," he sighed, at length, " it will be the most difficult thing young people on fire can do—nothing, and wait."

" Wait ? "   There was dismay in Peter's echo.

" The Finghetti business will be settled soon.   He will
go.   It will be easier then.   Delfino would never allow
himself to be forced.   He's the proudest man in Chioggia,
and the most stubborn.   How long can you wait ? "

" A lifetime ! "

The dottore stood up and placed a trembling hand on
the young man's shoulder.

" Santa Madonna ! " he cried in a voice of emotion,
" what a blessed thing it is to be young !   We have such
faith in Fate."

He repeated the last words to himself and appeared to

fall into a reverie for a few moments. Then he chuckled and beamed on his young friend, who began to tell him all he planned in their radiant future.

II

It was about this time that Finghetti, consumed with hate from the moment he had seen the *Celavasansdire* enter the harbour and heard the crowd greeting Signor Neville, received a summons from Delfino, and, in response to an imperative message, moodily entered the old fleetmaster's house. Half-an-hour later, livid with rage, he strode out again into the Corso. Had anyone stared at him in that moment he would have smashed in his skull. There had been a tense duel between the fiery old fleetmaster and the younger sullen man. The bill of damages from Ancona, together with the legal costs, had arrived that morning. For half-an-hour, in high altercation, the two men had bandied their accusations of bad faith, broken promises, incompetence and drunkenness. Finghetti, losing all control of himself, drenched the whole house of Delfino in a stream of abuse.

"That English dog's prowling here again. He knows what he can get, he knows all he's offered!" stormed Finghetti.

Delfino stood like a rock before the flood of slander, and no glimmer of surprise at Neville's return was allowed to show in his fierce, narrowed eyes. But forty years of command rang in his voice as he dismissed Finghetti from his house and his fleet. Before the tempered steel of this adamant will the Sicilian had no courage to stand his ground; the bully collapsed before the righteous fury of the old man, quivering from the insults heaped upon him.

Outside in the Corso, Finghetti stood a few moments, dazed, maddened, like a bull seeking a victim of its fury. He could not yet realise he had sacrificed everything to that paroxysm of abuse, that Delfino was now his enemy, that his position was taken from him, his ambitious hopes of Lucia shattered beyond repair. A sense of injustice added to his rage, for three of his own boats had been damaged in that collision with the Ancona fleet, and Delfino was fully aware that Ancona grew more aggressive and encroached every day.

Reviewing his wrongs, his brow black as a thundercloud, he made his way along the Corso to his house. He wanted to think. He had his own boats. Why not go over to the enemy and harass Delfino off the sea ? He almost exulted in the thought. They should see if they could treat him in this manner ! A hate of Chioggia and every living soul in it glowed in his heart. By the time he had reached the house his plan of revenge was complete. No, not complete. It did not embrace one he hated more than all the others. That sneaking Inglese had evaded him twice—once in the storm, and again on that dark night along the fondamenta. His brain worked on the problem. Somehow he must settle the score.

Entering the house, he went straight to the cupboard and mixed himself a drink. He must think this out, with no blundering this time. Again and again he filled his glass, his mind feverishly rejecting plan after plan. And that brat Marco, he too must remember Finghetti ! For an hour he sat there, drinking and evolving scheme after scheme. When his aunt entered the room he looked at her with glazed eyes, his massive head bent as he watched her from under a heavy brow. She knew well that sign.

" A waiter from the hotel has just left this," she said, throwing a packet on the table, and hastily withdrawing.

He let it lie there, still brooding over his scheme, deep in confusing thoughts. After a while, curious to know what was in the packet, he broke the string and unrolled it. The blade of a knife gleamed dully in his shaking hand.

With a cry of rage, stung by the insult, he flung it viciously across the room, then picked it up and examined it before collapsing in his chair. Drinking and brooding, he sat scheming. The Inglese was laughing at him, was taunting him! Dio! Him, Paolo Finghetti! With a sudden resolution he got up and staggered out of the room.

Even then he had evolved no clear plan, but he could not rest. Something would come to him soon. He stood blinking in the sudden glare of the sunlit street, and then lurched away down a narrow calle towards the canal where his boats lay. On the fondamenta he walked by the women as they sat mending the nets. A brown urchin, naked as he was born, catching sight of Finghetti's scowling face, dived into the canal. Experience had taught him not to get in the way of Finghetti. The women watched the hulking fellow pass.

" There's a storm brewing," cried one.

" And reason," replied another, " if all that's said be true."

Their tongues, busy as their fingers, retailed the gossip along the fondamenta. Had Delfino dismissed him? Why had Lucia Delfino gone to Venice, and why had she returned—just before the English signore had come again? Santa Madonna! there was something happening. Finghetti's luck seemed ended at last. He had the evil eye. The fleet had not prospered. The men hated him.

The noise of laughter came through the open window of the *Buon Pesce*, the little wineshop where the boatmen congregated. Finghetti stood and surveyed two of the bragozzi along the canal. Lazy devils ! Why weren't they overhauling the nets ? He turned in at the dark doorway.

A wooden partition separated the passage from the low-ceilinged room, thick with tobacco smoke, the smell of stale wine, and the polenta which some of the men had brought off their boats and were eating. Unshaven, clad in greasy red or brown shirts, with seasoned faces and throats, they looked a wild crew. Two of them, shock-headed deck hands, were gesticulating and arguing at the top of their hoarse voices, so that it was impossible to know whether they were friendly or quarrelling. Unseen, Finghetti paused behind the partition.

" I tell you he's finished ! Delfino's no fool," shouted a voice.

" Nor the Signorina. The Inglese's back ! " cried another.

" Ah, la bellina ! " added a maudlin voice.

" Santo Dio ! Here's luck to him ! " growled a fellow in the corner.

Suddenly a frightened hush fell upon them. The huge form of Finghetti towered over them, his face distorted with rage.

" Who's finished ? " he asked, in a voice of thunder.

There was no reply to the menacing figure. The silence was as that of a bird-haunted wood whereon the shadow of a hawk has fallen. They drew back apprehensively into their seats. Finghetti advanced to the centre of the room, facing the open window overlooking the sunlit canal.

" Luigi Casolotto, who says I'm finished ? Beppo Balsari, did you ? Angelo Zappa, answer me ! " thundered the angry giant.

Fear gripped them in silence. The next moment

Finghetti had seized Casolotto, who had risen apprehensively to his feet.

" Get out ! " bellowed his captor, but the command was a mockery, he could not get out of the way, held as a rat shaken by a dog. The next moment he was lifted shoulder-high and hurled like a sack through the open window. The strength of the enraged bully carried the victim clear of the fondamenta ; he dropped with a resounding splash into the filthy canal.

Before the noise of his striking the water had reached the dark tavern parlour, Finghetti, the veins on his brow suffused, had turned upon another victim.

" And you, Beppo Balsari. Get out ! " he cried, as the helpless figure shot from those ruthless hands. There was a scamper to the door, but the quick arms of the drunken fleet-master pinned another in flight.

" I'm finished, eh, Giovanni Ferluga ? Dio mio ! We'll see ! "

The terrified victim followed the others in flight through the window. Finghetti heard the splash of his fall as he stood in the deserted tavern. The padrone had vanished with his customers. With unsteady hand he filled a mug from the bronze wine bin on the counter, and took a great draught. He was parched and breathless after his herculean exertion, and his eyes were bloodshot around the distended glowering pupils. He lurched out of the tavern and halted, like a dazed animal, on its threshold. Not a soul was on the fondamenta, but, had he known, curious eyes watched him from their retreats. Cursing, he went away down the alley, past the Fishmarket, towards the Corso.

Despite the advent of October the noonday heat was oppressive. On the far horizon, out at sea, grey-black thunder-clouds were massing, and scirocco was in the heavy air. Hardly a human being traversed the Corso as Finghetti emerged from the shadowy calle, and his eye, surveying the broad road, detected a figure moving in the direction of the Pontelungo. There was something familiar in the gait and he watched bemusedly. Slowly his clouded brain recognised the figure. It was the Inglese! This was Fate surely. Keeping in the shadow of the arcades, he stalked the unconscious object of his hate.

Where was he going? Stealthily Finghetti followed, until the Englishman turned off into the Campo Duomo. Hastening after him, Finghetti paused at the corner of the little church of San Martino, and watched cautiously.

The Englishman was crossing the open square in the direction of the Campanile. In a moment Finghetti had guessed his object. He had heard the gossip about the meetings in that gallery. So he had trapped them now! With a curse, he checked his impulse to follow. His brain was working at last. The form of his revenge was taking shape. It would be better if fulfilled before her eyes.

When his destined victim had disappeared through the door at the foot of the Campanile, Finghetti scurried across to the Duomo. The side door of the cathedral was open, and he entered, leaving it slightly ajar, so that he could survey the Campo unseen. Lucia Delfino would pass that way. It was essential that she should be in the Campanile when he carried out his design. So intent was his vigil, he was unaware that his entrance had attracted the attention of other eyes, lowered before an altar where a youth repeated his prayers. The creaking of the door had disturbed the worshipper and he watched the lurking figure anxiously.

Finghetti had not long to wait before he saw Lucia Delfino turn into the sunlit square and hurry across towards the Campanile. In the moment of seeing her, hatred and jealousy almost compelled him to wreak his vengeance on her. That was the Sicilian way, to disfigure forever the beauty that was not for him. He had often seen girls in his native isle marked for life with the ugly cicatrices scarring their faces, the emblems of outraged love. Finghetti's hand instinctively sought the knife sheathed in his belt. But no, the Inglese had returned it to him. It should be for a purpose. The handsome Inglese, the Chioggiotti called him ! He would end that.

A few minutes passed, then stealthily he moved, in the shadow of the Duomo, towards the Campanile door. He entered swiftly, shutting it behind him and, removing his sandals, began the noiseless winding ascent in the gloom of the tower.

III

Tumult was in the heart of Peter as he waited on the open gallery for that great moment of reunion. Here he had held her to his heart, here their first kiss had been tremulously given and taken. It was hallowed to him for its memories. It would be more sacred henceforth as the scene of a great moment in their lives. He could not doubt, with such letters given and received, that his quest would be fulfilled. Their only uncertainties were those of time and ways. The dear old dottore had assured him that both served love, if awaited in patience. He had faith in the dottore, who might assist the way of patience and even shorten it with skilful advocacy of their love in the proper quarter.

The bells in the town below noisily proclaimed the noon. She would be here at any moment. His eyes swept the vast expanse of blue sea and silver-grey lagoon. Along the canals veining Chioggia, the clustered boats lay deserted and still. A ship out at sea caught the sunlight on its sails as it veered in the breeze. To the west, the exposed shoals of the dead lagoon were purple with sea-lavender, and across the golden Venetian plain, the Euganean hills lay distinct and dark under a storm cloud. Nearer, he could hear the faint clatter of a donkey barrow passing down the Corso. At the bar of the Porto, where they had escaped the hand of Death, a few boats lessened sail as they took the channel. Below him, wave on wave, flowed a sea of red tiles, chimneys, and the white campanili of the churches along the street.

The Campo at his feet glared deserted under the noonday. A diminutive figure moved, fly-like, along by the shadowed wall of the Duomo. He saw it cross to the Campanile ere losing it. Surely it was not coming here ? It might be a ringer. No one came up to the gallery, only a few tourists, and that was later, when the afternoon boat came in from Venice. Another figure left the side door of the Duomo. How cautious these Chioggiotti were to keep in the shadow ! He watched it curiously, but the sound of footsteps along the gallery made him start up in joyful expectation. A moment later, Lucia came round the corner of the tower and with a cry was in his arms.

" Lucia ! tesoro mio ! " he whispered.

Her dark eyes looked on his a space in silence, and then, suffused in tears of joy, closed in the ecstasy of their uniting kiss. The height of the blue heaven domed them in its silence and brightness. Unheeded, Time flowed on apace ere words and the world were again with them. How much they had to ask, how much to answer ! They wondered at the richness of their sorrow—now it was only a memory. Little by little they reconstructed their lives apart, lived with such longing, heavy with such loneliness, and now eager with the hopes that would surely be fulfilled.

IV

Whatever of steadiness and cunning drink had robbed
Paolo Finghetti, as he crept noiselessly on to the dizzy
height of the stone gallery surrounding the old Campanile,
hate had supplied. Madness was in his brain but the
strength of a fearful purpose was in his limbs as he
approached on the task of vengeance. For a moment he
paused in the open doorway of the room above the belfry,
letting the breeze play upon his flushed face. He was on
the windy side of the gallery, and therefore could not hear
the voices of the lovers. He must approach at the back
of the Inglese ; she must have no chance to intervene.
The gallery assisted him in this, for he could choose the
side from which to spring, once he had found Neville's
position. It would be the work of a few seconds. A
swift seizure by the throat, a quick laceration of the face,
and he would carry the marks of vengeance through life.
The handsome Inglese ! Per Cristo ! They should see !

Finghetti drew out the knife in readiness, and pressing
his body against the wall of the tower, his left hand flat
to the surface, he advanced on silent naked feet. At the
corner, a cautious glance revealed the back of the unconscious man turned towards him as he bent forward,
talking.

Gripping the knife, for a second Finghetti controlled
the tumult of his hate, then moved to his foul intent.
But a swift shadow fell upon the bright blade. The knife
clattered noisily on to the stone, involuntarily released by
the surprised hand seized in a fierce grip.

The astounding clatter broke the silence of that eyrie.
The startled lovers heard a cry of rage. Alert, Peter
sprang apart, stepped swiftly round the tower, and then
stood amazed by the sight before him. Two men, locked

in a fierce embrace, fought on the narrow gallery. The next moment there was a sound of crumbling masonry, a cry of terror, and two indistinguishable forms shadowed the sun from his eyes. Relentlessly grappled to each other, he saw them fall outwards with the broken balustrade, down through the bright air.

Peter turned from the sickening sight as Lucia came towards him.

" Pee-tar !—what is it !—what is wrong ? " she clamoured.

But no word shaped itself on his parched lips. She could only read the horror in his eyes as he stood there, the broken balustrade gaping behind him.

CHAPTER XXVII

I

THE last days of October passed with the richness that closes the pageant of the Venetian year. November would follow with its mists, when the lagoons, steely and dull, were smitten with the chilling winds from the hills of Trieste, with that *bora* so fierce, and yet preferable to the banks of mist that shut off the landscape and sent the ships perilously groping through the gloom. It was then that the Chioggiotti needed all their courage in stern warfare with the sea, which changed from a sunlit azure mistress, and lashed bitterly those who braved her hard, frowning face.

But October, as if conscious of her farewell gesture to beauty, decked her brows in orange and crimson and purple. Spring and high Summer had their triumphs. Wayward April with her bursts of sunshine, her scudding clouds that sent waves of light rippling over the water and marble façades of the palaces, gave a fresh life to the faded *intonaco* upon the walls of Venice. Every tone, ranging from sea-green to that beloved Venetian red, rose under the sudden splash of rain, and for a space one discerned the glimmering wonder of the City, when the hands of the great masters had painted the walls of its houses with frescoes. Here a garland of cherubs, festooning the eaves of a crumbling palace, briefly glowed from the faded past ;

here the brush of Giorgione, with rich suggestion, had left a trace of its labour on the face of a palazzo.

Venice glowed with her old gaiety in the brief space of those rapidly drying showers. There would float, ethereally pure, on the cold green lagoon, the islands of San Clemente and San Servolo, or San Giorgio Maggiore in its veil of grey and silver, intangible as a dream. In the Forte at the north extremity of the Littorale, the grass was then green as in an English meadow, and the passing boats caught the perfume from the violets and acacia blooms. There lay the City, like a lily on the water, crowded about with the crimson and orange masts of the fishing boats, and, beyond, the floating heights of the snow-crowned Alps.

Such had been the first prelude in that long symphony enchanting Peter Neville ; but Summer, drenching the air with its scents, caught a more passionate note with her flaming colours. There had been the hot days, hazy at early morn, when he had wandered with Marco along the Littorale, or drifted into waste backwaters of the lagoons. Sand lizards had shot from their sun-bath into the crevices of stone, or to banks where the pale sea-holly raised its violet bloom above the yellow of the evening primrose. The little gardens of Chioggia, bee and butterfly haunted, glowed with their oleander blooms and trailing honeysuckle covering the yellow walls, creviced with ivy or flame-spotted with the pomegranate flower.

How happy poor Marco had been in that riot of Summer. Peter could see him now, running through the sward where the narcissus swung its white-petalled head under the breeze, or, again, as he splashed through the limpid blue water, a diamond spray about his shoulders, and then rose, breathless on the golden marge, to fling himself down amid the bent-grass and the heather covering the sandy dunes.

And now the solemn cypress, with the withered flame-coloured trumpets of the bignonia climbing through it, kept watch over this child of the sun. Here, in the quiet of the Campo Santo, he had been borne through the splendour of the Autumn. A great concourse stood about his grave, but there was no sadder heart than the one which, in his devotion, he had served faithfully unto death. Later, in the quiet of the evening, Peter had returned to the cemetery, and stood awhile amid those great wreaths of flowers with which the Italian betokens his sorrow.

Beyond the low wall of the Campo Santo, the great lagoon stretched westwards towards the marsh and the dark hills that skirt the Venetian plain. A row of stately cypress trees, bordering the cemetery, cut sharply against the last crimson glow of the evening. Around him, like a silent multitude, glimmered the white marble memorials, pathetic in their incongruous mixture of pomp and crudity. Later, another memorial, more pompous than these, would cover the grave, for Peter would deny nothing to those who mourned him, and when Marco's parents had gratefully accepted his offer, he had let them give to it the shape of their own desire. Marco would rest honoured and revered among his countrymen with such a magnificent and costly testimony from his padrone.

Nor did Peter's thought of the dead cease there. That dear lad's memory called for his care of the living. To the end of their days Marco's parents would find the struggle of life lightened by the small pension Peter had settled upon them, and there was also Marco's only legacy of the treasured *Celavasansdire*.

Standing there in the evening calm, land and sky and lagoon so peaceful under the waning light, the old, old query filled the mind of Peter. How much did that dear lad know now, how much was he conscious of their grief and gratitude ? Were his ears sealed to the prayers, his eyes shut to the sight of that slim girl who, on her knees by the grave's edge, spoke her trembling words for his repose ? In the burden of the mystery, Peter wanted to believe, simply, wholly, as Lucia believed.

Kneeling at her side he caught and re-echoed the closing words of her prayer, which was not of his faith and yet, somehow, spoke from the depths of his sorrow—

. . . che la tua anima riposi in pace.

II

The sensation that had shaken Chioggia in those days soon passed into the quiet storage of the memory. The tragedy of that day when Marco and Finghetti had been hurled to death in their last desperate embrace, became part of the history woven around the old Campanile, companion of the stormy clouds and the sunny sky. It stood there, resolute to the elements, with its repaired balcony and its loud bells, a dignified survival of the centuries that had flowed about its walls. To others, in the due length of time, the story of that tragic day would be one of the many stories of battles and sieges, hates and loves, to be told with legendary embellishment. Poor Ursula Bossi ! poor Marco ! The Campanile was their monument.

Meanwhile the living faced their daily problems, toiled for the means of life and seized its fitful pleasures. The seasons and the diurnal round called men from their private griefs to follow the tide of life. Love shadowed so closely by Death, was deeper and lovelier. In those days following the tragedy the young lovers felt their troth sealed by the devotion of that dead boy. For a few days Peter saw little of the distraught girl he had brought down from the terrible scene, and taken home to the Palazzo Delfino. The police enquiries, the inquest, the funeral, the fantastic accounts winging their way from café to café, all highly circumstantial and highly contradictory, these things filled his days.

There were interviews with the Pretore and the Sindaco, questions and depositions and all the preposterous ponderings of the Law. He shielded Lucia from these. Evidence arose from unexpected sources, corroborating the simple story, and clearing it of the suspicions and suggestions the Law amassed in its process of investigation. A witness came forth, a poor laceworker seated late at her door on the fondamenta, who had seen the knife hurled by Finghetti on that dark night, as Neville walked by the canal. Luigi Spinelli reported Marco's strange premonition of impending tragedy, his certainty that evil for him lay in the hands of Finghetti.

He had been constant in his visitations to the Duomo, where he prayed often. The wild joy in the Signorino's return had been clouded by foreboding disaster. His own end might never have been encompassed but for his presence that very morning, when he had turned from his contemplation at the altar, and discovered Finghetti lurking behind the cathedral door. He had followed his enemy forth to death, impelled by devotion to his padrone.

There was one painful scene with Signor Delfino, painful in that Peter confronted a man no longer angry, but broken. With what words the gracious old dottore had prefaced his visit Peter never knew, but he was sent for, and was received with a quietude that made his host a figure of compassion. With characteristic courage, Delfino broke through the conventional phrases with which they sought to overcome their reserve.

" Signor Neville, it is useless for me to ignore the object

of this visit. It is to make my peace with you. I opposed you, I opposed my daughter, I was wrong. Perhaps an old man, too conscious of the values of the world, is apt to ignore the blind impulses of the young, who feel, while we rely on experience. My blindness had brought anguish and death. Forgive me, I was too ambitious. I sought to build Lucia's happiness on foundations of my own choosing. It was not to be."

The proud old head and the eagle eye looked un-flinchingly towards the young man, who heard these words conscious only of the courage they denoted. They made him feel ashamed of his defiance, with all its contemptuous indifference of youth towards age.

"Signore," said Peter earnestly, "it's I who should say these things. My love of Lucia I would not, and cannot, disclaim, but, believe me, the manner of it, and the words you have just spoken, shame me. I opposed you ungenerously. Even now I am bold to ask my favour —but I ask it, Signore, I don't demand it."

For a long moment Delfino regarded him in silence, and then a smile softening the steel of his eyes, he placed an affectionate hand on the young man's shoulder.

"You make my surrender easy—let us call Lucia and show her I am no heartless father," he said.

III

The golden Autumn passed in its farewell pageant. The water-meadows, with the feathery plumes of the sea-lavender, glowed purple under the weakening sun. The early morning had a snap of cold in the air, and the mists came earlier, and clung later, as each day advanced towards the winter season. There were signs of a Chioggia which Peter could not recognise. The women

along the canal were no longer barefooted and stockingless ; the brown bodies of the men were clad in bright
jerseys.

But his farewell to Chioggia was made in brilliant
sunshine. It seemed as if the season had endeavoured to
pay its last tribute of gold to the young lovers. The mist
lifted early from the lagoons, and the sun, triumphing,
took everything in its warm embrace.

Long before the hour of noon it was obvious that
Chioggia had decided to do no work that day. A request
had been made for a quiet wedding, but a ceremony of this
nature was beyond the understanding of the Chioggiotti.
Yet they respected the wish, prompted by the memory of
Marco, asleep there amid the dark cypresses. They
refrained from turning the day into a festa, but bright
clothes they wore, and with flowers they were laden.
The boats lay empty along the Vena, and the crowd
thickened about the office of the Sindaco, where the
official ceremony was to be performed.

Peter was amazed at the size of the crowd which opened
up a way for him as he came on foot, accompanied by his
compare, or best man. Amid the babel of cries wishing
him good-luck, he entered the Municipio, but the best
man was held back and was compelled to make a speech
from the steps, for it was the Signor Dottore, loved by all.

Per Bacco ! He was a great orator, and he thanked
them on the bridegroom's behalf for their welcome ; a
few words of tribute to Marco brought tears to their eyes,
of which, in simple peasant fashion, they had no shame.

After a few minutes of waiting, a fresh outburst of the
babel of voices, and a stirring and a stretching of necks,
proclaimed the arrival of Lucia with her father, in the old
landau, which was almost in the nature of a State carriage,
since Vittorio Emanuele had once ridden down the Corso

in it. Peter, watching the arrival from an upper room, turned to the dottore.

"I believe all Chioggia's out there this morning—if this is a quiet wedding, what is a normal one, I wonder!"

The dottore laughed gleefully, so that Peter suspected him of being a conspirator in this ovation.

"My dear young man, you don't expect to carry away our beautiful Lucia without all Chioggia coming out to see? It will be nothing compared with this evening. Dio mio! it is hard to ignore any wedding, but one like this, so romantic, so touched with tragedy, so unique in—"

He spread his hands in a loss of adequate expression. His oratory on the steps, which he had thoroughly enjoyed, had whetted his appetite. They would call for him this evening. Bene! They should hear him as never before. He would speak freely when the Signorino and his bride had departed in their gondola for Venice. And he would speak for Delfino also, who was no orator. He would speak from the balcony of the Palazzo Delfino, overlooking the Corso. It was a fine setting for an occasion for eloquence. Per Dio! they should remember this day!

CHAPTER XXVIII

IT was all as the dottore had prophesied, and perhaps wished. The route of their carriage down the Corso had been strewn with blossoms. Amid shouts and hand-wavings they had disappeared in the Palazzo Delfino, to appear a few minutes later on the balcony, in response to the calls from the crowd below that showed no sign of dispersing. So they bowed and waved their hands, and then Signor Delfino made a courtly bow, and also the dottore, who, of course, made a little speech, not too splendid—he was reserving himself for the evening—in which he spoke now of la bella Signora Neville, of the caro Signorino, and, dramatically addressing himself to the bridal pair, warned them that Chioggia would only forgive the theft of their Lucia if the Signorino faithfully made an annual pilgrimage to this town, whose hearts they commanded. Bravo ! Bravo ! Bene, per Dio !

At this conclusion, and with many bows, the old fellow retired, to return, introducing, with gracious flourishes, Lucia and Peter, and Delfino. And then, when the window was closed and the noise shut out, he mopped his brow.

" Per Bacco ! it's hard work for an old fellow. Friend Delfino, you escape your share, and our young man is quite tongue-tied ! "

Signor Delfino raised an accusing finger.

" My dear dottore, you are a humbug ! You are enjoying yourself tremendously ! "

369

With a great smile Galuppi acknowledged his guilt.

" Eh—and why shouldn't I ? God bless these children ! " and almost beside himself with good humour, he embraced both bride and bridegroom.

It was a true Venetian departure that evening. The journey from Chioggia was to be made in a gondola, rowed by two gondoliers at the prow and stern. The night was to be spent in Venice and early on the morrow they would leave by boat down the Adriatic, en route to Egypt.

By six o'clock on the molo there was no standing room. The gay gondolieri, in immaculate white sailor-suits, with blue and red bonnets, and swathed in crimson sashes, proudly awaited their happy passengers. The long black gondola, trimmed with rosettes, carried a line of coloured lanterns from prow to stern, in readiness for the falling darkness. The glow of evening was in the upper sky when the carriage slowly made its way through the concourse in the Piazza and along the harbour front.

" I never knew so many people lived in Chioggia," whispered Peter to his bride. Every window of the hotel was full, for the waiters, the maids, and the padrone, particularly, claimed a personal interest in this departure of their patron.

Neither Delfino nor the dottore had accompanied them to the harbour. There had been a tender farewell between father and daughter. Peter felt some remorse in taking away from the old man one so dear to him, and Delfino must have seen this thought in his face, for his last words to him were—

" Take care of her, caro, and come back whenever you can, but don't be unhappy for my sake. This is the way of life, one should not be blind to it. In youth, the world is a bright place, full of friends and interests. In age, it is a lonely land, peopled with memories and grey with shadows. I would not deprive you of your sunshine. Live in it while you can."

His voice had broken at the last words, and Peter gripped his trembling hand, promising to return. As for the Dottore, he had remained with his old friend Delfino, to keep him company—and prepare his ovation.

The young lovers had passed down the steps now, amid the cries from the crowd. Surely some of them would fall over into the water in their eagerness! Peter handed Lucia into the black cabin, with its crimson cushions, gleaming brass-fittings and flower-cut glass windows.

" Addio ! " he called, with a final wave of the hand, as the gondoliers pushed off.

" A rivederci, signore! A rivederci, signora! Ritornate presto ! " came the answering cries from the molo above.

They had left the harbour now, and rocked slightly as they crossed the open mouth of the Porto. Suddenly there was a whistling in the air, and a rocket soared up into the darkening sky to burst high over their heads in a spray of stars. Away there, on their right, ran the long line of the murazzi on the Littorale. It was deserted, save for a single figure, moving slowly away from the Forte, indistinct in the lessening light. But Peter recognised it, and turned away his face with a slight shiver at his heart. In his memory he could still hear the tap-tap of that blind man's stick.

Now they were alone in the dusky cabin of the gondola, a curious shyness overcame them. Peter's eyes lingered on the beauty of Lucia's profile, clear against the blue-grey water. She became conscious of his scrutiny, and turned towards him with a nervous little laugh as his hand closed over hers. He was just about to speak when they were surprised by a distant sound of music. Through the vent behind, where the gondolier stood on his raised *poppa*, Peter saw a gleaming crescent of coloured lanterns riding through the gathering dusk, their vivid lights staining the dark water around.

" Lucia !—look, they're following us ! "

She turned, to see a hundred yards distant, a fairy fleet riding in their wake. There were minstrels aboard, and to their ears floated the plaintive music of the mandolins. Presently, a voice soared up into the calm night, singing its serenata.

" That's Luigi Spinelli—I know his voice," murmured Lucia.

> *Volème ben, che sarò sempre vostro,*
> *Sino che durerà, l'aria del cielo.*

" What's he singing ? " asked Peter.

She turned to him. " A folksong," she said, paraphrasing the words, as from her own heart—

> *Love me but well, I will be thine forever,*
> *As long as shall endure the winds of heaven.*

He kissed her then, strangely moved, as he saw the tears glistening in her eyes.

Slowly the night curtained them in with tranquillity. The far sunset had flamed to death behind the dark Euganean hills, and the horizon changed and waned from orange to gold, from crimson to purple. The upper sky darkened to its dome, where the first bright star rode on the tide of night. Still behind them, at their fixed space of a hundred yards, followed the lanterned barques, music-laden, wafting to them catches of happy laughter in the pauses between the singing. But off Pelestrina there were cries of *Addio ! Buona notte ! A rivederci !* The fairy fleet had halted. Lucia and Peter went outside the cabin and waved a last farewell.

Alone now, the gondola took the channel to Venice. The dark water flowed mysteriously around them, for the moon had not yet risen from her Adriatic bed. The only sound upon their ears was the rhythmical beat of the oars, and the soft lap-lap of the water on the boat's side. A lantern glimmered at the steel prow, below the dusky figure of the front gondolier ; away on the Littorale, the lights of the lagoon villages speared the dark flood.

Through the vast still night they floated, towards the far, jewelled horizon, where ancient Venice shone upon her waters.

THE END